THE BLACKSMITH PRINCESS

TWELVE DANCING PRINCESSES BOOK 1

ROWAN MALLORY

ISBN 978-1-956158-01-4
eISBN 978-1-956158-00-7

Be the first to learn about Rowan Mallory's new releases by signing up for the newsletter. You'll get brief months emails about new releases and receive exclusive content.

www.rowanmallory.com

Far Shore Design Publishing

For Ari
Your determination to forge your own place in this world inspires me every day.

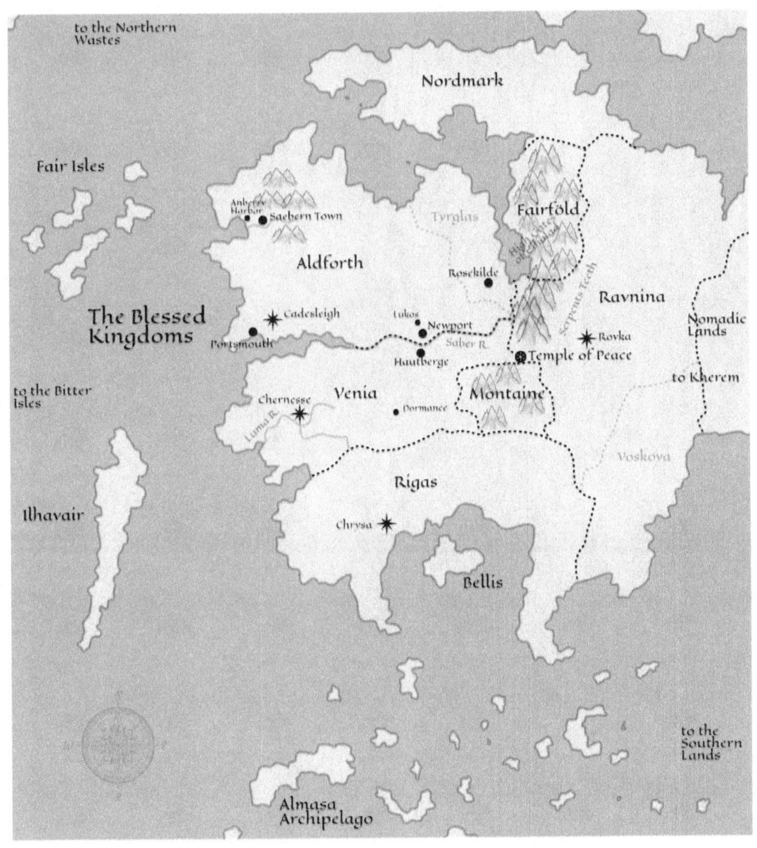

MAP OF THE BLESSED KINGDOMS

O, Sorrow! Speak, for I have not the words
To set the scene of a tragedy so vast.
Fair prince, or if not fair, at least endowed
With handsome face and tiger's fearsome strength,
Beside fair bride, a maid of raven locks
And heart so pure, the two destined to rule
With iron fist and gentle smile. Alas!
Twas not to be.

— From "The Death of Prince Guntram," by Foolscap
the Bard

CHAPTER ONE

Curse the trader whose eagle brought the news of King Wulfric's ball to Kherem. May he and all his retinue be lost in the desert and die of thirst mere steps from a caravan well.

— Princess Anara of Kherem

"Pardon me, *milady*." Sarcasm dripped from the word like spoiled honey. "May I beg a moment of your time?"

Jax steeled her face, though her ears burned as she turned from her father's forge to face Hubert, the miller's oldest son. The large wooden shutters along the smithy walls had been raised to let in light and air. Unfortunately, they also let in pests.

Hubert leaned his bare forearms on the open half-wall, eyes glinting. If it weren't for the knowing smirk, Hubert might be handsome, with his thick, curling hair and even features.

"I know you're too high and mighty for the likes of us," he said, with a sly glance at his younger brother, Eric, who hovered behind him like a nervous shadow. Hubert always had an audience. "But perhaps you could humble yourself to pass a message to your father."

Hubert no longer called her "bastard," as he had when they were children. His needling had become less crude, but he still knew just how to remind her she didn't belong.

Jax brushed her sooty hands on her apron, her palm resting reflexively on the hammer at her waist, reminding herself who she was. She couldn't alter her height or the color of her skin. She refused to exchange her short tunic and breeches for a dress while working—long skirts might catch a spark.

But she could stand confident as her father's apprentice and treat Hubert as a respected customer. She crossed the smooth-swept dirt floor to face him.

"How can I help you?"

"My father's horse lost a shoe. He wants me to bring her in tomorrow, and he wants your father to do the shoeing. He doesn't want an apprentice mauling his prize mare."

Hubert hunched a little closer over the half wall as if to share a confidence, but he didn't lower his voice. "He says it's shameful to see a girl working like a mule, even if she does look like one. He's thinking of complaining to Count Renaud."

That brought a grunt of surprise from Eric that became an anxious chuckle when Hubert elbowed him.

So, maybe Hubert was making up his father's complaint to goad her. But maybe not. Jax clutched her hammer. Blacksmithing was the only thing that offered her a place here in Dormance.

"We'd best be on our way." Hubert pushed himself up, grinning with the knowledge his barb had struck home. "I've promised Eric a pint at Dame Clothilde's. He's been accepted at the Court School in Chernesse."

He clapped his brother on the shoulder hard enough to knock the boy against the wall.

"Good for you," Jax told Eric, squelching the curl of old

yearning in her heart. "You must have worked hard to earn that place."

Eric flushed and nodded nervously, caught between her praise and Hubert's narrowed eyes. He had recently turned twelve, the minimum age to be accepted at the Court School, and he still looked awfully young, all knees and elbows and big eyes.

"Mama always wanted him to become a jumped-up noble," Hubert said with a sneer. "After all, I'm the one who will inherit the mill and take Papa's place as bailiff."

A flash of alarm crossed Eric's face at his brother's darkening mood. Jax managed to bite her tongue before it could remind Hubert of his childhood boasts that he would be the one to go to school in Chernesse and come back as a lord to rule the rest of them. How he had rubbed her nose in the knowledge that her birth made her ineligible to attend the Court School, no matter how well she did in Father Donat's classes. How the only pang she had felt when the priest told Hubert he hadn't passed his exams had been regret that he wouldn't be leaving Dormance, after all.

"You'd better go get that pint," she said instead.

"None of that watered-down child's swill." Hubert thumped his brother again. "You're off to become a man, boy. I'll get you a man's ale and give you some advice for when you meet those noble ladies at the capital."

"Only if they aren't all man-eating giants like Jax," Eric piped up with an exaggerated leer.

So much for gratitude.

Hubert roared with laughter and wrapped an arm around his brother's head.

"Fee fi fo fum," he chanted, dragging Eric giggling and struggling out into the square toward Dame Clothilde's inn.

"Too bad there's not a real giant around to crack your skulls," Jax muttered, her stomach churning with familiar mortification at Hubert's nastiness and new anxiety over what his father might say to Count Renaud.

Work. That's what she needed to settle her mind.

Her father kept a few ready-made shoes displayed on the smithy's support beams, but the miller's mare had small feet. Jax could prepare a smaller shoe before her father returned from his work at the manor that afternoon.

She found a suitable piece of iron stock in the boxes below one of the workbenches and brought it to the brick forge near the stone wall the smithy shared with her family's cottage next door. She pumped the bellows to raise the heat in the coals and pulled on her leather glove. She thrust the length of iron into the fire with a pair of tongs.

As soon as she had the metal hot enough to forge, she moved it to the anvil on its tree stump pedestal nearby. Her hammer struck the bright yellow iron with a satisfying thunk that jarred her bones.

What had she ever done to Hubert, to deserve his cruelty? She swung again, in a swift, driving rhythm, pounding the hot metal. *Other than be more useful than he was.* With a wrench of her tongs, she shifted the shoe from the anvil's flat face to its cone-shaped horn. *And smarter.* Another series of hammer strokes curved the metal around the horn. *And stronger.* Even as the stock cooled to orange and then red, it bent like butter under her furious blows—

"By all the gods, girl. What has that poor scrap of iron ever done to you?"

Jax struck one more blow for good measure before setting her hammer down on the anvil's face. She swiped her glove across her forehead, brushing away the hairs that had escaped her plait, before glancing up at her father.

Bahar's own dark hair was pulled back in a ponytail, showing off the tiny gold hoop in his left earlobe. With his southern skin burnished bronze by the sun, his powerful arm muscles bare beneath his leather apron, he looked more pirate than smith. Only the amusement that warmed his light brown eyes spoiled the villainous image.

Jax sometimes wondered if her father had chosen smithing

over piracy simply because no pirate captain would take on a man with such a good-natured smile.

"Hubert said he would bring his father's mare in for shoeing tomorrow," she told him. "We didn't have any shoes small enough."

"It's true the miller's nag has dainty feet, but I never noticed they were so misshapen."

Jax eyed the twisted piece of metal she held in her tongs. With a grimace, she thrust it into the quench bucket, her sigh matching the hiss of steam as the hot iron hit the cold water.

"A hammer is a powerful tool." Bahar spoke the words like a proverb. "But not as powerful as the mind that wields it. A strong arm is not what makes a good smith. Even working iron, your greatest strength comes from your mind and your heart, not your muscle."

"So you always tell me, Papa." Jax pulled the horseshoe from the bucket. The water didn't evaporate, so she knew the metal was cool enough to touch. "I *was* using my mind. It told me that it was better to hammer the shoe than Hubert's head."

"Did it now?" Her father took the horseshoe and made a show of examining it. "I can't say I agree with your reasoning. A few hammer strokes might actually improve Hubert's looks, but they've done nothing for this poor shoe."

Jax made a face, but when Bahar wrapped an arm around her shoulder, she leaned against him. He smelled of coal-fire and sweat and horse, the smells that had always meant home and safety. Yet, the comfort he offered didn't seem to spread as far as it once had. Maybe it was just that she'd outgrown it, like a childhood cloak.

He squeezed her shoulder and released her. "There's no sense in upsetting yourself over an oaf like Hubert. If he didn't get a reaction, he'd stop teasing you."

Jax didn't bother arguing. Even her genial father, who saw the good in everyone, had to know that wasn't true.

"Isn't seventeen years long enough to live down the

scandal of my birth?" She turned to the forge, away from her father. "He said it was shameful for me to be working for you and that his father is going to complain to Count Renaud. What if the count decides he disapproves of your having a girl for an apprentice?"

"Why would he change his mind now? He's had no objection for the past three years."

"It might be that no one wants a woman smith." Jax fed the forge fresh coal from the edges. A sprinkle of water cooled the spread, to keep the heat concentrated in the coke at the center.

"There are women blacksmiths doing good business in Venia," Bahar reminded her. "Why, there's a pair in Chernesse—"

"Blacksmiths' widows," Jax said. "Keeping on their husbands' business."

"And you're a blacksmith's daughter, who's going to continue her father's business," Bahar said in exasperation. "I'm a free man. Milord Count isn't going to tell me who I can and can't have as my apprentice. Besides, I'm the best blacksmith this village has had in the gods' own memory, and he knows it. The only thing that would make me give up on an apprentice would be if she couldn't produce a decent horseshoe after banging her hammer around my forge since she was old enough to walk. Maybe she can do something about that before supper, eh?"

Bahar handed her the misshapen shoe, and Jax gave him the smile he wanted.

Her father loved solving problems and making things right. Jax had always believed he could fix anything, but even he couldn't force the villagers of Dormance to accept a woman blacksmith. He couldn't make Jax into a fair-skinned, graceful, marriageable girl.

She thrust the poor horseshoe back into the heart of the fire. Her father's love of his work had been what drew Jax to the smithy as a child. Bahar loved shaping metal. He loved making powerful tools like plowshares and axes, loved making small, beautiful things, like hooks decorated with delicate vines or the boar's head knocker on the village inn.

She'd absorbed that love and felt at home at the forge. She relished the way her hammer became an extension of herself. How together they shaped something useful from an unpromising hunk of metal.

It was the world outside the smithy she couldn't shape herself to fit.

Jax worked the bellows to intensify the forge's heat and swiped her glove across her face again. She envied her father's bare arms. Her stepmother, Agnes, forbade her to remove her sleeves for smithing, even though some of the other village girls did when they worked the harvest. Agnes said it wasn't proper for a young woman. As if anyone in Dormance thought of Jax as a proper young woman.

She moved the hot shoe back to the anvil. *Use your mind. Strike from the shoulder, not the wrist. Let the hammer do the work.* A few swift blows flattened out the unsightly twist. She grabbed a wedge and hammered a groove along the shoe to punch the nail holes through.

The world narrowed to fire and metal, muscle and skill, the ringing of her hammer, the fiery breathing of the bellows. Jax's turmoil settled to satisfaction as the horseshoe took form, fine-looking as any in the shop.

"What's this, now?"

She glanced up to see her father wiping his hands on his apron and moving to the smithy entrance. A pair of riders were crossing the village square toward them. Strangers. The men reined their snorting palfreys to a stop before her father.

Bahar nodded to them. "Good afternoon, milords."

Lords they obviously were, their horses glossy and sleek, their clothes of fine cloth and well made. The older man in front held himself tall, with a superior tilt to his long, hatchet-nosed face. He wore sleeves trimmed with white lace and sported gold buttons on his tailored surcoat, but the jagged scar from his jaw to his left ear and the well-worn pommel of his sword marked him as a soldier, not just a dandy.

"Are you looking for the manor?" Bahar prompted, though the strangers must have passed Count Renaud's great house on the crest of the hill above the village.

"I seek Bahar Smith." The man's voice was as sharp as his nose.

"The gods' blessings on us both, then," Bahar said amiably. Jax guessed only she saw the wary tightening of his shoulders. "You've found him."

The stranger's mouth pinched as if to say he'd feared as much. "I am Anatole, constable to Her Most Illustrious Majesty, Queen Léonie of Venia, Our Gracious and Just Sovereign. I come by the queen's order to discuss business she has with you."

A trickle of dread slithered down Jax's back.

Bahar bowed, though his muscles hardened further. "I am at the queen's service, though I can't imagine what business she might have with me when she has the finest blacksmiths in Venia to command. Please, come into my shop."

"Our business is private." Constable Anatole's big horse shifted uneasily beneath him as the man glared around the square. The innkeeper had stepped out to sweep her stoop when the strangers arrived. A pair of women whispered together outside the bakehouse, their loaves wrapped in their baskets. A gaggle of small boys showed off their stick-sword skills by the well, glancing over to see if the lords were impressed.

"No one will come into my workshop while you're here," Bahar said dryly.

The villagers might be burning with curiosity, but they also had a hearty distrust of outsiders. They'd want to hear all about whatever business these wealthy queensmen had with their smith—at a safe distance from any trouble that might be involved.

And there was trouble involved. That much was obvious.

"It's private business," Anatole repeated as he dismounted, gesturing his companion to do the same. "Send your boy home."

Heat burned Jax's cheeks, though she was used to being teased for her unconventional clothing. The brief nod from her father fueled her embarrassment, but also her fear. He wanted her safely away.

Her hand tightened on her hammer, but she dropped her chin in assent and set the half-finished horseshoe on the floor to cool.

"That's not a boy." The mild voice pulled Jax's gaze to the second stranger. She had barely noticed him behind the gaudy, ill-humored Anatole. She saw now he was a young man, probably close to her own age, though his shrewd eyes held a composure the older man seemed to lack.

He stood taller than the constable, though slender, and his clothes were equally well-tailored. Yet, in his plain brown surcoat, his ruddy brown hair nearly matching the wool, he almost disappeared beside his companion.

If not for those sharp, midnight blue eyes.

"What do you mean, Nicolas?" Anatole demanded.

"I believe we owe our apologies." The young man, Nicolas, offered Jax a respectful bow. "Please forgive our lack of proper courtesy, Your Highness. We meant no disrespect."

"*Your Highness?*" Anatole's eyes widened. "*That's* the girl?"

Nicolas nodded and bowed again. "It is an honor to make your acquaintance, Princess Jaclyn."

CHAPTER TWO

… Death struck, a blow so cruel
E'en Death would pause to mourn. Yet not the king.
The kingdom all his heart, he issues forth
The call: "Whoe'er can save my people from
This foe, this one shall all my people rule
In law. My only heir shall marry her,
A crown be hers, all honor on her fall.
Come dance for me, be chosen at my ball."

— From "The Death of Prince Guntram," by Foolscap
the Bard

The Kingdom of Montaine hosted Prince Guntram on his way home from his campaign against the Almasa archipelago, you know. Just think of it. We were among the last people—of any consequence—to see him alive.

The Almasans threatened to sink Aldforthian ships that didn't pay the outrageous tolls they charge for passing through their waters. When Prince Guntram returned from his campaign, he had the Almasan crown prince's head in a silver-plated box. I saw it myself. He planned to present it to his father as a birthday gift.

Such a valiant man.

— Princess Isolde of Montaine

The two men hadn't come for Bahar.

Princess Jaclyn. No one but Hubert called Jax that —and only when he was certain Bahar couldn't hear. Nicolas's voice held none of the miller's son's mockery, yet it frightened Jax in a way Hubert never had.

"You'd best come into the house." Bahar threw off his apron and pulled a linen tunic over his bare chest. "My family is not business."

He put a hand on Jax's shoulder and squeezed it, a reassurance he would protect her. To the death, if need be. She prayed it wouldn't come to that.

She could imagine the gossip in the square. *Bahar Smith took those strange city men into his house. What do you suppose they want with him? Problems from his past, no doubt. That business with his daughter. You have to keep your eyes on foreigners …*

Jax's stepmother turned from the hearth as they entered the cottage, baby Denis clutching her skirt, his thumb in his mouth. Agnes's fair, heart-shaped face, lined with the worry Bahar cheerfully refused to feel, paled beneath her white wimple. Sidonie and Lili moved closer to their mother, ten-year-old Siddy taking the younger girl's hand.

"We have guests," Bahar said dryly. "Milords, my wife, Agnes."

Agnes's disapproval easily matched Constable Anatole's. "Sidonie, take your sister and brother to your grandmother's house."

Of Jax's three siblings, Sidonie looked the most like Jax, with her long, dark hair and light brown eyes, but where Jax was too tall and too serious, Sidonie was a lovely dark sprite with the easy manners of their father.

"Yes, Mama. Good day, sirs," she said brightly, bobbing a pretty curtsy for the queensmen. "Come along, children."

Denis and Lili looked like smaller versions of their mother, with their fine fair hair and big gray eyes. But while toddling Denis let Sidonie lift him into her arms without complaint, five-year-old Lili scowled mulishly.

"I don't want Siddy," Lili said. "I want Jax."

Jax crouched down, her heart squeezing with love for the cross little waif with her fierce eyes—for all three of her siblings, however trying they could be at times. "I'll come get you when I'm done. Go with Siddy now, and I'll let you help me groom Bruno."

Lili's eyes widened. She had inherited her father's way with beasts, if not with people, and she loved grooming Bahar's mild-mannered old cart horse.

"I can ride him when we're done."

"We'll see."

The little girl nodded. "By myself."

"Lili! Come along." Sidonie tugged her away.

As the door banged shut behind them, Jax rose reluctantly to her feet.

"Take a seat." Bahar gestured the queensmen toward the sturdy oak table, as much a command as an invitation.

Jax stifled her nervous amusement as the constable and his companion sat themselves stiffly on one side of the table while she and her family watched warily from a distance.

Agnes sniffed. "I'm sure the gentlemen have had a long journey. I'll get some cider."

Jax followed Bahar to the table. Her hammer knocked against the bench as she sat beside him, and she realized she still wore her leather apron.

For a long moment, the only sound was the rattle of mugs and the slosh of liquid as Agnes poured the cider. The sour-sweet scent of it cut through the smell of the stew bubbling on the hearth. Jax's father and the constable looked ready to sit in silence and battle each other, stare for stare, until the end of time.

The younger queensman, Nicolas, finally spoke. "Master Smith, I'm sorry we've surprised you like this. There was no time to send advance word. We've come directly from the queen in Chernesse—"

"Just tell me why you're here," Bahar interrupted. "I'm a simple man. Say it straight."

"King Wulfric's son, Crown Prince Guntram, is dead." The words dropped like stones from Constable Anatole's mouth.

Braced for distressing news from their own kingdom, Jax's memory stumbled on the foreign names. King Wulfric … of Aldforth, Venia's nearest neighbor to the north.

"The prince was killed at Newport near the spring equinox," Anatole said. "May the gods rest his spirit."

"*Killed*, you say?" Bahar asked. "In his own country?"

"By a manticore."

Jax turned to Nicolas. The crown prince of Aldforth killed by a mythical monster? Surely the constable must be joking— or raving. But the younger queensman nodded grimly.

"At least, that's the story," Anatole said. "Body of a lion, wings of an eagle, a dozen rows of teeth. Some such garbage. Idiot probably fell off his horse, and Wulfric's covering it over with this ridiculous tale. True that he's dead, though."

"But what's that to do with us?" Bahar demanded, cutting to what seemed to Jax the heart of the matter. "Rough on King Wulfric, but hardly Venia's problem."

"Wulfric has made it Venia's problem, the old bastard." The thump of a cider mug at his elbow made Anatole start. "Forgive my language."

With pursed lips, Agnes passed around the remaining tankards and sat beside Bahar.

"King Wulfric is a difficult neighbor," Nicolas said.

An ironic understatement. The uneasy peace between Aldforth and Venia had lasted for nearly a century, but Aldfor-thian aggression remained an ever-present threat. Still, unless Queen Léonie planned to offer her as manticore bait to appease King Wulfric, there wasn't much Jax could do about it. A flutter of bitter laughter died in her throat. She wouldn't put it past Constable Anatole to suggest it.

"Prince Guntram's death has only made the situation more precarious," Anatole said.

"He has other sons, hasn't he?" Bahar asked.

"More's the pity," Anatole said bluntly. "Wulfric's a brutal man, and Guntram was worse. I doubt we can expect better from the ones that are left. Prince Theodor is next in line for the throne, and there's a younger boy from the king's mistress. Too bad the manticore didn't take them all."

"Constable," Nicolas warned. "Venia mourns King Wulfric's loss—"

"Yes, yes." Anatole waved him off. "Officially, it's a great tragedy, and Queen Léonie has extended her deepest sympathies to the old—" He glanced at Agnes. "To the old man. In return, Wulfric has sent an invitation."

At the constable's nod, Nicolas reached into the leather pouch that hung at his side and pulled out a cream-colored roll of vellum.

"Her majesty asked us to share it with you," Nicolas said. With long, deft fingers, he unrolled the scroll and held it out to Bahar.

"The queen knows I can't read," Bahar rumbled. "Show it to Jaclyn. She's studied with the priest, like all my children. She'll tell me if you're saying it true."

Nicolas's dark blue eyes met Jax's with a look of comradely embarrassment at having to perform for their elders. He smoothed the vellum on the tabletop and turned it so she could see the bold, elegant script of whatever Aldforthian official had taken down King Wulfric's words.

The scroll was written in the Common Tongue of the Blessed Kingdoms, not Venian, but Jax had no trouble following along as Nicolas began, " 'From His Royal Majesty, King Wulfric of Aldforth, Lord Protector of—' "

"Skip the bedamned salutations," Anatole commanded. "We don't have all day."

As if he weren't the one babbling on about politics instead of explaining what any of this had to do with Jax's family.

Nicolas skimmed down the page with his finger. " 'Due to the tragedy that has befallen our House, we find ourselves with a second son thrust to the fore, in dire need of a wife to continue our line. Knowing, therefore, of the great love the Venian people and their monarch hold for us, we extend this invitation to bring our two countries yet closer in bonds of mutual affection and future prosperity.

" 'We hereby announce a royal ball to introduce Prince Theodor to the most eligible maiden princesses in the nine Blessed Kingdoms and beyond. From their number, one will be chosen to marry our son and heir.' "

Jax snorted, then flushed at the sudden sharp stare from the constable. *But really. A ball? The king might as well have put out a call for "the fairest in the land."*

Nicolas cleared his throat and continued, " 'Had Prince Guntram's wife been capable of her own defense when the manticore attacked, Prince Theodor might have had enough sense to go to his brother's aid, rather than hers, and our heir might yet live.

" 'Thus, our ball shall be enlivened by a series of preparatory events. Each princess shall submit to instruction in the arts that will allow her to protect herself, her future husband, and their heirs. She shall engage in lively competition with her peers in said arts, including, but not limited to, archery, sword-play, and hand-to-hand combat.' "

"Ridiculous," Anatole interjected. "Girls as soldiers."

Jax looked to Bahar. He'd told her the legends of the fabled women warriors of Asbahr, his home country, that war-ravaged land beyond the Almasa archipelago, caught between the sea and the desert kingdoms beyond. But he ignored the constable's words, his grim focus on the vellum in Nicolas's hands, as though it were a dangerous animal that might decide to bite.

Dread curled in Jax's heart.

" 'The princess who proves herself best able to perpetuate and protect the royal line of Aldforth,' " Nicolas plowed on, " 'shall marry our heir and rule at his side as co-regent, fully equal in power to our own son.

" 'By sending participants to our ball, our neighbors may prove their love and friendship for us and assert their innocence of involvement in the foul murder of Crown Prince Guntram.

" 'While acknowledging Venia's peculiar laws of succession, our own customs require blood lineage.' "

No. Jax's heart seemed to slow. *The queen's blood.* He couldn't mean …

"Therefore, we are pleased to understand that a suitable Venian candidate exists to fulfill this display of affection and honor. We eagerly await your daughter's—' "

"Horse apples!" Bahar exploded to his feet, nearly spilling Jax and Agnes off the bench. Towering over the queensmen, his face thunderous with fury, he looked fully capable of storming a ship or raiding a town. "Please forgive me. My Common Tongue must be rusty, because what you're saying is outrageous nonsense."

Nonsense. It was nonsense. A legacy that was no legacy. A past that was never supposed to touch her. Any moment, the queensmen would explain the misunderstanding, and Jax's breath would return, the hollow ringing in her ears would fade away.

"Her Majesty felt much the same way," Anatole said dryly. "After reading this letter, she ordered Wulfric's messenger drawn and quartered, with the further instruction that his head be sent back to Aldforth on a pike. The poor man had a bad few moments before she recovered herself."

Bahar leaned forward, hands flat on the tabletop.

"The ruler of Venia has no children," he said, slowly and distinctly, as if the queensmen were very young children needing a lesson. "Every monarch forfeits all claim to any issue from any union they may make. Children born from such unions are forbidden from benefitting in any way from their parentage or pursuing any claim to nobility or rule. That is the *peculiar* law of succession that allows Venia to choose the most qualified candidate to rule in the event of a monarch's death or abdication."

"Yes," Anatole agreed. He drained the cider from his tankard and clapped it on the table. "Yes, it is."

"The queen wants me?" The idea was so ludicrous Jax's ears burned with embarrassment. The queen had *never* wanted her. "The queen wants me to go to Aldforth and represent Venia at this … ball?"

For the first time, Constable Anatole met her gaze directly. "Princess Jaclyn, you are Queen Léonie's only natural child."

"I'm not a princess." A flare of bitter anger whipped the words from her tight throat. "Or hadn't you noticed?"

"What I notice is immaterial," Anatole said. "I am merely an old soldier who must fulfill his duty to his queen and his country to the best of his ability."

Jax shook her head. "Then it is your duty to tell King Wulfric that Queen Léonie's only natural child is an unlovely, low-born blacksmith."

"You think that would curb his insistence on your attendance?" the constable demanded. "Don't you understand? He *wants* to humiliate the queen."

The stark truth lodged in her chest like a knife thrust, choking her reply.

"King Wulfric is well aware of your status under Venian law, Princess Jaclyn," Nicolas said, his pragmatic calm not blunting the sting. "This invitation is not an overture of friendship. It's a threat. If Queen Léonie doesn't send a representative to King Wulfric's ball, he will use it as an excuse to accuse her of conspiring to murder Prince Guntram."

"That's the queen's problem, then, isn't it?" Agnes snapped. "That law she's been so pleased to abide by these past seventeen years—she doesn't get to just throw it aside when it becomes inconvenient."

"That's not … She doesn't …" Anatole sputtered. "The gods only know what flimsy pretext Wulfric used for sending Guntram to murder the Almasan king's son this past winter. It's not just Queen Léonie's problem if Wulfric decides to invade—"

Agnes rose beside Bahar. "This is *my* family. Not hers. No child in a freewoman's family can be taken from her without her consent. You won't get mine."

Jax stared at her stepmother. Had Agnes really just claimed family-right to her? She saw no more tenderness in Agnes's eyes than usual. Yet the same fierceness burned in them as the time a rabid fox had cornered Siddy near the henhouse and Agnes had gone after it with a soup ladle.

Having seen the remains of the fox, Jax figured Agnes could hold her own against Anatole.

"Agnes—" Bahar looked nearly as astonished as Jax.

Agnes glared at him. "Do you dispute that Jaclyn is a child of my family?"

His wide mouth softened for the first time since the queensmen had entered the house. "No, mistress. I'm just not sure it's quite so simple—"

"It seems simple enough to me." She pointed her sharp chin at the strangers. "You needn't think you can take advantage of us just because we're not city-bred. We know our rights. Pack up your fancy message from that foreign king and get out of my house."

The queensmen pushed back their bench and rose to their feet. Belatedly, Jax scrambled to hers, as well.

"Gentlemen." Bahar nodded toward the door. "I believe my wife has revoked her hospitality."

The constable's face reddened. "This isn't over, Smith."

"I think it is," Agnes said. "I've made myself clear. Will you challenge my rights?"

"No, Mistress Agnes," Nicolas said, inserting himself between her and his master. He didn't lack bravery. "The law on family-right is clear."

Anatole looked as if he might murder the young man himself, but he addressed Agnes. "What do you think will happen to your family if you don't comply? If Wulfric knows about the girl, he knows where she lives. If he decides she's insulted him, do you think he'll let that go? I've seen the heads displayed on the city gates of Cadesleigh, the Aldforthian capital. If you value your family—"

A cold chill ran down Jax's back, but Agnes fairly burned with fury.

"Is that a *threat?*" her stepmother demanded.

"Family-right is clear," Nicolas repeated. "But in this case, the consent is not yours to give, Mistress Agnes."

Agnes turned on him. "The queen has no right—"

"Not the queen," Nicolas interrupted. "Princess Jaclyn. As you pointed out, she has reached seventeen years. Under the law, she is a freewoman herself. The choice whether or not to attend King Wulfric's ball is rightfully hers alone."

CHAPTER THREE

I had no choice. Holy Mother thought it prudent to grant King Wulfric's request for a candidate from the Temple of Peace. I am the most expendable of the royal acolytes, so she sent me.

Of course, I'm happy to go. My sworn duty to the Temple is to defend Peace against all enemies.

As for the contests, I hope to do well. Before her death, my mother ensured I was well versed in archery, light swordplay, and hand-to-hand combat.

I'm not sure what you mean about that being ironic.

— Eira, acolyte of the Temple of Peace and (former) princess of Nordmark

"I don't want to go to Aldforth." Jax's words hung in the soft, honeysuckle-scented evening air.

Bahar looked up from his workbench, where he was filing the blade of a plow he'd repaired. "They can't make you go." The hint of a smile touched his lips. "Your stepmother will see to that."

Indeed, that was all the discussion Agnes had allowed on the matter after she ushered the queensmen out the door. She'd sent Jax to fetch the children with strict instructions not to worry them with "the queen's foolishness" and simmered in tight-lipped righteousness all through supper.

Jax had been glad to escape to the smithy to tidy up the shop and ready the forge for the next day's fire. Even so, the routine hadn't brought its usual calm.

She swept the top of the anvil with a wire brush, though it was already clean. "I'm not a princess. I couldn't be what they want me to be."

"Mmm." Bahar rubbed at the plowshare with a rag, frowned, leaned into the file. "Seems to me those are two different things. What you want and what you think someone else wants of you."

"I'm a blacksmith's apprentice. I don't know how to act at court or how to be a lady. I'd be an embarrassment to the queen. To you and Agnes."

"Agnes taught you manners fit for any lady," Bahar reproved her. "Father Donat taught you your letters. I taught you to dance." A sparkle lit his eyes. "I won your mother's favor with a dance. I'd say you could hold your own at a ball."

"Papa. This is serious."

"I'm well aware." He rubbed the plowshare again, eyed it critically, and set it aside before turning to face her. "It's not the manners or the dancing that worry me. I don't like the tone of that letter. Wulfric's veiled threats and his talk of archery and swordplay. I've seen well-trained knights killed in 'lively competitions.' There's something not right about that man."

"You agree, then." She swiped the brush more forcefully, caught between dread and relief. "I shouldn't go."

"You're my daughter. I would slay dragons to keep you safe."

"I don't think a dragon would bother with Dormance." Jax hung up the brush and sat on the bench beside him. "But King Wulfric might. The constable said you and Agnes and the children might be in danger if I don't go."

"Bah," he scoffed. "That Anatole earns his bread as

queen's constable by imagining all the ways things can go wrong. That's his job. He'll do whatever it takes to protect the queen. Did you notice how he turned your love for your family into a weapon to convince you to do what he wants?"

She had. She also noticed that her father hadn't answered her question. "You were the one who said there's something not right about King Wulfric."

"I almost hope the old villain does send a little muscle. I haven't had a good fight in ages." Bahar flashed his pirate grin, but his next words sounded less sure. "You *want* to stay here in Dormance?"

Jax glanced at the wall between the smithy and the house where she'd grown up. A house filled with good memories—laughing at her father's terrible jokes, making ginger cakes for winter solstice, telling fairy stories to her younger siblings.

Grateful her stepmother wasn't wicked, and yet envying the children their easy love for their mother.

The woods beyond the smithy held memories, too. Memories of hunting berries and mushrooms, wading the creek, pretending to be a character from one of Agnes's bedtime tales or Father Donat's legends. Jax had rescued many a prince from enchantment and saved many a kingdom with a sword or a song.

While she hid from Hubert's taunts and the whispers of the villagers.

"This is my home. I belong here." She said it as if it were true. She was making it true, being her father's apprentice. The village blacksmith always belonged.

Bahar took her work-roughened hand in his. "I knew you'd be safe here, at the least. The most fearful thing a parent can imagine is their child in danger."

"My …" Jax couldn't say *mother*. "The queen isn't worried about the danger. She wants me to go, or she wouldn't have sent Anatole."

Her father sighed. He'd told her stories of her mother, of

course. Fairy stories of the beautiful queen and the rakish, charming foreigner who'd won her love for a season.

Jax no longer believed in fairy tales.

"I said I would slay dragons to keep you safe, and there's nothing truer," Bahar told her. "The queen … I think Léonie knows me well enough to trust that I've raised you to slay your own dragons if you need to."

Such a kinder interpretation than the one twisting its knives in Jax's heart. *Better to sacrifice a daughter she's never known than risk a war she probably couldn't win.*

Jax leaned her head on Bahar's shoulder. Her earliest memories flickered through her mind. Traveling from place to place with her father, before they came to Dormance and he met Agnes. The crowded marketplace in Chernesse, the castle towers rising above the capital city. Splashing in a bright pool below a little waterfall in the forest. A frightening standoff when bandits tried to take her father's horse. An orange for which her father paid more than he could afford, so she would know what his homeland tasted like.

As the light faded and the song of the night insects began, she wondered what Aldforth tasted like.

JAX'S POKER clanged discordantly against the forge as she aerated the coals. All morning her skin had itched with dread at the queensmen's impending return. At the same time, she desperately wanted them to *arrive* already, so this whole business would finally be settled. So she could give them her decision, no turning back.

"Shall I tell you what Laure heard?"

Jax turned to see Hubert leaning against the post at the smithy entrance, eyebrows raised archly. Just what the morning needed.

"Your father's mare is ready." She gestured toward the horse shifting nervously at the hitching ring.

When he'd brought the mare by earlier, Hubert had made a fuss about her high-strung temperament, but the horse had never twitched, even when Bahar hammered in the horseshoe nails. Maybe it was just the sound of Hubert's voice that unsettled her.

"Laure served at the count's table last night," Hubert pressed on. His older sister worked at the manor. "She heard those queensmen didn't come to Dormance to see your father. She heard they came to see *you*, Your Majesty."

And Hubert would make sure everyone in the village heard it, too. Jax bit back an angry reply—it would only encourage him. She turned away to thrust her poker into the central coals of the forge.

"Laure thinks they've come to take you away, to get you married." Hubert sidled around the side of the forge, probably hoping to see his words hit home. "She says one of the queensmen is a jumped-up churl, one of those *learned* lordlings. That seems about right. A grubby lord to marry a grubby princess."

Jax forced herself to loosen her death grip on the poker. He was jealous. Of Nicolas's title, his sword, his court clothes. She should have known Hubert would need to take Eric's acceptance to the Court School out on someone. Should have guessed it would be her.

"Everyone says the queen is beautiful," he continued. "It must be embarrassing for her to have such an uhhh … *unmarried* daughter."

Jax jabbed harder at the coals. "I'm working. You should return your father's horse to him."

"Of course, the queen herself has never married," Hubert mused.

"By law," Jax snapped. "Venian rulers can't marry, any more than they can acknowledge children. She has a consort."

"A lover." Hubert leered at her. "She can have all the lovers she wants. I guess that means you could, too. Maybe she didn't bestow you her features, but you might have inherited her ...” He leaned toward her ear. “... proclivities.”

Jax stumbled back, lifting the poker between them. “Leave me be!”

He laughed. “You wouldn’t hit me. Look at you, shaking. Don’t worry, I won’t hurt you.”

Jax’s arm *was* trembling, with rage and embarrassment. He was so smug, so sure of his right to torment her. She had never before been so close to striking him. No one would go to a blacksmith who attacked a customer. Yet how could she earn her place in the village if her customers did not respect her?

“You need to leave,” she said, steadying her hand. “You have a count of five.”

“Or what? You’ll call for your father?”

I’ve raised you to slay your own dragons if you need to.

As hard as her heart was pounding, Jax had to stifle a smile. Hubert wasn’t really much of a dragon. More like a rabid weasel. She couldn’t risk hurting him, but he didn’t have to know that.

“I don’t need to call my father.” She tilted the red-hot tip of the poker toward him. “Five. Four.”

Hubert stepped back, his face darkening. “You think you’re so high and mighty. You think you’re too good to talk to me?”

“Three.”

“You’re not a princess. You’re just the common daughter of a grubby whore!” He spun on his heel and nearly plowed into the young queensman, Nicolas, who had just stepped through the smithy entrance.

“Watch where you’re going, beggar lord,” Hubert snarled, pushing past Nicolas to fumble the mare’s reins free from the hitching ring. “You’re welcome to Her Royal Highness. You may think she’s close enough to a princess, but she’s still an ungainly cow.”

The mare snorted and danced, dragging Hubert out across the square.

Jax watched them go, choking down laughter and a sickening dread. Hubert would be fuming to get back at her for chasing him away. But it still felt awfully satisfying.

She took a breath and faced Nicolas, who was watching her with thoughtful eyes. The moment had finally come. She lifted her chin. "Are *you* going to call me 'princess' now?"

His lips twitched. "Not until you put that poker down."

She huffed a surprised laugh and hung the poker on its hook. Her hands only shook a little, whether from the encounter with Hubert or dread of facing Anatole, she wasn't sure. "Where is your constable?"

"He sent me to find you. He's already inside with your father and stepmother."

"He sent you to 'talk some sense' into me," Jax guessed. "You're going to remind me of the dire consequences to my family and Venian sovereignty if I don't do what the queen has asked."

"That's Constable Anatole's job." He studied her with unsettling frankness. "I was actually planning to tell you not to listen to him."

"What?"

"I was going to tell you that a royal court is not like a fairy tale. That the princesses attending King Wulfric's ball will be fully versed in politics and intrigue, happy to tear a shy, innocent country girl to pieces. No one, not even the queen of Venia, has a right to ask you to sacrifice yourself on a king's cruel whim."

His pity burned.

"I am not a naive child," she told him.

"I can see that now." A spark of humor lit his cool blue eyes. He gestured toward her poker. "Village life is not so safe and innocent as I believed. And you are neither timid nor helpless. If King Wulfric hopes to humiliate Venia by inviting you to his ball, I think he will be sorely disappointed."

CHAPTER FOUR

I couldn't stop crying when I got the news about Prince Guntram. Have you ever heard of anyone being killed by a manticore? I didn't even know they were real! He was so handsome. Not as handsome as Prince Theo, though.

I do feel lucky to be here. Who wouldn't want to marry Prince Theo? Isolde's sister, Ivonne, had to marry a Venian count who's nearly forty and looks like a toad. Her life might as well be over.

It's just like a fairy story. The king holding a ball, so the prince can marry the most beautiful girl in all the lands. Isolde says I shouldn't even qualify since my father is only a duke. She and I are cousins. You probably know that. Ha ha. People say we look like sisters, though Isolde will tell you that she's the pretty one.

But Papa says any prince would be lucky to have a sweet dumpling like me.

— Princess Pia of Capra

Nicolas opened the cottage door with a perfect, courtly bow. Jax hesitated. Only one stride across a single threshold, yet it felt like a crossroad without signposts. But there was no point in standing still. She'd decided which path to follow. She stepped inside.

As she entered, she caught the lightning in Agnes's eyes, felt the storm brewing between her stepmother and the constable.

"Coward," Jax muttered to Nicolas behind her and was rewarded with a stifled chuckle.

Constable Anatole gestured impatiently for them to close the door.

"It's the girl's *duty* to go to Aldforth," he was telling Bahar, obviously well into his argument. "It's not just the outside menace that Wulfric poses. Queen Léonie's rivals could use his threats as an excuse to seize her throne. I don't suppose you're old enough to remember the last time a reigning Venian monarch was deposed."

He touched the jagged scar on his jaw. "Rivers ran with blood. Even out in the county manors."

"I'm sure clever men like you will find a way to keep the queen on her throne," Agnes said with a sniff. "Jaclyn stays with us."

"Is that your choice, girl?" the constable demanded.

Their eyes turned to Jax, like foxes who had just noticed the rabbit in the meadow. She spent so much effort deflecting attention from herself—her height, her trade, her history. Strange what a relief it was to have them remember she was there to speak for herself.

How unnerving and extraordinary it was to have something to say. As if her sense of herself were being unraveled.

"I'll go."

Nicolas sucked in a breath behind her. Constable Anatole's mouth opened in wordless surprise, as if he were so primed to argue with her, he couldn't think what to say.

Agnes had no such trouble. "You will not! You don't owe this man anything, nor Queen Léonie. Duty." Her mouth twisted on the word as if it were bitter. "What about your duty to this family?"

Jax risked a glance at her father, saw the dismay, pride, fear darkening his eyes. Saw his resolve to let her make her own choice of where her duty lay, regardless of what he would choose for her.

"This isn't her mess." Agnes pointed a fierce finger at the queensmen. "It's wrong of you to ask her to clean it."

"She's the only choice we have." The constable found his voice, still threaded with surprise. "Do you think we would have asked if there were a less humiliating option?"

Jax dug her nails into her palms, on the knife-edge of taking her words back, as she'd been on the knife-edge of not saying them in the first place. Still, she survived humiliation in Dormance every day—like the incident with Hubert just moments ago. She could survive it again to protect her family.

Her father's hand on her arm startled her. She'd been so focused on the constable, she hadn't seen him move. His eyes searched hers as though he might read her heart. All he said was, "Are you sure?"

No. Of course she wasn't sure. She couldn't leave her father, leave Agnes, leave the girls and Denis, leave everything she'd ever known since she was five years old.

She nodded.

He held her gaze for another long moment, then squeezed her arms and nodded back.

Jax realized suddenly that Bahar believed the constable's fears were credible. He would never have told her so. Would never have suggested she risk her safety for the queen's sake. Would prefer to protect his family himself.

Yet, he understood why it was necessary for her to go.

Warmth lit her father's suddenly damp eyes as he leaned toward her ear. "If I were choosing a girl to save Venia, you'd be first on my list."

~

"THIS IS NEWPORT CASTLE, just across the Aldforthian border." Constable Anatole placed his tankard of cider beside the empty trencher he was using to represent the Saber River. "We must reach it within the fortnight."

Ever a scrupulous hostess, Agnes had proved unable to refuse even unwelcome guests an invitation to stay for supper, and after the meal, the old constable had turned the dinner table into an impromptu geography lesson.

Jax tried to gauge the distance of the tankard castle from Nicolas's spoon, standing in for Dormance. She couldn't see the tabletop clearly from her stool by the hearth, but she didn't dare move closer. Lili had raged for an hour after hearing Jax was going away, growling viciously if either of the queensmen came near. She still clung tightly to Jax's neck, though her breathing had settled toward exhausted sleep.

Disgusted with her little sister's histrionics, Siddy sat beside Bahar, her eyes sparkling with the thought of castles and balls and princesses. Denis sat in Nicolas's lap, silently sharing the treasures he had collected throughout the day—feathers, rocks, beetles that hadn't quite survived being put in his pocket with the rocks—hoping they might be used for whatever game the adults were playing. Nicolas attentively considered each one, earning the boy's worshipful devotion.

"King Wulfric's invitation mandates that all the princesses must be in Newport for a 'presentation ceremony' by midday on the summer solstice," Anatole said. "The queen's council wasted so much time arguing over Jaclyn's candidacy that it will be a rush to get her there in time. The ball itself will be held on the night of the winter solstice."

Half a year. Jax squeezed Lili tighter.

"Why Newport?" Siddy asked the constable. "Isn't Cadesleigh the capital of Aldforth?"

"It is, indeed. But Cadesleigh"—Anatole pulled Denis's bowl into play—"is in the Saber's delta. King Wulfric moves court to Newport in the summer to escape the heat—and the pestilence. Fever was bad in Cadesleigh last year. Fortunately,

Newport is just across the Saber from our river port, Hautberge, so we'll have good roads getting there."

"River might still be high this time of year," Bahar pointed
out, leaning over the table. "Still getting snowmelt."

He and Anatole looked like two grizzled generals planning
a campaign. Or two pirates, out to plunder an unsuspecting
merchant ship. If only Bahar had chosen piracy for a living …

"Ferries run all year," Anatole said. "I don't suppose the
girl's horse has ever traveled by boat? Makes some animals
nervous."

"Horse?" Agnes banged down the pot she'd been scrub-
bing by the hearth. "Why would a blacksmith's daughter have
a horse?"

"The previous monarch's by-blows all have a horse and
cart," Anatole said in consternation. "Old King Felix's consort
saw to that."

He glanced around the cottage as if a small jennet might
be hiding under the rafters.

"Her Majesty's not sent Jaclyn so much as a word of cheer
at midwinter," Agnes said tartly.

Jax knew why. Bahar had explained it to her when she was
six and he'd discovered she still expected her mother to write
to her someday, to tell her she loved her. Queen Léonie had to
follow the law to the letter, he'd told her. As the first woman
chosen monarch in a hundred years, she had to be careful to
play by the rules, even if Old King Felix hadn't.

Jax had nodded as if she understood. She'd never told him
how much it hurt that the queen had chosen the rules
over her.

"I suppose there's the baggage cart," Anatole grumbled.

"Princess Jaclyn can't ride into Newport Castle on a
baggage cart," Nicolas objected.

"She can take Bruno," Bahar said. "My cart horse."

"No." Agnes stalked to the table. "How will you take wares
to market without a horse? How will you bring back supplies
for the smithy? They're already taking your apprentice!"

Anatole slammed a hand on the table. "We have no choice! What about that don't you understand?"

"You'll not speak to my wife that way, not in my house," Bahar stated, voice low but no less threatening.

Well, that was the problem with pirates.

"I might have a solution." Jax's heart pounded as all the combatants turned toward her. "By law, I am not allowed the accoutrements of nobility. Isn't that right?"

She addressed the question to Nicolas, the only one she thought she could rely on just then for a sensible answer.

"That's right," he agreed.

"That's a convenient excuse—" Agnes began.

"King Wulfric hasn't given us any other options—"

"Unless," Jax spoke over the red-faced constable. "Unless the queen intends to *hire* me to perform the duties of a princess for the duration of King Wulfric's challenge. If that were the case, the queen might pay me a portion of my wages in advance so that I could purchase a horse for my journey."

Nicolas shot her an approving look. "That would be within the letter of the law."

The constable chewed his cheek a moment before nodding. "It's not an untenable position."

"It still begs the question of where you'll find a horse on such short notice." Bahar's eyes sparkled as he winked at Jax. "It happens I know a fine old gelding that might be for sale."

"A palfrey fit for a princess would bring a high price, indeed," Jax put in, earning a grudging nod from Agnes. "I'm sure the queen's gentlemen would agree."

Her father laughed. "My daughter's wits are as sharp as another's sword. For the price of a princess's mount, I could replace my cart horse, even this time of year, and alleviate the hardship on my family."

"By all the gods." Constable Anatole turned a ferocious glare on Jax, then burst into an abrupt guffaw. "That's a neat trick. I suppose it's the least the queen can do to recompense you for your trouble. Nicolas can write up some showy contract for the sale. We'll bring payment in the morning, along with a trunk for the girl to pack."

"What is she supposed to pack in this trunk?" Agnes demanded. "Don't tell me you hadn't planned to provide her with proper clothing, either?"

Jax glanced down at her tunic and breeches, Lily's sleepy drool adding to the work stains. At least she'd put away her forge apron and hammer.

"Of course we brought clothing," Constable Anatole grumbled. "We aren't going to present her to King Wulfric in rags."

"You didn't bring a horse."

"Clothing is different. Obviously, the girl's never been to court. The queen commissioned proper attire." The constable frowned at Jax. "I hope it will suit. We'd heard she wasn't petite, but we weren't prepared for a giantess."

Jax's face burned.

"The gowns contain material for alterations," Nicolas jumped in, saving her from further discussion of her inconvenient height.

Anatole grunted. "I suppose it's too late to start work on them tonight ..."

Bahar clapped him on the back. "You'd better get out while you can, or you might find yourself in debt to my daughter for more than a royal palfrey."

The pride in his voice warmed Jax's heart. But looking down at her plain, oft-mended clothing, her courage finally failed her. She was a smith's daughter. A smith's apprentice. No amount of fancy clothes could turn her into a princess. When the queensmen saw her in the gowns they'd brought, they'd realize how impossible the whole thing was, and they'd leave her behind.

Surely the emotion she felt must be relief. Even if some part of it felt oddly like disappointment.

CHAPTER FIVE

I insisted on all new gowns for the trip to Aldforth. Once I explained to Father that you don't go into battle with dented armor and a rusty sword, he agreed to provide me with the proper weapons.

He can afford it. Montaine isn't called the "Jewel of the Blessed Kingdoms" just for the beauty of our mountain valleys, you know.

— Princess Isolde of Montaine

My uncle says simple clothes don't call as much attention to my disfigurement. They lessen the discomfort of those who must be in my company. We in Bellis pride ourselves on our diplomacy.

— Princess Beatrix of Bellis

Nicolas and the constable arrived with their cart and driver just past daybreak the next morning and carried the largest, most ornate chest Jax had ever seen into the cottage.

"Ohhhh." Sidonie knelt beside it to run a small hand over its fine oak-leaf carvings. "It really is fit for a princess."

Reverently, she raised the lid, revealing a glimmering dragon's hoard of treasure—jewel-toned silks, shimmering velvet, soft furs. Against her will, Jax drew closer.

"Feel this." Siddy lifted a simple shift from the chest. A simple shift of linen so fine and white that Jax was afraid to touch it, for fear the calluses on her fingers might tear the fabric.

"Lili!" Siddy called toward the cupboard where their youngest sister had hidden when she heard the queensmen's cart arrive. "Come see these beautiful clothes. They're going to make Jax into a princess."

"No!" The cupboard did not muffle the fierceness of the reply.

Denis obediently trotted over, but Siddy dropped the shift back into the chest and scooped him up before he could reach it. "No, Denny. Your hands are sticky."

"I can't wear those." Jax stepped away from the glorious fabrics. They might as well be taunting her. "I'd look ridiculous. Besides, they're doubtless too small."

"The designs are all simple," Nicolas said with calm assurance. "Made to be easily altered since no one knew your measurements. A little needlework is all that is needed."

"And who will do these alterations?" Agnes demanded. "Do you see any royal dressmakers in this house?" She stared down into the chest with an expression approaching awe. "I'm half afraid just to look at them."

"Nico will see to it," Anatole grumbled. "Boy's father is a tailor. He's got some skill. How long will it take?"

Nicolas considered. "If Mistress Agnes and Princess Jaclyn help with the stitching, we can have most of it done in a couple of days. I can complete some things on the journey."

"I'm good with a needle, Lord Nicolas," Siddy spoke up eagerly. She gave him a dimpled smile and a curtsy, Denis still clutched in her arms.

"I would be grateful for your help, Mistress Sidonie." He bowed back.

"Well, get to it, then," Anatole ordered. He eyed the girls

and the clothes and edged toward the door. "Is Bahar in the smithy? I'll go see about the horse and provisions and … such things."

Agnes watched him with narrowed eyes as he hurried out the door. "If that man is an example of courtly manners, I'm glad to be from the country."

"He's an old soldier, Mistress Agnes," Nicolas said. "He's used to giving orders. Asking for help makes him uncomfortable."

"Aren't you the diplomat." Agnes eyed him up and down. "Your manners are fine enough."

His face stilled, as if only the surface of a deep pond had frozen for the winter. "I was schooled in them."

At the Court School in Chernesse, of course, where Hubert's brother Eric would be heading soon. Jax would have liked to ask him about it, but something about his expression stopped her.

Nicolas opened the bag at his waist and pulled out a measuring tape. He caught Jax watching and flashed her a wry smile. "Comes in handy more often than you might think."

"I'll take charge of that." Agnes whipped the tape from Nicolas's hand. "Tailor's son you may be, but I'll not have you putting your hands on any daughter of mine."

"Of course not!" Nicolas flushed, and Jax found her own cheeks heating.

"I will need a measurement from the base of the neck to the waist and to the ankle, shoulders, chest, waist, hips," he told Agnes. "Perhaps you would help me sort the clothing, Mistress Sidonie, while your mother and Princess Jaclyn are busy."

"Princess Jaclyn," Siddy repeated with a sigh. "Does that make you her fairy godmother, Lord Nicolas?"

Jax choked a laugh as she followed Agnes into the small bedroom her father and stepmother shared, the only private room in the cottage.

"Turn around," Agnes commanded. Her thumb pressed the end of the measuring tape against the top of Jax's spine. "Stand straight. Slouching won't improve matters."

"It will take more than a fairy godmother to make me look like anything but a blacksmith's daughter," Jax said wretchedly. "Surely they can see that."

"Most people see what they want to see," Agnes told her. "Hold still. The queen's men want to see a princess, so that's what you'll be. They're not going to change their minds now. Besides, there's no law saying nobility must be beautiful. You're a good sight prettier than Count Reynaud's daughters, even in those old breeches."

Jax shot a surprised glance over her shoulder.

"Arms up." Agnes grabbed Jax's plait and pulled her head straight. "Oh, you're handsome enough in your own way. But it's not what's outside that matters. You'll be representing your father and me, as well as the queen, when you're way off in Aldforth. I expect you to remember that and act accordingly."

"Yes, milady."

Agnes gave her a gentle cuff before pushing her arms back down. "Don't be pert with me, girl. I can still take a willow switch to your backside."

Agnes had never once taken a willow switch to Jax's backside. Even at five years old, Jax had recognized she would never break through the invisible wall between herself and her new stepmother, but she understood that Agnes meant well. She had tried her best not to be any trouble.

Agnes rested a hand on her shoulder. "If you must go through with this, don't let them change you into someone you're not. You've a right compass on you. Follow it. And be sure it brings you home, if just to let us know you're all right."

Hesitantly, Jax settled her own hand on Agnes's slenderer one. "Thank you." Somehow the words came more easily, with her stepmother behind her. "For trying to protect me, to keep me here, despite the danger it might bring."

"That surprises you." Agnes sighed. "I never knew what to

do with you. You never rebelled against me, but you refused to let me raise you to be a gentlewife and mother, as my mother raised me. I wanted you to be Siddy, yet you've become yourself, anyway. I hope I've learned enough to do better with Lili."

Jax smiled wryly. "*I've* never threatened to run the queen's constable through with a dinner spoon."

"I should have let her. That man." Agnes pulled her hand free and smoothed Jax's plait down her back before turning her around. "No, you haven't Lili's brashness, but I fear you've more of your father in you than I realized. I shouldn't have expected to be able to hold you here."

Unexpected tears stung Jax's eyes. "Papa's never wanted to leave Dormance, not since we got here. He wouldn't return to the queen, even if she asked. He loves you. You and the children."

"Is that what you think? That you remind me of his love for her?" Agnes's expression caught between surprise and pain. "I was never jealous of Léonie. He could have stayed with her, you know, been her consort. She expected it, I think. But he would have had to give you up to do it."

Agnes shook her head. "I never feared he would leave me because of *her*."

For a long moment, Jax couldn't reply. Her lungs hurt as if she'd taken a blow to her stomach. "He wouldn't …"

"Wouldn't have moved on if Count Renaud hadn't agreed to allow the queen's bastard to live in his demesne?" Agnes asked. "Wouldn't have fled with you if one of the queen's enemies had tried to steal you to use against her?"

"He wouldn't leave you and the children," Jax repeated. "He loves them every bit as much as he loves me."

"He does," Agnes agreed, her mouth softening. "But they have a mother he trusts to protect them."

Unable to turn away from her stepmother's clear gray gaze, Jax whispered, "Then why would you want me to stay?"

"Why? You fool girl. Because you're *my* daughter. Not the queen's." She gave Jax's shoulder a shake before stepping away and swiping a sleeve across her eyes. "There now. We'd better get your measurements to that lordling tailor, or you'll never leave at all."

CHAPTER SIX

Have you listened to those silly girls complain about the
difficulty they had reaching Aldforth by Presentation Day?
Rovka is farther from Aldforth than any other capital in the
Blessed Kingdoms, yet I had a pleasant, easy journey.

Of course, Ravninan horses are not only the strongest
and swiftest in the world. They have the smoothest gaits, as
well.

— Princess Raisa of Ravnina

That preening devil from Ravnina is so proud of her
prancing, long-legged horses. Let her try crossing the Yxen
Desert in less than a seven-day on one of those water hogs.
Only Kheremese ponies could have brought me to Aldforth
by Presentation Day. I cannot blame them for getting me
here in time. I cannot blame them for being the best in the
world.

— Princess Anara of Kherem

Thick clouds muffled the sunrise, matching the
heaviness in Jax's heart the morning she and the
queensmen were to leave for Aldforth. An early

summer rain hushed against the thatched roof, a soft, misty river falling from the sky.

"I know that constable is in a powerful hurry, but anyone sensible would wait another day," Agnes grumbled as Nicolas and Emile, the baggage cart driver, hefted Jax's trunk. "This is no weather for setting out on a journey."

That might be true, but the climate inside the blacksmith's cottage wasn't much better.

"I'll find you!" a furious voice hissed from the rafters above. "I'll kill you and bring Jax home."

The skinny, stoop-shouldered cart driver made a furtive sign against evil spirits, but Nicolas stopped and looked up toward the demon's hiding place.

"I'll bring her back to you myself, Mistress Lili," he said solemnly. "You have my word."

"You won't!" Lili howled. "Not if she marries that beastly prince."

"Prince Theodor isn't going to marry Princess Jaclyn," Nicolas said, his surprise somehow increasing the ache of Jax's unshed tears. "You don't need to worry about that."

"I'll kill you," Lili spat back. "Maggot."

"Enough of that," Bahar said mildly. He lifted Jax's old woolen cloak from its hook by the door and wrapped it around her shoulders. "A little water never hurt anyone. The rain will be gone by noon."

"Jax should be wearing her princess clothes." Even Siddy looked mulish this morning, clutching Denis to her chest, as the fairy tale dazzle gave way to the reality of Jax's departure. "She doesn't look like a princess in her old breeches."

"There's no sense letting the rain ruin my fine new clothes." Jax tried for a reassuring smile. "And no sense in you getting soaked seeing me out. I'll just say goodbye now."

Her stepmother reached her first, pulling her close with surprising fierceness. Agnes's head came only to Jax's shoulder, yet for an instant, Jax felt like a child enfolded in a mother's arms, wrapped in the familiar scents of cook smoke and fresh herbs and the cow her stepmother had milked at dawn.

Then Agnes stepped back, her face stoic as ever, and Siddy took her place, tears spilling down the girl's smooth cheeks. Jax kissed the top of her head and then Denis's, too, drinking in the milky-stinky toddler scent.

"Come say goodbye to your sister," Agnes ordered the shadows in the roof, but the only response was a muffled, hiccuping sob.

"I'll give you Lili's hug, too," Jax told Sidonie, loud enough for Lili to hear, as she squeezed Siddy and Denis again. "It's a special kind of hug since we're both her big sisters. That means you can give it to her again and again, whenever she needs one, and she'll know it's from both of us because we love her so much. Right?"

Siddy nodded, eyes steely despite her sniffles. "And if Nico doesn't bring you back like he promised, I'll help Lili kill him."

Jax couldn't entirely smother the laugh that burst through her own suppressed tears.

"That's enough talk of violence," Agnes said severely.

Jax turned blindly toward the door. Bahar's hand found her shoulder and guided her out into the gloomy, sodden morning. Constable Anatole already sat astride his big bay gelding, the horse as restless as his master to be on the road, despite the drizzle. Nicolas stood nearby, holding patient Bruno's reins, as well as his own glossy chestnut horse. The cart had disappeared over the hill past the manor; they would overtake it soon enough.

Bahar reached into his cloak and pulled Jax's forging hammer from his belt, his sturdy fingers almost dwarfing it. "You can't go out into the world without your hammer."

"But—" Jax shook her head, her heart suddenly aching for the forge. "But I can't take it. It's yours."

"Mine!" He shot her a flash of that pirate grin. "What would I do with this puny thing?"

"Apprentices don't own tools. Tools belong to the master."

"Ah. You have me there." He rubbed his free hand across his mouth—whether to cover a smile or some other expression, she couldn't tell. "Still, this hammer wouldn't suit any hand but yours. I suppose I've put off noticing, but you've grown into a fine young woman and not a bad blacksmith, if I may take some credit for that. You're no more an apprentice than you are a little girl."

He fit the hammer into the loop on her belt. "It's past time I made you a journeyman smith. The hammer is yours."

Jax touched the cool iron of the hammer's head and bit her lip. She couldn't begin to separate the surge of gratitude and independence that crashed over her from the savage undertow of grief.

"There now, none of that. Blacksmiths don't cry." Bahar pulled her close, and Jax thought not all of the moisture falling on her hair came from the rain.

"There now," he said again. He lifted her hood over her head and adjusted her cloak, as he hadn't done since she was small. He led her to where Nicolas stood with the horses and took Bruno's reins.

The young queensman mounted and edged his chestnut away, giving Bahar room to help Jax up onto the big gelding's saddle. Bahar placed the reins in Jax's grip, wrapping her hands in his.

"A hammer is only a tool," he said. "The good or ill it does comes from the one who wields it. Your heart won't steer you wrong, and you've a good mind. Use them to create your place in this world. I knew when I brought you here, Dormance couldn't hold you. It was only a place I could keep you for a while."

"I'm going to be a blacksmith in Dormance like you trained me to be." The edge of panic in Jax's voice made even staid Bruno twitch nervously. She was leaving to *save* Dormance. Didn't that prove she belonged there? "I'm coming back. Just as soon as King Wulfric's ball is over."

"It will be over before we get there if we don't leave soon,"

Constable Anatole snapped. His horse danced out into the square, Nicolas's mount close behind.

"Of course you'll come back," Bahar said, sounding so certain it settled both Jax and her horse. "You don't want those sisters of yours hunting you down."

He stepped back, and she nudged Bruno after the queensmen. The old cart horse stepped out almost smartly, ears swiveling forward as if he were eager to see what the road would bring.

Jax glanced back. Bahar waved and grinned, a fierce piratical grin that didn't hide his fear or his pride. Jax straightened in her saddle and held her head high. She might not be a princess, but she was the daughter of Bahar Smith, stepdaughter of Agnes, sister of firebrands. If old Bruno could step bravely into this adventure, she could, too.

She'd be back in Dormance in six months with a lifetime of stories to tell the children—and their children. Living the life she knew. The life she was meant to live.

❧

HER FATHER WAS RIGHT. The rain ended by noon, leaving the sky washed a clear, bright blue. Sunlight shone gently through the early summer green of the forest.

Of course, by noon Jax's buttocks, thighs, and knees ached so badly she didn't give a fig about the weather. She had come to hate poor Bruno's back with a driving passion, and she feared she would never walk straight again.

When Nicolas reined his horse back to ride beside her, Constable Anatole turned to glower at him. "Keep up the pace, boy. We'll be lucky to reach Newport in time as it is."

"We won't get there at all if we break down the horses," Nicolas argued. "Bruno isn't used to—"

"That old cart horse is strong as an ox," Anatole said. "It's not the animals you're worried about. Just come out and say it."

"Princess Jaclyn isn't used to riding like this. I'm saddle sore myself."

"I'm all right." Jax shifted her weight. The pain didn't actually bring tears to her eyes—but only because she was too tired to cry.

Anatole harrumphed. "If she couldn't handle the riding, she would have asked to go in the cart with Emile."

If she'd thought of it. Jax glanced back at the empty road behind them. They'd passed the plodding baggage cart hours before. If she got off Bruno now and just sat under a tree by the side of the road … It would mean a longer day of traveling, but it couldn't possibly be more uncomfortable.

"I expected the girl to be complaining like a scalded cat by now," the constable continued, "but she's not said a word. She's showing us how tough she is. Don't take that away from her, boy. She's going to need her toughness in Aldforth."

Jax narrowed her eyes at him. Devious old scoundrel. "*She* is going to need more than that." She gritted her teeth and settled in the saddle. "I need to know about Aldforth, what I'll find when I get there. Which princesses are going to the ball? Where are they from?"

"Nico and I aren't diplomats—" Anatole ignored her snort of agreement. "But we'll teach you what we can. We're bound to know more about the world than you."

"I'm not a fool," Jax said. "I studied with Father Donat."

Anatole grunted dismissively. "No disrespect to your local priest, but his knowledge of the world probably dates from before you were born. Who is the current ruler of Rigas?"

"King Kleon."

Venia's nearest neighbor to the south, Rigas prided itself on being a key trading partner to all the Blessed Kingdoms. With the best harbors on the Central Sea, Rigan merchants controlled lucrative trade routes to Almasa and the Eastern Empires. Even in a backwater like Dormance, Count Renaud imported silks, medicines and olive oil from Rigas.

"King Kleon succeeded his father, King Andreas, six years ago," Jax added. "*After* I was born."

Anatole's bristly eyebrows rose. "So, which of his daughters do you suppose Kleon will send to King Wulfric's ball?"

Jax's mouth opened, then snapped shut. The Rigan king's heir was also named Kleon, but his other children …

Anatole gave a satisfied snort at her lack of response.

"It's a trick question," Nicolas said. "Kleon doesn't have any daughters. The Rigan ambassador says Kleon's sending his niece, the daughter of the younger brother he poisoned."

"*Poisoned?*" That surprised her out of her pain.

"There's no proof of that," Anatole said. "Not that there would be. The Rigan practitioners of *pharmacia* are the best in the world with poisons—and potions of all kinds. Besides, the brother tried to assassinate Kleon first."

He ignored Jax's shudder. "Can you list all the Blessed Kingdoms?"

"And recite your alphabet?" Nicolas murmured, so only she could hear.

Jax stifled a laugh and gave the familiar class recitation. "The nine Blessed Kingdoms are Venia, Bellis, Rigas, Aldforth, Ravnina, Nordmark, The Fair Isles, Montaine, and Ilhavair."

"The Fair Isles have been a protectorate of Aldforth since old King Walther's reign," Anatole corrected, "and Wulfric forced the king of Nordmark into vassalage nearly five summers ago. Your priest is behind, after all."

"But the Blessed Kingdoms are blessed because there are nine of them," Jax objected. Father Donat had taught his pupils a song to that effect. "After the Devastation, when the Santi Empire collapsed, the nine kingdoms banded together—"

"There were *twelve!*" Anatole thundered in sudden exasperation. "Twelve Blessed Kingdoms. Don't children learn anything these days?"

"There haven't been twelve kingdoms in a long time," Nicolas said.

"Mostly thanks to Aldforth," Anatole growled. "Ravnina conquered Voskoya, but Aldforth overpowered Tyrglas, as well as the Fair Isles and Nordmark. Power-hungry imperialists. That's why it's so critical we keep Wulfric's eye off Venia—"

"That's only eleven."

Anatole blinked at Jax as if he'd forgotten she was there.

"I *can* count," she said dryly. "Father Donat taught us that much. There's a kingdom missing."

"Hmph." Anatole frowned at her. "You may be ignorant, but at least you pay attention. Fairföld was one of the original Blessed Kingdoms, but they withdrew from the alliance after Ravnina subjugated Voskoya. Said they wouldn't associate with backstabbers."

"Fairföld?"

"You've never heard of Fairföld?" He rolled his eyes. "She's never even *heard* of Fairföld. The giants' kingdom, girl. Surely you've heard of the giants? They were the heroes of the Battle of the Serpents Teeth, kept the steppe warriors from overrunning the twelve kingdoms before we even got blessed."

"There are actual giants?" She'd heard a ballad about that battle, a legend, no more real than a fairy story. Although, if one were to believe the fairy stories ... "Those monstrous, dull-witted creatures that eat humans? Men fifty feet tall?"

"More like ten. Or so they say," Nicolas said. "I don't know anyone who's ever seen one. They never leave Fairföld."

"Just because they never do, doesn't mean they never will," the constable said grimly. "And don't assume they're slow-witted. Military commanders still study the tactics they used at the Serpents Teeth."

Jax shook her head, caught between delight and a shiver of dread. "What is their ruler's name?"

Anatole and Nicolas shared a look.

Nicolas leaned toward Jax as if sharing a confidence but

spoke loudly enough for Anatole to hear. "We may know more about the world than you do, but how *much* more …"

"The kingdom of Ravnina," Anatole snapped. "On our eastern border. There's always a threat of invasion there. Who rules Ravnina?"

"King Petrov?"

"Excellent. If I'd asked for a ruler from a century ago." Anatole shook his head in disgust. "The current monarch is King Korol."

Jax bit off a sharp reply. However gruff the constable might be, however lacking he found her, he wasn't out to hurt and humiliate her. He truly wanted her to succeed. She could almost enjoy the novel experience, if the consequences of failure weren't so stark.

So don't fail.

"King Korol of Ravnina," she repeated.

I remember my journey from Ilhavair to Aldforth last summer. I was so excited and full of hope. I had been betrothed to Prince Guntram since I was ten years old. I prayed he would be a handsome prince and a powerful knight, and when I met him for the first time in the Great Hall of the King's Palace in Cadesleigh, I saw my prayers had been answered.

Only later did I realize I should have prayed for other things.

— Princess Ellycia of Ilhavair, Dowager Crown Princess of Aldforth

By evening, the travelers passed out of Count Renaud's demesne. They stopped for the night at a small inn. Grateful to be off Bruno's back, Jax ate what her anxious stomach could handle of the simple, hearty supper and escaped to the inn's rear yard. She found a narrow bench by the inn's vegetable garden where she could sit and watch the summer twilight pool under the trees beyond the stable.

The evening peace had quieted even the birds and the insects. Everything but her own troubled thoughts. She was almost relieved when Nicolas tracked her down, a long, narrow bundle under his arm.

"We have another all-day ride tomorrow," he said. "I'm sure you're tired."

Jax strangled a laugh. "You have a talent for understatement. But the more information you and Anatole pound into my head, the more I realize how much I don't know. I wish I were the princess you need me to be."

"*I* wish you didn't need to be a princess at all," Nicolas said, surprising her with his vehemence. "Venia is just fortunate you were willing to fulfill Wulfric's demands. Anatole, the queen—they couldn't ask any more than that. Yet you're smart and determined. You're clever enough to defuse even Anatole's temper. You'll be a better representative for Queen Léonie than anyone had a right to expect."

Grave earnestness sharpened Nicolas's strong cheekbones and darkened his arresting blue eyes.

Stop staring. Jax jerked her gaze away, her cheeks warming.

"I do understand something of what you're feeling," Nicolas continued. "Some people will never accept a tailor's son as a lord."

"But you graduated from the Court School! That makes you as much a lord as anyone. My … Queen Léonie's great-grandfather was a common soldier." It wasn't as though Jax believed the world worked by fair play. Still … "Corrupt rulers drove my father's home kingdom into debt and poverty. It's why he came to Venia, where the ruler is chosen for their aptitude. Venians never have to be governed by a despot or a fool, simply because that person was born a prince or princess."

"I'm not saying a commoner can't rise. I'm fortunate the constable chose me as his aide. But I don't expect to be treated the same as a landed lord." Nicolas took a deep breath, as if loosening something tight in his chest. "It doesn't mean we quit trying to make the world better."

Jax touched the hammer in her belt. "I still think I'm more

suited to smithing than princess-ing. I'd rather be pounding on something."

"As it happens …" Nicolas unwrapped the long bundle he carried, revealing a sword in a dark leather scabbard. "King Wulfric said his guests would be competing in swordplay. I thought it might be good if you've held one before you get there."

Fascinated and unnerved, Jax rose to get a closer look. The simple metal pommel and cross-guard gleamed against the dark, leather-wrapped grip. The scabbard hid the blade. It still looked deadly.

She stepped back. "I don't think you can teach me enough in a week to keep me from getting myself killed."

"Probably not."

Not if that's what King Wulfric wants to happen.

They hadn't talked about that possibility, but if it had occurred to her, it must have occurred to the queensmen. King Wulfric might see his proposed competition as a grand entertainment for his court, a diversion from his grief. Or he might see it as a way to punish his suspected enemies. There was no way to know until they reached Aldforth.

"Even so," Nicolas said, "I might be able to teach you enough to prevent you from killing anyone else."

That had not occurred to her. But it should have. There would be girls there who had never lifted anything more dangerous than an embroidery needle.

Jax shuddered. That long, deadly blade in the hands of a girl with the strength to wield it, but no idea of how to control it … "Show me."

She took the scabbard from Nicolas's hands. The sword slipped from its sheath with a soft whisper of metal on leather. She expected it to feel awkward, heavy, but it weighed hardly more than her hammer and was so well balanced that the blade felt almost like an extension of her hand.

"Careful," Nicolas cautioned. "It's sharp."

"Ha." Jax set the scabbard on the bench and rested the

sword's blade on her open palm. A keen edge indeed. A village smith did not receive commissions to make swords, but her father had taught her to forge a knife, and she could recognize the craftsmanship that had gone into this weapon. It showed an eye for the beauty in simple, good work that reminded her of Bahar.

She tilted the hilt, eyeing the length of the blade. "There's an inscription, but I can't read it."

"It's in an old Santian script," Nicolas told her. "It means, 'protector.' It belongs to the queen. She sent it for you."

Jax almost lost her grip on the hilt. The queen had never given her anything. Now she sent this deadly thing? "The queen carries a sword?"

"Venian monarchs wear a sword when inspecting their soldiers." Nicolas nodded at the weapon in Jax's grip. "Queen Léonie said she has never needed to draw it in anger, and she hopes you won't, either, but she trusted it would recognize your hand and serve you as faithfully as the smith who forged it had."

Jax eyed the blade wryly. No wonder it had reminded her of her father. *Protector.* That could be meant in so many ways. And probably was.

"What is she really like?" she asked. "Queen Léonie?"

Nicolas's brows drew together in thought. "She is a strong, intelligent ruler. She can have a quick temper, but she treats those who come to her for help with compassion. I wish I could tell you more about her as a person rather than a queen."

"It's all right." Jax swallowed the catch in her throat. She had no more claim on the queen's person than any other Venian. "I assume Anatole will have you send her reports on our progress. Please thank her for the sword."

"Most likely, you will never hold anything but a blunted blade in Aldforth," Nicolas said. "But we don't have any training swords with us. So everything we do, we're going to do very, *very* slowly."

He shot her a smile she couldn't help returning. She swept the blade out in front of her, making a swooshing noise, like the boys in Dormance playing knights with their sticks.

Nicolas laughed, his whole face suddenly boyish. It made Jax laugh, too, at the absurdity of the situation. And with something almost like happiness, just to be alive on a soft summer evening with a full stomach and a warm bed waiting, despite the dangers that lay ahead.

"All right, then." Nicolas put on a sober, instructor face that made her laugh again. "You need to be able to move quickly and easily in any direction, so you don't want to stand with your feet together like that. Put one in front, both knees bent."

Jax shifted her feet. "Should I put the sword down?"

"Yes, but don't. You're not going to have enough time to get used to it as it is." He stepped behind her and tapped her sword arm. "Pull your elbow in closer, angle the sword's tip up." He touched her hand where it held the grip, his fingers as callused as her own. "Arm lower, hand a little higher. There."

"I feel like I'm going to tip over."

"Stand on the balls of your feet. You can widen your stance just a bit. Here, turn your hips." His hands touched her hip bones, then jerked back as if they'd been burned. He held his hands high as he stepped away, his cheeks flushing red. "I only meant … I was treating you like I would any … My apologies, Your Highness."

Jax's own cheeks flamed. She wasn't sure if she were pleased he'd treated her as he would a male pupil … or disappointed.

He gestured vaguely toward her legs. "Bend your knees a little more, Princess Jaclyn."

She dropped the point of her sword. "Jax," she said. "My name is Jax."

"You need to get used to being treated like a princess—"

"I'm Jax when you're teaching me sword fighting," she said firmly. "You can princess me all you want the rest of the time, but if you don't treat me like a student when you're training me, I won't learn enough to prevent me from skewering some poor girl. I refuse to be a killer, Lord Nicolas."

Humor softened his stiff, proper expression. "Nico. Out here, I'm no lord. I'm your brutal combat instructor."

"Nico isn't a very brutal name."

"Wait until you've been holding that sword for a while." His smile didn't look so harmless this time. "My sword master's name was Isidore. Still gives me chills."

Jax narrowed her eyes. "Do your worst."

Nicolas laughed. "Right. Head up. Shoulders back. Let's get you standing like a warrior."

CHAPTER EIGHT

Holy Mother told me I should try not to speak my mind so much while I'm in Aldforth. She's not sure I understand the potential dangers. I reminded her that my uncle is king of Nordmark because he plotted my mother's death and my banishment. I don't know why she thinks anything King Wulfric could do would shock me.

— Eira, acolyte of the Temple of Peace and (former) princess of Nordmark

"There." Constable Anatole gestured at the sleek blue-green ribbon carving the wide valley before them. "The Saber River. Cleaver of Mountains."

On the near bank lay the Venian port town of Hautberge, its wooden palisades and bustling docks faintly hazed by the afternoon light. A league away, Jax guessed. Maybe more. Farther yet, across the breadth of the great river, rose the cliffs of Aldforth. The stone buildings of Newport harbor straggled up the steep heights to the walled town at the top.

"The Saber comes down from the Serpents Teeth," Anatole said, nodding toward the cloud-wreathed fangs of the mountains to the east. "Downriver, when it enters the canyons of the Lower Narrows, it runs so fast ships have to be pulled upriver with mules and winches."

But for once, Jax couldn't focus on the geography lesson. She had eyes for nothing but the castle, a glimmer of white stone and spires perched just beyond Newport Town. They had pushed so hard to reach this destination over nearly a fortnight of travel, yet it was hard to believe it was real.

King Wulfric must be there, right now—and the prince. Kings and balls and monsters, human and otherwise. Like a fairy tale made real.

"And who will win the prince's hand?" Jax intoned. "The fairest of them all."

"The most politically valuable," Anatole corrected. "The match King Wulfric finds most advantageous."

"What about the competition?" Jax demanded, rubbing her aching sword arm. "Nico has been working me as if you think he'll make us fight each other. Why would he have this ball if he's already decided on a bride for Prince Theodor?"

"Who knows for sure?" Nicolas said grimly. "To force the rest of the Blessed Kingdoms to acknowledge they're afraid of him? For entertainment? Whatever the reason, you can be sure he's already chosen the winner. Or at least narrowed it down to the top two or three."

The prince isn't going to marry Jax. You don't need to worry about that. Embarrassing how much it had hurt that only Lili had ever thought she might be chosen to marry the prince. And how it lightened her heart to know Nicolas's appraisal had been due to her abject lack of political importance, not her personal worth.

"Well, that's a relief," she said wryly. "I hate to think what my sisters would do to you if I became queen and didn't return home."

"I shudder at the thought," Anatole said.

Nicolas's midnight eyes darkened. "I assure you, whatever happens in Aldforth, I intend to return you safely to your family."

"I thank you, kind sir." Jax sketched him a mock bow from horseback, suddenly grateful for the chance to break eye contact. "All I have to do is be inoffensive and uninteresting enough to prevent King Wulfric from invading Venia. That shouldn't be so difficult."

"I just hope he hasn't already made up his mind about that, too," Anatole said. The old constable stared out across the Saber as if trying to peer through Newport Castle's walls into King Wulfric's mind. "A decade ago or so, Wulfric got it into his head that the Duke of Tyrglas was plotting a rebellion against him, hoping to make Tyrglas an independent kingdom again. Maybe the rumors were true. Maybe they weren't."

"I never heard about an uprising in Tyrglas," Nicolas said.

Anatole shook his head. "Never got that far. Wulfric had taken the duke's two sons as wards, companions for the royal princes. He brought the boys to Tyrglas with his army. Launched the oldest one's head over the castle walls with a catapult. Duke surrendered to save the other boy's life."

"Then he killed the duke?" Jax's stomach lurched.

"No." Anatole leaned from his horse to spit the taste of the tale on the ground. "He graciously allowed the old duke to continue governing Tyrglas in his younger son's name until the boy reaches his majority at twenty—after castrating the father to ensure he couldn't sire any more rebels."

"You waited until *now* to tell this story?" Nicolas demanded.

"Wouldn't have changed her mind," Anatole said. "Would it, girl?"

He *had* warned her. Wulfric's enemies' heads on the gates at Cadesleigh. That's why she'd come. Fear of what the Aldforthian king would do to her family.

"No," she said. "It wouldn't."

"Lord Amaury has a small manor not far from here." Anatole nudged his horse into a walk. Used to traveling with his little herd by now, Bruno stepped along with him. "We'll spend the night there and cross the river in the morning."

"Tomorrow is the solstice. Shouldn't we catch the ferry this afternoon?" Jax asked. They'd been pushing so hard to reach Newport before the deadline, it felt disconcerting to stop before suppertime. "We could be there before dark."

"Everyone in Hautberge will know about Wulfric's bedamned ball by now," Anatole said. "Every princess traveling to Newport has to cross the river."

Jax looked down at her mud-spattered breeches, the hammer stuck through her belt. "You want to put me in Nicolas's fancy clothes before anyone sees me. It hardly matters. I'm not going to make a pretty comparison with those real princesses, however clean I am."

"We're not here to be pretty," Anatole snapped. "We're here to protect our kingdom from a tyrant."

"You won't look like a Ravninan princess or a Montainan princess," Nicolas said. He gave her a quick smile. "But I doubt Ravnina or Montaine has any blacksmith near as pretty as you."

Jax huffed a laugh, and even Anatole smiled.

"We won't be what's expected," the constable said. "Well, that's all right. You're not exactly what I expected when Nico and I got sent off to the middle of nowhere to collect you for this farce."

He nudged his horse into a trot and pulled away.

Jax glanced at Nicolas riding beside her. "That makes me feel so much better."

The warmth of his laugh eased the chill in her heart. She looked back at the river valley, the castle on the cliffs. Tomorrow, she'd be within its walls, in the power of a brutal king. And her best hope was that she might not be what he expected.

It would have to do.

CHAPTER NINE

No Almasan suffers from seasickness. We are born on the
sea. If I appeared unwell when I arrived, is it not natural to
feel sick at heart, traveling so far from home?
— Princess Marjani of Almasa

The steward's wife at Lord Amaury's manor, appalled
that Jax traveled without a maid, took it upon herself
to dress and coif her the next morning. Jax's plaits
were tight enough to pull the skin back from her eyes.

"My poor little cabbage," Mistress Steward fussed as she
cinched Jax's bodice laces. "We'll have you right as rain, soon
enough."

She'd been appalled that Jax's gown was secured with
laces rather than expensive buttons, but with another yank,
she managed to bind Jax's waist even more tightly than her
hair.

When Jax tried to tug up the front of the bodice, Mistress
Steward slapped her hand away.

"Leave that be. It's perfectly modest. Lady Amaury wears
hers much lower than that. It's appalling they haven't bothered to dress you in the latest court fashion."

Mistress Steward was appalled by nearly everything about Jax's situation.

Still, her outrage was all for Jax's sake, and when she stepped back with a smile of approval at her handiwork, Jax was glad for the knowledge her appearance passed the woman's exacting muster.

"That's better," Mistress Steward said. "You're as much a grand lady as I can make you."

Jax felt about as grand as a scarecrow stuffed into human clothes and held upright with a pole. At least her split riding skirt included breeches for modesty.

"Now go find those queensmen of yours," Mistress Steward commanded. "They'll be waiting in the courtyard. But don't let that constable leave without my Luc's escort. We've heard plenty about the royal delegations crossing to Newport on the ferries, and you can be sure they're not traveling with only two guards. King Wulfric is limiting each princess to no more than a dozen retainers at the presentation ceremony, and Hautberge is overflowing with the leftovers."

Emile had left with the cart before sunrise, but Jax found Anatole already mounted and waiting in the yard as Mistress Steward had predicted. Nicolas led Bruno to the block and held him while she swung astride.

"I knew that green silk would be a good color on you," Nicolas told her.

A perfectly natural comment from a tailor's son, but her cheeks warmed, anyway. Maybe his did, too.

"Don't argue with me!" Mistress Steward appeared, sweeping her husband and two gangly sons into the courtyard with her apron as if she were shooing hens. "She should have a proper retinue to escort her, but you sorry lot will have to do. She's a princess! I won't have her shown up in front of all those foreigners."

"Princess!" Master Steward puffed indignantly. "Venia doesn't have princesses! Nor princes, neither. No offense to the girl, but it isn't right for free Venian folk to be bowing and scraping to some chit, just because her mother happens to be queen. If Léonie thinks she can make us—"

"King Wulfric demanded a princess, so we're bringing him a princess," Constable Anatole barked. His anxious bay danced toward the short, round steward. "Unless you want to be first to fall when he sends an army across the Saber, you free Venian folk—those of you who want to stay free—will damned well show your respect to Princess Jaclyn—"

"I'm just Jax!" Horrified, Jax drove Bruno between the affronted steward and the constable's snorting horse. "I'm a blacksmith's daughter. A free Venian, like you. You have no obligation to bow to me, Master Steward. None of you do."

"King Wulfric—" Anatole huffed.

"To all the hells with King Wulfric," Mistress Steward snapped. "We live every day in the shadow of his menace, here by the river. He's got half an army of the dead prince's soldiers there in Newport. Gods know they'd love nothing more than to come whet their swords on us. And this girl is crossing over to keep them in their place. What do you think, Luc Steward? That free Venians would have some mincing, high-and-mighty lady as their princess? Not us! We've got a blacksmith's daughter. You heard her. Just like us."

We've got a blacksmith's daughter. The pride in Mistress Steward's claiming of her stole Jax's voice away.

"Princess Jaclyn is too modest," Nicolas said. "She's a journeyman blacksmith in her own right. More useful than a princess."

"Not afraid to put herself between a free man and a knight's horse," Mistress Steward added, with a glare at Constable Anatole. "To protect her own people. She's one of us."

"She does look more like a blacksmith than a princess." Slowly, the steward's frown untwisted. "Wonder what old Wulfric will make of that? Might make him think twice about threatening us if our princess looks like she could crack a few heads."

He turned to his two teenaged sons, as tall and bony as he was short and stout. "Come on, boys. Let's take our girl down to the ferry. Give Princess Jax a proper Venian sendoff."

The younger son stared up at Jax. "You really a blacksmith, milady?"

"Your Highness!" Constable Anatole corrected.

The boy blanched, but Jax edged aside her fine woolen cloak to show him the hammer tucked into her belt.

He grinned. "A blacksmith princess. That's all right, then."

His mother grabbed his ear, making him squawk. "Her Royal Highness is waiting on you, scamp."

In short order, the steward and his boys were mounted on their own horses and leading the way to town. The knowledge that she would be in Aldforth by mid-morning strung Jax's nerves tighter than her gown laces.

"That was cleverly done," Anatole conceded grudgingly. "Winning over the steward and his boys."

"I wasn't being clever," Jax said. "I was being honest."

"Call it what you like. Just don't expect Wulfric's court to be as easily charmed," he warned. "No one will be rooting for you on the other side of the river."

The sun hung bright with midsummer promise over the distant Serpent's Teeth by the time they reached Hautberge. Jax guessed the ferry town would be bustling at any time, with its docks and barges and ferries. Currently, it looked as though it had burst its seams. Clusters of tents had popped up in the fields around the town like colorful mushrooms after a rain.

From her lessons with Nicolas and Anatole, she guessed that the crimson banner with the rearing black horse marked Ravnina's tents. And the sky-blue banner with the green mountain on it must be Montaine. But the others were a swirl of strangers, tall and short, dark and fair, colorful and plain.

The people standing around the cookfire of a group of red tents nearby had darker skin than even her father, from deep umber to ebony.

"Did Almasa send a delegation?" she asked. "They're not part of the Blessed Kingdoms."

"Crown Prince Guntram spent the winter slaughtering Almasans," Nicolas said. "Maybe they're afraid Wulfric thinks they had something to do with his death."

"It might take more than their princess to appease him," Anatole muttered.

A makeshift market catering to the visitors was doing a thriving business outside the town walls. As they rode past, Jax smelled cooking meat, old ale from the night before, and a rich mixture of unfamiliar spices. The clanging of metal pulled her gaze to a blacksmith stall just off the road. A large man in a leather apron rained quick, expert blows on a horseshoe.

Jax stifled a wave of sudden, desperate homesickness. The hammer in her hand, the heat of the forge, the steady presence of her father. Siddy, Lili and Denis were aching holes in her heart.

The visiting foreigners barely glanced at Jax's group as they rode by, but as they neared the town gates, she noticed curious looks from the farmers and villagers they passed.

"What's your business with those queensmen, Luc?" A rough-clad giant of a farmer stepped in front of Master Steward's horse, forcing him to a halt. "That's never Lord Amaury's chit with you."

"Queen's business, Gabin," Master Steward called back. "Hence the queen's men."

"We heard Léonie was trying to raise up her bastard daughter," a gray-haired woman spoke from the edge of the road. "I said she'd never. She's been a good queen. A fair one. But we all know her paramour was a foreigner, and there's that girl, near tanned enough to be a southerner herself, riding with the queen's guard, bold as brass."

Jax watched the woman's anger radiate into the curious passersby. Nicolas moved closer to her. Anatole's horse skipped to the side, giving him more room for his sword if he needed to draw it.

"That's right," Master Steward said, appearing unperturbed. "This here is Princess Jax, Queen Léonie's daughter, heading for King Wulfric's ball."

"We've had enough fancy folk come through Hautberge this month to last a lifetime." The old woman spat on the ground. "Fine examples of why Venia wants no princesses."

The sweetness of belonging that Mistress Steward's approval had brought her soured in Jax's stomach. More farmers and townsfolk were gathering, and an ominous murmur rustled through the crowd.

"Fancy folk," Master Steward agreed. "With their fancy carriages and fancy servants and fancy tastes, demanding the best of everything and never satisfied."

It made Jax wonder what Lord Amaury was like when he was visiting his Hautberge estate. And what Master Steward was thinking. Did he plan to throw her to the mob, hoping they'd let him and his boys go? Surely the crowd wouldn't challenge Anatole and Nicolas, with their swords and their horses. How much blood would she be responsible for?

"All those kings sending their perfumed pretties to tempt King Wulfric," the steward continued. "Hoping he won't send his armies pouring into their lands like ravaging wolves, slaughtering their villagers, destroying their crops, carrying off their flocks and herds. Like he did to Nordmark not so long ago. Or his father did to the Fair Isles. They're all thinking, better a tribute of one girl than rivers of blood and gold."

His words hung in a sudden breath of silence. His audience's faces changed, remembering just how close they lived to King Wulfric's armies. Thinking of Prince Guntram's hardened men just across the river. Jax would not have imagined the round, balding steward had such simple eloquence in him, but his words held his listeners captive.

He laughed, breaking the spell. "Well, we're sending a girl, too. A Venian girl. She's not going to wilt like some delicate flower in front of old King Wulfric. She's no princess."

Dozens of eyes turned toward Jax, curious, judging, suspicious. She forced herself not to flinch, not to show the raw edge of her unease. Her apprehension of them. Her fear for them.

"She's a blacksmith," Master Steward concluded. "One of us. She'll show him what his neighbors to the south are made of."

The steward's younger son spoke up, his voice breaking in excitement. "Show them your hammer!"

Taking a steadying breath, Jax shrugged her cloak back. Her lips pulled wryly at the corners. No delicate flower had shoulders like hers, that was certain.

She might not have Master Steward's gift for storytelling, but she didn't need to speak to serve his flair for the dramatic. Or show her pride in being a blacksmith. She pulled her hammer from its loop. Staring directly at the angry old woman, she slapped the handle into her right hand and raised it high over her head.

Someone barked a laugh. Another whistled.

"Did I say bold as brass?" The old woman spat again. Then waited. She knew how to work a dramatic moment, too. "More like bold as iron!"

The huge farmer laughed, and a child whooped.

"Princess Jax!" Master Steward shouted. "Make way for Princess Jax!"

"Make way for Princess Jax!" The crowd jostled and pushed each other back. "Princess Jax! The blacksmith princess! Princess Jax!"

Master Steward urged his horse forward, his sons on either side to form a wedge. Nicolas and Anatole dropped back, leaving Jax … *alone, protected, on display* … in the middle as they rode in formation through the town gate and down the main street of Hautberge.

Children ran ahead, and the grownups followed behind,

cheering and laughing. The way cleared before them, people moving aside in confused curiosity until the crowd explained. Jax didn't lower her hammer until they reached the waterfront. There, an eddy of the great river created a calm docking place for cargo barges and ferries alike.

Master Steward rode his horse right onto the largest ferry, where Emile and his cart had already been secured for the passage to Aldforth. Jax feared Bruno might balk, never having traveled by boat, but he seemed as relieved as she to escape the crowd. Nicolas dismounted to take Bruno's reins, and Jax slipped from the saddle. The boat shifted as she touched the deck, and she had to grab Nicolas's shoulder to steady herself, but at least she didn't get tangled in her new skirts or fall on her face.

"Your Highness," Master Steward addressed her from his saddle. "Do you want my boys and me to cross with you?"

Yes. She wanted his sturdy support, his boys' grinning admiration, to bolster her on this last stretch of her journey. But they'd already risked enough for her, more than she'd known they would have to. And Mistress Steward would be waiting for their safe return.

"Thank you," she said, trying to convey how much she meant it. "For all your help and kindness. We will be fine from here."

"Very well, Your Highness. We'll wish you luck, then."

"I will take all the luck I am offered," she said fervently.

He gave a deep, court-perfect bow. "Gods be with you, Princess Jax."

The boat shifted again as the steward and his sons rode back across the boarding ramp, and Bruno nickered. She laid a hand on his neck to steady them both as the ferrymen pulled the ramp aboard and the boat moved away from the dock.

"Wave." Nicolas nodded toward the crowd.

Jax raised a hand, and the people on the bank cheered.

"Princess Jax!" came the ragged call. Someone shouted, "One of us!"

Jax watched the deep green water widen between the ferry and the docks. How strange to hear anyone call her their own. Strange to be a princess who had never been wanted by her mother, her village, or her kingdom until she left.

It should feel good, to be claimed, acknowledged. But instead, it was terrifying. It wasn't just her family counting on her protection, not just Siddy and Lili and Denis who would suffer if foreign soldiers marched into Venia.

The lives and livelihoods of everyone in Hautberge, of everyone in the kingdom, rested on her shoulders.

"You can do this," Nicolas murmured beside her.

"Do what?" Jax stuffed her hammer into her belt. "If it hadn't been for Master Steward, those people would have pelted me with rotten fruit instead of cheering my name."

"True enough," he agreed wryly. "But those people are your people now. You're their princess."

Constable Anatole huffed. "Gods help us all."

CHAPTER TEN

As Dowager Crown Princess Ellycia's stepsister, I should have been allowed into Newport Castle as soon as I arrived, not made to wait with all the other girls. I bet Ellycia told them to keep me out, but she's already had her prince. Now it's my turn.

Everyone knows King Wulfric still needs the alliance between Aldforth and Ilvahair if he wants unrestricted trade routes for his fleet. I am the obvious choice to marry Prince Theodor. There's no point in pretending otherwise.

— Princess Lidia of Ilvahair

Jax craned her neck to watch the walls of Newport Castle loom closer atop the cliffs downstream from the ferry docks. Bare rock spires jutted from the forested hills behind it, like the remains of ancient ruins. She narrowed her eyes. One spire had windows.

"Is that a tower?" she asked. "On that hill past the castle?"

"Lukos," Constable Anatole said darkly. "The northernmost stronghold of the Santi Empire, before the Devastation."

"They called it the Light in the Darkness," Nicolas said. "An outpost of civilization and learning. Gold gilded the great hall. Hot and cold water ran through pipes to the kitchens and bathing chambers. There was a library as big as a stable."

Jax had heard the same yearning in Father Donat's voice when he spoke of the knowledge and beauty lost during the century of the Devastation.

"Why didn't the Aldforthians rebuild it?" she asked.

"Cursed." Gruff, practical Anatole made a sign against evil. "Legend says that's where the Devastation started. Digging up things better left buried. Demon magic, maybe."

"*History* says all the Santians in Lukos died trying to stop the Devastation and find a cure," Nicolas said.

"Maybe." Anatole shrugged. "Served them right if they started it."

Jax hid her smile. No wonder Queen Léonie trusted the constable. You always knew where you stood with him. "I suppose a civilization-ending plague is too much to hope for to get us out of this mess."

"The boat could still sink," Anatole said. A fortnight ago, Jax wouldn't have caught his dry humor. Now it buoyed her.

In the end, the ferry docked smoothly. Warehouses, merchants' offices and public houses crowded the narrow curve of the docks, then stacked themselves haphazardly up the steep road leading to the clifftop where the rest of the town perched. The waterfront milled with activity—workers loading barges, men and women mending fishing nets, tavern keepers sweeping their stoops, children chasing each other up and down the narrow streets. They all kept an eager eye on the arriving boats, enjoying the excitement of foreign royalty come to parade through their town.

Jax stiffened in anticipation of their judgment, but their eyes slid away as she and the queensmen rode their sturdy horses up the steep, cobbled streets. The denizens of Newport had spent the past fortnight gawking at beautiful girls in beautiful clothes, escorted by knights and fanfare. A trio of decently dressed minor nobles didn't rate a second look.

Jax might have laughed if her thudding heart hadn't made simply breathing a struggle.

Newport's upper town overflowed its wooden palisade on the rocky clifftop, prosperous and lively. The road passed around the town wall, leading through a grassy dale toward the castle on the low hill beyond.

"King Wulfric's 'summer palace,' " Anatole growled.

Jax pulled Bruno to a halt to stare. The stone curtain wall shone white in the sunlight, its circular guard towers as graceful as they were imposing. The castle itself rose behind the walls in a confection of turrets and fluttering flags, bright against the forested crags beyond. The fairytale beauty intensified Jax's sense of unreality.

In the broad meadow before the castle stood smaller versions of the tent cities around Hautberge. Groups of brightly dressed people sat on horseback or in carriages or covered palanquins.

Princesses, waiting to make their entrance.

Thank goodness Anatole hadn't given her time to eat breakfast. She couldn't be sick if there was nothing in her stomach.

"You might not want to wait there too long," a thin, leather-skinned man leading a mule called to them. His Common Tongue held the clipped accents of the north. "You're dallying right where the manticore done for Prince Guntram, and they never did catch the thing." He grinned around jagged teeth. "Still blood on the rock if you look close enough."

Jax couldn't help glancing at the sky, as if even now a winged monster might be plummeting from the high, blue expanse. The scene played in her mind's eye—the residents of Newport cheering their returning prince, the courtiers there to escort him to the castle.

The rocky cliff offered no shelter from an aerial assault.

Bruno sidestepped uneasily, and Jax patted the horse's warm neck to reassure him. If only she could reassure herself.

A manticore attack sounded no more frightening than the gathering of royalty on the grassy swale below.

A trumpet's brassy call carried over the open ground. The castle drawbridge began lowering across the deep ditch surrounding the curtain wall.

"It's time." Anatole gave a battle-ready smile. "There are more delegations here than I expected. Maybe they won't notice us."

If there hadn't been a cliff and a swift, deep river behind her, Jax might have been tempted to flee home to Dormance. But poor Bruno couldn't outrun the queensmen's horses, and Jax knew with a sick certainty that she couldn't outrun her birth. She touched her heels to Bruno's sides and followed Anatole.

Ahead, the bright clusters of royals and retainers moved toward the castle gates. Some crowded to be first, while others held back as if hoping to make a grand entrance. Soldiers with gleaming pikes and plumed helmets planted themselves at the head of the drawbridge. A man in a black tunic stood beside them, attempting to organize the procession.

Jax wiped a damp palm on her cloak and hoped Bruno's reins wouldn't slide from her grip.

"There's Ravnina." Nicolas nodded toward the group now crossing the drawbridge. Jax recognized the rearing horse on the standard bearer's bright crimson flag from the Ravninan camp across the river.

"King Korol," Jax recited. The first lesson Anatole had given her. "Queen Irina died two years ago. He has five daughters and three sons. Crown Prince Andrey is eight."

"Ambassador Grigory told me he thought Korol would send his eldest princess, Raisa," Anatole said. "Prince Theodor would be the perfect match to take an unmarried, ambitious daughter off his hands."

"And Wulfric will surely be tempted by an alliance that would squeeze Venia between her two most powerful neighbors," Nicolas added. "Raisa will be a top contender for Theodor's hand."

There were several women in the Ravninan delegation, but only one glimmered like the sun in a surcoat of cloth of gold. As they watched, Princess Raisa's sleek black horse tossed its head and rose up on its rear legs. Jax caught her breath, afraid it might topple from the drawbridge to the rocks below, but the horse balanced perfectly, then leaped forward with graceful power, landing on all fours. The young woman on his back sat tall and proud, in complete control.

"Over there." Anatole pointed to the sky-blue standards flying above a gilded carriage that crowded toward the draw-bridge, cutting off the group of riders behind the Ravninan contingent. Shimmering gold curtains hid the passengers from view. "Who is that?"

Green mountain on a blue field. She'd known it an hour ago, outside of Hautberge. She closed her eyes, blocking out all the wealthy, powerful strangers. *Small kingdom nestled at Venia's south-eastern border with Ravnina and Rigas, protected by its ring of mountains …*

"Montaine," she gasped, opening her eyes. "King Henrik and Queen Clementina. They have two daughters?"

"This will be the younger one. Isabelle? Isadora?" Anatole grimaced. "Never thought I'd need to remember. The older daughter, Ivonne, married a Venian count. Her first-born son should inherit the Montainan throne, cementing our king-doms' alliance. But if the younger girl produces an Aldfor-thian prince first …" Anatole tilted a hand back and forth.

"Montaine may be small, but the gems they dig from their mines are big enough," Nicolas said as they watched the man in black direct the Montainan carriage across the drawbridge. "If Wulfric got his hands on Montaine's wealth, it could finance any number of Aldforthian wars."

"I've heard the Montainan princesses are comely, too," Anatole added. "Wulfric's a practical bastard, but I'm sure he likes a pretty face."

Jax worked to calm her breathing as they rode toward the gates, wending their way through the local townsfolk, farmers and villagers who had gathered on the grass to catch a glimpse of foreign royalty.

They passed a group of religious pilgrims, men and women in plain brown cassocks and hoods. A young priestess walked with them. Her white robes glowed in the bright sunlight, despite the travel dust around the hem, and her long, icy blond hair was pulled back with a silver band. Jax noticed with surprise that she carried a bow and quiver slung over her shoulder.

Ahead, a group of men and women in light blue tunics were also walking, but their fine clothes and haughty demeanor said these were no footsore pilgrims. They must have traveled to Newport by boat. They left a careful space around the figure in deep, sapphire blue at their center. She strode with watchful grace, head high, red hair spilling down her back in fiery waves.

"Where is that group from?" Nicolas asked.

"That hair," Anatole said. "It can only be Bellis."

"*Bellis?*" Jax repeated. Bellis was one of the Blessed Kingdoms, an island city-state just off the coast of Rigas in the Central Sea. But … "You said the Bellisian senate chooses the king's successor, so they don't have princesses, like Venia."

"Bellisian rulers style themselves emperors, not kings." Anatole snorted at the conceit. "And the senate almost always votes in favor of the reigning emperor's chosen heir. I thought Constans' daughter had died. I suppose one of his brothers must have a girl." He shook his head. "I never thought those arrogant weasels would send a delegation to the barbarian north. Maybe they couldn't bear to be left out."

Pounding hoofbeats pulled Jax's attention from the Bellisian entourage. A half dozen men on horseback appeared around the castle's north side, their mounts galloping full-out. The men all wore plain black tunics, and black masks covered their faces. They whooped as they bore down on the delegations crowding toward the drawbridge, their eyes and teeth gleaming.

Bandits. Jax grabbed her hammer as Nicolas reached for his sword.

"*Hold.*" Anatole barked. "They're unarmed. Mischief-makers, not outlaws, I'll wager."

Indeed, these rowdy young men rode sleek coursers. Their costumes boasted fine silk trim. In their sword hands, they held roses. Gawkers scattered as they charged into the crowd.

"Ilhavair!" cried the lead horseman, a tall, dark-haired gallant. He pulled his horse into a hard turn that brought it skidding to its haunches beside a covered palanquin carried by six men in sea-green livery.

Ilhavair, Jax's mind finally made sense of the word. An island country in the western ocean. The palanquin must hold the Ilhavairan princess.

A fair hand pulled aside the gauzy curtains. The horseman tossed a red rose into the compartment and spun his horse away.

"Almasa!" An auburn-haired brigand on an auburn-haired horse galloped past another sedan chair, this one open to the elements. He tossed a yellow rose to the single occupant, a tall woman in deep red robes with skin as dark as the tightly curled hair cropped close to her head.

A man with harvest-blond hair turned his silver-gray mount toward Jax. Her face burned—*I'm not a princess*—before she saw the man's eyes were focused on the Bellisian delegation ahead of her. Of course, they were.

The foxy-haired rider put heels to his mount and cut the blond rider off.

"Bella Bellis!" he cried, parting the sky-blue tunics like waves.

The regal, red-headed woman turned at his shout, and Jax gasped involuntarily. The right side of her face was a rough, faded tracery of flame that ran from her neckline to her forehead. The burn had spared her eye but taken part of her right eyebrow, giving her expression a sardonic tilt.

The horseman's mask didn't hide the sudden, repulsed twisting of his jaw. His shoulders jerked sideways in horror. His horse turned with him, its eyes rolling in surprise at the panicked yanking on its reins.

The Bellisian princess showed no emotion, as if her whole face were hard and immobile as her scars. Even her eyes, green as emeralds, gave nothing away.

Over the rustle of spreading murmurs, Jax heard one of the other horsemen laugh nervously. Nearby onlookers joined in. Someone shouted, "Young duke's courting monsters now!"

"Doesn't know the difference! It's not like his father can teach him what a real wench is like!"

Foxy-hair might have meant to ride away, to find another princess to shower roses on, but the mockery tugged him around. Fury distorted his masked face, reminding Jax of Hubert. He reached for his sword but found only a pouch of flowers.

"Can't find your shaft, Your Grace?" someone shouted, to coarse laughter.

The rider's visible skin flushed red as his hair. His gaze fell back on the Bellisian princess, his jaw set in humiliated fury. Even as he dug his heels into his horse, Jax threw herself from Bruno's saddle.

"No steel!" Anatole shouted, grabbing Nicolas's sword arm before he could follow her. "No weapons!"

Jax ran toward the red-haired girl as the princess's own retainers fled before the galloping warhorse. The scarred princess stood immobile, the only unmoving object on the lawn, focused on the enraged horseman bearing down on her. Maybe he only intended to scare her, to make her run, but Jax could tell the girl had no intention of running.

"*Princess!*" Nicolas's desperate shout turned the Bellisian girl's head.

Her green eyes widened as she saw Jax barreling toward

her. Jax reached for the girl's arm to drag her out of the horse's path, but her foot caught in her long riding skirts. She tripped straight into the motionless princess. Maybe the Bellisian braced herself, but Jax was bigger—of course—and she wrapped her arms around the girl as they collided.

A horse's scream pierced her ears as they tumbled sideways, both of them landing on Jax's shoulder, rolling and skidding as iron-clad hooves pounded past their heads.

CHAPTER ELEVEN

I can't believe we missed the Rose Knights. I would have swooned if one of them had offered me a rose! Isolde just *had* to be one of the first into the castle.

Still, I have to keep pinching myself. One of us princesses is going to *marry Prince Theo*. I joked to Isolde that I hoped our carriage wouldn't turn into a gourd, but she didn't think it was funny.

— Princess Pia of Capra

J ax lay sprawled on the ground, braced against the imminent pain of being trampled. But except for the wrenching of her shoulder and an ache in her ribs where the other girl's elbow had landed, she felt nothing except shock and the first prickling of mortal embarrassment.

A horse snorted, jerking her from paralysis. *He's coming back to finish the job.* As she struggled to disentangle herself from the Bellisian princess's blue robes, a calfskin boot planted itself in front of her nose.

The boot belonged to the white-robed priestess Jax had noticed earlier. She stood facing the heavy-breathing horse, reaching for the bow on her shoulder.

"No weapons!" Jax gasped, remembering Anatole's command.

The priestess shot her a questioning look from calm blue eyes, shrugged, and left the bow in place. Her stance shifted, and suddenly her hands looked as dangerous as the arrows in her quiver.

"Be easy. I mean you no harm." The masked rider dismounted.

Jax scrabbled for her hammer, panic overriding her own instructions. Yet as her hand closed on the haft, she realized the rider wasn't Foxy-hair. It was the tousled blond knight.

The priestess stepped aside to let him crouch beside Jax and the red-haired girl.

"Are you hurt, Princess?"

"I'm all right," Jax assured him, but the horseman was extending his hand to the Bellisian.

"Can you stand?" He sounded genuinely concerned. Even with half his face hidden behind the silken mask, he was a vision of a handsome cavalier.

For an instant, burning fury flared in the Bellisian princess's green eyes before her expression smoothed of emotion once again.

"If this giantess will allow me to rise," she said coolly, her Common Tongue smoothed and polished by the faintest of accents.

"She saved your life." The blonde priestess reached down to offer Jax a hand as the horseman helped the Bellisian to her feet.

"Should I thank her for that?" the redhead demanded, tilting as much of her scar as possible toward Jax and the priestess. Then she blinked, and something else flickered deep in her eyes, something that might be shame. "Please, forgive me. I do thank you for your quick action on my behalf."

"Jax!" Nicolas pushed past the horseman and grabbed Jax's shoulder, his midnight eyes wild. "Princess Jaclyn. Are you all right?"

Embarrassment burned through her as the others turned to stare. Or maybe the heat came from Nicolas's grip on her arm. Dragging her gaze from his, she realized that neither of the other girls' retinues had come to their aid. The Bellisians had scattered well out of the way, and the priestess's brown-clad companions stood where she had left them, showing no apparent surprise or concern at her actions.

"What were you thinking?" Nicolas demanded. "You could have been killed."

"She was proving she is capable of protecting Prince Theodor, of course," A sardonic smile touched the Bellisian princess's mouth. "As was Princess … Eira?"

The priestess's eyes widened. "I am impressed. I don't know how you guessed my name. Who are you?"

The red-haired girl tilted her head. "Beatrix of Bellis, in your debt."

More hoofbeats caught Jax's attention. The dark-haired rider who had led the masked brigands pulled his mount up several yards away.

"Kenrick has brought out the guards," he called to the blond boy. "We have to go."

The blond rider pulled a soft pink flower from his satchel and offered it to the Bellisian princess, Beatrix. "A gift from the Rose Knights. Welcome to Aldforth, Your Highness." His gaze shifted uncertainly. "Your Highnesses."

Princess Beatrix glanced down at the bedraggled blossom.

"Ra—*Hurry*," the dark rider ordered, glancing anxiously toward the castle. Three soldiers in chain mail hauberks struggled to get their mounts around the carriage blocking the gate.

With a sudden, impish grin, the blond boy tossed his rose to Beatrix and bolted for his horse. It didn't flinch as he vaulted nimbly to its back—perhaps used to such abrupt exits. The two horsemen spurred their horses after their companions, back the way they had come.

The mounted soldiers finally reached the end of the drawbridge, where the man in black urged them after the bandits.

"The Rose Knights' horses are tired," Beatrix said coolly, watching the soldiers chase the fleeing boys around the castle walls. "They'll be caught before they reach the postern gate."

"The soldiers' horses are carrying the weight of their armor," the priestess—or princess—Eira said. "It will be a good race." She turned to Jax. "Why wouldn't you let me draw my bow? A good scare wouldn't have hurt them."

Jax's breath left her. She had never in her life been within speaking distance of royalty—at least, not since the wet nurse had taken her from her mother's arms—and here she stood with one princess she'd tackled to the ground and another she'd ordered about. A blacksmith's daughter could be whipped bloody for less.

"*Princess* Jaclyn," Nicolas reminded her, steadying her.

"No weapons," she repeated. Anatole must have understood the situation immediately. "Those Rose Knights. Young lords making mischief at King Wulfric's court? One of them must have been Prince Theodor."

Pale Eira paled even further.

"Not even a princess would survive drawing a weapon against King Wulfric's heir," Beatrix said with a frown. "Thoughtless of him to put us all in danger like that."

"I hope he isn't the ruddy-haired boy." Eira wrinkled her nose. "I'd rather not have to marry *him*."

That was a thought.

"Princess …" Constable Anatole reined in near the group, leading Bruno and Nicolas's horse. Only the tightness around his jaw showed his tension. "…Prin*cesses*… We should continue to the castle."

"It is not diplomatic to cause a scene on your host's doorstep," Beatrix agreed.

For a moment, the three girls shared a glance. Then Eira laughed, openly delighted. Beatrix actually smiled.

Jax blew out a choked breath and made her way to Bruno's side, where Nicolas cupped his hands to help her mount. If he noticed her trembling legs, he didn't mention it.

He rested a hand on Bruno's neck, a hint of quiet humor returning to his eyes. "The next time you plan to do something dangerous and stupid, please hit me in the head with your hammer first, so I don't have to watch."

"It wasn't *that* dangerous."

Nicolas lifted the edge of her cloak. The muddy imprint of a horse's iron shoe marred the fine wool.

Jax struggled for a light tone. "Maybe Princess Beatrix was right, and I've just proved to the king I can protect Prince Theodor."

"Let's hope he doesn't get the idea you're dangerous instead," Constable Anatole said. "I assumed you understood that the one thing, the *one thing*, we wish to do here in Aldforth is *not* to draw King Wulfric's attention."

Jax bit her lip. They were right. She should not have interfered. Her only real weapon against the danger King Wulfric posed to her family was her utter lack of importance or interest.

She looked toward the castle to see the man in black waving the Ilhavairan delegation across the drawbridge. He hardly spared them a glance. He was too busy staring at Jax.

CHAPTER TWELVE

What did I expect? I expected Prince Theodor to be more mature, a pragmatic warrior like his brother. The Rose Knight charade was the game of a frivolous boy.

No, I am not disappointed. Every opponent's weakness is an opportunity. Yes, I did say opponent. Isn't marriage simply another kind of battle?

— Princess Raisa of Ravnina

When Jax and her companions reached the drawbridge, the man in black ignored her. He asked Constable Anatole for their names, wrote them in a leather-bound ledger, and instructed them to cross the bridge. His extravagant lack of interest didn't ease Jax's nerves.

"This is it," Anatole muttered as they rode beneath the heavy iron spikes of the portcullis. "We're in it now."

Jax shivered, grateful to pass out of the shadowed gateway into the sunlight of the castle courtyard. After the commotion outside the gates, she had expected chaos, but order reigned in the yard. The delegations already within waited in evenly spaced groups around the courtyard, like the markings on a sundial.

A recently erected wooden dais, the planks still fresh, fanned out in a semicircle from a narrow stone stairway leading to the entrance of the castle's looming keep. Two high-backed, velvet-cushioned chairs waited in its center. Red ropes marked off viewing galleries on each side of the dais. These were crowded with finely dressed men and women—presumably nobles summering in Newport with their king.

Soldiers in Aldforthian livery stood at intervals around the dais and galleries, so neat and orderly they might have seemed purely decorative if not for the gleaming pikes held at their sides.

A young page in the black and purple of the royal house of Aldforth led Jax and the queensmen to an open spot on the southern side of the yard, near the stables. After shooting a wary glance around the courtyard, Anatole nodded that they should dismount.

As soon as Jax's feet hit the ground, the page bowed. "The presentation ceremony will begin precisely at noon. Castellan Kenrick asks you to wait here, Your Highness."

"Who?"

"Castellan Kenrick, Your Highness." The page peeked up from the bottom of his bow. Probably thinking she was the most unlikely princess he had ever seen. "He runs the castle for the king. You met him at the gate?"

The man in black.

"Yes. Of course. Thank you." She feared she sounded as lost as she felt, but it was good enough for the page. He scurried off before she could ask anything else.

"Almost noon already," Anatole said. "Took them that long to get everyone inside."

Indeed, the sun seemed to have stalled directly overhead. Inside the walls, protected from the breeze, it beat on Jax's shoulders like a smith's hammer.

Nicolas offered her a waterskin.

"Drink," Anatole ordered when she hesitated. "Don't want you passing out in the middle of the ceremony."

As she lifted the skin to her lips, a trumpet blast burst the bubbling murmur of the courtyard. Jax choked, spitting water down the front of her surcoat. Anatole thumped her back, a little harder than necessary. She swiped self-consciously at the damp, but no one around them noticed her embarrassment. All eyes were on the keep entrance, where a herald blew another raucous call before descending the stairs to stand at one side of the wooden dais.

His voice rang nearly as loud as his horn. "His Royal Majesty, King Wulfric of Aldforth, Lord Protector of Nordmark and the Fair Isles, and His Lady, Her Grace, Duchess Bianka of Southsea."

The king—he had to be the king, though he looked more like a soldier than a monarch—descended the stairs before the herald could finish. His steps rang with impatience, and his eyes raked the courtyard from under thick, grizzled brows. His neatly trimmed hair and beard were equally shot with gray and black. He wore a simple black tunic, unadorned save for the silver wolf's head emblazoned on the front. A single glittering emerald embellished the plain gold circlet on his head.

To be fair, the emerald was large as a hen's egg.

Duchess Bianka, younger than the king by at least two decades, followed more sedately in a confection of periwinkle silk skirts beneath a white velvet cloak trimmed with ermine. Even in such a profusion of material, she managed to appear cool and unflustered, despite the heat. Her pale blue eyes focused somewhere above the gathered crowd as she expertly navigated the stairs without plunging to her doom, which Jax thought was an impressive feat.

The couple took their seats on the chairs at the center of the dais.

"Duchess?" Jax asked Anatole beneath her breath. "Why is she not called queen?"

"Old queen's still alive," he muttered back. "Joined some religious order years ago, after giving Wulfric his heir and a spare. This one's his mistress. He made her a duchess after she gave him an extra son."

The herald's voice rang out again. "Her Royal Highness, Ellycia, Dowager Princess of Harcastle, and His Grace, Prince George."

"The crown prince is always prince of Harcastle. The widow will lose that title when it goes to Prince Theodor," Anatole continued his lesson in Jax's ear. "Hadn't heard that Bianka's boy had been made a prince."

The dowager princess wore a black cotehardie trimmed with copper-colored silk at the neck and wrists. A simple black wimple covered her hair, exaggerating the pallor of her face.

Jax felt an unexpected stab of sympathy. For her, Crown Prince Guntram's death was a vexing problem: If only Guntram had possessed the good sense not to die, she would be safely home in Dormance, working in her father's smithy. She hadn't considered how ghastly King Wulfric's ridiculous ball must seem to Guntram's grieving widow, who couldn't be much older than she was.

A boy brushed past Princess Ellycia on the stairs, maybe a little younger than Siddy, perhaps eight or nine. Prince George stared avidly at the gathered delegations as he crossed to stand behind his mother's chair.

"His Royal Highness, Crown Prince Theodor," the herald called next. The low murmur of breath and bodies around the courtyard hushed in anticipation. Finally, the man the princesses had been brought to Aldforth to marry.

Listening to fairy tales, Jax had never thought, *maybe the princess would rather be a blacksmith.* She might even have dreamed of marrying a prince herself, of being whisked away from the loneliness and judgmental eyes of Dormance. Her father had loved a queen, after all. It hadn't seemed so far-fetched.

At least, not for a handsome rogue like her father. Jax had long since realized princes didn't whisk away girls who played with hammers.

Yet, she *had* been whisked away. Not by princes, perhaps. She flicked a quick glance at Anatole, glowering at the king and his family, and then at Nicolas, whose clenched fists belied his calm expression. No, not princes. Still, given a choice, she wouldn't trade them.

Nevertheless, she was curious to see this prince—who was taking a long time to make his grand entrance. Movement rustled the viewing galleries, several gallants pressing in for a better look.

"He's not made it back to the castle in time," Nicolas muttered.

The Rose Knights. "The guards caught them."

Nicolas shook his head. "They wouldn't keep the prince from this. They wouldn't risk angering the king."

King Wulfric's face had set hard as carved granite. As the silence lengthened, Jax could see the rage beginning to seethe beneath his skin. She thought he wasn't so much still as coiled, like a wolf about to lunge or a snake about to strike.

Motion in the keep doorway brought a collective release of breath from the onlookers. A young man dashed out onto the stairs, then paused, collecting himself before descending to the dais.

He wore a tunic of deep purple, emblazoned with a silver wolf like his father's, over black shirt and hose. Only the slightly off-center tunic and the tilted gold circlet on his tousled hair showed the haste with which he'd torn off his Rose Knight costume to rush to this ceremony.

Jax recognized him as the dark-haired bandit who had given a red rose to the Ilhavairian princess. He certainly looked like a fairy tale prince, tall and handsome and fit.

With a surreptitious tug at his tunic, he crossed the wooden dais to stand behind his father's shoulder.

"You deign to join us." The king's Common Tongue ground in his mouth like river rocks.

The prince offered a military bow, his expression combining contrition and mischief. "I apologize, Father. I only wanted to catch a glimpse of the beauty descending on our kingdom—"

"Even after what happened to your brother, you can't manage to show up in time."

The prince stilled. Jax had heard that tone of anticipation in Hubert's voice often enough to know nothing good would come next.

"Where is your esquire?" The king leaned forward, scowling out at the viewing galleries. "Where is that boy? Ralf!"

"Father, please. It's my mistake—"

The king leveled his glare on his son, and Prince Theodor froze, the color draining from his face.

"Here I am, sire." One of the young gallants who had pushed through the gallery leveraged himself up onto the stage. It was the blond boy who had offered his hand to Beatrix. Not as tall as the prince, but perhaps even more beautiful. "At your service, Your Majesty."

"Here, boy."

Jax wondered if anyone else saw the desperate look the prince shot his esquire or the tiny shake of the head in response. The young man strode across the dais and knelt before the king.

"By law, no one may raise a hand to a prince of the blood." King Wulfric curled his lip. "More's the pity. I wonder, young Ralf, if your father would have sent you to me if he'd known what a miscreant Theodor would be."

The king's arm lashed out with such sudden violence that Jax jerked as if she were his target. The back of his fist collided with the side of Ralf's head, lifting the esquire nearly to his feet before flinging him sideways. The youth crumpled in a limp heap on the wooden planks.

The king's teeth flashed as he turned to his son, but the prince made no move, holding himself preternaturally still. Jax guessed any protest would result in greater punishment for the esquire.

Breaking the stunned silence of the watching delegations, two more young men jumped onto the dais to lift the fallen boy and pull him, stumbling, back to the gallery. Blood streaked his cheek. Despite the heat of the midsummer sun, Jax shuddered with a bone-deep chill.

"Gods' breath," Anatole cursed softly.

"We can't leave Jax here," Nicolas whispered. "We have to go. Now."

"Don't be a fool," Anatole hissed. "They've already lowered the portcullis."

Jax saw he was right. She met Nicolas's gaze, his horror at the king's casual brutality mirroring her own. "I knew the danger," she reminded him.

"Well?" The king glowered at the herald. "Now that my worthless boy is here, we can finally begin."

The herald cleared his throat. "We will begin the presentation of the candidates."

Anticipation rustled through the courtyard, edged with misgiving. Blood rushed to Jax's face, then sank again, leaving her faint. She swallowed, her throat suddenly dry.

I can't do this.

Nicolas took her hand and squeezed it. "I'd get you out of here if I could. But Venia couldn't ask for a better princess. You're clever enough to deal with Wulfric. You have a talent for defusing fraught situations, and you'll keep your head if things get dangerous."

Anatole grunted. "We believe in you, girl."

Surprise jolted her from the edge of panic.

"Her Imperial Highness, Princess Beatrix of Bellis!" the herald cried.

"Bellis was the first of the Blessed Kingdoms," Anatole murmured, brushing aside his momentary sentimentality. "It's traditional to give them precedence."

Across the courtyard, the sky-blue tunics of the Bellisian delegation ebbed back to leave Princess Beatrix standing alone, her red hair shimmering over her sapphire blue gown.

She glanced neither left nor right as she walked to the front of the dais.

"What's wrong with her face?" Prince George's shocked voice echoed loudly from the stone walls.

King Wulfric's fist clenched dangerously on the arm of his chair, but no one responded. Beatrix paused at the foot of the wooden steps leading up to the platform and bent her head to the king.

"Don't bow," Anatole repeated his instructions for the hundredth time. "Or gods-forbid curtsy. You're the princess of a sovereign nation. Just a tilt of the head, like the Bellisian girl."

"Princess Beatrix," the herald spoke over the princess's head to the courtyard at large. "You have been invited to King Wulfric's ball to vie for his son's hand in marriage. How do you intend to protect Prince Theodor from those who wish Aldforth harm?"

The prince in question, standing behind the king, stood rigid as a statue. Only the color rising in his cheeks betrayed his mortification.

Beatrix's polished voice sounded cool and composed. "As the oldest of the Blessed Kingdoms, the birthplace of the Santi Empire, Bellis's history teaches that knowledge is the ultimate weapon. No one knows more about their enemies— or their friends—than the diplomats of Bellis. No one under-stands better how to use that knowledge to keep peace, wage war, and deflect any threats to their allies."

King Wulfric grunted acknowledgment and gestured her forward. Beatrix mounted the steps and crossed the dais to stand where the herald indicated, several paces to the right of Prince Theodor.

"Her Royal Highness, Princess Raisa of Ravnina."

"It should be Rigas next," Nicolas whispered.

"He's playing favorites. Princess Jaclyn will be last," Anatole warned darkly.

Jax thought of Master and Mistress Steward, the crowd in

Hautberge just that morning, her family in Dormance. All depending on her to shield them from this brutal king's wrath. Well, the more he dismissed her, snubbed her, *forgot* her, the better.

Princess Raisa's sleek black horse carried her smoothly to the base of the dais, then knelt on one knee, right leg stretched forward. The tall, amber-blond princess swung lightly off its back. She spoke before the herald could ask her his question.

"A well-mounted knight is the best defense a kingdom can put forth." She gestured to the magnificent animal still kneeling before the king. "I offer a gift to Your Majesty from your friend, King Korol, and the people of Ravnina. More will follow when I am crowned."

A murmur went through the crowd as King Wulfric nodded his thanks. Princess Raisa swept up the steps to her position at the left of young Prince George. A page darted out to take the stallion's reins.

"Ravnina doesn't *ever* give those horses away," Anatole muttered as the animal passed them on the way to the stables. "Old Korol is going all out."

"Her Royal Highness, Princess Lidia of Ilhavair," the herald called next.

The litany continued, the herald calling names, the princesses bringing offers of protection. Rigas, Montaine, Ilhavair, the Aldforthian protectorate of the Fair Isles. Jax tried to focus, but the herald's words flowed through her ears like sighing wind as she watched the girls pass, all so poised and elegant in silks and jewels. They showed no uneasiness over the king's brutality toward the prince's esquire, except for a dark-haired, fawn-skinned child of about eleven or twelve who looked so frightened that the herald waved her to her place without making her speak.

The Almasan princess, the dark-skinned girl in the deep red robes, vowed to show Prince Theodor her devotion with her spear.

"Prince Guntram was bringing home her brother's head in a box when he was killed," Anatole said.

Jax forced herself to breathe.

"Princess Eira of the Temple of Peace, formerly of Nordmark."

The blonde priestess-princess strode across the courtyard, pausing to offer a respectful knee, as well as her bow and sword.

"You're next, princess," Anatole warned. He gave Jax a tight smile. "Being last has its advantages. Less time to have to stand up there."

Jax could only nod. Nicolas squeezed her hand again and let it go.

"Princess Pia of Capra," the herald cried.

Jax stumbled a step forward before she could catch herself. Fortunately, all eyes were turned to the gilded carriage that had brought the Montainan princess—Désolée or Isabella or … what had the herald said?

"*Princess* Pia?" Nicolas asked as Jax stepped back. "Capra's a Montainan duchy."

"The Duke of Capra is King Henrik of Montaine's younger brother," Anatole said. "He's a prince, so I suppose his daughter can be a princess."

The young woman who descended from the carriage blushed furiously under the scrutiny of the crowd. Her masses of blonde ringlets bobbed about her round face as she gave a nervous curtsy before the throne.

"I'd do *anything* to protect Prince Theodor, Your Majesty," she burst out earnestly.

The king didn't quite roll his eyes as he gestured her to her place.

"Her Highness, Princess Jaclyn of Venia."

Even knowing it was coming, it still made Jax's pulse skitter with dread.

"We're with you," Nicolas said.

"Don't trip," Anatole muttered.

Caught between laughing and crying, Jax walked out across the hard-packed dirt of the courtyard. Hundreds of eyes pivoted toward her, curious, surprised, condemning, confused. She didn't need to hear the words to know what they murmured to each other. *A Venian princess? Commoner. Too tall. Ridiculous. Pretender. Bastard.*

Boring, she thought back at them, staring fixedly at King Wulfric's boots as she neared the wooden platform.

She walked like a blacksmith, not a princess, but she reached the dais without tripping on her skirts. Tamping down her panicking heart, she bent her head the precise amount Anatole had taught her. Then she looked up at the man on the throne, the man who had threatened her family. The man who had lost his son.

She expected rage or grief or cunning. What she saw in his narrowed, pale blue eyes reminded her instead of Hubert the miller's son—discontent, irritation, spite. The king's mouth curved up, but it wasn't a smile.

"Venia fussed they didn't have a girl of royal blood to send to my ball, but I see they managed to dredge one up."

"Dredged from the bottom of the Saber, apparently," some wit called.

A few obligatory chuckles rose from the galleries. Jax could only dip her head again.

"How do I know you're even Léonie's brat?" Vexation churned the amusement from the king's voice. "She might have sent her chambermaid, for all I know."

Jax's ears burned with humiliation and fear. She'd been Hubert's target long enough to recognize a bully and his tactics.

The king wasn't going to be satisfied with boring.

CHAPTER THIRTEEN

Who would I place coin on? Must you ask? It's obvious who the top contenders for Prince Theodor's hand are, and I can outdo any of them. I'm prettier than that Ilhavairan girl, and, anyway, King Wulfric already has one of them, so why would he need another? The only other real beauty is Pia, and she's a goose. My family is richer than even that merchant princess from Rigas. The Ravninan girl made a grand gesture with her gift, but I doubt King Wulfric would choose a fancy horse over enough gold to buy a herd.

None of the rest of them amount to anything.

— Princess Isolde of Montaine

Choose a front-runner? No. Until I understand King Wulfric's endgame, I cannot be certain any one of us is safe.

I mean safe to wager on, of course.

— Princess Beatrix of Bellis

"I'm a blacksmith, Your Majesty." Jax's voice rang out louder than she'd intended, and she had to force herself not to wince.

For a moment, silence filled the courtyard. Then someone on the dais tittered. Smothered laughter began to spread. A long heartbeat later, the king joined in, a burst of noise like a broken trumpet.

"By the gods, you are." His smile bared teeth. "Those arms! Even that Venian vixen wouldn't have the gall—or the imagination—to send a blacksmith unless you were her genuine bastard. Tell me, girl, how do you plan to protect my son and heir as a *blacksmith?*"

She'd had plenty of time while the other girls were presented to come up with a boring, vague answer, but those weren't the words that fell from her lips. "He'll need someone to keep his weapons sharp, your majesty."

Lightning flashed in Wulfric's eyes. *She'd gone too far.* But then the thunderclouds burst in another clap of laughter.

"Hear that, boy?" the king barked at Prince Theodor. "She's already offering to sharpen your sword."

The prince stared straight ahead, looking as horrified as Jax at the crude twist of her words. But the king's interest was already fading. He waved her impatiently away. Though her knees threatened to buckle, she managed to climb the dais steps and take her place beside Eira.

"Well done," the priestess-princess breathed.

Jax shook her head, grateful she still *had* a head on her shoulders. A minimal achievement for walking across a courtyard. She glanced toward the stables. Anatole looked pale enough to have just stared death in the face, but Nicolas gave her a firm nod of support.

The herald stepped forward. "Thus concludes the presentation of the candidates for the hand of His Royal Highness, Prince Theo—"

"Wait!" A guard called urgently from the castle entrance. "It's another delegation."

Jax could just make out movement through the portcullis. The black-clad castellan, Kenrick, hurried toward the gate.

"Fairföld," King Wulfric spat, his mouth twisted in grim satisfaction. "I warned King Frigyes he'd better have that ugly chit of his here on time." He leaned forward in his chair. "The ceremony is finished! Tell those cursed giants they're too late. Turn them away. They'll answer for this insult later."

Giants! Dread rippled through the courtyard. Heads tilted up toward the castle walls as if there might be monsters looming over them. Only ten feet tall, Nicolas had said. *Ten feet tall.* For the first time, Jax was glad of the portcullis.

Castellan Kenrick conferred with the soldiers, then hurried back across the courtyard to whisper in his monarch's ear.

Slowly, Wulfric's scowl relaxed. Jax could almost see the calculations running through his mind as he considered what his castellan had to say. He nodded to Kenrick, who moved to whisper to the herald.

The herald's thin eyebrows rose in surprise, but he stepped forward once more. "Her Imperial Highness, Princess Anara of Kherem."

"It can't be." Eira's gasp joined the swell of astonishment —and relief, *it's not the giants!*—that swept through the crowd. She leaned toward Jax to get a better view of the gates as the portcullis rose for the latecomer.

"Kherem?" Jax asked. She was sure Anatole had never mentioned Kherem. "Where is that?"

"It's one of the eastern empires," Eira said. "East of the tribal lands beyond Ravnina. The Ravninan sisters at the Temple of Peace tell all kinds of wild stories about the Kheremese Empress. That she's got three heads and a thousand consorts and rides around on a—"

Her voice trailed off as a dark-haired girl on a stocky white horse rode through the gates.

Every wide-eyed gaze in the courtyard locked on the small creature sitting on her right shoulder. Its scales shimmered in patterns of dark green and blue, accentuating the polished gold of its talons where they clung to Princess Anara's indigo jacket. A blue crest tipped with silver rose behind its narrow head, and its long tail draped around the princess's neck like a living torque. The beast tilted its muzzle, bright emerald eyes glittering at all the humans staring back.

Assured it had the full attention of its audience, it unfurled wings that spread like a banner at least three feet on either side of the princess's head.

"—on a dragon," Eira finished her breathy whisper.

One of Princess Anara's attendants leaped from his horse as if to take her reins, but she dismounted before he could reach her. The dragon fanned its wings, ruffling the princess's short, straight black hair, before folding them back against its body.

Compact and sturdy as her horse, Anara strode toward the dais. She stopped at the foot of the stairs, arms folded into her sleeves across her chest. She stared at the king staring speculatively at her shoulder.

Apparently, no one had told her she should bend her head, but King Wulfric didn't seem to notice.

"I see my invitation spread farther than I expected," he said finally. "Your mother, the empress, has sent you far from your own country to compete for my son's hand. How do you hope to show you can protect him?"

"Empress Khulan is my father's mother." Princess Anara's Common Tongue was as strangely beautiful as her dragon companion. Perfectly clear, yet with an unfamiliar music. She lifted a palm toward the dragon's head. "Tenzin and I have protected the eldest daughter of the crown princess of Kherem for the past two years. She is still alive."

King Wulfric gave a flat smile, clearly disappointed the dragon wasn't a gift. "Your *grand*mother, the empress, shows Aldforth great friendship. You may take your place on the dais beside the princess from Capra."

Fluttery Princess Pia squeaked with terror as Anara stalked toward her. The little dragon, Tenzin, flicked its tongue at her, but Anara hissed at it, and it hunched back onto her shoulder in a huff.

King Wulfric stared covetously after them for a moment,

then rose to his feet. The portcullis clanged down, and Jax suppressed a shudder at once more being trapped inside the castle.

"Welcome to Aldforth." The king's voice didn't seem capable of welcome, despite his words. "We are gratified by the love and respect so many kingdoms have shown for us by sending these candidates to win my son's hand in marriage."

Jax wondered if she imagined the fleeting expression of desperation, or perhaps desperate rebellion, that crossed Prince Theodor's face.

"How many princesses have come for our ball, Kenrick?" Wulfric asked the castellan at his side.

"Eleven, Your Majesty."

"Eleven?" The king frowned at the unfavorable number.

"Twelve." Dowager Crown Princess Ellycia stepped from behind the thrones and swept around to bend her head to the king.

"What? What is the meaning of this?" Wulfric whirled to glare at his son. "If this is one of your pranks—"

"No, Your Majesty." Princess Ellycia dropped into a full curtsy. "Prince Theodor knows nothing of my desire to enter the competition."

"*How dare you.*" Grief and fury finally surged to the surface, suffusing Wulfric's face. Jax caught her breath, terrified he would strike Ellycia as he had Ralf. "If it weren't for your pathetic helplessness, my beloved heir would still be alive. How could you think I would ever let you near another son?"

Ellycia held her curtsy, though her pale face had drained almost bloodless. "I failed my husband, Prince Guntram, when the manticore attacked. I have no excuse, save that I was never taught to defend myself. I have no martial skills, but I do have a motivation to learn them that none of these other candidates possess. I know the price of failure."

King Wulfric's wrath withered. "We already have a candidate from Ilhavair," he said peevishly.

Ilhavair. Jax glanced at the other princesses, trying to remember which one came from the island nation.

The girl beside Beatrix stepped forward. She was younger and slighter than Ellycia. Indeed, with her catlike green eyes, her gleaming brown hair gathered in a gold band at the small of her back, she looked almost nothing like the dowager crown princess.

"My father sent *me* to represent Ilhavair," the girl snapped, a blaze of indignation in her eyes. "*Not* my stepsister. *Not this time.*"

"I am no longer an Ilhavairan princess." Ellycia lifted her gaze to the king. "I am a princess of Aldforth now. Each of the other Blessed Kingdoms has a candidate for your ball. Should not Aldforth be represented, as well?"

The king's fist clenched threateningly.

"The original Blessed Kingdoms numbered twelve, Your Majesty," Castellan Kenrick interjected. "Twelve *is* a more auspicious number."

"Superstitious nonsense," Wulfric snapped. Yet he held his hand. Then shrugged. "Very well. You may participate in the ball. You are stripped of all privileges due your title as our daughter-in-law for the duration of the competition. Expect no special favors."

"Thank you, Your Majesty." Ellycia bent her head again and rose gracefully from her curtsy. She never looked at her sister—stepsister—but the younger girl's glare followed her back to her place.

"Twelve princesses!" King Wulfric rose to his feet and gazed down the line of young women curving around the dais at either hand. "I have one command for you. *Don't disappoint me.*"

CHAPTER FOURTEEN

Any girl who came to Aldforth not in fear for her life is a
fool.

— Princess Marjani of Almasa

"Your Highnesses." Castellan Kenrick stepped forward
and sketched a bow that encompassed all the young
women arrayed around the dais. "By the new year,
one of you will be married to the heir of the most powerful
kingdom in the known world."

This was the promise that had brought these delegations
to Aldforth. Jax watched the reality of it coalescing in the
princesses' eyes. Even the most coolly royal couldn't contain a
flicker of avarice or excitement or apprehension.

"Over the next six months," Kenrick continued, "one of
you will prove herself the most capable of protecting Prince
Theodor and ensuring the continuance of his royal lineage.
You will show your worth in archery, swordsmanship, and
more.

"To that end, you will live apart, as students of these arts,
dedicated to your studies. To eliminate distractions, your
retinues will be sent back to your home kingdoms. They may

return at the Winter Solstice to celebrate the choosing of Adlforth's new crown princess."

Sent back? Jax spun toward the stables. Nicolas's midnight blue gaze met hers as he tried to wrench free from Anatole's grip. The old constable held him grimly, his eyes flicking from the guards surrounding the courtyard to the archers on the ramparts to the soldiers with their pikes before the dais. Jax saw that the king and his family had already retreated into the keep.

As comprehension spread, a wave of protest rose from the princesses' escorts. Some pushed toward the dais, only to be rebuffed by lowered pikes. Several young Ravninan men put their hands on their swords, but none dared draw for fear of endangering their princess.

"Now, if you will come with me," the castellan said, so courteously it hardly seemed like a command. "I will lead you to your accommodations."

Some princesses threw their delegations questioning glances. Others hardened their faces, hiding their confusion or fear. Eira shrugged, as if such behavior were only to be expected from a king. Yet to Jax's dismay, they all moved obediently toward the keep stairs.

Any one of them could order a blacksmith's daughter to kiss her slipper if she chose. But not one dared to defy this ruthless king.

The young page who had directed Jax to her place in the courtyard earlier appeared at her side.

"Follow the castellan, Your Highness," he said, only a faint sheen on his upper lip betraying his nerves. "The king wishes you to be settled in your rooms as soon as possible."

The crowd shifted, blocking her view of Nicolas and Anatole. Her heart thudded heavily in her throat. "I can't leave my friends—"

"You don't want to be responsible for them getting hurt," the page said quietly at her elbow. It was so sensible, it hardly sounded like a threat.

There. Anatole's hand rested on Nicolas's shoulder, but the younger man had stopped struggling. They couldn't help her by getting themselves skewered. Jax's gaze locked with Nicolas's. She couldn't hear his words over the din of angry voices around the courtyard, but she knew what he said. *I will get you home.*

She nodded to him and to Anatole. Then she turned her back on her only two friends in the entire kingdom of Aldforth and climbed the narrow stairs into the keep's entrance hallway.

The sound of Castellan Kenrick's boots drew the line of flustered princesses through a wide, arched doorway into the cavernous great hall beyond. Shields in a confusion of colors and designs hung from gallery railings along both sides, the walls below decorated with rich tapestries of hunts and battles and bloody saints.

After the dizzying heat of the courtyard, the hall was cool enough to raise goosebumps on Jax's arms. Even with the two enormous fireplaces on either side, it was hard to imagine the room ever being truly warm.

The great hall in Count Renaud's manor in Dormance would fit inside this one with enough room left for the village inn and her father's smithy. None of the other princesses seemed overawed by the size or the decor.

"Where are we going?" Princess Raisa demanded as Kenrick escorted them out the hall's rear door into the castle gardens. She followed closely behind the castellan, far ahead of Jax, but her voice carried clearly. "You said you were taking us to our rooms."

"Newport is a small castle. There isn't space for so many guests in the keep itself," Kenrick replied.

Eira dropped back beside Jax. "Where do you think he's leading us? The barracks?"

The glittering blonde princess ahead of them, her hair gathered in a silver net glinting with chips of diamond, glanced back. "Such crass jokes are in extremely bad taste."

Jax wasn't sure Eira was joking. Her own raw fear had her listening for screams of agony from the courtyard they had left —or from the princesses ahead. Surely even King Wulfric wouldn't start a war with all of his neighbors at once.

"He's taking us to Lukos." Princess Ellycia spoke from behind her, the last in line.

"Lukos?" Eira asked.

"The old Santian ruin," Ellycia told her. "King Wulfric has been renovating it. He ordered the sisters from the Abbey of the Mother Goddess to move in a fortnight ago to prepare our accommodations. Kenrick must plan to take us out of Newport Castle through the postern gate."

They'd entered another hallway, cramped and dim. The only light came from narrow slits in the outer wall. Jax caught nothing but a glimpse of sky through them as she passed.

She looked back at Ellycia. Talking to Eira was one thing. She'd seen the priestess-princess with shoulders squared, ready to punch a knight. It was harder to address a princess who wore her very skin like royalty should—refined, remote. Regal.

Still, Ellycia had spoken first.

"I was told Lukos is cursed," Jax tried.

"A curse!" Eira brightened with interest. "Is sending us there some kind of test? Does the king hope one of us can break it?"

"The workers have spread odd stories," Ellycia said, "but King Wulfric doesn't believe in the curse. None of us speak of it. Particularly not since …"

Her voice trailed off, and a chill worked its way down Jax's spine. *Not since a manticore slaughtered Crown Prince Guntram on the cliffs of Newport.*

"May the deep emptiness of your loss be a receptacle for Peace," Eira said, the ritual words somehow both sincere and devoid of pity. "The Holy Mother has ordered Prince Guntram added to the litany of the departed at the Temple for a full hundred days. He is not forgotten."

"No, he is not," Ellycia said, lowered lashes hiding her eyes.

Sunlight brightened the corridor ahead. They rounded a corner to find a heavy iron grate pulled inward and a thick oak door pushed out. A narrow, wooden stair led down behind a curve in the outer wall to the ground outside the castle, a dozen yards below. The postern gate.

"The prince and the Rose Knights must have gotten back in this way," Eira observed. "They probably hid their horses in the woods for the grooms to fetch later."

Jax followed her cautiously down the steep, narrow steps.

"The stairs can be burned away if the castle falls under attack," Ellycia told them. "The postern gate is meant for convenience or quick escapes, not for welcoming guests."

The moat dwindled to a stone-jumbled gully on this side of the castle. Looking back across it, the postern entrance was almost completely hidden by the design of the wall. Ahead, a steep hill rose from a small wood. Jax could just make out the broken top of the ruined fortress at the hill's crest. *Lukos.*

"Isn't the castellan worried we might change our minds and leave?" Eira asked as they followed the straggling princesses into the trees.

"They won't allow your retainers out of the castle until Kenrick reports we're safely locked away," Ellycia said. "You couldn't leave without them."

Eira blinked. "Of course I could. If I didn't care to be here."

Considering Eira's self-contained confidence, that might be true. But Jax could tell Ellycia couldn't conceive of a princess going anywhere without guards and companions and servants. She was saying they were trapped.

Jax had felt trapped from the moment she'd stepped inside Newport Castle's walls, but to have someone say it out loud …

She wasn't a princess.

Jax had enough coin in her pouch to pay passage on a ferry across the Saber. Enough to feed herself on the long walk back to Dormance. She touched the head of her hammer. She could protect herself if she didn't encounter too much trouble.

Yet if she ran away now, she might as well never have left home. Being separated from Anatole and Nicolas and locked away in a cursed ruin might not be what she had expected. But it was hardly worse than what she *had* imagined.

The trees welcomed them into cool shade, conifer needles soft beneath Jax's feet. Pia, the pretty, plump Capran princess, sank down on a boulder ahead of Jax and Eira, her fair skin pink with exertion.

"Isolde!" She reached for the regal, glittering blonde. "Wait for me."

"For pity's sake." Isolde brushed past her without a pause. "This could be a test. I'm not failing it because you ate too many of those little cakes this morning."

Isolde, not Isabella. The Montainan princess. That explained all the jewels. And would make her Pia's cousin. *Isolde, Isolde, Isolde.*

Jax paused beside Pia's rock. "I can walk with you the rest of the way, if you like."

The slumping princess shook her head, her expression more resigned than surprised at Isolde's desertion. "I'll get there eventually. Just, please don't let them shut the door before I arrive."

Jax wasn't sure which side of Lukos's gate she wanted to be on herself, but she nodded. "I won't."

As they walked on, Eira asked, "Do you think that Montainan girl could be right? That this might be a test?"

"By King Wulfric, you mean? To see who can manage the climb?" It wasn't inconceivable.

"Probably not to see who offers compassion on the weakest."

Jax couldn't suppress an un-princesslike snort.

"What if it is?" she asked, watching Isolde stride

implacably up the hill ahead of them. "Do you want to win? Do you *want* to marry Prince Theodor?"

Eira looked at her quizzically. "Of course."

"Why?" Jax bit down on the word too late. *Such a stupid thing to say, giving away too much …*

But Eira seemed pleased to explain. "Aldforth has become more and more warlike in recent decades. More imperialistic, conquering Tyrglas and the Fair Isles. King Wulfric forced the current king of Nordmark to become his vassal."

She didn't use the Common Tongue for 'king' when she talked of Nordmark. It sounded more like *kerning*.

"Is that your father?" Jax asked hesitantly. The herald had said Eira was from Nordmark.

"My Uncle Einar," Eira said. "He made the peace with Aldforth, after my mother, the queen"— *kvenn*—"died in the fighting. I'm sure he thinks he can regain Nordmark's independence eventually, but none of Aldforth's other conquests ever have."

Her voice remained carefully serene. "As an acolyte of the Temple of Peace, if I became co-regent of Aldforth, I could counsel Theodor toward reconciliation, toward peace for all the Blessed Kingdoms. And beyond."

"That never even occurred to me," Jax admitted. "What good I might be able to do as a queen."

Not that she had any chance of becoming one. But still.

Eira's face broke into a grin. "Well, that's not the *only* reason I want to win. I love competition. The Temple hosts several game days throughout the year. My favorites are the running and archery contests. The Holy Mother says I might occasionally be overly enthusiastic, but she thought it would stand me in good stead in this case."

She scrutinized Jax as though sizing her up. "You're probably a good archer, aren't you?"

"I've never even held a bow."

"I can teach you," Eira said confidently. "You've got the

arm strength for it. You'll never beat me for accuracy before winter solstice, but you could challenge me for distance."

"I thought you wanted to win."

"I do. Winning isn't any fun if there's no decent competition." Eira's grin deepened. "How fast can you hike up the rest of this hill?"

Jax couldn't help grinning back. "As fast as you can."

Which turned out to be almost true. Eira was lighter on her feet, but Jax's longer strides kept her close. As the path steepened and bent back and forth on itself, they passed other princesses struggling up the slope. The mousy princess of Rigas—or the Fair Isles?—mouth in a fierce pout, and the youngest girl, princess of the Fair Isles—or Rigas?—focused fiercely on her feet. Beatrix, Isabella—*Isolde*, the Ilhavairan girl.

As they neared the Almasan princess, Marjani, Eira shot an assessing gaze at her effortless stride.

"Race us?" Eira dared her.

"This is no game," Marjani snapped, face steely with reproach. "You and your people are in danger, and you play like oblivious children?"

"And is your gloom making us safer?" Eira asked, her bright voice not hiding the spark of hurt. She brushed past the Almasan princess and pushed on even faster. Jax managed to keep up, but she'd lost the fun of the race. She wondered with a sudden, sickening chill if Marjani's brother's head had been sent to Cadesleigh after Guntram's death, to hang on the capital's gates.

She and Eira reached the base of Lukos Castle behind only Raisa of Ravnina, who looked as though she could continue for hours, as elegant and spirited as her horse, and Anara of Kherem, who wasn't even breathing hard, despite the extra burden of the dragon on her shoulder.

Jax suddenly felt the sweat beneath her arms, the loose strands of hair, finally freeing themselves from Mistress Steward's severe plaits, sticking to her face. Raisa assessed them coolly, her eyes narrowing at Eira's challenging grin. Anara barely spared them a glance, but her dragon watched them with curious, glittering eyes.

They had paused at the bottom of a stone staircase that climbed the sheer rock cliff supporting the ancient fortress above. Castellan Kenrick, black clothes stark against the pale stone, wended his way up the stair to an arched doorway at the base of the fortress wall. He chose a great, dark key from the ring at his waist and unlocked the iron gate, which opened with a groan.

He gestured to the princesses waiting below. For a moment, the four of them looked at each other. Then Raisa tossed her head and started up the steps. Anara motioned for Eira and Jax to go ahead.

Shrewd choice.

As Jax passed her, the little dragon unfurled its wings and leaped into the sky. Wind from its flight rustled Jax's silk hood. Heart skittering, she watched it mount to the sky. Its wings moved more like a great bat's than a bird's, yet its body flowed sinuously through the air as it rose above the tower wall and circled there. It chirruped sharply.

Anara huffed unhappily and followed Jax up the stairs. These steps were even steeper than those at the postern gate but less well-maintained.

"Was he checking to see if it's safe?" Jax risked a glance back at the Kheremese princess.

Anara's face colored a furious red. "Tenzin is female," she snapped. "Male dragons are not allowed in the Empress's service. You dishonor her."

"I'm sorry." Jax's ears heated in return. "I meant no disrespect. To her or to you."

"You know *nothing* of dragons."

"Nothing," Jax admitted. "Before today, I thought dragons were only legends."

As the words left her mouth, she realized they might be considered insulting, too.

But Anara looked mollified. "I am not yet accustomed to your culture's ignorance of such things."

"She's beautiful." Jax watched the dragon glide in large, lazy circles above the fortress. "Even more beautiful in the air."

"Don't let Tenzin hear you say that. She is vain enough already." Anara waved Jax forward. "She sees no danger. There may be some she cannot see, but that must be what it will be."

Jax didn't find that particularly comforting, but King Wulfric obviously enjoyed the idea of so many royal houses sending their daughters to compete for his son's hand. He wouldn't just throw such entertainment away.

The princesses should be safe enough—as long as they remained entertaining.

Twelve ladies from far kingdoms came,
Braved trials of road and wave,
To vie for prince's hand and heart,
A royal house to save.

To learn of sword and bow and fist,
They toiled all the while,
These maidens, whose first weapons were
A curtsy and a smile.

—From "The Ballad of King Wulfric's Ball," by Foolscap
the Bard

The narrow passageway through the fortress wall led into an elongated courtyard, its margins littered with stones fallen from the gap-toothed walls. Of the compound's original buildings, only the keep remained, the stone tower looming over the yard to Jax's right. The recently erected wooden stable and other outbuildings looked incongruous in the ancient space.

The main gate opposite the keep also showed signs of restoration. A new oak door sat closed and barred within the archway, and a guard paced in one of the watchtowers above. No doubt the road to *that* gate did not involve hazardous staircases.

Castellan Kenrick watched them enter, his dark eyes unnervingly keen. "Sisters from the Abbey of the Mother Goddess wait for you inside the keep. They will provide for your needs until the king's ball."

Raisa led the way, head high, and Eira followed, glancing about the walls as if judging the fortress's defenses. Anara gave a birdlike whistle, and Tenzin called back, a flash of blue-green lightning high above.

"She will fly a little longer," Anara said. "I will wait." She paced toward the center of the courtyard without looking back.

Jax paused. *Do not draw attention.* But she'd made a promise to Princess Pia. She raised her eyes, as a princess would do, and spoke to the castellan. "You will keep the gate open until all the princesses arrive, won't you?"

"Of course, Your Highness." Kenrick sounded shocked at the implication he might do otherwise, but the glint in his eye suggested laughter at her fears—or an acknowledgment of their validity.

She forced herself to hold her ground, and after a moment, he offered her an amused bow.

"I give you my word, Your Highness."

Trying not to think about murdered boys, castrated dukes, or ancient curses, Jax hurried after Raisa and Eira.

The keep's sweeping stone stairway offered a visible testament to the ancient Santi Empire's pride and confidence in its subjugation of the scattered tribes that had once roamed the north. Lukos had no moat or double walls or any of the extra defenses of the newer castle down the hill. Defenses that had become necessary when the empire fell, and all of its former subjects had learned its lessons in iron and war.

King Wulfric apparently felt secure enough in his own hold on his kingdom and the fear he inspired in his neighbors to rebuild this ancient castle for pleasure rather than protection.

Indeed, in contrast to the dilapidated courtyard, the keep doors opened into a great hall full of order and light. High windows paned with glass—a costly luxury—lit the tapestries scattered along the walls. These hangings were few but lovely, with scenes of the Mother Goddess and her children picked out in threads of silver and gold—the sisters must have brought them from their abbey. Sweet, fresh rushes covered the floor.

A round-faced sister in dove gray robes and wimple curtsied to Jax as she joined Eira and Raisa at the entrance. Jax barely caught herself from curtsying back.

"I am Sister Ursel," the older woman said, her expression somehow both amiable and commanding. "I will show you to your rooms."

"There are more of us," Jax told her.

"A good many more," Eira added cheerfully.

"And we have more sisters to serve them," Sister Ursel said. "Follow me."

She led them to a tightly spiraling staircase at the side of the hall. Jax's feet barely fit on the narrow steps. At the first small landing, Sister Ursel guided them out of the stairwell to a hallway that ran the length of the keep. Four doors opened off of it, two on each side, with another staircase at the far end.

"These rooms have been prepared for your comfort," the sister told them. "Your things will be brought up as soon as they arrive. We sisters have the rooms on the next floor, if you require us for any reason. The uppermost floor contains a small chapel, should you wish to pray or meditate."

Her tone suggested they should so wish.

"Which is the largest room?" Raisa demanded.

"They are all the same," Sister Ursel said evenly. "You may choose whichever you prefer. We were told to expect eleven girls, but there are twelve beds, three per room."

"There are twelve of us," Eira told her. "But two of them were extras. I wonder who we're missing."

"The giant princess," Jax reminded her.

"Oh, darling," Raisa scoffed, "you can't really think anyone expected giants."

"Only the Mother Goddess knows what we can expect around here these days," Sister Ursel said drily. "A midday meal will be served as soon as the rest of the girls arrive."

She curtsied once more and disappeared back down the stairs.

"I require a southern-facing room." Raisa opened the door nearest the staircase. "I don't wish to suffer from the dark and cold when winter comes."

"Rigan winters must be much milder than the ones here in Aldforth," Jax said in sympathy.

"*Rigas?*" Raisa's voice bit like an icy wind. "Did you just confuse me with that grubby merchant princess?"

Oh, gods. Raisa was from *Ravnina*, not Rigas. Grassy steppes and broad river valleys, not rolling coastal hills. Jax knew that. And now she'd offended a princess from one of the most powerful of all the Blessed Kingdoms.

"A south-facing room. Good choice." Eira came to her rescue. "A strategic move."

"Choose your own," the Ravninan princess replied coldly. "I mean no offense, but sharing a room with you would offer me *no* advantages, strategic or otherwise. You are an exile from your own kingdom. Honestly, I don't know what you are even doing here."

Eira smiled serenely. "I'm here for the same reason you are. To marry Prince Theodor. It is true my uncle banished me from Nordmark, but only because he had the good sense to fear me." She turned to Jax. "She's right about the light. We should take the other south room."

As Eira started down the hall, Raisa stopped Jax with a gesture.

"You don't want to throw your lot in with that one." She

said it offhandedly, but the tight twist to her mouth betrayed her anger at Eira's dismissal. "She's not going to last long in this competition."

"Neither am I," Jax said. She barely managed not to add, "Your Highness."

Raisa laughed. "You're not even *in* the competition, blacksmith. You're no threat to me. I'm giving you a friendly warning. Pick a north-facing room. You might enjoy the cooler air. You don't want to be too close if I decide the Nordish girl needs to go."

And why should you *be the one to decide?* Jax could actually hear Constable Anatole's voice in her ear: *Be quiet and invisible. The best we can hope for is that they'll forget all about you.*

"You think Eira's a threat?" Jax asked.

"Of course not." Raisa looked as shocked as though Jax had suddenly grown horns and a tail. "It's astonishing how little you know, you poor thing. Those savages in Nordmark may once have called her mother a queen, but her uncle is no more than a vassal to Aldforth. King Wulfric would never consider her an appropriate alliance.

"No." She offered Jax a condescending smirk. "That girl is no threat to anyone. But she *considers* herself a threat. She doesn't know her place, but I'm telling you yours. If you stay in it, you'll be fine. Princess Eira will not."

Keep your head down. You don't owe that priestess girl anything. She could even see Anatole's scarred face, contorted in dismay.

But she could also see Hubert's glee over some taunt he'd thrown at her, and the other village children joining in or turning away.

"I think you forget yourself," Jax said, her heart beating hard against her ribs. "We're all princesses here."

This time, it wasn't even hard to leave off the "Your Highness." Anatole would shake his head in despair.

She brushed past Raisa, who took a half-step back. Probably not used to women taller than she. Jax felt the Ravninan's gaze sliding thin daggers into her back, but she managed to make it to the next room without losing anything more than metaphorical blood.

Eira stood just inside, slender fingers over her mouth, her blue eyes dancing.

Jax pushed the heavy door closed, relieved to have its solid bulk between her and the Ravninan's ire. "She's going to kill us."

"No doubt," Eira agreed. "You could have taken another room. I wouldn't have held it against you."

"Do you think any of the others would let me stay in a room they wanted for themselves?"

"The outcasts," Eira said cheerfully. "That's us."

Voices rose in the corridor. Another group of princesses had come up from the great hall below.

Eira laid her bow and quiver at the foot of one of the three brightly blanketed beds and sat on a stool beside the cold fireplace. "Now we wait and see who is foolish enough to join us."

Jax dropped to a nearby stool. "Probably whoever is last up the stairs."

"Crossing Raisa is a bold opening strategy," Eira said. "Of course, anyone who wants to be queen of Aldforth had best be bold—especially if she doesn't match up to the perfect model of a princess."

So. Eira knew her story—or at least whatever version of it had swirled around the Newport Castle courtyard. Eira might think their outsider status gave them common ground, but the Nordish girl had been born a princess like the others. Jax didn't even know how to explain the gulf that gaped between them.

"Queen of Aldforth?" Jax shook her head. "A fortnight ago, I was working in a village smithy." She touched her hood. "I've never worn anything made of silk before today. Or velvet. Or silver or gold. I can't marry a prince."

She huffed a rueful sigh. "My father has received a single offer for my hand, from a widower farmer with only half his teeth and a son my age. He thought I would be a good match because I was big and strong and could help with the pigs."

"Surely Prince Theodor is more appealing than an elderly pig farmer—at least he's got all his teeth." Eira flashed her quick grin. "Admit it. He's just a little bit gorgeous."

Jax rolled her eyes. "This isn't about Prince Theodor—"

"Is it that boy?" Eira leaned forward. "The one who grabbed you after you saved Beatrix from being trampled?"

"Nicolas?"

"*Nicolas*." Eira drew out the name as if tasting it for flavor. "Poor boy looked like he'd just seen death pass before him. I don't know what he would have done if you'd been injured. He's not as dazzling as Prince Theodor, but he's got those amazing eyes. Do you have feelings for him that—"

"No!" Jax's cheeks burned. It seemed she blushed at everything these days. "He's one of the queensmen assigned to escort me here. I owe him a great deal, but I don't … he's not …"

"He doesn't have the rank to marry a princess," Eira guessed.

"I'm *not* a princess," Jax said. "I'm only here at all because King Wulfric threatened my mother—"

"The queen."

"King Wulfric threatened to invade Venia if Queen Léonie didn't produce a candidate for this ridiculous ball." Jax groaned in frustration. "You don't understand. It's not that Nico can't marry me because I'm a princess. He can't marry me because I'm *not*. He's worked his whole life to rise to the rank of a noble. By Venian law, if he married me, he would have to give up his title, give up everything."

"So, you've thought about it," Eira said. "Marrying him."

"I haven't thought about it at all!" Jax barked. She hadn't. *Had* she? The reasons against it had come awfully easily.

"Anyway, that's not the point," she said firmly. "The point is that I don't belong with a prince any more than Princess Raisa belongs with a pig farmer. When the ball is over, I will go home, and no one will call me a princess ever again."

Except Hubert. Her hand closed involuntarily on the hammer at her side.

"I think I understand," Eira said. "You want to go back where you belong."

Belonging is all I've ever wanted. Jax opened her mouth, but no words came, stifled by the thought that suddenly filled her head. *I never said I wanted to go back.*

Eira's eyes clouded. "Holy Mother is always saying I should learn to belong where I am. I figure I can do that here as well as anywhere."

Before Jax could respond, the door to their room swung open, and Princess Beatrix swept in, her scarred face held high. She stared at them defiantly for a moment before her mouth curled up.

"I should have guessed," she said. "What did you two do to get on Raisa's bad side already?"

"Easy targets?" Jax suggested.

"The initial sorting," Beatrix concluded. Despite her calm voice, banked fury burned in her eyes. "It appears you're stuck with me, as well."

"Could be worse," Eira said brightly. "Could be that Montainan girl."

That lit a flash of amusement in Beatrix's eyes. "Princess Isolde is setting herself up as queen of the room across the hall. Our dark horse, the dowager crown princess, has claimed the one across from Raisa."

"Princess Ellycia turned you away?" Jax asked, surprised. Then again, just because Ellycia had deigned to speak to a blacksmith's daughter didn't mean she would have agreed to share a room with her.

Beatrix shrugged. "To be fair, I don't think she would have, but she had already taken in that poor Almasan princess and the little Fair Island girl."

"Not her sister?" Eira asked.

"It would not be diplomatic to repeat what Princess Lidia said to Princess Ellycia in the hallway just now," Beatrix said primly. "I believe Raisa has pulled Lidia into her own hive, along with Dora, for some reason."

"Dora?" Not even the name sounded familiar.

"The Rigan girl," Beatrix said.

"The sour one," Eira clarified. She stretched her legs out and bent to reach for her toes. "Holy Mother is always exhorting us to have faith that things will order themselves in the way of peace, if we only allow them to. Our ending up together is a perfect example."

Beatrix frowned at her as if searching for mockery, but Jax thought Eira meant it. Of course, she suspected Eira would believe the same if she'd ended up in a room with Princess Raisa and the manticore that killed Prince Guntram.

"I'm not much for faith," Beatrix said finally. "But I will put in my pledge for peace between us."

Jax had never expected any of the princesses to befriend her, but to be able to sleep in a room with girls who didn't make it a point to humiliate her—it was more than she had dared hope for.

"Me, too," she said, releasing a little of the desperate isolation that had gripped her since leaving Nicolas and Anatole behind. "Peace."

"We'll need it," Eira predicted. "A place of our own where we can find respite and quiet—"

The door burst open once more, slamming against the stone wall. Princess Anara stood in the doorway, hands on her hips, dark eyes blazing. On her shoulder, the dragon, Tenzin, sat tall, her crest raised above her head like a silver-tipped crown.

Jax found herself on her feet beside Eira, as far as possible from the door, barely aware of having moved. Tenzin might be smaller than she had imagined dragons to be, but her heart skittered at the sight of those fierce, glittering eyes.

Anara's nostrils flared, her coiled wrath as menacing as the dragon's. "That yellow-haired witch across the hall said she refused to share a room with a nasty, barbarian beast."

"That would be Isolde of Montaine," Beatrix informed her calmly, backed against the opposite wall.

"I told her *I* would not share a room with one, either," Anara said.

Eira pressed a hand to her mouth, failing to stifle her laughter.

"I can't blame you," Beatrix said, "but I'm afraid she would be no more welcoming to any of us, and we have only three beds."

Which was undoubtedly true, and Jax had no more desire to sleep in the same room with a dangerous predator than Isolde did. But she couldn't help thinking how far the Kheremese girl was from home, the farthest of all of them. Couldn't help being aware of her own gratitude at being accepted in this very room.

"It's a large chamber," Jax said. Indeed, it was almost as big as the cottage she had grown up in. "We can move the extra bed from across the hall."

Anara glared at Eira and Beatrix's dubious expressions. "In Kherem, it is an honor to have a dragon in your house."

"If Tenzin will honor us with her presence, we welcome you both," Jax said.

Anara turned to the little dragon, who whistled and flared her crest. The Kheremese princess nodded. "We thank you."

"I'm sure the other girls will be green with jealousy," Beatrix murmured, raising her half-eyebrow at Jax.

Tenzin abruptly launched herself from Anara's shoulder. Without so much as a flap of wings, she glided across the room, landing with a light thud on the carved mantel of the fireplace. With a sinuous twist of her long neck, her nostrils were suddenly inches from Jax's face. Her bright emerald eyes, with their catlike pupils, stared intently into Jax's own.

"Hello," Jax managed.

Tenzin yawned widely, showing a long, forked tongue and an impressive array of needle-sharp teeth.

Anara whistled something short and sharp. The little dragon grinned at Jax—there was no other word for the curve of her mouth over those gleaming fangs—and leaped from the mantel to the bed nearest the fireplace. She curled up in the very center and tucked her nose under her long tail.

Anara spun on her heel and stalked back across the hall.

Eira laughed and patted Jax's shoulder. "We'd better go help her collect *your* bed from Isolde's room."

Beatrix gave the dragon's roost a wide berth as she joined them at the doorway. She shot Jax a look. "So much for peace and quiet."

CHAPTER SIXTEEN

It is obvious who belongs in the competition and who does not. There is no kindness in pretending otherwise. The ones who don't belong should return home while they can.

— Princess Raisa of Ravnina

The bell rang for dinner just as the four girls finished wrestling the soft featherbed into place atop the straw-filled mattress of Jax's new bed.

"I've never slept on a featherbed," Eira said cheerfully as they headed for the stairs. "Not even when I was an actual princess."

Jax chose not to mention she'd never slept on any mattress raised off the floor until she'd left Dormance with Nicolas and Anatole.

Sister Ursel and a cadre of gray-robed sisters welcomed them into the great hall. Twelve might seem an excessive number of princesses, even at a royal court, but they all fit easily around one long table on the stone dais at the head of the great hall while the sisters sat around another. Jax and the others from her room found themselves at the foot of their table, farthest from Raisa at the head and glittery Isolde at her right hand.

The sour-faced princess from Rigas—"*Dora,*" Eira reminded Jax in a whisper—fairly seethed with uneasy resentment when Anara sat beside her, despite the fact that Tenzin had not accompanied them to dinner. She spent the meal with her shoulder turned to the Kheremese princess, bitterly complaining to the dazed-looking Fair Isles girl on her other side about the blandness of the food.

Jax couldn't speak to the delicacies Dora described or the spices available to "even the lowliest servant" in Rigas, but the amount of meat served at that single meal was more than Jax's family would consume in a month, and they were considered well-off in Dormance. The bread was made from flour finer than any Hubert's father had ever milled, and there was a slice of orange floating atop the goblet of mulled wine one of the sisters placed by Jax's trencher. Even Eira seemed to take such luxury in stride.

Determined not to look as overwhelmed as she felt, Jax carefully copied the other girls' table manners and listened to the scattered conversations around her. The weather on their travels. Distant relatives they might have in common. The spike in silk prices after the winter storms. She couldn't be the only one wondering what had happened to their escorts or what King Wulfric planned next, but her tablemates seemed well versed in the art of speaking pleasantly about nothing.

"My daughters." A commanding voice interrupted the trifling chatter.

The woman at the head of the sisters' table wore dove-colored robes and an iron-gray wimple like Sister Ursel's. Yet she wore them with a cool, regal authority that made even Raisa appear unrefined in comparison.

"I am Abbess Sofia." She surveyed the princesses with calm, gray eyes. "I shepherd the Abbey of the Holy Mother, which lies some leagues north of Newport. King Wulfric has assigned my order to minister to your care while you are guests at Lukos Castle. The sisters are here to see to your comfort and serve you as would your ladies-in-waiting at home.

"The king has decreed that you begin martial training tomorrow morning. For the rest of today, you may get settled in your rooms and rest from your travels."

"Where will our advisers be staying?" Raisa demanded.

Marjani looked up from her barely touched food. "Can you assure us of the safety of our companions?"

Freed by their queries, the other girls' worries bubbled out, a cacophony of questions and fears and isolation.

"Can we not leave Lukos Castle?" Beatrix's voice cut through the rising confusion. "Surely, as guests, we may consult with our delegations."

"You are not prisoners," Abbess Sofia said. Yet, in her cool voice, Jax heard an echo of iron gates clanging shut. "You may leave this fortress at any time. However, the king will consider that a tacit withdrawal from the competition for the prince's hand. You will be expected to leave Aldforth immediately and return home."

Jax understood the implicit threat. Withdrawal from the competition could implicate the princess's kingdom in whatever wild conspiracy Wulfric chose to construct in the matter of Crown Prince Guntram's death.

A shiver passed around the table, the reality of being left behind, alone in a foreign land.

The abbess's voice softened. "I assure you that all who traveled here with you are safe and well. The king is hosting a feast for them at Newport Castle this evening. He intends to send them back to your home countries until the solstice ball, though that might be difficult for some."

Her gaze flicked to Anara, who stared back, face stoically unconcerned at how far from home she and her escort found themselves.

"Lukos Castle will be your home for the next six months," Abbess Sofia continued. "I hope my sisters can ensure it is a pleasant one. A simple supper will be brought to your rooms this evening. You will be woken in the morning to break your fast before your training begins."

With a dignified tilt of her head, she turned and left the hall.

"I guess we're on our own," Eira said, her smile only a little forced. "I'm sure Holy Mother will be glad to have my escort back at the temple sooner than she expected."

Jax pictured Nicolas and Anatole making their way back to Chernesse. They could be home within a sennight, not slowed by her and Bruno. Except, they'd have to take Bruno with them, wouldn't they? Somehow it was thought of the old cart horse that nearly brought her to tears. Would they deliver him back to her father? Would Anatole make Bahar refund the money they'd paid for him?

She thought not. The gruff constable understood what he'd asked of her and her family. He knew the queen owed them more than the price of a horse.

And Nicolas … She remembered the look on Nicolas's face as she'd followed the other princesses from the courtyard just a few short hours ago. Maybe there would be one person, besides her family, thinking of her, caring what happened to her over the long months until the winter solstice.

DESPITE HER HOMESICKNESS AND FEAR—NOT to mention the unsettling strangeness of sharing a room with a *dragon*—Jax slept hard and deep on her soft featherbed, between her smooth linen sheets. Still, the shadows of dark dreams lurked in her mind when Sister Ursel came to rouse the girls at the faintest rumor of dawn.

She dressed in the same split skirt and breeches she had worn the day before. Attempting swordplay in such fine clothes seemed akin to sacrilege, but nothing else in her trunk was any more suitable. Constable Anatole had forbidden her to bring her blacksmithing clothes to Newport. She supposed the steward's wife at Lord Amaury's manor would donate them to a family in need. Or burn them.

She managed her own laces—she liked breathing, as it turned out—but let Sister Ursel plait her hair. For just a moment, she closed her eyes and pretended the deft fingers weaving the heavy, dark strands were Siddy's and that the rustlings of the other girls were Agnes and the little ones.

Most of the princesses arrived in the great hall bleary-eyed and stifling yawns, but only Isolde came down so late as to nearly miss the morning meal. The Montainan girl had made the most of the extra time she'd taken. Not a fold of her blue silk gown was out of place. Her bodice dipped low enough to show off the delicate lace of her chemise along with a not-quite-scandalous expanse of skin. Her golden curls were pulled from her forehead by a band patterned with silver thread.

"Dressed for battle, I see," Raisa noted with cool approval. Like Jax, Raisa wore her riding outfit from the day before. Still, her own armor was impressive, her sleek, burgundy split-skirt gown highlighting her lithe figure and setting off her amber-blonde hair.

Several of the princesses had dressed elegantly, accentuating their weapons of looks, breeding, and wealth—though none quite reached Isolde's mastery. Several had chosen clothing that offered more freedom of movement for whatever the morning might bring. Eira had exchanged her acolyte's robes for a simple fawn gown with sleeves close-fitting enough not to interfere with a bow and skirts loose enough not to hamper her movements.

The rest, like the wide-eyed child princess from the Fair Isles, wore modest day dresses, shielding themselves from undue attention as they tried to feel their way through the labyrinth of King Wulfric's machinations.

Jax didn't find it reassuring that she was not the only one uneasy about what their "training" might consist of.

Abbess Sofia appeared as the sisters cleared the breakfast

tables. "Good morning, my daughters. I trust you slept well. For today—"

An insistent pounding at the great hall door interrupted her. Jax's heart thudded in echoing alarm, but Abbess Sofia merely frowned in disapproval as Sister Ursel strode to the door. If the dauntless sister hesitated to open it, perhaps it was only the weight of the thick wooden bar across it that slowed her down.

Jax heard a man's voice at the entrance, though she couldn't make out his words. Sister Ursel returned to Abbess Sofia at a pace as unruffled as her expression and murmured in her superior's ear.

Spots of color bloomed high on the abbess's cheeks, but her voice remained calm. "Marshal Oswald, Lukos Castle's master of arms, requests your immediate presence in the yard. He will be supervising your training."

From her emphasis on "request," Jax guessed that was not the word the man at the door had used. It was obvious Abbess Sofia did not appreciate being given orders by Wulfric's men, but it seemed she did not have the authority to refuse them.

It hardly mattered. Despite Jax's misgivings, most of the princesses appeared eager, or at least curious, to find out what the king expected of them in their competition to marry his son.

"Sister Ursel, please take the girls to the marshal," Abbess Sofia directed.

Eira nudged Jax with an elbow as they rose to follow the sister. "Don't look so gloomy. This could be fun."

"I think the word you're looking for is 'dangerous.' "

"The word *you're* looking for is '*exciting*.' Come on. This has to be more fun than pig farming." Eira grinned. "It's an adventure."

"Don't listen to her, Princess Jaclyn," Beatrix said. "The Nordish are notorious barbarians."

Tenzin whistled from Anara's shoulder a few paces ahead.

"Tenzin says you are all barbarians," Anara told them. "Though perhaps not without potential."

"Please tell her we are heartened by her generous judgment of our characters," Beatrix said, her voice carefully drained of irony.

"You may tell her yourself," Anara said. "She understands Common Tongue." Tenzin hissed in protest, but Anara frowned at her. "It is not honorable to deceive those you share a hearth with, *khaar mi'*."

The little dragon hooded her glittering eyes in what could only be called a pout, and Jax shivered with the sudden awareness of an alien intelligence she had never encountered before.

"My life was fine without this kind of adventure," she said weakly.

Eira laughed, and Jax felt a tiny, traitorous skip of her heart. Maybe, terrifying as it was, this *was* more fun than fending off Hubert's taunts or wondering if Count Renaud would accept her as a smith. A little more exciting than the predictable, unchanging, some might say *monotonous* rhythm of life in Dormance …

She glanced at Eira, the girl still grinning as she strode toward the great hall doors, and she couldn't stop the smile that tugged her own lips. Jax missed her family desperately. Her situation was perilous. She would be relieved when it was over and she could return home.

That didn't mean she couldn't appreciate the adventure.

CHAPTER SEVENTEEN

Is King Wulfric truly mad? It's only a matter of time before someone gets killed.

— Princess Pia of Capra

Jax's newfound optimism lasted until she stepped outside and saw the instruments of death.

Lukos's courtyard had been transformed. Coiled straw archery targets stood along the wall across from the stables, bows hanging on a rack close at hand. Another section of the yard looked like a recently logged forest, thick wooden posts driven into the ground at intervals to serve as practice butts for sword training. Mercifully, the barrel beside them held wooden training swords. Broken bones were preferable to severed limbs.

Most of the knives displayed nearby looked wooden, too. It was even conceivable the others were blunted.

A rack of spears, clubs, maces, and things Jax didn't even know the names for rounded out the dangers arrayed before them.

Princess Pia stared around the courtyard, her soft face pale. "Surely they don't mean for us to … use those?"

"If you're feeling faint, you can go hide in our room,"

Isolde said with dripping disdain. Yet even she brushed nervously at her skirt as though rethinking her elegant attire.

"Your Highnesses." A tall, thickset man with the widest shoulders Jax had ever seen apart from her father's stepped toward them and bowed. Fresh scars ran from a leather patch over his left eye down into his bushy, graying beard. In contrast to his savage looks, he wore a clean white tunic embroidered with a black wolf's head, a mirror image of King Wulfric's clothes of the day before.

"Marshal Oswald," Princess Ellycia greeted him cordially, as though he were not the most terrifying man she had ever seen.

The big man squinted up at the princesses, still crowded together at the top of the stairs.

"Me and my lads are here to prepare you for the king's competition." The marshal gestured behind him to the dozen or so men staring at them from around the courtyard, all dressed in a similar uniform, though few looked quite so … *marshal* as Oswald did.

Indeed, on second glance, they seemed a motley bunch, some in clothes too tight or too loose, more than one missing an ear or part of a nose, one missing a hand, one with a wooden leg. The few who appeared sound of body wore resentful scowls. One black-haired youth lounging against the stable wall saw Jax looking at him and smiled in a way that reminded her of Hubert.

"These men wear Prince Guntram's colors," Princess Ellycia said. "They served with you under his command?"

"Aye, Your Highness. The king retained the crown prince's guard. Most are reinforcing the kingdom's key defenses." His massive chest swelled with obvious pride at the trust put in his men. "The rest have been assigned to guard Lukos Castle while Your Highnesses are in residence and to teach you what fighting skills they can."

"I see." Ellycia raised her cool, clear voice. "I thank you all for your service to Crown Prince Guntram during his life and for the protection and training you provide to us now."

"They don't serve *you*," Princess Lidia snapped. The look she shot her stepsister was sharper than any of the available weapons. "King Wulfric said you weren't to have any advantages." She scowled at Marshal Oswald. "I will complain to the king. This isn't fair."

"I serve King Wulfric now," the marshal said mildly, "as do these men. We'll follow his orders, which are to protect and train the lot of you. He told us we're not to have favorites, and we won't."

Spots of color burned Lidia's cheeks. "I will hold you to it."

He pushed on. "With new students, I start by finding out what they need to learn. Or unlearn, just as like. We'll start with archery. I expect most of you have some skill with a bow."

Jax's heart dropped. She had no skill in anything Marshal Oswald might plan to teach them.

"Wait." Raisa's imperious order pulled the marshal up short. "I want my own bow. If I'm ever called upon to protect Prince Theodor, I won't be carrying one of those shoddy practice bows over there."

"I want my bow, too," Isolde said.

Eira grinned. "Competition."

"How many of you brought your own bows?" Oswald asked

At least half the girls nodded or raised a hand. Jax stifled a groan.

"Sister Ursel," Oswald called. "Arrange to have the princesses' bows brought to the courtyard, please."

"We weren't told to bring our own equipment," Dora complained as half a dozen girls crowded around Sister Ursel. "It's not fair. My personal bow is of the highest quality. It would give me an advantage if I'd been told to bring it with me."

"Oh, it wouldn't matter if I'd brought mine," Pia sighed. "I've never been as good as Isolde."

"My grandmother refused to send any weapons with me," the little Fair Isles princess said softly, her dark eyes anxious. "She didn't want King Wulfric to think I was dangerous."

Jax's heart squeezed for the young girl—and for her grandmother. Apparently, Jax wasn't the only one who'd been sent to deflect King Wulfric's fury from her people.

"I'm the dangerous one," she assured the girl. "I've never even held a bow before. I'm as likely to shoot myself as the target."

The little princess shook her head earnestly. "Don't worry. It's not hard to learn. I can show you how to draw it safely, Princess Jaclyn."

"Please call me Jax." Jax smiled at her, trying not to picture Siddy in her place, alone and afraid in a strange country. "I'm afraid I didn't catch your name at the ceremony yesterday."

"Ziva." The girl gave her a shy grin. "I had to ask Princess Ellycia everyone's name last night. I couldn't remember a single one."

"Thank you for offering your help with my archery, Princess Ziva," Jax said. "I don't want to kill anyone my first day."

"Perhaps you can show me, too." The Almasan princess, Marjani's voice was low and measured, her Common Tongue rounded like a lullaby. "In Almasa, we mostly hunt with spears, not bows."

"Could you show us how to throw a spear?" Ziva asked, her eyes gleaming.

"I think so. It takes strength, but you look strong." Marjani swept her red cloak off one shoulder, revealing a sleeveless tunic that would have horrified Agnes. She bent her knees and whipped her arm forward in a throwing motion that managed to appear both graceful and deadly.

"I want to learn to do that," Eira said. Her eyes widened

as she met Marjani's gaze, and she leaned toward the dark-skinned young woman. "You have wraith eyes!"

Looking more closely, Jax saw that Marjani's right eye was a warm amber brown. The left swirled golden green.

"The Nordish believe wraith eyes are the sign of a sorcerer," Eira said. "They think they traffic in demon magic. They used to kill them as witches at birth."

"What are you saying?" Horror threaded Marjani's voice. "I am no sorcerer."

"Of course not," Eira said. "I just meant the Nordish have no tolerance for witches—"

"For the gods' sake." Princess Lidia whirled on Eira. "It sounds like they missed one. Don't pay her any mind, Marjani. We're *all* grateful we weren't born in Nordmark."

Eira's icy skin paled even further. "That's not what I … I didn't think—"

"No, you did not think. You have no sense of propriety." Marjani jerked her cloak into place and followed Lidia toward the archery targets. Ziva ducked after them.

"In Ravnina, we honor those with ties to the spirits," Raisa chided, her voice pitched loud enough to carry. "My father has two sorcerers as advisers. Their wise counsel has served him well."

She shot Eira and Jax a smug smile as she swept past.

Eira started after Marjani, but Beatrix grabbed her arm. "Leave her be. You can't fix it now."

"I didn't mean to offend her," Eira said.

Jax stared at her. "You just implied she should have been murdered at birth."

"I didn't say killing babies was a *good* thing," Eira cried. "The Temple of Peace teaches that all human gifts come from the One Goddess and that it is up to us to use them for good or ill. Marjani would be welcomed there. That's what I wanted to tell her. She's just so *touchy*."

"I mean this with all kindness and respect," Beatrix said, "but the Temple of Peace is renowned as a place of learning.

Did no one there attempt to teach you tact or diplomacy? Or at least suggest you might not say *everything* that comes into your head?"

Eira sighed. "Holy Mother may have mentioned that, yes."

"Apparently, it bears repeating." Beatrix sniffed. "Diplomacy isn't just good manners. It can keep you alive in dangerous waters like these. If you can't think of your own good, think of those who must share a room with you."

Raisa had caught up with Marjani and linked arms with her. She leaned in to whisper in the Almasan girl's ear, shooting Eira a gloating smile.

Jax winced. Beatrix had a point.

Eira's shoulders sagged. "I've made things more difficult for you both—and Anara, too. It's not as though that's likely to change. You'll have better luck in the competition if you don't associate with me."

"Of course, I'll associate with you," Jax said. Changing rooms wasn't going to change her fortunes in the competition. "I already told you I won't be marrying Prince Theodor."

"Because of that boy?" Beatrix demanded, her green eyes suddenly glittering like Tenzin the dragon's. "The one who wanted so desperately to kiss you after you almost got trampled yesterday?"

"Yes!" Eira said, her irrepressible enthusiasm returning.

"No!" Jax paused in confusion. "He didn't want to kiss me."

Eira and Beatrix shared a look.

Jax fought the blush that threatened to suffuse her entire body. She was *not* going to imagine kissing Nicolas. "We're talking about Raisa. She's never going to accept me. Why should I try to appease her by cutting myself off from someone who's befriended me?"

Blacksmith. Commoner. Bastard. What hubris had caused her to imply a girl of royal blood might be her friend? But Eira's troubled blue eyes cleared.

"I would be honored to have you both as friends," Eira said, looking, for an instant, every inch a Nordish princess.

"I have no intention of shunning you," Beatrix sighed. "Raisa and Isolde will pick us off one by one if we don't stick together. Still, if you could avoid saying anything outrageously idiotic for an hour or two, I'll feel better about throwing my lot in with the two of you."

"*That's* diplomatic?" Jax asked.

"Part of diplomacy is knowing when only blunt talk will get the results you desire. You're out of your depth, Princess Jaclyn. I only have so long to teach you how to swim with the sharks."

"There are sharks this far from the sea?" Anara asked, joining them as they began walking toward the archery range. She had taken a moment to send Tenzin off into the sky and looked oddly vulnerable without the little dragon on her shoulder.

"No," Jax told her. "Just Raisa and Isolde."

"Them?" Anara said dismissively. "I expect such sharks at any court. But these men." She frowned around the court-yard. "These are the men sent to guard us? In Kherem, only the finest warriors are allowed to serve a princess."

Most of the men had returned to duty at the gates or on the walls, some with a disheveled sluggishness suggesting they had been rousted from bed earlier than they would have liked. The few remaining in the courtyard all had some physical infirmity, though the man pounding a last practice post into the ground with his single arm looked more than capable of breaking a few heads.

"They're from Prince Guntram's personal guard," Eira said.

"The dregs of Guntram's guard." Beatrix pitched her voice low. "The infirm and malingering. The ones King Wulfric doesn't trust with the kingdom's defenses."

"If he doesn't trust them, why would he put them to guarding us?" Jax asked.

"Guard us from what?" Beatrix asked. "We're in a fortress in a peaceful region of a powerful kingdom. These men don't need to be able to fight off an army. They barely need to be able to fight off a wandering drunkard."

"Considering all the girls who brought their own bows to a ball," Jax said, "we could probably fight off our own drunkards."

"Oswald's men aren't here to protect us," Beatrix said flatly.

"What do you mean?" But the answer whispered in Jax's mind, even before Anara spoke.

"You use your finest warriors to guard your greatest treasures," the Kheremese princess said darkly. "You use the dregs as jailers."

CHAPTER EIGHTEEN

I would have done as well as any of the other girls if someone had told me I should bring my own bow.

— Princess Dora of Rigas

The bald, one-legged man Marshal Oswald introduced as their archery master, Dirk, distracted Jax from the threat of imprisonment with the threat of imminent death—although not her own.

"These bows ain't toys," Dirk growled. "They're for killing. If they do what they're made to do, it's your own fault, not theirs. Don't draw your bow 'less I tell you. Don't nock your arrow 'less I tell you. Don't *touch* your damned arrow 'less I tell you. You loose before I tell you, you're done on my archery range."

Jax stood at the mark for her target, awkwardly holding the bow he'd thrust at her. The princesses who had neglected to bring their own instruments of death got first shot at displaying their skills.

Lucky us.

She tried to copy Dora's stance at the next mark over, but the Rigan princess didn't look all that confident herself, despite her boasts about the superior equipment she'd left at home.

Ziva stood at the end of the row, past Beatrix, Pia and Marjani—too far to ask for help, even if she were still willing after Eira's gaffe with Marjani.

"Let's see where you're at." Dirk stood well off to Jax's right, with a good view of both the princesses and the targets. He sounded more uneasy than enthusiastic. "Ready your bows."

Jax lifted hers, one eye on Dora—

"Wait!" Marshal Oswald's formidable voice filled the courtyard. "Bows down!"

Jax complied, relieved at the reprieve, however temporary. A pair of guards swung open the heavy wooden doors of Lukos's main gate to reveal a sweeping view of the forested hills that spread beyond the fortress's plateau.

A half-dozen men strode through the gates, leaving others with their horses on the swath of grass outside. *The princesses' delegations.* Jax's breath caught as she searched for Nicolas and Anatole among them, come to take her home.

Then she saw the circlet of gold on the tallest man's head and the silver wolf on his tunic. King Wulfric. She recognized Castellan Kenrick beside him, once again all in black. The men with them must be Aldforthian courtiers—friends, advisers, hangers-on.

"Your Majesty." Marshal Oswald dropped to one knee. "I didn't know you'd be joining us this morning. I've not had time to set up a reviewing stand. I'll send some of the lads for benches from the keep—"

"Rise, man." The king waved his hand. "Don't let us interrupt. We were riding to the hunt this morning and thought we'd stop to see how our candidates are faring."

The king smiled as he appraised the princesses arrayed before him. But no amount of joviality could hide the predatory gleam in those pale blue eyes.

Jax swallowed the panicked constriction of her heart and

bent her head with the rest of the girls. Down the row, little Ziva looked as terrified as she. Raisa smiled with satisfaction—undoubtedly relishing the thought of proving her skill before the king. And Isolde's stunning gown now appeared an excellent move in the chess game to win a prince.

"We were about to test their highnesses' ability with the bow," the marshal said.

The king's smile showed the tips of his teeth. Jax suspected he knew perfectly well that the six girls up first were the least likely to be any good. He looked delighted by the prospect.

"Carry on," he ordered. "I am eager to see this demonstration."

"Ready your bows!" Dirk seemed as undaunted by the king's presence as he was at ordering princesses around.

Jax lifted her bow. Humiliating herself in front of the king on the first day. Things could hardly get worse.

"Wait!" Another cry, this one from above.

Jax bit her lip on a word no princess would say. A second group of well-dressed men had appeared on the gap-toothed parapets overlooking the archery targets. They leaned precariously out over the ancient crenellations, the sun behind them making it impossible to see their faces.

But Jax didn't need to. Few people would have the temerity to spy on the king's guests without permission. And considerably fewer would demand the king wait for anything.

"We'd prefer not to be behind the targets when the shooting starts," the central figure called down. "Give us a minute, Dirk. We'll be there in a trice."

Stomping boots and laughter tracked the progress of the young men as they ran to the nearest tower and clattered down its circular stairway. They spilled from the tower door like a half-dozen hound puppies, the dark-haired prince in the lead.

Jax recognized the thick auburn hair on the tall boy closest to Prince Theodor. With no mask to hide behind, his sharp nose and narrowed brown eyes added to his foxy appearance.

She might have thought him handsome if she hadn't seen the disgust on his face when he'd tried to trample Beatrix the day before.

Ralf, the esquire the king had struck so brutally during the presentation ceremony, loped beside him. The blond boy flashed a charming grin undimmed by the purpling bruise across his cheek. How did they dare risk the king's wrath again? Was it courage or just resignation to his brutality?

Which was worse?

The three men behind the ringleaders looked slightly older, their eyes more watchful—undoubtedly more experienced knights assigned to keep the prince and his friends from getting into too much trouble. It must never be far from King Wulfric's mind that the manticore that killed his oldest son remained at large.

Then again, at the moment, the king looked more than ready to hand his current heir over to a man-eating monster.

"Let's get on with it," he snapped.

"Right." Dirk pivoted back to the girls and their targets. "Ready your bows!"

Jax now had plenty of practice with that, at least.

"Nock!"

She fumbled an arrow from the bucket beside her. Small blessings—the slit at the end made it obvious how to fit it to the bowstring. She peered down the row of princesses arming themselves beside her.

One finger above the string, two below. Hold the end of the arrow ...

"Draw!"

Her arrow bounced away from the bow as she pulled the string back. She glanced at Dora again. *Oops. Arrow on the* other *side of the bow, resting on the top knuckle ...*

"Loose!"

Not yet! But her fingers reacted to Dirk's order, not her brain's. The string slapped her forearm as she jerked the bow to face the target, but much too late. By grace of the gods, she'd dipped the bow when she drew, and the arrow dropped, too, skittering wildly across the uneven courtyard to flip to a stop at Dirk's feet.

He gaped at her, and she could only gape back in horror.

After a long, silent moment, the prince's voice rang out. "Good thing you've got that wooden leg, Dirk!"

Jax's ears burned as laughter rippled through the courtyard. One of the prince's friends brayed like a donkey he laughed so hard. Raisa's cool amusement rang lightly from the walls. Even Eira stifled a giggle in her fist.

"The rest of the shots look halfway decent by comparison," Foxy-hair smirked.

Even Marjani's arrow had struck the outer edge of her canvas. Ziva must have coached her through the shot.

"We'll know which girl to call if Theodor gets attacked by a garden snake," King Wulfric chortled. "Or a rabid hedgehog."

Laughter was fine. The more the king laughed at her, the less likely he was to order the invasion of her kingdom and the murders of her entire family. It didn't matter if it stung. A king, a dozen princesses, a handsome prince and his handsome friends all laughing at the big, awkward peasant girl.

"Three arrows each. Ready your bows!" Dirk ordered. He pointed a stubby finger at Jax. "*Not* you. I plan to keep the foot I've got left. You wait back with the rest."

Jax carried her bow to the stand. Her hand shook so badly she had to grab the frame to steady it, to renewed howls of laughter. She backed quickly from the firing line, just managing not to trip over her feet.

Eira caught her elbow, steadying her—and preventing her from running for the keep.

"That wasn't so bad with no instruction," Eira said loyally, though her mouth twitched at the corners. "Think of it this way. You'll be the most improved archer in the castle by the Winter Solstice."

"Loose!"

The second round of arrows sped toward the targets,

mercifully pulling everyone's attention from Jax. Marjani missed her second shot, but her third struck the target, just shy of the outer circle. The other girls scattered theirs unevenly through the rings. Only Beatrix placed an arrow in the central yellow bullseye.

"St. Aelfred's ears," Dirk swore. "What a sorry lot."

"I would have done better with my own bow," Dora protested.

Dirk turned his head and spat. "If this was a Nordish raid, we'd have our entrails spilled all over the ground. Let's see if the rest of you can manage not to embarrass yourselves."

The sisters had returned, laden with bows. Sister Ursel handed Anara a small, deeply curved black bow. Raisa's had a similar shape, though hers gleamed nearly white. Isolde's bow was the tallest, and she smiled at the attention the boys paid her when she took it from one of the sisters and strode toward the practice line.

"I'm so sorry." A short, plump sister stopped beside Eira. A gracefully curved blond bow sagged awkwardly in her arms. The snapped wood reminded Jax of a broken bone, and the way Eira's face paled at the sight, it was nearly as painful.

"Your beautiful bow," Beatrix mourned, coming up beside them with Anara.

"It was fine this morning, before breakfast." Eira's fingers hovered over the break.

"It was like this when I found it," the sister squeaked. "I was so careful with it."

"This couldn't have happened by accident," Eira said. "Someone did it on purpose."

"But … who would do something like that?" the sister asked, aghast.

"Raisa," Beatrix murmured.

"The mountain girl was the last to come to breakfast," Anara said, glaring toward the archery butts, where Isolde stood with her bow, a perfect picture of beauty and confidence.

"Marjani is strong enough," Eira said darkly.

"Why would *Marjani* do something like that?" Jax asked.

"You didn't even offend her until after breakfast," Beatrix pointed out.

"Raisa might have told her to. They seem awfully friendly."

"Whoever did it was very foolish." Anara raised her voice, so it carried through the courtyard. "Dragons are highly territorial. Anyone who damaged something in our room while Tenzin was nearby would not have enough fingers left to draw her bow."

Jax saw Raisa flick a nervous glance toward the skies, but most of the other princesses did, too.

"I think no one will bother your things again, Princess Eira," Anara said. "I am sorry it is too late for your bow."

"No matter." Eira caressed the smooth wood one last time before gently pushing it back to the sister. "I don't mind using one of the practice bows. It will make the competition more challenging."

"Avoid the one I used," Jax advised. "I think it's defective."

That pulled a smile from her … friend? Unlikely as it seemed, Eira *was* a friend.

"Not defective," Beatrix corrected. "Cursed."

"Was that a curse Jaclyn said?" Anara teased. "It wasn't Common Tongue, so I couldn't be sure."

Even Jax laughed. Somehow, her humiliation didn't hurt quite so badly anymore.

"Use the one I had," Beatrix suggested. "It's decent enough. I wouldn't have done any better with my own bow."

"Will you be gracing us with your presence this morning, ladies?" Dirk called. "Ladies" probably had a more insulting effect on his usual trainees.

Eira and Anara took their places between Ellycia and Lidia—the stepsisters had stayed as far apart as they could get.

"Ready your bows!"

The six new archers complied with significantly more confidence than the first group.

"Why are Raisa's and Anara's bows smaller than the rest?" Jax asked.

"Better for horseback," Beatrix explained. "You lose distance, but with the targets as close as they are, it won't hurt them."

"Nock! Draw! Loose!"

In three rounds of firing, not a single arrow missed a target. Anara whisked her arrows out as though her life depended on her quick reflexes, while Ellycia took her time with each move, checking for the breeze, striving for perfection. Lidia focused her ferocity as if the target were her worst enemy. Eira coolly adjusted her aim after her first mediocre shot with the practice bow to score as well as Raisa, who dazzled with her flair. But it was Isolde who bunched all three of her arrows in the center of the bullseye.

"Fine shooting!" Prince Theodor and his friends hooted and clapped their approval, which transformed more than one of the fierce archers into fluttering maidens.

"I guess our entrails are safe from those Nordish raiders, after all, Dirk!" Ralf called.

"Except for that one." Foxy-hair nodded toward Eira. "She looks pretty dangerous to me."

"She's welcome to *your* entrails, Your Grace," Dirk jibed back.

"I'm sure you could out-shoot all of us, Prince Theodor." Isolde's lashes glittered gold as she batted them at the prince.

"Not I," the prince said cheerfully. He thumped Foxy-hair's shoulder. "Jordis is the best archer among us."

"Gods help the rabbits!" King Wulfric snapped, his voice soured like curdled milk. "If any of you callow boys could shoot straight in a fight, I wouldn't need a daughter-in-law who could use a bow in the first place. This isn't a *sarding* entertainment."

Jax didn't need a translation of the curse to know it was crude.

The king turned his ill humor on Marshal Oswald, his eyes nearly disappearing into the dark tunnels of his brows. "I'll be back tomorrow morning to see their sword work. I expect that viewing stand to be ready."

The king spun on his heel and swept toward the gates, not sparing a glance for the princesses who had shot so well or the young men he'd just humiliated.

After a moment of embarrassed silence, foxy-haired Jordis tossed out a cocky grin.

"*I* certainly feel safer surrounded by all of Your Highnesses," he called. "The more closely you want to surround me, the better. Isn't that right, Theo?"

"Absolutely," the prince agreed. But his forced smile couldn't hide the red burning his cheeks.

CHAPTER NINETEEN

It's true that some of the other girls are nearly as talented
with the bow as I am. What they don't grasp is that it's not
simply the assets you possess. It's how you present them. I've
made sure Prince Theodor is well aware of my … assets.

— Princess Isolde of Montaine

King Wulfric's promise—or was it a threat?—to
return the following morning thoroughly diverted
Marshal Oswald's attention to the creation of His
Majesty's viewing stand. It was only a delay in the feast of
embarrassment, but Jax was happy to set down her fork for
the time being.

As the marshal's men began clearing ground and hauling
planks, Isolde, Raisa and most of the other girls descended on
Prince Theodor and his friends with sideways glances and shy
smiles—like ravening wolves sidling up to a flock of sheep in
the guise of friendly puppies.

"It all sounds like a fairy tale," Eira mused. "The one
where the king invites the maiden daughters of his jarls and
thanes to a feast, so the prince can choose the most beautiful.
But King Wulfric acts as though the whole thing is meant to
insult us, and Prince Theodor, too."

"I don't think it's an act," Beatrix said darkly. "Nonetheless, diplomacy requires me to pay my respects to the prince. Might as well get it over with."

"That's the spirit." Eira grinned. "Come on, Princess Jaclyn."

"I think it's better if I stay out of the way." Jax nodded toward the prince's entourage. Jordis, the foxy-haired youth, was pantomiming awkward bowshots, making Raisa throw back her head with laughter.

Eira winced. "I can see how that might be the wiser course."

"We'll test the waters," Beatrix said. "If no one eats us, you can wade in later."

Jax watched her friends stride over to the boys. Prince Theodor welcomed them with a smile, as though nothing could please him more than the company of a scarred Bellisian girl and a Nordish exile. As though his father hadn't just shamed him in front of a dozen princesses.

"Why would King Wulfric want to humiliate his own son?" she muttered to herself.

"The king blames Theo for Guntram's death."

Jax whirled to find Princess Ellycia standing nearby.

"The ball is his punishment," Ellycia explained.

"He blames Prince Theo?" Jax repeated. "For the manticore attack? I thought he suspected a rival kingdom of plotting to murder Prince Guntram."

"Oh, I'm sure he does. He doesn't hold Theo responsible for the attack; he blames him for failing to stop it." Ellycia's gaze grew distant. "Theo and I led the welcoming party that met Guntram and his men in Newport on their return from Almasa. The king stayed behind in the castle. He wanted Guntram to receive all the attention, to enjoy being cheered as a conquering hero. And the people did cheer him."

She blinked hard. "I rode beside him as we returned to the castle. When the manticore dropped from the sky, my horse panicked. *I* panicked. The air seemed filled with wings. Claws. All those teeth. Thousands of teeth.”

Until that moment, Jax hadn’t quite believed the manticore could be real. Surely it must have been a wandering panther misinterpreted by frightened men or even a story fabricated by the king to cover up a drunken stumble off a cliff.

Watching the shadows flicker in Ellycia’s eyes, Jax knew the dowager crown princess wasn’t fabricating anything.

“Theo thought the monster was attacking me,” Ellycia continued. “He pulled me from my horse and got me to safety before going back to face the manticore. By then, it was too late. The creature got past Guntram’s sword and slashed his throat.

“The king thinks Guntram died because I was a coward and Theo was a fool. He believes that if Theo had stayed with his brother, Guntram would still be alive.”

“Do you believe that?”

Ellycia met her gaze. “Guntram was the best swordsman I’ve ever seen. If he couldn’t stop that beast, no one could. It killed two of Guntram’s knights. Marshal Oswald lost his eye trying to drive it from Guntram’s body. And still it escaped.”

Jax glanced at the sky, clear and blue above them. She didn’t want to believe in monsters bringing death from above. But she’d seen a dragon with her own eyes. Was a manticore any more improbable?

“If I had been less of a coward—” Ellycia’s voice betrayed only a hairline crack. “If Theo had tried to save Guntram rather than me … King Wulfric would have lost two sons that day.”

“The king must realize how fortunate he is that Prince Theodor wasn’t killed.”

Ellycia gave a short, sharp shake of her head. “Guntram was the golden son, the king’s right hand. His heir, not just in name, but in spirit. I almost think Wulfric would rather Theo had died with Guntram than to survive as a reminder of the son he lost."

The grief in her voice squeezed Jax's heart. "I'm sorry. I didn't mean to make you relive it all."

"I remember it all the time. I can't seem to stop. I sometimes think it would have been better …" She turned troubled eyes on Jax. "You need to know that if this seems like a fairy tale, it's not one with a kindly king and a fairy godmother. No impoverished, good-hearted peasant girl is going to marry the prince and live happily ever after."

She turned softly on her heel walked away.

JAX STOOD ALONE and forgotten in the center of the courtyard, but she couldn't remain invisible forever. Eventually, someone would notice her, and based on how the morning had gone so far, that wouldn't end well.

She touched the hammer in her belt. If only she had work to do, something useful to keep her mind from the things she couldn't control. There must have been a smithy in Lukos once, back when the Santians had built it, but with the new castle and its forges so close, she supposed it wasn't necessary now.

She slipped into the shade of the stable. Out in the yard, Jordis had succumbed to the girls' pleas to show off his archery skills. His hair gleamed copper in the sunlight, and he looked like a prince himself as he took aim with a borrowed bow.

Isolde's bow, Jax saw, though it seemed smaller in Jordis's hands. The Montainan princess sparkled brightly beside him, smiling coyly. Ralf clowned nearby, teasing Jordis, drawing giggles from the other girls.

Raisa, though, stood a pace apart, scanning the courtyard as though searching for something. Or someone. Jax jerked her gaze away before the Ravninan princess could catch her looking. Her skin prickled, like a rabbit touched by a hawk's shadow. She slipped through the half-open stable door feeling as if she'd escaped by a whisker.

The gloom inside smelled as much of new wood as animals, but she heard a soft whicker and the sounds of shifting hooves. As her eyes grew accustomed to the dim light, she saw several horses sticking their noses over their stall doors, checking to see who had entered. A groom ducked into a stall at the far end of the building, but the stables were blessedly empty of knights and princesses.

A blocky, frost-gray muzzle nodded at her over the nearest stall. The top of the mare's shaggy mane was gathered into a tassel tied with green silk. Jax recognized her as Anara's sturdy little horse.

A familiar whicker hurried her to the next stall.

"Bruno!" She laughed at her own joy at seeing the old carthorse's homely, angular face.

He wuffled her hand, obviously pleased to see her, too. He didn't even seem overly disappointed she hadn't brought him a handful of clover or an apple core.

"Good old Bruno," she murmured, speaking to him in Venian, glad of a chance to use her native language. "I thought they'd sent you home with Nicolas and Anatole. Have they been taking good care of you?"

It was obvious "they" had. Bruno's rough coat gleamed from a recent grooming, and he stood in thick, fresh straw. Flecks of his breakfast oats spotted the bucket that hung from his stall door. Seeing her examining it, he took another swipe with his tongue, just in case he'd missed anything.

"Look at you," she crooned around the homesickness swelling her throat. "Are you enjoying being a princess's palfrey? Don't get used to it."

Straw rustled in the next box down, and a thump rattled the wall. A sleek black head rose over the stall door, jerking up and down in irritation. Princess Raisa's stallion. There was no mistaking the sculpted muzzle, the aristocratic curve of his neck.

He looked as though he had walked out of a story, black as ink, his mane spun of silk and shadows, his eyes deep as a woodland spring at midnight.

"Ellycia's right, you know," Jax sighed to Bruno. "No fairy godmother could make either of us look like that."

For the span of a breath, yearning for it pierced her soul. The noble, perfect horse. Raisa's effortless grace and confidence. Knowing her worth and having everyone around her know it, too. To be able to enter King Wulfric's ball with her head high, the most gorgeous gown in the kingdom swirling about her feet, every eye on her, not with scorn, but with admiration, jealousy, longing.

Bruno's cheek bumped her hand, and he tilted his head for her, sighing in pleasure when she scratched his ear. She couldn't help noticing the blocky set of his features. His over-sized ears. The mild eyes holding no dreams of running free on the Ravninan steppes. He only hoped for another bucket of oats.

Jax's heart squeezed with her betrayal. From now on, when she looked at Bruno, would she always see what he could never be?

"That your horse. He knows how happy. *To be* happy." The groom's halting, bare-rock accent ground awkwardly on the soft Venian words.

Jax ducked her head to hide her embarrassment. No one was supposed to hear her confiding in her horse. She hoped the man's understanding of Venian was as limited as his grammar.

"Yes, Bruno is rarely discontent." She switched to Common Tongue for courtesy. "I think he finds each moment to be just as it should be somehow."

"An admirable philosophy. I envy him." The voice, now confident in the language being spoken, sounded smoother, richer ... oddly familiar.

Jax glanced over at the groom and abruptly stumbled back, slamming into Bruno's stall door. Sick horror washed over her, along with a blush hot enough to set the stable on fire.

Despite the threat of sudden death—either from pure terror or spontaneous combustion—she couldn't help agreeing with Eira's assessment. Prince Theodor really was a little bit gorgeous.

Oh. My. Gods. He's *so* adorable.
— Princess Pia of Capra

"Oh! I didn't … I'm sorry," Jax stammered. "Pardon, Your Grace. I mean, Your Majesty." No, "majesty" was for the king. "Your High … Your *Royal* Highness—"

No, no, no, she was *curtsying*, for gods' sake. Anatole would be frothing. She jerked herself upright, knocking her head against Bruno's chin.

The horse snorted and took a prudent step back.

"Princess Jaclyn." Prince Theodor bowed with graceful courtesy. "Please accept my apologies. I didn't mean to startle you. I thought you saw me earlier."

"I thought you were the groom!" *Oh, gods.* By now, everyone in Aldforth must know her father was from the southern deserts. Perhaps they would assume her skin was meant to glow red.

"Blast!" The prince laughed. "I only came out because I thought you'd discovered my hiding place."

Up close, Prince Theodor looked almost as legend-worthy as Raisa's horse, his dark hair rakishly tousled, blue eyes sparkling with self-deprecating humor. He leaned forward as though divulging a confidence. "I excused myself from the melee in the yard to find the privy and couldn't force myself to return. The horses don't expect as much from me as everyone else does."

"Bruno expects the same thing from everyone—a pat and some hay."

"Exactly!" He smiled at her as though she'd said something brilliant. "The horses treat me like any other person. All those princesses treating me like a crown prince—it makes me feel like a fraud."

"Like me." Her tongue felt leaden as the drop in her heart. She had been a fool not to brace herself for his mockery.

"You?"

"I am the fraudulent princess, Your Royal Highness. The one who doesn't belong here."

"But you *are* a princess. You're the Venian queen's daughter, aren't you? Even if you are a ..." His voice trailed off, whether stumbling over *blacksmith's daughter* or *bastard* or *hulking peasant*, Jax didn't know. "I only meant me. It was a silly thing to say. I apologize if I've offended you."

Experience had made her wary, but his eyes wore the traces of weariness and doubt. A boy scarce older than herself who had always been the spare, suddenly thrust into the shoes of his larger-than-life brother ... He might indeed feel himself a fraud.

"You have no need to apologize," she told him, dizzy with the audacity of saying such a thing to a prince. "But isn't it better to be treated like a crown prince than an imposter?"

His smile tilted, less dazzling but more genuine. "Probably. Still, I wonder if you might not be better equipped to play a princess than I am to play a crown prince."

"I don't think either of us has the luxury of playing, Your Highness."

"Ouch." He pressed a hand to his ear. "That's a proper dressing down if I've ever had one, and I've had my share."

If only she'd hit Bruno's chin hard enough to knock herself unconscious. "Please forgive me, Your Highness, I didn't mean to—"

"Oh, I suspect you did, and I suspect I deserved it." He gave such a look of penitence that she could only laugh and shake her head, as if he were Denis, not sorry for the snails so carefully saved in Agnes's favorite cup, but heartily sorry Agnes wasn't pleased with them. "And now that we're on such familiar terms, you must call me Theo, as my friends do, and I shall call you Jaclyn."

"My friends call me Jax." What had come over her? She did *not* have friends who were princes.

"*Jax?* That's an outrageous name for a princess," he said in approval.

"You're incorrigible," she replied without thinking.

"So I've been told."

"Prince Theodor! There you are." Princess Raisa's voice lifted the hair on the back of Jax's neck, and the dire gravity of her situation flooded back in a wave.

"Princess Raisa! You caught me." The prince flashed his jaunty smile. "I couldn't resist sneaking a look at your stallion. What a breathtaking animal."

So. A different tale of impish naughtiness for the Ravninan princess. Jax narrowed her eyes at him. He winked.

"There's no need for guile, Your Highness." Raisa glided gracefully between him and Jax. "He is your father's stallion now. A gift."

"And the promise of more. A tempting bribe."

"A gift of brotherly love from one great king to another," Raisa rebuked him with a playful tap on his shoulder. "Our fathers are kinsmen, you know."

"Of course," Theo agreed. "Great-great-great-grand whatsis or something. On behalf of my father, I must express Aldforth's gratitude that our cousin, King Korol, has sent us such a magnificent beauty." He grinned wickedly. "And the stallion, too, of course."

The horse in question kicked the door of his stall and whinnied in irritation. Jax had no such outlet for her emotion. She edged sideways, an eye on the stable door.

"And you, Princess Jaclyn." Raisa managed to make *Jaclyn* sound almost as uncouth as *Jax.* "Are we not cousins, also? I am sure I have heard of some connection between the house of King Felix of Venia and my family."

Anger flared beneath Jax's fear and embarrassment. Shouldn't Raisa be out crushing the real competition beneath her heel? Isolde or Lidia or someone?

"Queen Léonie, my … mother—" Jax stumbled over the word. "She is no relation to King Felix's family."

As Raisa undoubtedly knew full well. Raisa probably knew more about the lineages of Venian nobility than Jax did.

"Oh, yes." Raisa's smile could have cut flesh. "Venia has that quaint system for determining succession. I understand … perhaps you can correct me if I am mistaken? I understand that even a *peasant* may become king?"

Raisa obviously meant to highlight the social chasm between them. But her words reminded Jax of Nicolas and the Court School.

Just because it's not perfect doesn't mean the ideal isn't worth believing in.

"I suppose it would seem quaint," Jax said, "to choose a monarch based on merit if you were used to your rulers being chosen by an accident of birth."

Outrage bloomed along Raisa's cheekbones. She put a hand on the crown prince's arm.

"Is Princess Jaclyn questioning your fitness to rule, Your Highness?" she purred. "That is a capital offense in Ravnina. We execute those who say such things."

Cold dread sank in Jax's throat like a millstone, yet she barely bit back her reply. *I suppose that's easier than earning their respect.*

"Fortunately, we have no such laws in Aldforth," Theo said lightly. "We'd be forced to execute half my father's council.

They can't understand why I find politics so dull. Besides, I am sure visiting royalty must be exempt from capital punishment in all the Blessed Kingdoms. Much as young princes are exempt from corporal punishment—as you saw yesterday, to my esquire, Ralf's detriment."

Anguish flashed across the prince's face, and he checked himself, as though he hadn't meant to say so much. "Enough of such tiresome topics. I want to know more about this splendid bit of horseflesh."

He guided Raisa to the stallion's stall and begged the details of the animal's parentage, his speed, his training.

Raisa smiled, triumphant at capturing the prince's attention. Yet even as she tossed her long, shining hair and pulled Prince Theo's arm closer, he shot an irreverent grimace over his shoulder at Jax and mouthed, *You owe me.*

Clenching her trembling hands in her skirts, Jax escaped through the stable door into the blinding sunlight of the yard. She paused to let her eyes adjust. And to settle the bile in her stomach.

Idiot. Fool. Dreaming of ball gowns and teasing a prince. Hadn't Anatole taught her better than that? She didn't have the luxury of flirting and sniping like Raisa. The wrong words could get her killed—or give King Wulfric the excuse he wanted to invade her homeland, destroy her village, kill her family.

She was ridiculously lucky that Theo—*Prince Theodor*—was not as easily provoked as his father. She had better count her blessings and be sure she didn't make any more missteps.

From now on, she would keep her head down and her mouth *shut.*

CHAPTER TWENTY-ONE

Why shouldn't I flirt? Sure, some of these princesses, you'd think their fathers would have been too embarrassed to send them, but the rest are comely enough. Even if Theo has his usual devil's own luck and the king picks the prettiest and richest for him to marry, there will be plenty of pretty, rich girls left. I guarantee you, most of their fathers would be only too happy to have an Aldforthian duke for a son-in-law.

— Duke Jordis of Tyrglas

"There you are!" Eira pounced as Jax walked away from the stable. "Marshal Oswald has forgotten all about us. There's nothing to *do.*"

"Who knew being pawns in a brutal game of dynasty building would be so dull?" Beatrix murmured, raising that sardonic eyebrow.

"I thought you were flirting with the Rose Knights." Jax rubbed her arms, hoping the sun's heat would dispel the chill from her encounter with Raisa. She needed to put some distance between herself and the stables.

"There's no point trying to get a word in, with Isolde and

Dora around," Eira complained. "Besides, Prince Theodor disappeared. It hardly matters what the other boys think of us."

"Who do you think has the prince's ear?" Beatrix asked. "*Those other boys.*"

"It doesn't make any difference," Eira said. "King Wulfric will choose his bride."

"She has you there," Jax said.

"Not such a harmless dimwit, after all," the Bellisian agreed. Her voice turned brittle. "And since the only criterion Duke Jordis and the others seem to notice is physical attractiveness, I am absolved of any need to waste my time on them."

"That absolves all three of us," Eira said cheerfully.

"Don't," Beatrix growled, low and feral. "Don't you *ever* tell me your eyebrows are too pale or your elbows are too sharp."

She whirled on Jax. "Don't go on about how you're too tall or your nose is too big. Not until a complete stranger tries to trample you with his horse because someone taunted him that he might be attracted to you."

The flat chill in Beatrix's gaze made Jax's neck prickle with unease, even as her heart ached for her.

"Well, yes, it's a good thing *you're* here," Eira said, ignoring the violence rippling under Beatrix's skin. "Otherwise, Jax and I would be the homeliest princesses in the Blessed Kingdoms. The known world, really. Marjani is breathtaking, after all, if you don't mind all that obnoxious gloom."

Something dangerous flared in Beatrix's eyes, but anything was better than that dead stare.

"If this were a fairy tale," Jax picked up Eira's lead, "we'd be the wicked stepsisters. And Isolde would end up as queen of Aldforth."

"Maybe we could try pricking her finger with a spindle," Eira suggested. "Put her to sleep for a hundred years."

"Oh, for the gods' sake." Beatrix's snarl would have done a lion proud, but the snort at the end ruined it. "You win. You're definitely the most obnoxious princesses in the known world."

Eira's smile was angelic—nearly.

"Unless you've got that spindle ready, we should keep walking," Jax warned, shooting a wary glance over Eira's shoulder. "Isolde and Jordis are headed this way."

"That's a dangerous combination." Beatrix picked up her pace around the practice posts, angling away from the foxy-haired duke, the golden princess, and their retinue of Rose Knights and ladies fair.

"Isolde's probably hunting for Prince Theodor," Eira said, adding dryly, "At least she's not carrying her bow."

"Prince Theo is in the stables with Raisa," Jax told them.

Beatrix hissed in alarm. "If Isolde knows Raisa's cornered the prince all to herself, she'll be out for blood. And Jordis has already figured out she loves seeing other princesses humiliated. We'd have to walk right past them to get to the keep, so we can't hide in our room."

"I'm not afraid of Isolde," Eira said. "And Jordis doesn't have his horse today."

But Jax knew exactly how much damage a bully could cause without ever raising a fist. Seeing the dread in Beatrix's face, she glanced around the courtyard for somewhere to slip her friend out of sight …

"Look there." She nodded toward the jumbled ruin of a turret built along the curtain wall nearby. She had thought the ruin connected the wall to the keep, but now they were closer, she could make out a narrow opening between them.

"Don't rush. We don't want to attract attention," Beatrix advised.

Still, they moved quickly, slipping into the narrow corridor of shadow between the keep and the old ruins. The opening continued a dozen yards before running up against another collapsed turret at the rear corner of the keep. The rubble reached nearly to Jax's shoulder.

"We have to go back," Beatrix said. "If they see us in here, we'll be trapped."

"Wait!" Eira eyed the pile of stones. "We can do this." She scrambled to the top of the rubble like a squirrel, hopping lightly from rock to rock.

"You're going to break your neck," Beatrix warned. But Eira had already turned the corner out of sight.

She reappeared a moment later, grinning wickedly, the sunshine behind her lighting her pale hair. "There's another courtyard back here. It must have been a garden in the Empire days. Come and see."

She disappeared again.

Beatrix glared at Jax. "You're not."

"Isolde would never follow us over that."

Beatrix tapped her fingers as she considered. "All right. Fine. You first."

Jax tucked her skirts into her belt, glad of her riding breeches underneath, and started up the pile. She was afraid the rocks might shift, but they must have been settling into place for centuries. They remained secure beneath her feet. Around the corner of the keep, the rubble sloped down, depositing Jax in the courtyard Eira had described.

"What a mess," Beatrix said, climbing down beside her.

The secluded yard was a dumping ground of broken stone, castoff timbers, and drifts of dead leaves. Beyond the worst of the debris, an orchard of ancient, gnarled fruit trees bent over stone pathways that wound between jagged outcroppings of rock. Tangled briars and climbing vines wrenched apart the remains of what must have once been an elegant garden.

Eira stood in the center of the main path with her head cocked, near a spreading weeping willow. She looked as though she ought to have little forest animals dancing around her feet.

"It's like an enchanted garden from a story," Jax said. For the first time since arriving in Aldforth, she felt a stirring of pure delight. "I half expect to see a unicorn or stumble over a spellbound princess."

"You're liable to stumble over a princess everywhere in this place," Beatrix pointed out darkly.

"Listen a minute," Eira said. "How quiet it is."

The thick stone walls muted the noise from the main courtyard, stilling the very air to a hush.

"Too quiet," Eira whispered.

Beatrix snorted. "No brainless chattering?"

"No birds."

A shiver ran down Jax's spine. Ruins. Briars. The mossy arm of a toppled statue protruded from an ancient fountain. It looked like a lost soul grasping desperately for help from the depths of the underworld. Not all stories were filled with light.

She touched her hammer. "Constable Anatole told me Lukos is cursed."

"That old poem? 'Death's Rule'? Superstitious nonsense," Beatrix scoffed. "The Devastation was caused by plague and war. Not the curse of some buried god or angry demon."

"The Temple of Peace teaches that human hatred is the greatest source of evil in the world," Eira said.

Jax wasn't inclined to believe in curses, either. Still … "The manticore that killed Prince Guntram came from somewhere."

No one squealed or even moved quickly, but suddenly they were all much closer together, backs to each other, facing the hidden places of the deserted courtyard. Eira's hand moved to her shoulder as if reaching for her broken bow.

"Good place for monsters," Beatrix observed coolly.

A sound came then, when Jax had so hoped everything would remain silent—a rustle in the leaves of the old willow just yards away. She yanked her hammer from her belt.

"That's not a very big weapon," Eira said.

"It's not supposed to *be* a weapon," Jax hissed back.

"Maybe you shouldn't mention that to the monster."

"There is no monster," Jax said firmly.

"Yes, there is." The irritated voice came from the depths of the willow's boughs. "You are correct to think a monster has frightened away the birds. She's been eating them."

CHAPTER TWENTY-TWO

So. The awful power of perfect princes
Fell broken and foul-fleshed
Before the savage soul-ravener.
Darkness loosed light-winged
From depths below the brightest Light
To swallow a hundred sun-wanderings.
A somber warning for all secret-seekers.

— From "Death's Rule," an epic from the time of the Devastation, Author Unknown

A sharp whistle tugged Jax's gaze upward. Green and
blue scales flashed against the sky, and a rain of
small, blackened feathers pelted her face.

"Finding privacy is no easier here than in the Imperial
Palace." Princess Anara stepped from the willow's bower, slipping a small scroll into a pocket of her tunic. She frowned at
the little dragon flying overhead. "You need not fear. If there
were a manticore nearby, Tenzin would have warned me."

The other girls sheepishly abandoned their defensive
formation. But it took Jax three tries to get her hammer shaft
through the loop in her belt.

Tenzin landed on Anara's shoulder with a self-satisfied warble.

"She says if you're trying to avoid that viper-tempered, ember-haired boy, she knows a better place than here."

"You're hiding from Duke Jordis, too?" Eira asked.

"I am not *hiding.*" Anara gave a sharp toss of her short, dark hair. "I am exploring to keep from breaking my vow to Empress Khulan. The things that boy said about Tenzin would require a challenge of honor in Kherem, but the empress commanded me to kill no foreigners while I am here."

Jordis outmatched the compact princess by at least a foot in height and fifty pounds in weight. Still, the girl's ferocity warned Jax not to discount her.

"Duke." Anara curled her lip. "A silly name."

" 'Duke' is a title," Beatrix explained. "A duke ranks just below a king or prince. They're often members of the royal family."

"Men's titles," Anara said dismissively.

"The Holy Mother made me memorize the Aldforthian royal family," Eira said. "Jordis wasn't one of them."

"No, his is a separate royal line," Beatrix said. "Our viperous Jordis is Duke of Tyrglas."

She paused dramatically. Jax glanced at the others. Maybe it sounded familiar? But they only shrugged.

"Tyrglas," Beatrix repeated, eyebrow raised incredulously. "One of the original Blessed Kingdoms? Gradually lost influence as Aldforth rose in might. King Wulfric's great-grandfather annexed it as a duchy with little resistance, although the previous duke, Jordis's father …"

Jax's skin grew cold as Beatrix's story merged with the one Anatole had told. "The previous duke of Tyrglas rebelled. His oldest son was killed—"

"King Wulfric shot the boy's head over his father's walls with a trebuchet," Beatrix finished for her.

"The duke surrendered to save his younger son's life.

Jordis's life." The pity Jax felt for that little boy, made duke after the murder of his brother and the mutilation of his father, warred with her loathing of the young man who had nearly trampled Beatrix to protect his vanity.

Tenzin launched herself from Anara's shoulder with a long-suffering sigh. She circled overhead, then swooped down a broken path leading deeper into the garden.

Anara rolled her eyes. "Dragons are supposed to be renowned for their patience. She wants us to follow."

"Fine with me," Beatrix said. "I'm up for hiding—I mean, *exploring.*"

"Holy Mother says curiosity is one of my most maddening qualities," Eira said.

Despite the shadow of the dark stories she'd heard that day, Jax felt a flicker of happiness. The ruined beauty, the hidden secrets, the simple pleasure of the garden's seductive wildness drew her in. Tugged by an unfamiliar, reckless sense of freedom, she followed the others past the strangled, broken statuary, the thickets of wild roses. The path wound through a cluster of natural rock formations as decorative as any statues before entering a tangle of hawthorns.

Hopping and gliding through the branches, Tenzin led them around the base of a great spire of rock, down into a small, mossy hollow hidden deep in the hawthorn thicket. Eira stepped into the center of the circle.

"There should be a fairy ring," she said, grinning with delight.

Tenzin whistled, the sound strangely muffled.

"We *did* follow you," Anara replied. She frowned into the tangle of thorny branches surrounding them. "There's no more path. We will not crawl under the trees to find you."

The little dragon's response sounded suspiciously like she'd stuck out her tongue and hissed.

"I think she's hiding in the rocks." Jax moved toward the rough spire that rose above their heads, the pale stone jagged and fissured from millennia of weather. One of the crevices curved inward, wider than it first appeared. "There's a cave."

A flash of glittering emerald eyes confirmed it.

No sensible person would walk into a dark hole where she knew an unpredictable dragon waited. Jax allowed the adventure to pull her in, anyway, Anara right behind her.

The narrow entrance opened into a small, bare space, dimly illuminated by a hole in the ceiling that let a shaft of sunlight through. Tenzin warbled and hopped to Anara's shoulder.

"Well, the cave couldn't be very big, could it, considering the size of the rock?" Eira said as she squeezed in behind them. "Silly to be disappointed. I thought it might be a hidden temple or a crypt. The Santians built a lot of underground shrines to their secret gods."

"Their demon gods?" Beatrix asked, entering more cautiously. "The ones they fed the hearts of their enemies to?"

Eira pressed her hands together in an attitude of piety. "The Temple of Peace teaches that all gods are manifestations of the One Goddess who permeates all things. The evil done in any god's name comes from the heart of the human supplicant, not from the god. Or demon."

"Lovely," Beatrix said. "I'm so sad that we won't have the chance to trespass in an ancient demon's temple to commune with Peace."

"How far underground do you think such a temple would be?" Anara asked from the far side of the chamber. "There are stairs leading down through the floor."

"Glorious," Beatrix muttered. "Of course there are."

Jax and Eira joined Anara to stare down at the winding stone staircase carved into the heart of Lukos's hill.

"Too bad we don't have a lantern," Beatrix said from behind Jax's shoulder. "I guess we'll just have to go back out into the daylight."

Anara stepped down the first few stairs, the brush of her slippered feet loud in the chamber's hush. "Tenzin?"

The dragon clambered headfirst down the front of Anara's tunic and hopped to the step below her feet. She hissed softly, and a small flame flicked from the end of her snout, casting a glimmer of light on the rough rock walls.

"Erk!" Jax jumped back. She might have knocked Beatrix over, but the Bellisian princess was already pressed flat against the farthest wall. *Fire-breathing dragon. That explained the singed feathers Tenzin had dropped on her head.*

"Amazing!" Eira exclaimed. "How does she do that?"

The little dragon gave a self-satisfied whistle and blew another gout of flame into the dimness below.

"The stairs do not seem very deep." Anara's voice rose in strange echoes from the hole. "They lead to a tunnel."

"A tunnel?" Eira scrambled down after her.

"We're not going down there," Beatrix said. "Who knows how stable it is? Princess Jaclyn? Jax!"

Jax adjusted her footing on the narrow steps. "It can't go far. We won't be long."

"Fine. Scream if the mountain collapses on you or you get eaten by a demon, and I'll go for help."

Jax grinned and ducked under the low lintel into the tunnel where the other girls waited. The intermittent light, which flickered out each time Tenzin drew breath, showed a narrow shaft that sloped downward into the earth.

"Not too fast," Anara warned as Tenzin scampered into the dark.

The air was cool after the summer warmth aboveground and smelled of stone and ancient dust. Jax could almost feel the rock pressing down on them as they traveled deeper into the hill. They passed a niche where the tunnel wall split open slightly. Tenzin breathed light into it, but the shallow space was bare of anything that might indicate a temple—or a demon.

"Part of the tunnel has been dug out of the rock," Eira said, "but some of it's natural. See how rough the walls are?"

"Do you think we're under the keep?" Jax asked, scanning

the low ceiling. Just because the great, heavy structure hadn't crushed the entire hill during its centuries of existence didn't mean it couldn't happen.

Around the next bend, the tunnel spilled into a large natural chamber with an uneven floor and jagged ceiling. Even Tenzin's flame couldn't illuminate all the crevices splitting the rock above their heads.

The little dragon cocked her head and whistled.

"Fine. Just don't wake them up," Anara answered. Then explained to the others, "Bats."

Even Eira ducked.

"Here is the exit." Anara moved to an opening at the side of the chamber. Tenzin's flame revealed a pile of rubble that spilled from ceiling to floor.

Buried under tons of rock with only a mischievous dragon for light and a horde of unseen bats sleeping overhead, a sensible person would be relieved to turn back. Yet, above-ground lay Lukos Castle, King Wulfric, and Jax's unwanted life being—*pretending* to be—Princess Jaclyn.

"Wait." Jax pointed to a small opening along the chamber wall. "That might be another way out."

The small fissure was barely as tall as Jax's hip. They had to crouch to peer inside, and when Tenzin sent her flame into the darkness, it revealed a sharp, steep drop more like a well than a tunnel. Not even the spirit of adventure could make entering that seem appealing.

"I see one more!" Eira called, leading them across the uneven floor to a larger gap of darkness.

It would have been wide enough for all three of them to enter side by side, but this tunnel was also blocked. The utilitarian iron bars of the gate that spanned it appeared out of place in the rough, irregular opening.

"A Santian artifact," Eira breathed. She reached out to brush her fingers over the rusting metal slats.

"I don't think *that's* a Santian artifact." Jax pointed at the decidedly less ancient chain and padlock securing the gate to its post. "Someone besides us has been down here in the past five hundred years."

"Most of the ancient sites have been looted. This was probably put in after everything of value was already gone." Eira sighed. "I wonder if there really was a crypt back there. Or a temple."

"Or a demon." Jax wished she hadn't said that.

"Maybe the gate was not put there to keep people out," Anara said. "Maybe it was meant to keep something *in*."

They were all quiet for a moment after that.

"Do you know that poem Beatrix mentioned?" Jax asked finally. A faint breath of cold air brushed her hand.

" 'Death's Rule.' " Eira tilted her head thoughtfully. "I had to read it once. Holy Mother insists all the acolytes be well versed in ancient religions, as well as modern ones. It's written in an archaic form of old Aldforthian, though, and translation isn't my greatest gift. There was a lot of ravening and carnage and the shadowy slaves of death laying waste to places that don't exist anymore."

"Constable Anatole said the Devastation started in Lukos." Jax steadfastly ignored the goosebumps traveling up her arms.

"No," Eira said, "Beatrix was right. The Devastation didn't have just one cause. There were wars, famine, natural disasters. The scholars at the Temple of Peace say even the plague wasn't just one disease, that there were different symptoms in different places. And 'Death's Rule' doesn't say it started here. It was someplace the Santians called 'The Light in the Darkness.' "

"Lukos." Jax gave up and rubbed her chilled arms. "That's what Nicolas said Lukos means."

The cavern went dark as Tenzin drew in a breath. Without the distraction of sight, Jax didn't just feel the brush of air from the gated tunnel. She heard something in it. A sound like a sigh.

Tenzin's flame flickered back, lighting Eira's sheepish expression. "I did say translation wasn't my greatest skill."

The cavern went dark again. Anara hissed anxiously, and Jax heard her scoop the little dragon into her arms. "She's spent too much energy making fire. She's getting tired."

Tenzin breathed a softer flame, lighting the worry on her master's face.

Although *master* wasn't the right word, considering the way the two worked together and watched over each other. Still, cradling the brightly colored creature in her arms, Anara looked every inch the dragon's guardian.

Tenzin gave a querulous warble that Anara hushed with her own whistle and a frown.

"No more exploring, *khaar mi*," Anara said firmly. "You need water and rest."

In the tentative light of Tenzin's now feeble flame, Jax and Eira stumbled after the Kheremese princess across the uneven floor of the cavern.

"The way up is not treacherous," Anara said when they reached the tunnel. "We can find our way in the dark."

Tenzin's light flickered out with a sigh.

Jax gulped down her sudden panic. She didn't believe in demons or curses any more than she believed in fairy tales. She wasn't certain she even believed in the Venian gods to which Father Donat prayed or the foreign ones her father still said devotions to every time the seasons changed.

Still, in the dark, where no one could see, she made the circles of the sun and the moon with her fingers and placed them over her heart. For balance, her father said. Being right with the earth and sky and all between. Something like the peace of Eira's One Goddess, she supposed.

It seemed a small gesture against that black, gated hole breathing behind them.

The return trek through the dark felt miles farther than it had with Tenzin's flame. But as nothing but the occasional jutting rock reached out to grab their skirts or pull their hair,

Eira began to laugh, apparently delighted by the fearful sensation of fleeing imaginary demons utterly blind.

By the time they reached the spiral stairs, Jax was giggling, too. And as they scrambled up the stairs and tumbled into the hushed chamber inside the rock spire, even Anara's stoicism cracked.

"I cannot express my gratitude at being invited on such a pleasant outing," she managed around strangled chortles, squeezing a puff of smoke from the sleepy dragon in her arms.

"It's just as well we didn't find a Santian temple," Eira said in mock offense. "I'm afraid you two wouldn't have had the proper reverent attitude."

Then she burst into another fit of laughter and gave Jax's shoulder a shove that would have knocked her sideways if she hadn't been three inches taller than the slender Nordish girl.

"Where is the fire-kissed one?" Anara asked, sobering. "Princess Bee-uh … trish?"

"*Trix*. Beatrix," Jax corrected.

"That's easy for you to say, *Yahks*." Eira shot a grin at Anara. "These barbarians with their outrageous names."

"*Jax*," Jax huffed. "*Civilized* people can pronounce jays properly."

"That's what I said."

"What if Beatrix tried to follow us?" Jax asked. "Could we have passed her in the dark?"

"Beatrih …*Bee* was frightened of the underground, the darkness," Anara said. "She would not have entered the cave."

Fear wasn't an emotion Jax would normally apply to someone who hadn't twitched an eyelash when a knight charged her with his warhorse. But Beatrix had been the last to enter this little chamber, had held back at the stairs, had nearly jumped out of her skin at Tenzin's first flame.

Was it going underground that had unnerved the scarred princess? Or the fire?

And if cool, caustic Beatrix could be frightened, what

about the other princesses who seemed so self-assured? What secret fears did they harbor that she'd never even considered?

Tenzin's soft whistle sounded exhausted, but she climbed onto Anara's shoulder and shook out her wings.

"Voices," Anara translated. "Tenzin says they are yelling at the flame-girl."

Jordis and Isolde. Jax's thoughts fled to the quiet, dark hole behind them and how easy it would be to hide until the bullies finished with Beatrix and moved on. Hadn't she vowed, barely an hour before, that she would keep her head down and stay out of trouble?

If Eira or Anara shared her craven impulses, they said nothing. They only followed as she rushed to the entrance and pushed her way out into the sunlight.

CHAPTER TWENTY-THREE

Why do people try to frighten one another with talk of imaginary demons when so many real ones walk freely among them?

— Princess Anara of Kherem

"I *told* you. It's dangerous back here." That was Jordis, Jax thought—curt, haughty. "Where are your friends?"

"That's none of your concern." Beatrix's voice matched his for hauteur.

It seemed such a shame to waste her efforts to protect the rest of them. Jax sighed and headed for the path through the hawthorns.

"I am a duke of the royal lineage of Tyrglas!" Jordis snapped. "You'll watch how you speak to me."

"I am an imperial princess of House Magna of Bellis," Beatrix's tone held a dangerous chill. "You should think twice about how you speak to *me*."

"We're only concerned about your friends' safety," another voice cut in. Jax recognized Ralf's lilting accent. "Please, Princess Beatrix—"

"Princess *Beast* is more like it," Jordis snarled.

"*Jordis*," Ralf chided. "The ground in this area can be treacherous, princess. If anyone were injured—"

He stopped, startled, as Jax came around the last bend in the path, Eira and Anara close on her heels.

"Princess Jax!" Another voice she recognized. Prince Theo stood between Jordis and Beatrix—probably to prevent them coming to blows. "We keep encountering each other in the strangest places."

"It's a small castle," Jax pointed out.

His face lit in a delighted smile at her irreverence, but Jordis's disapproving scowl reminded her of the dangers of unwanted attention.

"Princess Eira. Princess Anara." Theo greeted them all with an extravagant bow. "I am so grateful to find you alive and well and not trapped at the bottom of a sinkhole or buried in a pile of rubble."

"We're grateful for that, too, Your Highness," Eira said brightly, making Beatrix roll her eyes.

"I insist you call me Theo," he corrected. "Wait. First, I must introduce everyone." He gestured around him. "His Grace, Duke Jordis of Tyrglas. My Esquire, Ralf. Milords Sir Van, Sir Edgar, and Sir Ryder."

Jax had no idea which of the three older knights was which. She could only hope Theo did. They all wore identical swords and had identical arm muscles to prove they knew how to use them. Still, their relaxed posture suggested they saw themselves as part of the prince's pack rather than his babysitters. If the king had assigned them to keep his son in line, he must be sorely disappointed.

"You girls have caused a lot of trouble," Jordis said. "You don't belong here."

Beatrix raised an eyebrow. "The king put us in Lukos."

"I meant this *courtyard*," he spat.

"My father's restoration of Lukos hasn't reached this far," Theo explained, once more inserting himself between the two.

Jax gave him credit for courage. "The ruins are unstable. It's dangerous."

"Men have been killed working in this area," Jordis added.

"Seriously injured," Ralf, the peacemaker, amended. "A broken leg. A head injury."

"They thought that one was going to die," Jordis said. "He didn't wake up for two days."

"Workers won't even come here anymore." Theo lowered his voice. "They say there's a curse."

Eira sneezed. At least, that's what Jax hoped the boys thought.

"They've heard noises," Ralf put in, eyes earnestly wide. "Moans, cries from the pits."

"Terrifying," Theo said, adding a dramatic shudder. "They say it's like the voices of the damned calling from the underworld."

Jax dug her teeth into her lip. It wasn't funny—as long as she didn't meet Eira's dancing eyes. Boys telling spooky stories to frighten the girls. Curses and moans. *They can't expect us to believe all that?*

Unbidden, the memory of the chill breeze from the locked gate crept up her spine. The darkness behind that gate could be right beneath their feet. And whatever lurked in that darkness.

Nothing. Nothing lurked in the darkness. But the thought cured her of the urge to laugh.

"That sounds *awful*," Eira said. She actually batted her eyes. "We're so fortunate you came to warn us."

"Not as fortunate as we are to have found you lovely ladies," Prince Theo assured her. "Please allow us to escort you to safer ground."

"We are overwhelmed by your chivalry," Beatrix scoffed. But she allowed Ralf to take her arm and lead her up the path. Jordis stomped after them.

With a wink at Jax, Eira darted forward to take Prince Theo's arm. Apparently, she hadn't been kidding when she'd said she enjoyed competition. Jax wondered if Raisa had intuited the Nordish girl's fierce will to win. That would explain her choosing Eira as her first target.

Tenzin rested her chin on Anara's hair and gave a sleepy whistle.

"Tenzin says the prince is admirably handsome for a foreigner," Anara translated as they followed the others. "I say, he cannot tell us what to do."

"Of course he can," Jax said. "He's the crown prince, the king's oldest son."

Anara huffed disdainfully. "None of my grandmother's sons would dare command a Kheremese princess to do anything. These boys are trouble. Telling us ridiculous tales."

Jax couldn't argue. Prince Theo and his friends were obviously up to mischief, and mischief was a risky proposition. The ugly bruises marring Ralf's handsome face attested to that. Jax wasn't afraid of turning an ankle or falling debris, but she couldn't afford Prince Theo's kind of trouble.

Prince Theo ordered Sir Van—or maybe Sir Edgar—to return the four princesses to Sister Ursel at the keep. After cautioning them against venturing anywhere beyond the main courtyard, Sister Ursel sent them to their room for the rest of the afternoon.

"As if we're a bunch of toddling children, and she's our mother!" Eira complained, throwing herself down on her bed.

"No one in this kingdom shows proper respect," Anara grumbled, settling a sleepy Tenzin in her lap.

At least they were out of the courtyard, far from the hostile stares—and out of range of listening ears.

"Anara …" Jax didn't want to alienate the Kheremese princess, but her fear for Nicolas and Anatole wouldn't let her remain silent. "Please. Would you tell us what Tenzin's message said?"

Tenzin's crest rose with a hiss.

"What are you talking about?" Anara demanded.

"That scroll you were reading in the garden!" Beatrix snapped her fingers. "Tenzin's the only one of us who can leave the castle. Of *course* she'd bring you information. I should have put it together myself."

"But none of King Wulfric's men would ever guess," Jax said.

"Because no one but us knows how clever Tenzin is." Eira sat up. "It's brilliant!"

Which was just the thing to smooth Tenzin's crest. But Anara's jaw only set harder.

"Would you tell us what's going on?" Jax pleaded. "We just want to know if our people are safe."

"If you can," Eira begged. "We're dying to know what's happening out there."

Looking from face to anxious face, Anara's expression softened. "Oh, very well." She pulled the scroll from her pocket. "My honor guard sent word they have received permission to camp here in Aldforth for a few days before returning home. They say this king is *inhospitable*"—in a tone that suggested the word gave even more offense in Kheremese than Common Tongue—"but they have not been mistreated. As far as they know, it is the same for all the visitors."

The tight band around Jax's heart loosened a notch. Not that she thought Abbess Sofia would deliberately deceive them, but she didn't know who to trust here in Aldforth. On this point, at least, Anara's guard had no reason to lie.

"Do you think they could find out what our delegations are doing?" Eira asked wistfully. "I suppose my escort has already left to return to the Temple."

"I'm surprised your people risk written messages," Beatrix told Anara. "Can't Tenzin just relay what they said?"

Tenzin's glittering eyes narrowed.

"A dragon would never speak to a man!" Anara said. "And

the empress's men are forbidden to speak to dragons. My attendants would not dare to break that command."

"Your attendants are *all* men?" Eira asked, eyes wide. "No women traveled with you?"

"No women traveled with me, either," Jax said. "The Venian queen doesn't require a chaperone. Why should a princess?"

"For *companionship*," Eira said. "How long did you travel, Jax? A sevenday? A fortnight? It must have taken over a month for Anara to get here from Kherem. Without anyone to gossip with about Prince Theo or complain to if she got cramps during her moon time."

"Not all of us *want* to chat about our 'moon time,' " Beatrix said drily. "We weren't all raised in a convent."

"The empress could not spare any of her household's women on this foolish undertaking," Anara said, cutting them off. "If anything were to happen to me, I am an acceptable loss."

In the stunned silence, Jax felt a sudden kindred sympathy with the Kheremese princess. Hadn't Queen Léonie made a similar calculation about her? And yet, at least the queen had sent her own trusted constable to accompany Jax.

"Would Tenzin be willing to carry a letter to one of my people?" Beatrix asked, diplomatically skimming over the awkwardness.

"And mine?" Eira gave a little laugh. "I'm sure they have advice they want to offer me."

"I'd like to send a message to my family," Jax said.

"And Nicolas," Eira teased.

"*No*, I—" But she was already blushing. There was no point in protesting.

"A dragon is not a courier," Anara said stiffly.

"Of course not," Beatrix agreed. "She can't be carrying messages here, there and everywhere. But if your honor guard would be willing to introduce Tenzin to one of my father's contacts here in Newport, that person could gather information that would benefit us all, even after your people leave."

"It's a good idea," Eira admitted. "Bellisians have excellent spies. I bet he'd be able to tell us everything we want to know."

"*She* could," Beatrix corrected, and Jax couldn't help admiring her tactical maneuvering. "I wouldn't ask Tenzin to receive messages from a man."

After a long moment, Anara nodded. "If Tenzin chooses, she may meet this person you speak of and decide whether or not she is willing to carry such information."

Her stiff posture eased, and she gave the dragon a look of gruff affection. "If your contact can obtain candy, Tenzin is very fond of sweets."

The little creature's bright eyes gleamed.

CHAPTER TWENTY-FOUR

Raisa acts as if she's the only one who can possibly win the competition, so the rest of us will see her victory as inevitable and give up. Maybe it's working on the others. Some of them obviously don't have much confidence.

That's fine with me. I have no difficulty with *my* confidence.

— Princess Isolde of Montaine

J ax slept fitfully that night, dreading another day of humiliation on the training grounds. But when the twelve princesses made their way to the courtyard after breakfast, they found it deserted. The hastily erected viewing stand stood empty, presiding over the lonely archery targets. Even the birds were silent, probably owing to Tenzin circling lazily above.

Castellan Kenrick had ordered the gate guards not to speak to the princesses, but they had been Prince Guntram's men, and their loyalty carried over to his widow. They told Ellycia that the king had canceled his plans to visit Lukos that morning and called Marshal Oswald to Newport Castle for a council. Apparently, the court was buzzing with rumors of unrest on Aldforth's eastern border.

"Unrest in Tyrglas?" Beatrix demanded when Ellycia shared the news.

Ellycia raised a hand to quiet the swarm of princesses that buzzed around her on the keep steps. "The guards don't know any more than what I've told you."

"Who else could it be?" Raisa asked. "Ravnina protects the Blessed Kingdoms from the barbarian warlords of the eastern steppes."

"Nordish raiders might come down the straits," Beatrix muttered, tapping her fingers on her skirt.

Jax's Aldforthian geography was sketchy, but she knew the kingdom's eastern border was too close for comfort if trouble were brewing.

"Could it be the giants?" Ziva asked.

"Giants!" Marjani shivered, despite the red cloak she wore against the light morning fog. "Giants. Monsters. Nordish raiders." She shot a glance at Eira. "The north is the end of the world."

"The most agreeable end," Eira objected, bristling. "The Nordish have kept their pledge not to raid the Blessed Kingdoms."

"A pledge to this Aldorthian wolf king," Marjani spat. "The man whose army killed your mother. And you do nothing but speak of *peace*."

Jax moved between the two princesses, *accidentally* stepping on Eira's foot, cutting off her reply.

"We'd better hope it's not a problem with the giants," Beatrix said grimly. "The last time they fought a battle, they didn't leave a single enemy standing."

"No one has seen a giant in generations," Isolde scoffed. "My father says they've all died off. And good riddance."

"Aren't giants *supposed* to be hard to see?" Ziva asked shyly.

Dora gaped at her. "But … they're *giants*."

Ziva's cheeks pinkened. "But people are always surprised to see them, aren't they? In the legends?"

"I'd be surprised to see a giant, but I think I'd notice one if it were standing around," Dora replied.

"King Wulfric sent a ball invitation to Fairföld." Ellycia's quiet voice cut through the speculation. "His messenger wasn't allowed through the High Gates, so he didn't see any giants, either, but he said they *sounded* alive enough. King Wulfric was not best pleased."

In other words, the king had demanded the giant princess's participation, just as he had demanded Jax's, and her failure to arrive on Presentation Day had infuriated him. It proved the value of Jax's attendance, though she envied the Fairföldian princess, safe at home behind those High Gates.

"Maybe the giants sent the manticore," Raisa said. "Everyone knows there are monsters in the Serpents Teeth."

"Everyone knows Ravninans are treacherous backstabbers," Beatrix said coolly. "That doesn't make it true."

Raisa's amber eyes narrowed with fury.

"How dare you speak to Princess Raisa like that?" Lidia jumped to her defense. "Take it back!"

"Take what back?" Beatrix asked. "My assertion that something isn't true, just because it's what people say?"

"You think you're so smart, but you're just insufferable."

Someone muttered, "Princess Beast."

"What about us?" Jax broke in, startling herself with her own audacity. *Someone* had to break the tension. No storybook princess would resort to fisticuffs, but she wasn't so sure about these real ones. "Did Marshal Oswald leave instructions for what we're supposed to do this morning?"

"No." Ellycia gave her a grateful look for the change of subject. "No one seems to have given any thought to it. I suppose they expect us to occupy ourselves as befits high-born ladies."

Raisa sniffed. "We can't ride to the hunt if they won't allow us out the gates."

"I don't see any high-born gentlemen to flirt with," Isolde said, with an unexpected sly humor.

"Or low-born bards to entertain us," Lidia added.

"No merchants to trade with," Dora put in.

"Or entertainments to plan," Pia said wistfully.

"No books to read," Beatrix grumbled. "No history to study or strategy to learn."

"No prayer services to attend," Eira said, with a sigh that might have been serious—or not.

For just a moment, their differences seemed to fall away in the shared experience of being royal ladies. It struck Jax that their most necessary skill was not running a household, charming foreign dignitaries, ruling a country in a husband's absence, bearing a monarch's children or even keeping him happy, but doing all of it while appearing to be nothing more than a lovely decoration.

As good as their food was and as soft their beds, Jax didn't envy them. She'd much rather spend the morning in her father's forge, creating something useful, complaining about the heat and her aching muscles.

"Is there really *nothing* to do?" Dora asked plaintively.

"I can play," Pia offered half-heartedly. "If you want to dance."

"I brought an altarpiece I've been embroidering with my ladies," Ellycia said, not quite stifling a sigh. "I would be pleased to have you all join me."

"Shouldn't we practice?" Jax asked. "For the competition, I mean. Archery, maybe?"

"Oh, darling." Raisa gave her a narrow smile. "No amount of practice is going to help you shine in archery."

Jax managed to keep her tone even. "I'd still like to learn to draw a bow without shooting someone."

"Good luck." Isolde gestured at the deserted courtyard. "Who's going to teach you?"

"You outscored everyone yesterday." Jax didn't know where her courage came from. Two days ago, she wouldn't have dared to speak to a princess, much less to challenge her. "You could teach me."

Isolde stared at her blankly for a moment, then laughed. "Why would a princess teach a peasant to shoot?"

"Why would anyone teach an opponent anything?" Raisa asked.

Jax struggled to dig the right words from the depth of her frustration. "How good are you at swordplay?" she asked. Raisa's thinned lips were answer enough. "Have any of you ever wielded a sword?"

Only Eira raised a hand.

"I am proficient with a knife, both close and thrown," Anara said, "but not a larger blade."

"Does anyone else know how to throw a knife?" Jax asked.

"Not *throw*," Beatrix admitted, with an envious glance at the Kheremese princess.

"Is it like darts?" Dora asked. "I'm good at darts."

"*Poison* darts?" Isolde asked, bringing a mottled flush to the Rigan girl's face.

"No, that's just you," Pia muttered softly.

"Poison—?"

Beatrix made a violent slashing motion across her throat, silencing Jax's question. *Poison.* What had Nicolas told her? The Rigan king had poisoned his brother, Dora's father. That lesson felt so long ago now, before she'd met these girls, before they'd even seemed real.

"Can anyone besides Marjani throw a spear?" she pushed on. "Does anyone know as much about Aldforthian politics as Ellycia? About Blessed Kingdom politics as Beatrix? About money and trade as Dora? Can anyone control a horse like Raisa? Has anyone besides Anara been trained as a royal bodyguard?

"Did you all notice how much King Wulfric enjoyed my humiliation yesterday?" She had to find a way to make them understand what seemed so obvious to her and so incomprehensible to them. "I've been taught how to hold a sword. So which one of *you* is going to be shamed when we get to swordplay?"

Unease flickered over their faces.

"Better shame than manslaughter," Beatrix said. "I wouldn't let any of you come at me with a sword."

"But they're made of wood!" Pia cried. "They wouldn't let us hurt each other. Would they?"

"Of course not," Isolde said. "King Wulfric wouldn't risk starting a war."

Pia bit her lip. "My father doesn't have an army."

"The Fair Isles aren't even a separate kingdom." Ziva's voice dropped to a whisper. "Not anymore."

"What do you say, Ellycia?" Lidia glared at her stepsister. "You claimed to be the Aldforthian princess on Presentation Day. What does King Wulfric want? To humiliate us? To hurt us? Or to choose a suitable wife for his son?"

"Are any of those things mutually exclusive?" Ellycia asked.

Lidia stomped her foot. "You're the one who forced yourself into this competition, trying to take what's rightfully mine. *Again*. You wouldn't have done it if you thought it was dangerous."

"Not if I could avoid it," Ellycia muttered.

"They're supposed to train us." Dora's mouth turned down mulishly. "That's what the invitation said."

"King Wulfric's weapons master might not be here to teach you how to use a sword," Jax said. "But Eira could."

Eira's face lit up. "Oh, I could! That would be fun!"

"I'm willing to do whatever it takes to make sure I don't kill one of you," Jax pressed. "We all have different skills. We all have something we could teach. We could help each other through this."

Possibility hung in the quiet air for a long moment.

Then Raisa laughed. "You may be a peasant, but you are not the fool I took you for. Still, any alliance I made would need to be as beneficial for me as for my ally. I'm an excellent archer, and I'm sure Marshal Oswald will see to swordcraft, so I'm afraid that excludes you and that albino witch of yours."

Her gaze passed consideringly over the other girls, the perfect mixture of invitation and hesitation. *Could it be you? Could you be one of the favored ones? Don't cross me, and I might raise you up.* Even Beatrix and Anara received a questioning eyebrow.

"Come, darling." Raisa put her arm through Ellycia's. "Show us this altar cloth of yours. And Pia!" Her call pulled Pia's anxious gaze from Jax. "You must play for us."

The ones closest to agreeing to my idea, Jax thought. The fire that had lit briefly inside her flickered out as the crowd of girls headed back to the keep. Crowd of *princesses*. What had made her think they might listen to her? Nicolas telling her she was clever?

How ridiculous to think she could enlist a group of royal women to outwit a king.

Hubert's voice rang in her head. *You're not a princess. You're just the common daughter of a grubby whore!*

She could almost laugh, if it wouldn't have brought her to tears. *If only that were true.*

CHAPTER TWENTY-FIVE

I never knew hitting something with a stick could be so *satisfying*.

— Princess Dora of Rigas

"I thought you had a good idea," Eira said. "I hate embroidery."

"That's probably for the best." Jax turned to her friend with a reluctant smile. At least *one* girl hadn't followed Raisa. "I got the distinct feeling we weren't invited."

"You know, I think you're right." Eira's face brightened. "I bet the practice bows are in that shed by the archery range. I can teach you how to shoot."

Anara silently appeared at Eira's side. With her dark hair and black tunic, she looked like the Nordish girl's shadow. "If you teach me to kill with a sword, I will teach you to kill without weapons."

"That sounds more fun than sewing," Eira agreed.

Jax hoped Anara had confused the Common Tongue words for "kill" and "fight," but either way—*two* girls had stayed behind with her.

"I have no military skills to teach," she admitted as they

crossed the courtyard to the shed. "Knowing how to sharpen a blade isn't much use on a wooden sword."

"Any assassin planning to kill Prince Theodor will be bigger and heavier than me or Anara," Eira said. "If we train you, you'll make an acceptable opponent for us to practice on."

"Nice to know I'm good for something."

"You're certainly good at getting us into trouble with Raisa," Beatrix snapped, striding up behind them. *Three* girls.

"It's not Jax's fault Raisa is a snob," Eira objected.

"You don't get someone like Raisa on your side by challenging her in front of an audience," Beatrix said. "You pull her aside, ask her opinion, let *her* make the suggestion to the group. Then she keeps you close instead of exiling you to the outer steppes."

"Why are you here with us, then?" Anara asked. "Instead of inside embroidering?"

"Maybe I don't *want* to be close to Raisa," Beatrix said testily. "Besides, I need practice if I'm going to get more accurate with those second-rate bows."

Eira slapped the shed door. "We may have to take up needles, after all. It's locked. We can't get in."

"Yes, we can." Beatrix elbowed Eira out of the way.

From a pocket inside her skirts, she pulled a small ring holding a half-dozen oddly shaped keys. She flicked through them quickly, then slipped one into the lock. After a moment's probing, the mechanism gave a smooth click. Beatrix retrieved her key and swung open the door.

"What?" she asked. "They told us we needed to train. How are we supposed to do that if we can't get to the training equipment?"

"As long as we're sharing our skills, I want to learn that one," Eira said.

Inside the shed, they found the bows and arrows from the morning before, along with barrels of wooden swords and the deadly-looking spears and clubs that had been displayed in the yard. Jax touched a finger to the spikes on the head of an iron mace. She wondered if Marshal Oswald really intended the princesses to use cudgels like these or if they were simply props to appeal to King Wulfric.

Best to be prepared, either way.

"Let's start with archery," Beatrix said, with a nervous glance at the pikes. "Help me carry the equipment outside."

"There are only four of us," Jax reminded her as Beatrix piled all six bows into her arms.

The Bellisian flashed an enigmatic smile. "It doesn't hurt to be well equipped."

"Equipped for a giant attack?"

But when they followed Beatrix out of the shed, young Princess Ziva of the Fair Isles waited by the archery range.

"I've never held a blade bigger than a knife for cutting my meat," she said, a thread of steel in her shy voice. "I don't want my first time touching a sword to be in front of King Wulfric."

Jax quelled her urge to hug the girl and promise to protect her, as she would her sisters. This wasn't a thunderstorm or a spider or even Hubert the miller's son. She couldn't shield Ziva from a despot. She could only help the girl shield herself.

"We'll make sure you know what to do," she said.

"I can help you improve your archery scores, too," Eira told the girl. "Your technique is good. You just need more confidence. Come on. Everyone take a bow."

She clapped her hands, transforming in an instant from eager co-conspirator to self-assured instructor. "I'll start with Jax, but I'll be watching the rest of you."

"I am excellent with a bow," Anara objected. "I scored nearly as well as you yesterday, and I draw much faster."

"I would have beat you if I'd had my own bow." Eira burst into snorting laughter. "Sorry. But you need to practice with these larger bows, in case we have to shoot at a real distance. I can help you make the proper adjustments. All right. Jax, let's start with your stance."

Eira proceeded to teach Jax how to stand, how to hold her bow, how to nock the arrow and draw the bowstring back to her ear. How to aim lower than the target, not directly at the bullseye.

At the end of an hour, Jax's shoulders ached from the strain, and her left forearm stung from faulty releases, but she'd begun hitting the target almost every time she drew. Not necessarily the *scoring* portion of the target. But the sharp thwap of the point digging into the coiled straw mat pulled a smile from her every time.

She lowered her bow and just caught herself from swiping her fine linen sleeve across her forehead. She missed her old work tunic. She pulled a soft handkerchief from the pocket hidden in her skirts. It reminded her of the texture of Nicolas's sleeve when she would grab it to ask him a question about sword-fighting technique or riding a horse or … *Or pretty much any other excuse she could think of to hear his voice, meet his gaze, learn more about him.*

Heat rose in her cheeks that had nothing to do with the morning sun smoldering overhead.

Eira's slap on her shoulder brought her back to the yard. "Four out of the last five in the target. One in the blue! Well done."

"Dirk's remaining leg may be safe," Jax said. "You're a good teacher."

"It's good and right to share something you enjoy with other people." Eira grinned. "That's not one of the Temple's Nine Roads to Peace, but I've told Holy Mother I think it should be."

"Increasing one's skill with weapons of death would draw anyone closer to peace," Jax said dryly.

"Admit it, you feel more a lot more peaceful than if you'd had to spend the morning embroidering with Raisa and Isolde."

"When you put it that way …"

Jax regarded the other girls. They were using all six bows,

as Beatrix had predicted. Dora had joined them not half an hour after they'd begun, complaining, "I need time to practice if I have to use one of these poor bows."

They looked serious, fiercely focused on their stance, their form, their aim. Once they'd seen Eira strike the dead center of each one of the targets in turn, they'd listened closely to what she had to say. Even Dora had improved.

"Bullseye!" she whooped in triumph.

Jax called a break on that high note. After they scavenged a quick meal from the kitchens, Eira ordered a change of weapons and named Jax her swordmaster assistant.

"I know you're not skilled," Eira told her, "but at least you know which end of the sword to hold."

That seemed a little unfair. Only Anara had grabbed the blade end of her wooden sword, and only because she was using it as a staff to defend herself from Ziva's mock attack. It was good to see the shy Fair Isles princess laughing, even if she was swinging her weapon like a club.

Still, Jax felt grateful to have something to offer. However rudimentary her skill, she could at least help the other girls learn how—

She grabbed Dora's arm, preventing her from swinging her weapon into Beatrix's face.

—she could at least help the other girls learn how not to kill each other.

Which didn't mean no one got hurt. Beatrix dislocated her pinky, forcing her to switch her sword to her left hand. Princess Pia, defying her cousin Isolde to join them for the afternoon, scraped the skin off her knuckles. Dora wound up with the biggest bruises, proudly pulling up her skirts to show off her purpling left calf.

Despite her own aches, Jax took fierce pleasure in being able to hit something with her sword, maybe more pleasure than she should. Not that she was pretending the wooden post was Hubert. Or Raisa. Or King Wulfric. Or anything.

That night at supper, the seven princesses in sweaty, dusty

clothing sat in silent disgrace at one end of the table while the cool, clean, elegant princesses froze them out. Until Pia gathered the courage to suggest requesting practice shields from Marshal Oswald. And Ziva made everyone laugh by recounting Anara's frustration with her post's indifference to her wooden sword, which led to her stabbing it with her dagger instead.

"I know what I want to learn tomorrow," Eira said with a wicked smile. "I want Dora to teach us how to make a love potion."

"Rigan *pharmacia* is a subtle art." Dora frowned hesitantly, as if she couldn't quite tell if Eira were teasing. "It's meant to gently influence events, not bludgeon people into feelings they don't already have." Her lips twitched. "Unlike Montainan fashion."

The others stifled giggles at the sly reference to Isolde's gleaming finery.

"That's all very well," Beatrix interrupted, raising her voice. "But *I'd* like Marjani to teach me how to throw a spear."

Even Raisa's cold glare couldn't quell the rowdy chorus of agreement from the disreputable end of the table.

Jax thought Beatrix had broken her own rule against challenging the Ravninan princess, but the next morning at breakfast, Raisa herself announced Marjani should lead them in practice.

"The Almasans are renowned for their proficiency with the spear," Raisa said, placing a proprietary hand on Marjani's shoulder. "We should learn from the best."

"Well done," Jax murmured to Beatrix as they followed the others into the courtyard.

The trickle of defectors the previous day and the not-quite-disguised envy of the embroiderers must have pressured Raisa toward a change in strategy. But Beatrix suggesting Raisa's own protégé to lead the next lesson had allowed the Ravninan to save face and join in.

"Watch and learn, amateur," Beatrix told her. "Watch and learn."

Eira laughed. "Careful, Bee. That's exactly what she's doing—watching and learning. She says she's not here to win, but I don't believe her."

"Queen Jax?" Beatrix said speculatively.

"I can see it now," Eira said. "The Winter Solstice ball. Fires blazing in the great hall at Newport Castle, gems glittering on the courtiers' fingers, at their throats, in their hair—"

"Jax steps into the room," Beatrix took up the story, drawing an image Jax could almost see herself, "wearing a glorious gown of silks and satins. Every eye turns her way …"

Prince Theo, looking every inch a future king, offers her his hand, invites her to dance, draws her on with that mischievous twinkle in his eye.

Eira wrapped her arm through Jax's. "Raisa is purple with rage. Isolde swoons with jealousy."

Transformed from an ungainly peasant into the envy of every princess in the room, just like a fairy tale …

"Until I trip over those glorious skirts and knock Prince Theo on his royal bottom," Jax said, dispelling the vision with a burst of her friends' laughter.

She didn't tell them Eira was right. She was watching and learning everything she could. She *had* come determined to win. It was just that her idea of victory didn't include marrying the prince. She had only one opponent—King Wulfric. Only one goal—deflecting the king's wrath and returning safely home.

With her friends beside her, learning the skills the other girls could teach, she almost believed that she might, indeed, have a chance at victory.

CHAPTER TWENTY-SIX

O Mother of all, wake us, your children, in peace, that we may be alive to the beauty of your world this day.

Out of love for your children, feed us, that we may feed each other with your love.

In your pity, hold us in your embrace, that we may weep for the sorrows of this life.

In your wisdom, laugh with us, that we may leap for joy.

And at the evening's close, when darkness approaches all around, rest your hand on your children's hair while we sleep.

—From "A Prayer to the Mother Goddess," Traditional

Information is not just one weapon among many. Information is what gives a weapon its power. A sharp sword is better than a dull one. A dull sword is better than no sword at all. If you have no sword, you still have your hands.

If you have no information, your hands are tied behind your back.

— Princess Beatrix of Bellis

The next morning, the sisters of the Abbey of the Mother Goddess did not appear to wake and dress the princesses. Royal decorum kept speculation at the disconcerting break in routine to terse murmurs, but Jax found herself at the front of the anxious group of twelve as they made their way down the stairs.

Sacrifice the hulking peasant, she thought grimly, her stomach tight. But when they reached the great hall, she saw no sign of manticores or raging kings—and no sign of breakfast, either.

Abbess Sofia stood on the stone dais in front of the empty tables, a prayer book in her hands. She frowned at the girls' late arrival—or perhaps their worse-for-wear training attire—then gestured toward the floor before her, where the abbey sisters knelt in well-ordered rows.

"It's *Sevenday*?" Eira slapped a hand over her mouth, her eyes wide with chagrin.

Ellycia moved first, regal and dutiful, to kneel behind Sister Ursel. The other princesses followed, their rows as straight as the sisters'. Anara nudged Jax with her elbow, and Jax hurried to start a new row behind Princess Lidia. But rather than kneel beside her, Anara continued to the keep doors, Tenzin glimmering iridescently on her shoulder.

Jax breathed an envious curse before turning back to Abbess Sofia, whose gray eyes glinted with iron. The Mother Goddess might require a great many prayers of Her disappointing children this morning. With a sigh of resignation, Jax scrunched her skirts into a makeshift pad beneath her knees.

The prayers indeed stretched until noon, but the sisters interspersed them with song, their voices weaving haunting melodies in Old Aldforthian. Jax understood few of the words, yet the songs still spoke to her of love and pain, birth and death, a steadying hand in an uncertain world.

By the end of the service, she ached with grief for the mother she had never known—would never know—and missed Agnes with a fierceness that surprised her.

"Do not forget," Abbess Sofia admonished as they rose stiffly to their feet, "the Mother Goddess is not only a hearth keeper; she is also a warrior. She walks with all of her daughters, even unto death. In the eyes of the Mother Goddess, all of us are sisters. And all of us are called to guide and protect, as she does. The Mother's blessings on us all."

"The Mother's blessings on us all," the gray-clad sisters murmured in response.

"Sevenday is for rest and prayer," the abbess said, clearly a command. "Spend this time in quiet contemplation. We will break our fast this evening with a simple meal in our rooms."

Despite her determination to train as much as she could before King Wulfric's next test, Jax's body appreciated the break. Baths and gossip superseded prayer and contemplation, but the loose camaraderie among the princesses felt like a victory.

Clean and relaxed, Jax stretched out on her bed before supper, resting her aches and bruises. Eira sat by the hearth performing her Sevenday meditations while Beatrix pored over a tome of religious history—the only book she had been able to beg from Sister Ursel.

Five days in Aldforth. It hardly seemed possible. And yet

. . .

And yet, they made barely a dent in the six months until the winter solstice. Six months of this strange, soft bed. Of staring up at this finely milled wooden ceiling. A ceiling she'd heard Isolde and Dora complaining about that afternoon. *How could King Wulfric put us in such accommodations, where the rooms aren't even finished?* Apparently, the painted ceilings in Rigas were rivaled only by the ones in Montaine. Or was it the other way around?

Jax draped an arm over her eyes and pictured the rough beams back home. The smoke stains radiating from the opening above the hearth. The knots and swirls she had turned into friendly deer and sparrows for a three-year-old

Siddy when her sister had been frightened of the firelight shadows.

The door banged open.

"Our wayward souls return," Beatrix drawled.

Despite the warning, Jax had no time to react before four clawed feet landed solidly on her stomach.

"Ooph!" She threw her arm aside to find Tenzin's faintly smoking nostrils just inches from her own. The dragon's glittering emerald gaze and gold-tipped talons made her an image of deadly beauty, though she weighed no more than a bird her size might.

"Don't look so smug," Jax scolded her. "It's not fair you got to go out flying while the rest of us were stuck at prayers."

"Resign yourself." Anara landed as imperiously on Beatrix's bed as Tenzin had on Jax. "She will be appalling for days. She has news from Bee's friend in Newport."

Jax jolted upright. Tenzin spilled onto her blankets with a hiss of outrage.

"Your people found Margrit?" Beatrix snapped her book closed. Only one of Anara's men spoke Common Tongue fluently, and connecting him with Beatrix's father's spy in Newport had proven challenging.

"She sent us a message?" Eira abandoned her prayers and moved to perch at the end of Jax's bed.

"Let me read it," Beatrix demanded.

Anara brushed her hand away. "As your friend is female, Tenzin agreed to bring a verbal message. The sugared almonds Margrit brought as a bribe did not hurt, either." She turned to Jax. "*Your* spy brought candied lemon peel."

"My spy?" Jax frowned at her. "I don't have any spies in Aldforth."

"A young man," Anara said. "Apparently, he is quite charming. Tenzin says he has hair as brown and shaggy as a pony's, but—" She rolled her eyes. "His eyes are bluer than lapis lazuli."

"*Nicolas?*" Jax whirled on Tenzin.

"Oh, *definitely* Nicolas," Eira sighed.

"Nicolas is still in Aldforth?" Jax hardly dared believe it. "How did you find him, you amazing creature?"

Tenzin ducked her head in an elaborate display of false modesty. If she had been a cat, she would have been purring.

"The question is, how did *Nicolas* find *Tenzin*?" Beatrix demanded. That was *not* the question Jax wanted answered, but there was no point trying to distract Beatrix from an argument. "I thought you told your people to be discreet, Anara."

"*My* people?" Anara shot back. "How do you know this Nicolas didn't follow *your* spy—"

"None of my father's contacts would ever be so careless—"

Tenzin slipped onto Jax's lap. Her tail whispered across the coverlet with the unnerving, sinuous motion of a snake. Yet, her tiny sigh as she curled against Jax's stomach dissipated any perfectly sensible unease Jax might have felt.

"You're *impossible*," Jax said, leaving the dragon to decide if that were praise or rebuke.

Tenzin offered a contented puff of smoke in return. Jax looked up to see all three of her friends staring at her, quarrels temporarily set aside.

"Tenzin was impressed by your kindness, our first day here," Anara said, with an approving nod. "A dragon's trust is not given lightly."

"Jax does have a gift for dealing with difficult creatures." Beatrix's mouth twitched. "Myself being a prime example."

"Tenzin would not have agreed to meet Margrit if she did not find all of you worthy of trust," Anara said, mollified. "And neither my people nor Margrit were indiscreet. Jaclyn's friend saw Tenzin at the Presentation Ceremony, and he guessed I might use her to communicate with my delegation."

She gave Jax a sly smile. "Apparently, even your backward culture contains tales of the cleverness of dragons."

Tenzin's eyes had closed, her body relaxed into a warm ball in Jax's lap, but the corners of her mouth curled up. Jax decided not to mention that most Venian stories of clever dragons involved them eating fair maidens.

"This Nicolas came to my people seeking news," Anara continued. "Because I had asked for information about Jaclyn's delegation, they brought him to the meeting with Bee's spy."

Beatrix grimaced, but she let it go. "What information has Margrit gathered?"

"Eira's people left for the Temple of Peace immediately after the presentation ceremony. They gave alms at the Travellers' Temple in Lower Newport and prayed for grace on her life voyage."

"That's exactly as I expected," Eira said, her voice a little too bright.

"My delegation returned to Bellis, of course," Beatrix said with practiced indifference. "Did they leave a message?"

"They also departed before the banquet on Presentation Day. They did not contact Margrit," Anara reported. "My people leave for Kherem tomorrow. Now that they have connected Tenzin with Margrit, they have no reason to stay."

Jax lowered her eyes to mask her sympathy. Beatrix wouldn't tolerate it. Eira would insist she didn't need it. Anara would scoff at her cultural ignorance.

By all rights, Nicolas should not have stayed in Aldforth, either, and yet ... he had. She could just see him approaching the Kheremese tents, winning over the stony-faced guards with his admiration for their horses. Charming Tenzin with candy.

Almost see him—a flattened image, like the illuminations in Father Donat's books. Shimmering just a little at the edges, with gilt that might be real or imagined. What if—as with Bruno and Raisa's magnificent stallion—what if, when she saw Nicolas again, he seemed plain and ordinary compared to Prince Theo's dazzling looks and charm?

Shame burned her cheeks.

And what would Nicolas think if he saw her in the

training yard, her poor, lovely green gown sweat-stained and dusty, tendrils of hair stuck to her face …

Her mouth twitched. He would probably think she looked a lot more elegant than she had the first time he'd seen her.

"Did Margrit say anything else?" Beatrix asked.

"She heard …" Anara paused to consult Tenzin in a quick series of whistles. "She heard gossip that King Wulfric is strengthening fortifications along all his borders. He is obsessed with discovering who took his master's mind to send the monster that killed Prince Guntram—"

"Who masterminded it," Beatrix corrected. "That is the correct phrasing—"

"*Whatever*," Eira interrupted. "Get on with the gossip."

"The king is even more short-tempered than usual," Anara continued. "He is furious the giants did not send their princess for the ball. There is fear he might launch an attack on Fairföld."

Beatrix sniffed dismissively. "Fairföld is isolated and strategically unimportant. Attacking the giants would be foolish."

"His desire for retribution might cloud his judgment," Eira said. "Vengefulness is one of the Nine Roads to War."

"And Nicolas?" Jax couldn't wait any longer. "You said he had a message for me?"

One of Tenzin's emerald eyes blinked open, and she gave a little warble.

"She says he was very respectful," Anara translated. "He spoke his message to Margrit, as instructed, and Margrit repeated it to Tenzin, as was proper."

Jax leaned forward, making Tenzin squawk in protest. "*What did he say?*"

Anara tilted her head as if trying to remember, her eyes glimmering with mischief to rival Tenzin's.

"*Anara.*"

With a whip-flick of a grin, she relented. "He says to stay out of trouble."

"He doesn't need to worry about that," Jax said, stung. "If there's one thing I plan to do here, it's stay out of trouble."

Beatrix snorted. Not one of her friends tried to conceal their disbelief.

"He also says if you need anything, he can acquire it for you," Anara continued. "He intends to stay here in Aldforth as a dockworker."

A smart strategy. There would be plenty of Venian dockworkers in Newport. Even so, remaining in the kingdom against Wulfric's orders placed him in danger. He should have left with Anatole. But she couldn't wish he had.

"Is that all?" Eira asked. "No declarations of eternal love?"

Jax shoved the Nordish girl's arm, nearly tumbling her off the end of the bed.

Tenzin whistled brightly, and Anara rolled her eyes. "No, you greedy beast, she is *not* going to demand he bring you licorice drops. If you want more candy, you may barter your fire sweets for it."

"Fire sweets?" Jax asked.

Tenzin hissed dismissively.

"They are the most treasured candy in the world," Anara scolded her. "A single flower is worth more than a laborer's yearly wage. The empress's confectioners make them only for the palace dragons, who may eat or trade them as they wish."

Tenzin's warble sounded impudent.

"Just because you can breathe fire whenever you want …" Anara hopped off the bed and threw open the lid of her trunk. After some digging, she pulled out a small black bag embroidered with a gold dragon's eye. "We shall have our companions be the judges."

She reached into the bag and drew out a sparkling jewel the size of a wren's egg. Sculpted into the shape of a flower, it seemed to glow from within, as deep red and perfectly pure as the ruby on Raisa's favorite brooch.

Tenzin hissed.

"You have enough to share." Anara offered the flower to Beatrix.

The Bellisian shied away. "Thank you, but I avoid food with 'fire' in the name."

Jax also shook her head. If it were a choice between placating the knife-throwing princess or the fire-breathing dragon, she would have to choose the one sitting in her lap.

"I'll try one!" Eira leaned forward to pluck the gem from Anara's hand. She held it up to catch the gleam of evening light from the window. "It really is the most exquisite candy I've ever seen. It almost seems a shame to eat it."

Tenzin hummed appeased approval.

"Still …" Eira grinned and popped it in her mouth. She sucked it for a long, thoughtful moment as the others waited for her verdict. "Sweet," she mumbled around the candy, "and spicy. It warms your whole mouth. Sorry, Tenzin, but this is better than licorice."

"Yes, it is." Anara smiled a satisfied, catlike smile. "Now bite it."

"Shouldn't it be savored?"

Anara shook her head. "Bite."

She and Tenzin leaned forward with the exact same expression of anticipatory glee.

"Wait—" Jax warned, but too late.

Eira crunched loudly into the hard candy. Her blue eyes widened. She opened her mouth in an 'O' of shock … and a burst of red flame gushed out.

Jax jumped, dumping a hysterically snorting Tenzin to the floor. Beatrix yelped. Anara smirked.

Eira gaped at them for a long moment, then burst into delighted laughter, puffing smoke in everyone's faces.

"Fire sweets," Anara said smugly.

"Definitely," Eira said, between hiccuping snorts of laughter, "*definitely* better than licorice."

They all laughed then, even Beatrix, despite her pallor at the breath of fire. The strangest sensation warmed Jax's chest as she flopped, giggling, back onto her bed. It took her a moment to recognize it.

Happiness.

She was trapped in a despot's cursed castle, playing a sinister game with no apparent rules … But against all expectations, she had found friends. Friends to laugh with. Friends to commiserate with.

And Nicolas had stayed in Aldforth.

CHAPTER TWENTY-SEVEN

*Who knows what the poor, mad thing was thinking? Maybe
she doesn't understand the difference between bringing
attention to yourself and making an impression.*
— Princess Lidia of Ilhavair

Over the next sennight, the princesses settled into
something like a routine. Up early for breakfast,
then training. One group might practice swordsmanship with Eira while another threw spears with Marjani—
Jax found it best to keep those two clashing personalities as far
apart as possible. Raisa or Anara might teach archery from
horseback while Ziva explained the finer points of tracking. A
break for the midday meal. Then to indoor pursuits for the
heat of the afternoon—dancing instruction from Pia, elaborate hairstyles with Isolde, how best to wield a concealed knife
with Beatrix.

After the girls retired for the evening, Tenzin might bring
political news from Margrit or a word of encouragement from
Nicolas that made Jax so happy she hardly noticed her friends'
teasing. The two informants sent gossip, as well—the arch-
bishop of Cadesleigh was planning a visit to Newport Castle;
the king's mistress, Duchess Bianka, might be pregnant; an

anonymous wit had written some comic verses entitled "The Ballad of King Wulfric's Ball" that were hugely popular in Newport's taverns.

Tenzin taught Eira the tune, and for days afterward, the Nordish girl would break into raucous song at inappropriate moments.

Another Sevenday came and went. Firstday dawned bright and still, a beautiful summer day—for some quiet activity, done in the shade. By mid-morning, with the sun's heat pooling in the courtyard, Jax felt as though she were training in a bubbling cauldron. Even cool Princess Isolde was flushed and sweaty as she criticized Pia's archery technique.

No one complained when Sister Ursel brought out jugs of sweet sage water and ordered a break. The cool liquid felt like heaven sliding down Jax's throat.

Raisa tossed back her head and drained an entire goblet in a single long swallow, like one of Bahar's friends with a tankard of ale. The Ravninan princess noticed Jax watching and flashed an arch grin.

"Oh, this is *so* good," Pia moaned. She pressed her goblet to her forehead. "I feel like I'm going to melt, training in this heat."

"Why are we training at all?" Dora asked. She flopped down on the stairs beside Lidia and fanned herself with her hand. "Everyone has forgotten all about us."

"Do you think so?" Ziva asked hopefully.

Shouts at the castle gate preempted Dora's response. Guards rushed from the watchtowers to lift the massive crossbar and swing open the doors.

Jax's stomach sank. *Someone* had remembered them.

"The king!" A guard shouted. "The king is on his way from the castle."

"He won't like it that we're training without his permission." Ellycia set her cup on a tray and snatched up her bow. "We need to put the weapons away before he gets here."

"Oh, honestly." Lidia glared up at her sister. "What does it matter if he sees us? The guards will tell him anyway."

Ellycia grabbed a discarded pike from the ground nearby. "They've promised me they won't. They don't want to get in trouble, either."

Jax retrieved her wooden practice sword as the other girls began to stir, unsettled by Ellycia's urgency.

Lidia rolled her eyes. "You can't tell me what to do. You don't even belong in this competition. We're supposed to be training, aren't we? He can hardly get angry about it."

"I'm trying to protect you, but if you think you can predict what will make the king angry, then lounge there like a vulgar soldier of fortune and see how he reacts."

"Which one of them is the wicked stepsister?" Beatrix muttered.

"Ellycia is right," Raisa said. "Only a fool would risk making the wrong impression on a future father-in-law. Better to surprise the king with our proficiency. Quickly, darlings. Everything in its place."

At Raisa's command, even Lidia got to her feet. Despite a moment of anxious confusion, the girls swiftly fell into their cleanup routine. Jax organized the bow stands and barrels of practice swords. Raisa and Anara made sure the horses were settled in their stalls. Eira put the weapon shed in order. Beatrix locked up.

Isolde bossed everyone around.

For once, Jax didn't mind. The Montainan princess had a keen eye for perfect order. If the king didn't find out about their clandestine training, he couldn't find out it was Jax's idea.

"What about us?" Ziva asked as they regrouped on the keep steps. "Shouldn't we tidy ourselves up, too?"

Jax glanced around at the dust-streaked faces, the hastily mended training gowns, the disheveled hair. As one, the princesses edged toward the door, but a horn at the gate cut off their escape.

"Too late," Dora whimpered as Castellan Kenrick strode across the courtyard toward them, Marshal Oswald stomping at his heels.

"Why are the girls out in the yard?" Kenrick demanded. "Did you tell them the king was coming, marshal?"

Oswald's one eye widened. "How could I, when I didn't know it myself until a quarter hour ago? Did the king tell *you* he planned to visit Lukos?"

"If the king had it planned, he chose to surprise us all." Kenrick twisted his scowl into an unconvincing smile and offered the princesses a curt bow. "Your Highnesses, King Wulfric will be here momentarily."

He paused, eyes narrowing on their bedraggled appearance. His displeasure seemed to linger on Jax's hair. She'd plaited it herself that morning, and she could feel sweaty tendrils sticking to her face and neck.

"What in the hells have you girls been doing?"

The princesses shot panicked glances at each other, unsure how to answer. Jax made a desperate face at Eira, who smiled brightly.

"Dancing!" the Nordish girl exclaimed. "We've been doing a *lot* of dancing. We want to be ready for the ball."

"Yes, dancing!" Beatrix jumped in valiantly.

"We love dancing."

"We can hardly bear to *stop* dancing."

"We're going to need a shoemaker," Dora broke in. She lifted the edge of her skirt to show her silk slippers, the uppers scuffed, the heels almost worn through. "I didn't bring enough dancing shoes."

"Dancing shoes," the castellan repeated in disbelief.

Marshal Oswald swiped a sleeve across his face, whether to combat the sweat trickling down his forehead or to hide his amusement, Jax couldn't tell.

"King's called for swords this morning," he said. "You're to gather near the viewing stand."

Jax pushed her loose hair behind her ears and followed the

others across the yard. Two of Marshal Oswald's men were hurriedly unrolling the canvas awning above the stand. Another man hung a banner from the railing, the king's silver wolf's head on a purple background.

The archery master, Dirk, wrestled a barrel of practice swords out of the shed and settled it near Jax.

"Don't go swinging one of these around before your turn," he warned her. "I don't want my leg in any danger." His grin was almost affable, but it quickly faded. "Someone's bound to get hurt today. You're the strongest one out here. Don't you be the one doing the hurting."

Fair enough. "I'll do my best."

He nodded approval and walked away.

"Do you think the king is going to make us duel each other?" Pia asked nervously.

"He could call for a melee," Eira said. "One big battle. The last person standing wins."

"He wouldn't!"

"Perhaps two teams," Marjani suggested.

"You're on my team," Isolde said hastily. She made a sad face at Pia. "Sorry, there won't be room for you."

"That's all right," Pia said. "I want to be on Eira's team."

Jax ducked her head to hide her amusement at Isolde's vicious snarl. The Montainan princess hadn't thought far enough ahead. There was no chance of Eira and Marjani agreeing to be on the same team, and in a sword fight, Eira's team would be guaranteed a victory. Unless all eleven of them were on one side and Eira on the other. Even then, the odds were probably in her favor.

"Don't be silly," Raisa scoffed. "One of Marshal Oswald's men will test our skills. It will be perfectly safe. Stop acting like nitwits."

Isolde's eyes flashed at being lumped in with the nitwits, but before she could respond, the atmosphere in the courtyard shifted, like a storm blowing in. The men working on the viewing stand dropped to one knee.

Jax bent her head as the king of Aldforth and a handful of courtiers rode through the front gates. Marshal Oswald's men ran to take their horses as the king and his men dismounted. Castellan Kenrick strode over to join them.

The king clapped him hard on the back as they walked toward the viewing stand. "Not bad, Kenrick. Getting everything ready on short notice." Wulfric gazed around at his courtiers, his smile predatory. "Prepared for any eventuality, my man Kenrick. You can't catch him off guard, unlike you lot. It's why I keep him around. Not for his looks, is it?"

Kenrick smiled as the courtiers laughed, but Jax didn't think either the courtiers or the castellan enjoyed the joke. The men followed the king up onto the viewing stand, leaving several guards waiting below.

As the king settled into his chair, a rumble of hurrying boots echoed from the guard tower by the storage shed. The guards stiffened, then relaxed as the boisterous cadre of Rose Knights spilled into the courtyard.

"*Prince Theodor,*" Pia breathed, not the only princess sighing over the three handsome youths and their three handsome minders.

"Tell us we're not too late, Your Highnesses," the prince demanded, sweeping a bow to his adoring admirers.

"You were *born* late, boy," the king snapped, glaring down on his son. "And you were not invited."

"Surely Prince Theodor should be here to witness his future bride prove herself worthy … whoever she may be." Theo's esquire, Ralf, performed placating sincerity much more believably than the prince. "Otherwise, the princesses will be so busy trying to impress Your Majesty, they might forget him altogether."

"Enough of your cheek. You're no better than he is," Wulfric growled. "You ruffians stay out of the way. And don't complain about the heat. There's no room for you up here."

"Thank you, Sire." Ralf gave the king a respectful bow, echoed by the other Rose Knights, including Prince Theo.

The boys crowded up against the viewing stand, stealing the scant shade from the guards even as they blew kisses at the girls wilting in the sun a few yards away.

"Where did they come from?" Eira whispered to Jax. "Over the wall?"

"So much for our high-quality security team," Beatrix murmured.

Marshal Oswald stepped in front of the viewing stand. "Your Majesty, you asked to see the princesses' skills with the sword—"

"Swords!" Prince Theo straightened. "Oswald, you old fox. Have you been training the princesses in swordplay?"

"No, Your Highness," the marshal said. "I've been busy, as you know."

"You're just going to give them blades and let them whack at each other?" The prince's grin looked forced. "That sounds dangerous. Maybe you should put me and the boys through our paces today. Show the ladies what they can aspire to."

"Sarding hells!" King Wulfric roared to his feet and slammed a fist on the railing. "I told you to be quiet and stay out of the way! It might be dangerous? I'll tell you what's dangerous—battling a vicious monster while your *guards*, your *wife*, and your own *brother* stand by and watch. *That's* dangerous."

Jax dug her nails into her palms to keep from flinching at his sudden fury.

"I've got my best trackers trying to find a bedamned manticore," the king raged. "I've got hysterical reports of giants wandering the countryside. I didn't bring these girls here to drink my wine and look *pretty*."

"Of course not, Your Majesty," Castellan Kenrick said, steady in the face of the king's storm. "The prince's marriage is a serious matter, and your wisdom is irrefutable. As I am sure Prince Theodor would agree." He gave the prince no time to argue. "Just as I am sure Marshal Oswald is capable of demonstrating the princesses' abilities without placing them in any danger."

"That I can, Your Majesty," the marshal said.

"*You're* not going to spar with them, surely, Oswald?" Jordis called from his lazy slouch against the viewing stand. "Raising a hand against a princess—that could cost you more than your eye."

Jax winced. *Shut up, you fool.*

But Jordis knew the game better than she.

Oswald bared his teeth in a grin. "No one's royal during training, milord. 'Course you and yon prince sounded like princesses plenty of times as lads when my sword smacked your backsides, or don't you recall? Maybe I should refresh your memory."

That brought a laugh from the king and a smile of relief from Castellan Kenrick. Jax released her held breath.

Jordis pushed himself upright to sketch an ironic bow at the marshal. "Any time, old man. You won't find it so easy to knock me down anymore."

"Are you claiming you can hold your own against Guntram's marshal?" the king asked. "A stripling duke against a real soldier?"

Jordis stiffened. "I don't back down from a challenge if that's what you mean."

"Oh, it's a challenge you're looking for, is it?" The king leaned forward, eyes narrowing in delight. "Maybe *you* should be giving the demonstration. Why don't we try it, eh? See if you can hold your own against a pack of girls."

Marshal Oswald blanched. "Sire, I don't think—"

Castellan Kenrick's laughter rang through the courtyard. "Your face, Oswald! His Majesty was joking. Find a spot in the shade, Duke Jordis. You're looking over-hot."

"*Mind your tongue, Kenrick,*" King Wulfric spat. "You may run my castle in my absence, but do not presume to speak for me in my presence."

"Of course not, Sire." The castellan's face paled beneath his black hat. "I just thought … The girls' families—"

The king whirled on him, and his voice ground too low for Jax to hear, though the courtiers' expressions were clue enough. Despite the prickling heat, a nervous chill passed through the princesses around her. Pia whimpered softly, and Ellycia quietly pulled Ziva behind her.

Jax watched the hot embarrassment flooding Jordis's face. Another pawn in the king's cruel games. She couldn't believe that even the ill-humored duke wanted to harm any of them, but if the king goaded him into losing his incendiary temper …

A wooden sword wouldn't behead or disembowel an opponent, but it could break a rib or crack a skull. Helpless fury burned through her. Why should one capricious despot have absolute control over all their lives?

She fingered the hammer in her belt.

"Don't be a fool," Beatrix hissed, catching her sleeve. "He'll bludgeon you."

Better me than Ziva. Jax shook off Beatrix's hand and stepped forward. "I'll fight Duke Jordis, Your Majesty. You must agree that's a better challenge than a smaller girl."

"I *must?*" The king's chair toppled backward as he leaped to his feet. "No one tells me what I should and should not do! I won't have it. This is my kingdom, or *have you all forgotten?*"

He sent a withering glare at Kenrick and the courtiers, at the Rose Knights, at Jax. Her stomach curdled, and she dropped her eyes, the mouse's defense against the lion.

"What does it profit me to watch Oswald treat these girls like fine porcelain?" Wulfric snapped his teeth, for all the world like an angry wolf. "Or set the braggart duke against a bastard giantess? If these girls mean to marry my son, they should relish the chance to show me what they can do."

"I'm sure one or two of them could charm a man to death," Prince Theo called with a broad wink at Isolde. A show of courage, though Jax couldn't help thinking it was Ralf who might have to pay.

"One more word out of you, and I'll throw you out the gate myself," King Wulfric bellowed. "Where's your sword, Jordis? Or are you afraid of a bastard girl?"

Prince Theo grabbed Jordis's sleeve, and Eira wrapped both arms around Jax. The young duke snarled and tried to pull away as the king yelled for the two nearest guards to hold the prince.

"I'll be careful. I'm not a halfwit!" Jordis jerked free.

"Unhand me!" Theo ordered the guards, while Sir Van and Sir Edgar—or was that Sir Ryder?—tried to wrestle them away from the prince.

A flash of burnished red caught Jax's eye. Beatrix pushed past her, a wooden sword clutched in her hands. Her green eyes blazed as she stalked toward Jordis. Despite her scars, she looked like the warrior Mother Goddess Abbess Sofia prayed to.

No. Not *despite* her scars. Marshal Oswald had lost an eye. Dirk had a wooden leg. Warriors had scars. If the Mother Goddess were going to manifest as a warrior, surely she'd do it right.

"You want to duel against girls, Your Grace?" Beatrix jeered, her anger cold and clear. "Will that make you feel like a man? Come on, then. You can start with me."

CHAPTER TWENTY-EIGHT

The king to keep his kingdom safe
Called twelve to shield his son,
Unmindful that severest risk
Could come from untrained fun.

—From "The Ballad of King Wulfric's Ball," by Foolscap
the Bard

Do you think Prince Theo noticed me? I'm almost sure he
looked right at me before he went down.
— Princess Pia of Capra

Beatrix charged Jordis with a shout of fury that raised the hair on Jax's neck. Though caught off guard, the young duke deftly unsheathed his sword and stepped clear of the other Rose Knights, giving him room to defend himself. He looked more confused than angry as he knocked her first blow aside.

The other princesses, the Rose Knights, the courtiers all stood frozen in disbelief, too stunned by Beatrix's suicidal folly to react.

Jax wrenched free of Eira's hold. "He's going to kill her!"

"Not on purpose," Eira said as Jordis spun away, his foot-work graceful as a dancer's.

Jax yanked her hammer from her belt and flashed her friend a look.

Eira rolled her eyes. "No, of *course* that doesn't mean we just let it happen."

Beatrix's second wild swing pulled her off balance, leaving her open for a finishing blow. Again, Jordis backed away rather than attack.

Utterly focused, the two combatants never noticed Jax and Eira barreling toward them. As Beatrix lunged forward with her heavy wooden sword, Eira grabbed her shoulder, ruining Beatrix's attack. But Jordis had already begun a slashing defense meant to counter a weapon that was no longer there between his blade and Beatrix's neck.

No one in their right mind would meet a sword with a hammer, but Jax didn't need her mind. Even desperate, back-handed and running, her arm knew the perfect arc to draw to strike her target. The hammer shaft caught Jordis's wrist. His sword clattered to the ground as Eira and Beatrix tumbled away from the fight.

Using a trick Anara had taught them, Jax swept her leg around, hitting Jordis behind the knees. Already off-balance, he windmilled backward, right into Ralf and Sir Van—Sir Ryder? The three of them plowed into Prince Theo and the other two Sirs, who stumbled into one of King Wulfric's guards who'd stepped forward to help. The entire lot of them collapsed in a heap at the base of the viewing stand, directly beneath King Wulfric.

Jax's hammer fell from her nerveless hand, thudding softly to the ground in the moment of breathless silence.

"By all the fire-blasted gods of hell. The level of gross incompetence with which I am surrounded ..." The king's pale gaze lifted from the scrambling pile of young men to fasten on Jax, standing frozen and alone. "You have taken out my son and all of his men. With a *sarding hammer*. Have you nothing to say?"

Struggling to control her panicked gasping, Jax could only shake her head. *What had she done?*

"Seven in one blow, Sire," Castellan Kenrick said dryly. "Princess Jaclyn seems to have taken your command to prove her deadliness to heart."

"She's not supposed to prove it *on my son*," the king ground out. "I only have one legitimate son left."

"It was an accident, Father." Prince Theo pushed himself to his feet, brushing dirt from his fine linen tunic. "A rather amusing accident."

"An accident!" Jordis clutched his forearm to his chest. "She could have broken my wrist!"

"Better your wrist than Beatrix's neck," Jax told him. Hot horror flooded through her. If only she'd lost her tongue instead of her senses!

"*No one's* safety is more important than that of the crown prince." The king's icy malice was more terrifying than his earlier raging. "Raising a weapon against a royal prince of Aldforth is punishable by death."

Prince Theo's laughter sounded forced. "It's a good thing she was attacking Jordis, then."

"You were knocked to the ground because the girl raised a weapon." Wulfric's glare pinned Jax in place. Despite her terror, she could not look away. "That is no different from raising a weapon against your person."

"Visiting royalty is exempt from capital punishment in all the Blessed—"

"I told you to be quiet!" the king snarled.

Marshal Oswald had said no one was royal during training, but he wasn't speaking up for her now. Castellan Kenrick. The courtiers. Even her friends were silent.

It hurt. Shockingly so. But she had only herself to blame. Jax had always been the disposable princess. She knew it, and still she had brought herself to the king's attention.

"You remain on your feet before me, girl?" he demanded. "You should be on your—"

A frantic shout at the gate tore his gaze from her, and Jax stumbled as if his hostility had been a hand at her throat, holding her upright.

"What's this?" Wulfric roared. "Who interrupts the king?"

Undeterred, or perhaps riding too fast to change course, a mounted messenger galloped across the courtyard, scattering princesses as he came. He pulled his wild-eyed horse to a skidding stop before the king.

"Your Majesty," the messenger gasped, more winded than his horse.

"What is it?"

"Sire." The man sucked in another breath. "It's the giants, Your Majesty."

Wulfric glanced at the castellan beside him with a mixture of malice and satisfaction. "I told you, Kenrick. Those treacherous, lying bastards have shown their hand at last." He turned back to the messenger. "How large is their army? I assume they've crossed the border into Tyrglas. Have they reached Rosekilde?"

Jordis made a strangled sound. Duke of Tyrglas, Jax remembered through her dizzy terror. Rosekilde must be the duchy's seat. His family would be there.

"Your Majesty?" The messenger's brows wrinkled in confusion.

"Have the giants taken the castle at Rosekilde?"

"Oh. No. No, Your Majesty," the messenger assured him. "The giants are here. Outside Newport Castle. The king has brought his daughter, the princess. She's come to join your ball."

Hand. Hart. Hawk. Horn
Iron fist and battle-worn.
Horn. Hawk. Hart. Hand.
Never moved from oath or stand.

—From "The Giants' March," Traditional Aldforthian
Nursery Rhyme

And I thought Oswald was big.
— Prince Theo of Aldforth

The babble of stunned voices washed over Jax like a wave.

"Here? The giants are *here*?"

"The giant king himself?"

"A giant princess!"

"How did they—"

"Good gods, you fools," Kenrick shouted. "Shut the gates!"

As Oswald's men ran to close the great doors, the princesses edged closer to each other.

"You there!" Kenrick leaned over the viewing stand railing

to yell at the guards below. "Two of you get up on the wall. Are there no lookouts in this place?"

"What are we to look for, sir?" one of them asked.

"Giants!" the castellan snapped back. "Look for giants. They should be somewhat obvious, I would think. They're *gigantic*. You'd think someone might have noticed them *before now*."

"Giants!" Prince Theo's delight was as sharp as Kenrick's alarm. "We'll spy them quick enough. Come on, lads." He dashed toward the stairs, the Rose Knights at his heels.

"How many men?" the king asked the messenger. "How many men does Frigyes have with him?"

"I'd guess fifty or so, Your Majesty."

"I suppose your *guess* will have to do for now," the king said, his icy self-control underscoring the danger.

Jax guessed that fifty men, even giants, could hardly be a threat to Newport Castle. But King Wulfric wasn't in Newport Castle. He was in a derelict ancient fortress with a handful of guards and a small crowd of frightened princesses.

Jax wondered if she were the only one less terrified of giants than of the king.

"I see them!" one of the guards shouted excitedly from the wall. "The giants! They're setting up tents in front of the castle."

"They don't look so big from here," Prince Theo added from beside the guard. He sounded disappointed. "Oh, wait. That's a *horse* he's leading, not a dog …"

"We'll leave through the side entrance," Wulfric said. The viewing stand shuddered as he stomped down the stairs. "We'll return to Newport Castle through the postern gate."

"Sire!" Kenrick protested, close on his heels. "You'll be exposed going down the cliff."

"They won't see us from the front meadow." The king spat on the dirt. "Besides, they won't expect to find a king scuttling back to his castle like a beetle into its hole. Oswald, go make sure the path is clear."

"What about us?" demanded a balding courtier, hurrying to catch up. "I can't go down those stairs with my gout."

"The rest of you ride back, enter through the front gate." The king barely spared him a glance. "I can't imagine the giants care where you go."

"But …" The man paled. "I thought an armed escort … surely for Prince Theo—"

Wulfric shot a cool look toward the wall where the prince and his entourage were jostling for the best view. "If my son can't make his way safely home from a half-mile distant, he's not fit to rule Aldforth."

"Your Majesty." Princess Ellycia rushed into the king's path and dropped into the deep curtsy of a supplicant rather than the respectful nod of a princess. "Would it not be safer for the princesses to follow you to the postern gate?"

Wulfric frowned. "Follow me? No one has given you permission to leave Lukos."

"You can't leave us here!" Dora protested as a murmur of dismay rose from the other girls. "It's not safe."

Jax marveled at their surprise. Hadn't they just heard the king throw his own son to the wolves?

"I determine what is safe," the king snarled, whip-sharp enough to make the Rigan princess cringe. His gaze landed on Jax, poisoning her with its venom. "You've got your champion here to protect you. Just have her knock the giants down. *Seven in one blow.*"

He spun on his heel and strode toward the cliff gate, Castellan Kenrick close behind.

Jax gasped, as if a noose had loosened around her neck. Her fear, held stiffly at bay by sheer force of will, sank into her skin like needle-sharp teeth. Her legs wobbled.

"Horses!" the balding courtier squawked, pushing through the girls toward the front gate. The other courtiers scuttled after him. None of them spared the princesses so much as a word of sympathy.

"There are giants out there!" Dora said, her voice sliding upward. "*Giants!*"

"They eat people, don't they?" Pia asked, her eyes dark with fear. "That's what they do in the fairy tales."

" 'Fee fi fo fum, I smell the blood of a human man,' " Isolde chanted, but her mockery sounded forced.

With a rumble of hoofbeats, the Aldforthian courtiers rode out the main gate. Oswald's men rushed to close it behind them. The huge wooden bar dropped with a resounding thud.

"They're leaving us *behind*," Dora wailed.

"It's all right," Ellycia said sharply. "The giants have not come to make war. They've brought their princess to the ball. They have no reason to attack us, and we have no reason to fear them."

Considering how Ellycia had begged the king for refuge, Jax knew she was as anxious as the rest of them. Still, her show of confidence checked Dora's rising hysteria.

"We'll return to the keep," Ellycia said. "The marshal can bring us news."

"You're such a boring stick-in-the-mud," Lidia told her. "I want to see the giants. I'm going up to watch them with Prince Theo."

As one, the girls glanced toward the wall where they had last seen the prince, but he and the rest of the Rose Knights had disappeared. Jax hadn't seen them return to the court-yard. They hadn't followed the courtiers through the gate. They might as well have vanished in a puff of smoke.

"Princess Ella is right," Anara said. "There is no help in worrying until we have more information."

She strode toward the keep, drawing the others behind her. Jax noted her empty shoulder and the flash of blue-green high above, winging toward Newport Castle.

"Don't fret, darling." Raisa hooked Lidia's arm with a sly look at Jax. "We don't need to go anywhere to see a giant."

" 'Seven in one blow,' " Isolde said with malicious delight.

"Why would the giants attack? They've already got an assassin on the inside trying to murder the prince."

The other girls hurried after, avoiding Jax's gaze. Maybe they feared her disgrace might be contagious.

Only Beatrix stopped beside her.

"Why did you interfere?" Beatrix demanded, her hair a wildfire around her scarred face. "I knew exactly what I was doing, but you had to step in. Always out to *help*. Always trying to *make things better*. As if a simple peasant could have any idea what is best for the rest of us."

She stormed after the others, almost levitating in her fury.

"She nearly took my head off, too," Eira said, slipping closer once Beatrix was well away. "If the Temple of Peace believed in demonic possession, I'd know what was wrong with her. She's obviously battling *some*thing. She doesn't mean to take it out on us. She'll forgive us for saving her life by suppertime."

When Jax didn't respond, Eira peered more closely at her. "Are you all right?"

Jax lifted her gaze to the sky. If she didn't blink, no tears would fall. She didn't mean to speak, but the words tumbled out anyway. "No one even spoke up."

"To King Wulfric?"

"He was threatening to—" What? Behead her? Hang her? How did the king of Aldforth murder girls? Drawing and quartering?

"Forget possession," Eira said with a shudder. "King Wulfric might actually *be* a demon. Even Kenrick is frightened of his rages."

"So no one wanted to join me on the gallows."

"He probably wouldn't dare bully anyone else like that, but who could be sure?" Eira paused. "He was angry enough to threaten you, but he wouldn't have followed through. How many of the girls' families would have let them stay if he had? It would ruin his ball. But if we had challenged him, it might have pushed him even farther …"

"So you were trying to *save* me from the gallows?" The words tasted bitter.

"Beatrix said keeping quiet was the best way to help you, and even furious, she's usually right." Eira touched her arm. "Come inside. For once, I agree with Lidia. I want to see the giants. And we have a south-facing window."

"You go ahead."

Eira sighed and headed for the keep, leaving Jax alone in the empty courtyard. No, not completely alone. Dirk had roused the watch—there were several guards walking the walls now, one still trying to fasten the straps of his boiled leather breastplate.

Jax couldn't bear to return to her room, but she couldn't collapse in the middle of the courtyard, either. She forced her shaking legs to carry her to the stables.

The tears came as she crossed the threshold, so thick she could hardly see. She stumbled to Bruno's stall. He nickered in greeting as she groped for the latch. Entering the stall, she wrapped her arms around his great, bony withers, buried her face in his soft, warm neck and wept.

CHAPTER THIRTY

Personally, I think there are far too many princesses around
here as it is.

    — Princess Isolde of Montaine

Hours later, Jax returned to the keep, drained of
everything that might have held her together
through King Wulfric's ball. Her spirit. Her
strength. Her hope that she would ever see her family again.

It took the last dregs of her courage to enter her room,
return Anara's cautious nod, ignore Eira's wince at her red
nose and puffy eyes. Beatrix didn't even look up from where
she lay rigidly on her bed, facing the wall.

Jax sat on her own bed and closed her eyes, like her little
sister Lili used to do before she learned to hide properly. *You
can't see me.* It didn't work for Jax, either. Eira padded across
the room to her, the featherbed puffing softly as she sat.

She placed something in Jax's lap. Something unexpect-
edly heavy.

Her hammer. Jax's eyes flew open, and her hand closed on
the empty loop in her belt. She'd dropped her hammer in the
yard and forgotten all about it. The hammer Bahar had given
her. Her journeyman's hammer.

She touched the cool metal of the head, her throat tight with deferred grief. "Thank you."

"Beatrix grabbed it," Eira told her.

"I meant to clobber you with it." Beatrix's pillow didn't muffle the lingering resentment in her voice. "But I got tired of waiting for you."

Jax wrapped her hand around the handle and paused, looking down at the once-smooth wood. Short, shallow lines had been cut crosswise near the end of it, evenly spaced and parallel. Someone had rubbed charcoal into the cuts, darkening them against the pale ash.

"Seven." Eira ran a finger over the notches. "Don't let someone else tell you what you're worth. You knocked down seven knights to save your friends."

"Whether your friends wanted you to or not," Beatrix grumbled indistinctly. "And look what it got you."

"Being sentenced to execution can free you from fear of other things," Anara said.

"What would you know about it?" Beatrix flipped over finally, her eyes flashing. "When was the last time you were condemned to death?"

"When I bonded with Tenzin, of course." Anara frowned at their stares. "You heard me tell King Wulfric I am the daughter of the empress's son. Only a girl descended through the empress's female line may bond with a dragon."

"So your grandmother …" Not even Eira could finish that sentence. "How did you …?"

"Tuya, daughter of the Imperial Heir, was supposed to bond with the newborn dragonet," Anara said. "The silly fool panicked when Tenzin snapped at her. She threw her at me! Was I supposed to let a helpless hatchling fall to the floor? Tenzin could have died."

"If the empress condemned you for it, then why aren't you dead?" Beatrix challenged.

"Dragon law forbids killing a bonded human. Even an empress must obey." Anara looked appalled at their breathtaking ignorance. "She suspended the sentence for the space of Tenzin's lifetime."

"You'll be executed when Tenzin dies?" Jax asked in horror.

Anara lifted her palms as if letting the weight of the sentence fall away. "Dragons may live hundreds of years. I do not waste my time in fear of her death." Her eyes met Jax's. "Or of what others think of how I look or what I do."

"I wish I could be like that," Eira said wistfully.

"You never care what people say about you," Jax argued.

"I know I *shouldn't*," Eira corrected. "Holy Mother says it's awfully vain of me, so I try not to let it show."

Beatrix groaned. "That's right. You're all selfish and horrid. Now shut up about it, so I can suffer in peace."

"*That* didn't get to me," Eira said. "I know she doesn't mean it."

"I do," Beatrix snarled.

Cheerfully ignoring her, Eira tugged Jax's sleeve. "Come look at the giants."

"You can barely see them from here," Beatrix warned.

Eira moved to the nearest window and leaned halfway out the opening. "They've finished setting up their tents. I heard trumpets earlier. Their princess could already be in the castle having an audience with King Wulfric."

"Poor girl," Jax muttered. She glanced at her hammer, ran a fingertip over the seven precise notches. The abyss still loomed beneath her feet, the death King Wulfric had so spitefully threatened her with and so casually tossed aside. She had never felt so alone, standing forsaken in the center of his rage.

Beatrix said keeping quiet was the best way to help you.

The Bellisian's red hair spread around her head like a pool of fire as she glared up at the ceiling beams. What had she said? *Always trying to make things better. Damn you.*

A wry smile tugged at Jax's mouth. She let out a long breath and stood up to hook her hammer into her belt. "All right. Let's see those giants."

Eira scooted over to make room at the windowsill, and Jax leaned in beside her. Below their window, the keep wall ended flush with the cliff on which Lukos perched. The rocky spire dropped nearly a hundred yards before meeting the shallow valley between the fortress and Newport Castle.

On the edge of the grassy dale between the castle and Newport Town, a cluster of tents had appeared. Drab green and faded brown, they almost disappeared against the trees beyond. Horses grazed in a makeshift corral of stakes and ropes. Large carts rested nearby, many already emptied.

"But where are the—"

"Keep looking," Eira prompted.

There. Two men dressed in tunics of odd, drab colors talking next to the corral. Prince Theo was right. From so far away, they didn't seem particularly large. Yet, beside them, the draft horses looked like ponies. Now her eyes had adjusted to the distance, she could pick out more figures around a cook fire on the other side of the tents, tending pots and carrying wood.

A short man—Jax caught herself with a smothered laugh —a *shorter* man with wide shoulders strode rapidly through the center of the camp, a cluster of taller people chasing after him.

A sharp whistle jerked her head up as the open window suddenly filled with golden talons and blue-green wings. She and Eira tumbled aside, and Tenzin swooped into the room, hissing and spitting at their slow reaction.

"There *is* another window!" Jax pointed out indignantly.

Tenzin landed on Anara's bed, shaking out her wings and checking ostentatiously for scrapes. As Jax neared, the little dragon snorted a warning puff of smoke. Curbing a smile, Jax settled on the floor beside the bed.

"What's happened?" she asked. "I bet you know every-thing that's going on down there already."

Tenzin sniffed as if to say she saw right through such

shameless flattery. But her crest settled on her neck, and she tucked in her wings with a self-satisfied warble.

Beatrix heaved an exasperated sigh. "We don't need a dragon to tell us what's going on. King Wulfric has refused to allow the giant princess to participate in his ball."

Tenzin's crest snapped back up, outraged at being upstaged.

"Why would he do that?" Eira plunked down beside Beatrix. "He was furious King Frigyes didn't send a princess to the ball."

"*Freegyesh*," Jax murmured to herself. The giant king was King Frigyes. She wished she could tell Constable Anatole.

"The giants are *late*. Wulfric considers that an insult. He said so at Presentation Day." Beatrix sat up, dragged from her eternal sulk by the bitter pleasure of politics. "Now they've come without any warning, and he's had to sneak back into his own castle like a fugitive. Of course, he wants to humiliate their king. I'm sure Frigyes wasn't happy."

Tenzin tucked her nose under a wing. Anara rolled her eyes, but she pulled the little dragon closer and ran a soothing hand down her back.

"Nice work, master diplomat," Eira singsonged at Beatrix under her breath.

"How can we guess what the giants think?" Jax asked. "We've never seen a giant before, much less talked to one. We don't even know the giant princess's name. Not even Beatrix."

Beatrix opened her mouth, but Eira hissed at her, and she closed it again.

A warble escaped from beneath Anara's arm.

"Hajni," Anara translated. "Princess Hajni."

Emerald eyes peeked out, glancing toward Beatrix's bed.

"Clever dragon," Beatrix said, her eyes glittering almost as green.

Tenzin blew a smoke ring and whistled some more. Anara's smile faded.

"Wulfric refused to meet with the giant king," she

reported. "He said he would not tolerate their rudeness in arriving so long after the appointed time."

Beatrix raised a smug eyebrow.

"The giant king responded that he had not wanted to come at all, knowing of King Wulfric's warlike and uncivilized nature, but his daughter, Hajni—"

Tenzin flashed her tongue at Beatrix.

"—told him neighbors should not live in fear and ignorance of one another. She asked to attend the ball to forge a new relationship of peace and understanding between Fairföld and Aldforth."

"I gather that's off the table," Beatrix said.

Anara nodded. "The giant king said if Wulfric did not repent of his inhospitable behavior and allow Princess Hajni to attend the ball, the giants would return home, and Fairföld would consider themselves neighbors to Aldforth no longer."

"*That* was his ultimatum?" Jax asked.

"I guess the giants don't want war," Beatrix said.

"He said they would no longer be neighbors," Anara repeated. "You expected *worse?*"

"You can't blame them," Eira told her. "They're barbarians." She tucked her feet under her skirts and settled in for a sermon. "Neighborliness is what holds a civilized culture together. Your neighbors are the people who trade their mead for your butter. You observe the holy days together. If your house catches fire, they run for the well. When you go to war, they fight beside you."

Eira had a natural storyteller's rhythm. The picture she wove brought a lump to Jax's throat. Hospitality, warmth … *belonging*. It made her miss her neighbors desperately. Or, at least, made her desperately wish she had neighbors she missed.

"Now imagine," Eira's voice dropped, so they had to lean closer. "Imagine your neighbor does something so horrible, so wicked, so *un*neighborly that you can never forgive them."

You're just the common daughter of a grubby whore! Oh, yes, Jax could imagine.

"You will never trade with them again. You can't bear to celebrate with them. They'd let your house burn to the ground without lifting a hand, and you wouldn't trust them beside you in battle."

"They've become your enemy," Beatrix said.

"Worse than your enemy." Eira's pale eyes darkened. "An enemy who lives beside you. An enemy who shares your well, who has a seat on the thane's council, who is never more than a hundred yards from your gold, your animals, your children."

The room felt shadowed suddenly, though the summer sun had hours before it set.

"A neighbor who is no longer a neighbor," Eira intoned, "is not an enemy to raid, an enemy to pillage, an enemy to battle in the season of war. A neighbor who is no longer a neighbor is an enemy who must be destroyed."

Jax's scalp prickled, and she shivered despite the thick, lingering heat.

Tenzin chirped, and Anara nodded approvingly. "So it is in Kherem."

"Barbaric." Beatrix shuddered. "In Bellis, we turn those people into councilors and keep them even closer."

Eira's fierceness melted away. "This is why the Temple of Peace teaches love and forgiveness. How much better to return to neighborliness than for a village's streets run with blood."

"The giants wouldn't attack Aldforth over something so ridiculous as a ball," Jax said. "Would they?"

"We'd better hope they don't," Beatrix said grimly. "If King Frigyes decides to disrupt King Wulfric's ball, terrorizing a dozen princesses would be a great way to do it."

CHAPTER THIRTY-ONE

Guntram would never have done something so reckless and foolhardy. He had no imagination and no sense of humor. Only now do I understand his father's disappointment that Theo is not more like him.

— Princess Ellycia of Aldforth

The sisters served a late supper, after the day's high temperature should have eased. Instead, the sultriness settled into the stones of the keep, a smothering blanket of misery. The cheese was warm and sweating, the beef over-spiced to hide the rancid taste, and the mood at the princesses' table was as sour as the meat. Waves of apprehension rose from them with the heat.

"Abbess Sofia?" Pia implored after the abbess finished the blessing prayer. "What's happening with the giants? Will their princess be coming to the ball?"

Tenzin gave a smug warble from Anara's shoulder, and Eira stifled a smirk.

"King Wulfric has not seen fit to send word," the abbess said coolly.

Pia drooped with a sigh. If the giant princess joined the ball, Pia and Isolde would have to house her in their underoccupied room. Much as Jax had become fond of Pia, she couldn't help feeling the arrangement would have been worse for the giant girl.

"Yet, rumors still reach us," Abbess Sofia relented. "It seems the king has turned the giants away. You will return to your normal routines tomorrow."

Normal? Jax flinched at the memory of the day's debacle in the courtyard. Would the other girls even come out for training in the morning?

A sudden pounding rattled the great hall doors. Everyone in the room, even the haughtiest royal princesses, looked anxiously to Abbess Sofia.

After the briefest hesitation, she nodded to Sister Ursel. "See who it is."

"What if it's the giants?" Dora burst out.

"Don't be silly," Sister Ursel chided. "The gate guards wouldn't let a giant in."

Several girls laughed in relief, but giants were not the worst monsters Jax could imagine. Maybe King Wulfric had remembered his fury at her. Maybe he'd sent guards to take her into custody, drag her to Newport Castle …

Sister Ursel lifted the bar from the heavy double doors, and they flew open, nearly tossing her to the floor. A laughing, shouting mob of masked ruffians forced their way past her into the hall.

Ruffians with a familiar, rakish charmer at their head.

"*Prince Theodor*," Pia sighed.

"Good evening, Your Royal Highnesses!" Prince Theo swept off his mask, revealing the wicked glint in his eye. "Good evening, Mother and Holy Sisters."

"Crown Prince Theodor!" Abbess Sofia rose to her feet at the prince's entrance, yet she appeared anything but deferential. "What is the meaning of this?"

"We've brought another guest to join my father's ball." Theo swept his arm toward the rabble behind him, and Jax saw that for all their rowdiness, it was only the five Rose

Knights and another man, tall as Jordis, in a deeply hooded, fawn-colored cloak.

The stranger lifted his hands to his hood, taking a visible breath before throwing it back.

Jax started in shock as Eira gaped beside her. Pia squealed. Even cool Raisa gasped.

"He's a girl!" Ziva exclaimed.

The stranger reddened, peering at them through thick, dark lashes with eyes such a strange, deep blue they looked almost violet. They were certainly the most striking feature of her plain, round face—not just their vivid color, but the curiosity that sparkled in them as she took in her surroundings.

Jax shook her head as if that might reverse the transformation of the tall, adult man into a self-conscious young—

"Giant," Lidia said blankly. "She's a giant."

"Oh, Theo," Ellycia murmured. "What have you done?"

The prince guided the towering girl to the dais. "Allow me to present Her Royal Highness, Princess Hajni of Fairföld."

"Saint Winfred's—" Abbess Sofia caught herself before the curse's end. "Tell me you have not abducted King Frigyes's daughter."

Prince Theo winced. "Abduct is such a harsh word."

"I wanted to come." Princess Hajni spoke in a clear, high tenor, full of music. "It broke my heart that King Wulfric said I was too late to attend the ball. When Prince Theodor sneaked into my tent and offered to bring me here to join you, of course I came."

"Sir Van." Abbess Sofia pointed at the Rose Knight with the broadest shoulders and the honey-colored beard. "You and your men are sworn to protect the prince with your very lives. How could you fail to prevent this?"

Sir Van dropped to one knee, head bowed, just on the edge of cowering at her fury. "I am sworn to follow Prince Theodor's orders. He's the crown prince, Your ... um." He glanced up. "My lady—er ... Your Holy ..."

"She's an abbess now," Prince Theo said helpfully. "You can call her Mother."

"Abbess Sofia will do," the abbess said, ice in her voice. "I cannot credit the enormity of your collective stupidity. You must return Princess Hajni immediately."

"No!" Hajni clasped her hands, eyes pleading. "Don't send me home! I know I haven't a chance of marrying Prince Theodor, but this is the grandest adventure I've ever had. Don't make me go back before I get to attend the ball."

The abbess's eyes narrowed. "How old are you, Your Highness?"

"I'm fourteen. I know I look younger, but I *will* grow." As though she could decree it so.

The girl's height had tricked Jax into thinking she must be older, seventeen or eighteen. From the dismay dawning on Prince Theo's face, he had assumed the same.

"Old enough to be betrothed!" Hajni declared defiantly. "I'm not a child."

"By Aldforthian law, you are," Abbess Sofia said. "Is the age of majority so different in Fairföld?"

Hajni glanced down, her lips pursed mutinously.

"I thought so. Prince Theodor must rectify this catastrophic folly immediately."

"Come, now," Theo objected. "You heard Princess Hajni. It's a grand adventure—"

"*You.*" The abbess's voice sliced the air like a knife. "You are *not* a child."

"No." The mischief slipped from Theo's face. "I am the crown prince. No one seems to remember that."

"Maybe they would if you started acting like one," Abbess Sofia snapped. "Your brother—"

"If my brother believed my father wanted a war with the giants," Theo said bitterly, "he would not have sneaked into their camp and whisked away their princess as a lark to lighten the mood. He would have sneaked into their camp and slit her throat."

Hajni paled, and several other girls gasped in disbelief. But Jax noted that neither Princess Ellycia nor Abbess Sofia looked shocked by the prince's statement.

"We will never know what Guntram might have done," Abbess Sofia said stiffly. "Whatever you may think of him, do not forget that he was my son, too."

Jax swallowed her squeak of surprise. She heard the echo of Anatole's gruff voice. *Old queen's still alive. Joined some religious order years ago, after giving Wulfric his heir and a spare.*

Who else would King Wulfric trust to supervise the crown prince's prospective brides? No wonder the abbess seemed so unintimidated by a keep full of princesses.

"It doesn't matter." Prince Theo shifted uncomfortably in the face of his mother's grief. "There won't be any war. Princess Hajni is here for the ball, just as King Frigyes wants. Father won't send her back now she's here."

"Of course, he won't," Abbess Sofia snapped. "Sending her back would mean acknowledging that his son made a mistake. That the crown prince of Aldforth acted dishonorably, putting him under obligation to the giants he despises. No. Once he discovers the princess is here, he will not allow her to return to her father. How do you think King Frigyes will react to that?"

She turned her gaze to the Rose Knights. "Duke Jordis, remind my son how King Wulfric treats his hostages."

Jordis's face flushed red, and he looked as though he might be sick. Jax felt a pang of pity for him—until he opened his mouth and the poison dripped out.

"She's a *freak*," he spat. "We saw how much the king loves freaks in the training yard this morning." Maybe he thought the more vicious his words, the fewer people would notice the wretchedness in his eyes. "Princess Beast was spoiling for a fight this morning. Put the two of them together, you've got a battle of the monsters. He'll like that even better than a war."

The other Rose Knights ducked their heads in embarrassed confusion, as though they had started the evening as adventurers in a rollicking ballad and blundered straight into the opening stanzas of an epic tragedy.

"Father won't hurt Princess Hajni," Prince Theo said irritably. "She's too valuable ..."

"As a hostage?" Abbess Sofia pressed him.

He gave her a curt bow. "Mother Abbess, I offer my apologies for interrupting your meal. I thank you for your counsel, and I respectfully prefer my own. Good evening."

The prince and his knights swept from the hall. At least, the prince swept. The others scurried after him in their haste to escape the abbess's disapproval.

The door slammed, leaving Hajni awkward and alone before the dais. If she felt abandoned, she didn't show it. She raised her chin and attempted a smile. "It appears I will be staying for the ball, after all."

"Absolutely not," Abbess Sofia said. "My son's foolish actions have put you in grave danger."

"I'm not afraid."

"You are not the only one imperiled, Princess Hajni," Ellycia told her, nearly as stern as the abbess. "If your father discovers you're being held in this poorly defended ruin, he might try to break in to free you."

A current of fear swept around the princesses' table.

"Prince Theo *told* us this place was cursed," Dora moaned.

"Marshal Oswald and his men are here to protect us from any threat," Abbess Sofia said.

"Prince Theo didn't have any trouble getting in," Eira whispered to Jax.

"Nonetheless," the abbess continued, "we must rectify this situation. Sister Hella, please fetch my cloak. Sister Ursel, find the marshal and request an escort for myself and Princess Hajni."

"But Mother Abbess!" For once, Sister Ursel's sturdy calm deserted her. "You're forbidden from leaving the keep! If the king discovers you've defied his orders, your very life will be forfeit."

"I still have friends on the Alforthian council. I doubt they'd allow him to hang me for an evening stroll."

"Burn you at the stake for a witch, is what he said," Sister Ursel responded. "Mark my words, that man is seeking an excuse to be rid of you. I'll take the girl back to her father."

"I won't let you put your life at risk over my son's thoughtless prank—"

"I won't let you walk out that door—"

Their argument pounded in Jax's ears like the beating of a drum. *Cruelty. Malice. War.*

Thousands could die in a war between Aldforth and Fairföld, women and children as well as soldiers. But Jax felt as if she were drowning in her hatred for King Wulfric and his churlish spite, for the councilors who supported him. For King Frigyes, who had no better sense than to bring his daughter to Aldforth in the first place.

Why should she care if the whole lot of them slaughtered each other?

"I can take Princess Hajni back." Beatrix rose from her seat, her scars lurid in the candlelight. "You said we princesses were free to leave Lukos whenever we pleased. The worst King Wulfric could do to me would be to send me back to my father."

Jax thought she heard more truth in that statement than Beatrix meant to express.

"I'll go with you, Bee." Eira hopped up from her chair.

"The point is to return Princess Hajni to her tent without being seen," Marjani scoffed. "You are so pale you practically glow in the dark."

"And I'm still stealthier than you are with that big dark cloud of misery you drag around with you."

"Witch!"

"Killjoy!"

"I don't need help," Beatrix interrupted. "I'm a trained diplomat—"

"You are the daughter of the Emperor of Bellis," Abbess

Sofia said, silencing them all. "If anything happened to you, Aldforth could face war with your father as well as King Frigyes."

"Oh, no." Raisa rolled her eyes. "All ten of Bellis's fearsome warriors marching on Newport. What a terrifying thought."

"Bad things happen to those who cross the Bellisian emperors," Abbess Sofia said sharply. "Anyone who wishes to rule one of the Blessed Kingdoms should remember that."

Raisa's mouth pinched in anger, but she held her tongue.

Eira did not. "The Holy Mother of the Temple of *Peace* would hardly start a war if I were killed—"

Jax grabbed Eira's shoulder and pushed her back into her chair. It turned out there were some people she couldn't bear to watch get slaughtered, after all. "I'll go. Send me."

CHAPTER THIRTY-TWO

How could I have stopped her from going? She is foolhardy
and stubborn. Fate tallies our actions, and eventually, we
must pay the reckoning.

— Princess Anara of Kherem

Jax would never achieve Prince Theo's nonchalant
grace, but she managed to hop off the dais without
sprawling headfirst on the floor.

"I'm neither too valuable nor too pale." For once,
her dark hair and southern skin would be an asset. As would
her bastard status. She was the disposable princess, after all.

After a reluctant pause, Abbess Sofia seemed to reach the
same conclusion. "May the Mother Goddess watch over you,
my daughter. Sister Ursel, accompany Princess Jaclyn and
Princess Hajni to the gate and inform Marshal Oswald's men
they require an escort."

"I volunteered before she did!" Eira objected.

Beatrix shook her head at Jax, but she pulled the Nordish
princess back into her seat before the abbess could turn her
disapproval on them.

"Your cloak, Abbess!" Young Sister Hella burst from the
stairway at the head of the hall.

"Give it to Princess Jaclyn," the abbess ordered. "There's no time for her to retrieve her own."

"Come along, girls," Sister Ursel urged as Jax slung the dark cloak around her shoulders. "The sooner we begin, the sooner this will be accomplished."

"But I want to stay for the ball!"

Jax turned to Princess Hajni, disconcerted to have to look up to meet her eyes. Still, the awestruck, frightened girl reminded her of her sisters. She had to capitalize on that vulnerability before the giantess caught her balance and dug in her heels.

"You said you wanted an adventure. This is it. Come with me." She used the same tone she would with Lili on the verge of a tantrum—half command, half a sympathetic accomplice. "I can't wait to get out of this castle for an hour or two. You would not believe how dull it is here."

But Hajni's startling violet eyes flashed with rebellion. "I want to stay," she repeated.

Jax swallowed her growl of frustration. Surely *some* of Abbess Sofia's dire warnings must have gotten through to the giant princess. The girl just needed a salve for her pride, something to change an embarrassing retreat into a continuing adventure.

"Jaclyn!" Anara called.

A burst of flame lit the arched beams of the hall ceiling. Glittering blue-green wings broke the light into ten thousand shards, momentarily illuminating a deathly beautiful, mythical beast. Tenzin screamed, drawing answering gasps from her audience, before swooping down to land with a flapping, hissing flourish on Jax's shoulder.

The little dragon lifted her crest and stretched her neck to stare directly into the face of the wide-eyed, open-mouthed giant princess. She blinked her emerald eyes, loosed a tiny puff of smoke, and settled her wings on her back.

Jax raised her eyebrows at Hajni. "You don't mind Tenzin joining us, do you?"

The wonderstruck princess could only shake her head. Jax mouthed a heartfelt *thank you* to Anara before striding away down the hall. This time Hajni followed without protest, and they caught up with Sister Ursel at the door.

The night air was warm and thick, but it was fresher than in the keep, and Jax pulled in a deep breath. She hadn't lied to Hajni about wanting to get out. Her skin prickled with the need to escape Lukos, to walk free of its cursed walls, even for an hour.

"Oswald will send his best men with you," Sister Ursel puffed as they hurried across the empty courtyard. "I'll make sure of that."

"No," Jax spoke hurriedly. There was no time for argument. "Princess Hajni and I will go alone. It's the only way we can sneak into the giants' camp undetected."

"I can't let you go without an escort. If the giants catch you—"

"If the giants catch us, they'll see a helpful peasant girl who found their princess wandering lost in the woods and brought her home, not a dangerous band of rough-looking villains."

Sister Ursel narrowed her eyes, obviously picturing Oswald's men with their ill-fitting tunics and missing limbs. "I see your point."

The night watch would be on high alert for giants, but they weren't expecting anyone to approach the gate from the inside. Sister Ursel had to pound repeatedly on the door to the watchtower before someone finally stomped down the stairs.

The door swung open, and Dirk, the archery master, glared out at them. "What do you want?"

"Open the gate," Sister Ursel commanded. "These ladies have business in Newport."

"Gate doesn't open this time of night." Dirk frowned at Jax and Tenzin before his gaze slid to Hajni. He paused, whistled softly, then flicked a look back at Jax. "What trouble are you after getting yourself into now, girl?"

"Prince Theodor's trouble," Jax said flatly. "You opened the gate for him."

"This gate hasn't opened since those lily-livered lords rode back to Newport Castle this morning," Dirk assured her. "You'd've thought the giants were right behind 'em with knives and forks out. *If* the prince came in, he must have used the cliff gate."

"He's definitely been in—and back out," Sister Ursel said. "And brought a mess with him, as usual. We need to clean it up before it gets any bigger. Before it gets *gigantic*, if you catch my meaning."

Dirk scratched the back of his head and cast another appraising glance at Hajni.

"I s'pose I do," he said finally. "Got that hammer with you, Princess Jax?"

An unexpected wave of emotion washed over her at the laconic archer's question—a tacit acknowledgment that she might have prevented bloodshed that afternoon by disarming Jordis. She tugged aside the abbess's cloak, so he could see the hammer tucked in her belt.

"Right." He spat into the weeds withering beside the door. "Anyone asks, it weren't me that let you out."

"Of course not," Sister Ursel said. "And it won't be you that waits here to let Princess Jaclyn back in, either."

"What princess?" Dirk grumbled. "I haven't seen any princesses tonight."

With an impressive show of strength, he shifted the massive bar across the wooden doors. "Knock here when you're back. I'll let you in. And I'll let the boys know not to raise the alarm on you."

"I'll wait, too," Sister Ursel said. "May the Mother Goddess's protection go with you."

Jax pushed open the gate just far enough to squeeze through, Tenzin tucked tightly against her neck. Hajni slipped out behind her. The door closed on the giant princess's heels, and they heard the heavy bar thud into place.

In the sudden, giddy rush of freedom at being outside Lukos's walls, Jax gazed out over at the dark, forested hills that rose in the distance against a star-scattered sky. The road led them around the castle wall to the right, sweeping down the least precipitous slope of the fortress, back toward Newport and the giant camp.

"Prince Theodor's men blindfolded me when we entered the forest," Hajni said, her voice a bare murmur in the night silence. "It was spooky. I could feel the trees pressing in so tightly in places, it was like walking through a tunnel. But they said they couldn't let anyone know their secret shortcuts through the woods. We'll have to take the road."

Jax was just as glad. The trees dropped off sharply beyond the edge of the road. One misstep in the dark could mean a dangerous fall.

"How did those boys find their way through the woods?" she muttered, picking her way on the hard-packed gravel. "I can barely see my feet."

"They had a lantern."

Jax choked on unexpected laughter, startling Tenzin into a hiss on her shoulder. "I guess they make better highwaymen than I do. Not that we could use a lantern here on the road."

"There's plenty of light for me," Hajni said. "Giants see quite well in the dark."

"But I thought giants …" Jax paused, embarrassed. "I'm sorry. I thought giants were nearsighted. All I know about you is what I've heard in tales."

"Our tales say humans smell like rotten cheese," Hajni replied, "and that doesn't seem to be true, either. Besides, giants do have sensitive eyes. Bright sunlight is uncomfortable. We often travel at night."

"Is that how you got to Newport without King Wulfric knowing?" The darkness seemed to swallow their whispers as the road dropped into the forest.

"It's amazing what you wee people don't notice. As long as

we're quiet and not what you're expecting, you hardly seem to see us at all."

Jax bristled. "If you wanted attention, you wouldn't wear cloaks that blend into your surroundings——"

"Shh." Hajni touched her shoulder, bringing her to a halt. "I think something is following us." And then she disappeared.

Jax could still feel the giantess's fingers light against her arm, but she couldn't see—*there*. A hint of the drape of Hajni's cloak from the corner of her eye. She couldn't hear the girl, either, her own breathing a raging windstorm in her ears.

She glanced behind them. Lukos loomed high overhead, its shadow lapping at the road. Anything might lurk at the base of its rocky spire or in the shelter of the trees—ancient boulders, a frightened deer.

A manticore.

Jax pulled her hammer from her belt. Nothing would turn *her* invisible, out on the moonlit road. She wished she had Queen Léonie's sword. What had she been doing all that training *for*?

"Is someone there?" She hoped her harsh whisper sounded more confident than she felt inside. "Show yourself."

A shadow moved across the road. "Princess?"

That voice. The darkness was playing tricks with her ears as well as her eyes. *Something* was playing tricks. Weren't there legendary creatures who could mimic the voices of their victim's loved ones, luring them to their deaths? Maybe manticores were among them.

With a gleeful warble, Tenzin launched from her shoulder, landing awkwardly on the shadow's head. After a tangled struggle of arms and wings, muted curses and miffed whistles, the shadow stepped onto the road, resolving into the outline of a lanky young man with a very smug-looking dragon on his shoulder.

"Princess Jaclyn?" he asked tentatively, as though she might vanish at his whisper. "Jax?"

"*Nico.*" She launched herself at him with no more dignity than Tenzin, though he caught her more deftly than he had the dragon. She threw her arms around him, nearly knocking the indignant Tenzin from her perch. Jax laughed with the joy of seeing him again.

"It really is you," he said, his voice a mixture of elation and disbelief. "I thought I'd lost my wits, conjured you out of the night like a will-o'-the-wisp."

He pulled her close and rested his forehead against her hair. "Gods, Jax. I nearly did lose my wits when Tenzin brought the news about Wulfric's threats this afternoon."

The warmth in his voice ran like honey into Jax's very bones, threatening to melt her against him as she breathed in his scent of leather and horse and pine. It suddenly occurred to her that, as it turned out, Prince Theo's bright, shining *princeliness* didn't make Nicolas seem at all dull or homely by comparison.

Rather, Nicolas made the rest of the world seem brighter and clearer, as if a film of dust had been swept from the surface of her soul.

It also occurred to her, much too late, that Nicolas wasn't Bahar or Agnes or one of the children, someone she had any right to embrace. Maybe she shifted or stiffened. Nicolas stilled, and his grip on her loosened, though Jax could still feel the pounding of his heart against her own.

"Princess," he said softly. A reminder this time, to her, to himself.

I'm not a princess. But she didn't say it. She wanted to hold onto him, never let him go. Yet, in that moment, she *was* a princess. She could feel the weight of it pressing on her shoulders, hardening her spine. The duty, the restraints, the responsibility for others.

She lowered her arms, and Nicolas let her step back, the balmy night air suddenly cold in the empty space between them.

CHAPTER THIRTY-THREE

The best of intentions can sometimes lead to the worst consequences. Am I responsible for my children's actions? Is the Mother Goddess responsible for the deeds of hers? Does she despair of us?

— Abbess Sofia of the Abbey of the Mother Goddess

"Aflter I heard about Wulfric's threats, I thought if I could just find a way into Lukos, I might be able to rescue you." Nicolas gave her a wry smile. "I should have known you could rescue yourself."

Jax breathed in the night air, trying to clear her head, but her skin still sparked with his nearness. "I'm not escaping. I'm taking Princess Hajni back to her father."

"Princess who?" Nicolas asked in confusion.

And just like that, Hajni appeared where Jax had left her, a soft outline in the moonlight. "It isn't fair I have to go home when the rest of you get to have all kinds of exciting adventures."

"Gods." Nicolas barked a laugh. "She's half a head taller than you are, Jax, and I didn't even see her." Collecting himself, he sketched a respectful bow. "Princess Hajni. Of Fairföld, I assume?"

"Because it's the farthest place in the world from anywhere interesting?" Hajni asked crossly.

"Right," Jax scoffed, losing patience. "Not because you're so tall."

"Don't mock me," Hajni snapped back. "I know I'm small, but Mother always said she grew ten inches at fifteen."

"Princess Jaclyn was not teasing you," Nicolas assured her. "You seem astonishingly tall to me."

"Truly?" Apparently, Hajni was no more immune to Nicolas's infectious warmth than Jax. "You people really are hopelessly ignorant about giants."

And becoming ever more inclined to remain so. Jax bit her tongue.

Nicolas frowned. "I thought Wulfric turned King Frigyes away."

"He did," Jax said. "But Crown Prince Theodor abducted Hajni from the giants' camp—"

"I *ran away* with Prince Theodor to join the ball—"

"He refused to see reason when Abbess Sofia warned it could start a war—"

"He made some good points—"

"*Someone* had to return Hajni to her father, and after Theo stormed out, I was the logical choice," Jax concluded.

"*Theo?*" Nicolas asked.

"Prince Theodor insists we call him Theo."

"Charming," Nicolas observed, carefully bland.

"Oh, he's very charming," Jax agreed drily. "He reminds me of Denis."

Even the shadows couldn't hide Nicolas's smile. "Brings you dead beetles, does he?"

"Giant princesses."

"Ha ha," Hajni grumbled. "Let's go. You're the one who said we had to hurry."

Nicolas fell in beside them, Tenzin perched contentedly on his shoulder. "I've done quite a bit of reconnoitering over the past fortnight. There's a trail through the woods just ahead.

One branch of it leads to the lower meadow where the giants are camped."

He ducked into the shadows at the side of the road. They'd come far enough down the hill that the trees loomed above them rather than falling away beneath. "It's just along here somewhere. We can't ask Tenzin for light until we're completely hidden in the trees."

"She's breathed *fire* for you?" Jax asked. "I thought she wouldn't even talk to men."

The dragon's warble sounded flustered.

Jax stifled a laugh. "Don't worry. I won't tell."

"Is this the path you mean?" Hajni pushed past Nicolas into a darkness that looked like all the rest. "I can lead you until a light is safe."

Good sense might balk at following a stranger blindly into the woods. Even *bad* sense might balk at that. But when Hajni thrust out her hand, Jax took it, still surprised at a young girl's palm being larger than her own. Nicolas gripped her other hand, his sturdy and strong. The warmth of it flowed up her arm into her chest, brightening the darkness just a little. Letting her know she was not alone.

Not that she'd been alone much this past fortnight. She was more than happy to escape a few of the princesses for the night. But the truth was, she hadn't really been *lonely*. She had *friends*. Friends she would miss when all of this was over and she had to go home.

Had to? She stumbled over a root.

Hajni huffed with irritation. "It's like trying to sneak through the woods with a troll. Even blindfolded, I climbed over all that rubble better than you two walk a smooth path."

Jax wanted to ask if Hajni had personal experience with trolls—it seemed no more fantastic than giants, honestly—but she was distracted by the girl's words. Something about Hajni's blindfolded arrival in the fortress, the Rose Knights' pranks, a nagging question about that day when she and Eira and Anara had explored—

"There's a clearing ahead," Hajni warned, breaking into her thoughts.

Jax sensed the thinning of the trees, as much a pool of silence as a softening of the darkness. Were the woods always so quiet at night?

"Two paths converge at this clearing," Nicolas said. "One leads to the upper meadow. If we follow that one, the first fork will take us to the lower meadow and King Frigyes's camp."

They stepped from the shadows into a well of silvery light. The moon spilled over the tops of the trees, shimmering on a broad carpet of deer-cropped grass, soft beneath Jax's boots.

Hajni stopped abruptly, her sturdy form barely shifting when Jax stumbled into her.

"What—" Jax asked, but Hajni squeezed her hand hard, cutting her off.

Nicolas released her other hand, perhaps catching Hajni's tension. Jax heard the faint whisper of his knife leaving its sheath.

Once again, Jax wished she'd remembered her mother's sword—Nicolas couldn't wear one, pretending to be a dock-worker. She dropped Hajni's hand and tugged her hammer from her belt. She was a smith, after all. This was the tool her father had given her—although she doubted he could have foreseen the uses she'd been putting it to.

The moonlight failed to pierce the shadows beneath the trees surrounding them, but it settled dangerously on her companions' shoulders as they stood breathlessly in the center of the clearing.

For a long moment, the silence held. Then Hajni shifted.

"Sorry," she whispered, her voice higher and younger than before. "I thought I saw something shift, but there's nothing—"

A blinding light flared from the edge of the clearing.

"Halt! Don't move!"

Jax couldn't see, much less move, but Nicolas stepped

swiftly between her and the lantern. Beside her, Hajni spun in a panicked circle.

"We're surrounded!" The giant princess cried. "They must have heard us coming—"

"Princess Hajni?" a familiar voice asked.

"Prince Theo?" Hajni squeaked.

Jax closed her eyes, swallowing a curse and the receding gush of her terror. When she opened them again, she saw a masked figure stepping from the trees.

"They're armed," the voice with the lantern warned. Now that her heart wasn't pounding out of her chest, Jax recognized it as Sir Edgar's—or Sir Ryder's.

"Move away from Princess Hajni, you blackguards!" Theo ordered, placing a hand on his sword. Three more masked knights stepped into the clearing around them. "How did they abduct you from Lukos, Your Highness? Are you hurt? Wait, is that Princess Anara's *dragon*?"

"*We* haven't abducted anyone," Jax snapped, throwing off her hood and forcing herself to add, "Your Royal Highness."

"Princess Jax?" Prince Theo let his sword slide back into its sheath. "What are you doing here? What is the meaning of this?"

"Your mother—" Was it acceptable to refer to the abbess that way? "Abbess Sofia charged me with returning Princess Hajni to her father's camp." *To prevent you from accidentally starting a war*, she did not add.

"Mother." The word fell somewhere between a blessing and a curse. "She's always so sure she's right about everything."

It seems to run in the family.

"Who is that churl?" Jordis's voice came from the tall, masked figure to Theo's left. He pointed his sword tip at Nicolas.

"Dirk sent Nicolas to protect us." Jax's heart skittered in fear at what might happen to Nicolas if the Rose Knights learned his true identity.

Nicolas reacted to her ruse quickly, taking a respectful step behind her, disappearing nearly as neatly as a giant. Hajni's shoulder shook with suppressed giggles, enjoying the intrigue now the danger was passed.

"Why would Abbess Sofia send *you?*" Jordis demanded.

"Because Prince Theo refused to do it." Maybe the ambush's terror had pushed her past fear. "Fixing this situation is your responsibility, Your Highness."

"The straight truth I would expect from you, Your Highness." Behind his mask, Prince Theo sounded rueful. "It is indeed my duty. Sir Ryder, bring my horse. Princess Hajni, I will deliver you back to your father if that is truly what you desire."

Jax gritted her teeth at the way he leaned into *truly*.

"I would love nothing more in my whole life than to dance at your father's ball, Prince Theodor," the giant princess said earnestly. "But your mother is right. My father will worry if he finds me gone."

Apparently, even Hajni had a limit to her thirst for adventure

Sir Ryder appeared from the trees with a handsome bay gelding. The horse's eyes gleamed as he tossed his head and snorted.

Hajni eyed the skittish beast with equal parts curiosity and apprehension. "I've never been on a horse. Giants grow too big, so we don't train our horses for riders."

"Havoc will hardly know you're there." Theo's breezy assurance didn't appear to convince either Hajni or the horse, but the princess gamely took hold of Havoc's mane and placed her foot in the prince's hands for a boost.

Havoc danced sideways. Hajni flopped into the saddle with a squeal and wrapped her arms around the horse's neck. Sir Ryder worked to calm the gelding and the girl as Theo turned to Jax.

"Tell my mother I will complete your mission. Jordis can take you back to Lukos."

"That's not necessary, Your Highness," Jax said hastily. "It's not far. Dirk's man will see me safely to the keep."

Fortunately, the prince showed no interest in "Dirk's man" beyond a quick nod. "Very well." He flashed his mischievous grin. "Do be safe, Jax. This ridiculous contest of my father's might go more smoothly if you were eaten by a bear, but it would be a good deal less entertaining. Let's go, lads."

He took Havoc's reins from Sir Ryder. The gelding shied, his eyes rolling white in the lantern light. Another horse whinnied anxiously nearby.

"Easy there." Theo tightened his grip as the horse pulled him sideways. He shot an apologetic grin at Hajni, but the girl's eyes were squeezed shut in fear. "He's not usually like this. Try not to grip his neck quite so hard."

"Calm your brute, Theo," Ralf's voice called. "He's upsetting the rest of the horses."

Nicolas edged toward Jax, hand once more on his knife. "It's not Princess Hajni's horsemanship that's bothering him. That animal's frightened."

Tenzin warbled from his shoulder, and a shiver trickled down Jax's spine. With the lantern's light drowning out the moon, the shadows beneath the trees looked blacker than ever. She glanced at the sky. Manticores were supposed to have the body of a lion. Could they see in the dark like a cat?

"Shutter the lantern," Hajni commanded, straightening in the saddle. "Let me see."

In that moment, Jax saw *Princess* Hajni, a sovereign's daughter used to giving orders. Sir Edgar, used to receiving orders from royalty, obeyed. In the sudden darkness, Jax couldn't even see Nicolas beside her. But she heard Hajni gasp, a sound echoing with enough dismay to fill the clearing.

"No! Stop! Please, stop!" Hajni shouted. "Prince Theo! Look out!"

Tenzin squawked in alarm. A gout of flame burst from the little dragon's mouth as she lifted from Nicolas's shoulder. In the flickering span of Tenzin's breath, Jax saw new figures ringing the clearing, thick and sturdy as the tree trunks. Clubs clenched in white-knuckled fists, the giants—what else could they be?—towered over the prince's men, their faces ghastly in the dragon light.

Roaring with outrage, the giants flung their arms across their eyes against the sudden, blinding light. All except for the mountainous man with the flaming red-gold beard who had crept within ten feet of Jax without her ever noticing. He bellowed a war cry, swinging a club like a tree trunk over his head. Every muscle in his massive arm quivered with fury, and there was death in his black eyes as he took aim at Prince Theodor's skull.

Tenzin's fire flickered out.

CHAPTER THIRTY-FOUR

Then the giant king roasted the stalwart hero over his cookfire and ate him bite by bite until all that was left was the shining gold of his hair. The giant wove a crown of the hair and wore it as a warning to all the world to stay away from his farm.

— From "The Giant King's Three Goats," an Aldforthian fairy tale.

Hajni screamed. Havoc screamed. Jax couldn't make a sound, the muteness of her nightmares made real.

"Light!" Sir Edgar yanked up the shutter of his own lantern, and Tenzin flamed again, shooting tongues of fire at the prince's attacker. The giant roared and swung at her. She dodged the club, but the turbulence of the strike spun her off balance.

In the wavering light of the Rose Knight's lanterns, Jax saw Nicolas deflect another giant's charge with a well-timed slash of his knife. She was startled to find her hammer already in her hand.

Shouts filled the clearing. Rose Knights and half-blinded giants swung wildly at each other. Even the trees seemed to stamp and shudder. Or maybe that was Jax's careening heart-beat as she whirled, trying to figure out how to help.

"Don't hurt them! Please don't hurt them!" Hajni shouted, her voice high and desperate. Whether she meant the giants or the knights, Jax didn't know.

Havoc jumped sideways, knocking Sir Edgar to the ground. The knight's lantern rolled away, spilling oil and fire. For a moment, the burning grass slowed the red-bearded giant pursuing the prince. But Theo couldn't release his panicked horse to defend himself without endangering Hajni.

In the frenzy of the melée, no one else saw the danger, but Jax had no sword, no arrows, no experience with the roaring, unfathomable chaos of battle …

Theo is going to die. Breath shuddered into her lungs.

"*Tenzin!* Help the prince!" Jax shifted her weight to her back foot and hefted her hammer.

From the starry blackness above, Tenzin shrieked and dove at the prince's attacker. The giant reflexively raised his arm. Tenzin pulled up, just in time. Flames licked the giant's beard as she streaked over his head. He blundered back, eyes skyward.

Now. Jax whipped her arm forward, smooth as one of Anara's knives. Her hammer flew from her hand and struck the very center of the giant's forehead, true and clean as it had ever struck her father's anvil.

Jax tripped to a halt, suddenly weaponless mere yards from a furious, club-wielding monster. The giant stumbled back, trying to regain his balance. But his eyes were still going up, rolling into his head. Slowly, he tilted backward. Slowly, he began to fall.

He hit the ground with a crash that shook the clearing. Dust rose up around him. A faint curl of acrid smoke rose from his beard.

"Gergely!" Hajni cried.

Jax stared at the fallen man, legs shaking, her heart gripped in horror. He was someone Hajni knew, someone

Hajni cared for. Jax had felled him with a tool never meant to be raised in anger.

"Prince Theodor!" Sir Van's voice rang with authority. "Get Princess Hajni to safety! Retreat to Lukos, boys!"

Havoc had dragged Theo and Hajni away from the guttering flames of the spilled lantern. Jax could barely make out their shadowy forms. The Rose Knights waved lanterns and makeshift torches to keep the giants at bay.

"Jax!" Nicolas shouted.

A shadow rolled toward her in the flickering madness. Nicolas had both arms wrapped around a giant's waist, trying to wrench the huge man off-balance. The giant came on, as little bothered as a mother ignoring the tug of a toddler. He waved a bronze-headed mace that Jax doubted she could even lift.

Tenzin dove at him, shrieking. He spun with shocking speed, tossing Nicolas aside like a toy. He swiped at Tenzin with his mace, missing her badly. Her fire sputtered with laughter as she barreled by.

"Jax! Run!" Nicolas struggled to his feet.

Jax stumbled toward the giant she had felled. She might have killed him. Or he might be dying. In pain. He might need help …

Tenzin's impudent whistle made her look back. The dragon dove at the mace-wielding giant again, executing an acrobatic spin over his shoulder before diving down his back to smack his buttocks with a crack of her whiplike tail.

Yet as the little dragon swept around for another pass, the giant's stance changed. The off-balance ungainliness melted from his honed muscles.

"Tenzin!" Jax cried, suddenly recognizing his guile. "No! Back away!"

Tenzin snorted a scornful burst of smoke into the giant's face as she dodged a clumsy swing of his mace. But there was no clumsiness in his bare-fisted backhand. The blow hit the little dragon with all the speed and power of a horse's kick.

The force whipped Tenzin's head, wings and tail around the giant's fist. When his momentum finally released her, she tumbled limply through the air to smack against a tree.

"*Tenzin!*" Jax screamed.

The giant pivoted toward her.

Another giant shouted something in a language like a creek pouring over tumbled rocks. The only word Jax understood was "Hajni!"

The sound of hoofbeats gave her a fraction of a second to jump aside as Havoc thundered past. She saw the flash of the horse's rolling eye, the deceptive ripple of Hajni's cloak flaring out over his back as he galloped across the clearing and up the path toward Lukos. Tenzin's attacker charged after them.

"Follow the prince!" Sir Van shouted. "Retreat!"

Nicolas grabbed Jax's arm, but she jerked free. "*Tenzin.*"

The light from the Rose Knights' torches barely dimmed the shadows beneath the trees. Jax would never have seen Tenzin's body if not for the slightest wisp of smoke curling from her nostrils.

"She's alive!" That had to be breath, didn't it? Not just the little dragon's inner fire dying out. Jax dropped to her knees and ran her hands over the still form. "Tenzin? Can you hear me?"

She might have imagined the slight rise of the chest beneath her fingers if not for the smell of sulfur.

"Princess." Nicolas crouched beside her. "We have to get out of here."

Jax swiped at her face, her hand coming away wet. She hadn't even realized she was crying. "I don't want to hurt her."

"She'll be crushed if we don't move her."

That was true enough. The giants blundered about, arms over their eyes, swinging blindly at the Rose Knights trying to mount their terrified horses.

Gently and swiftly as she could, Jax folded Tenzin's wings and scooped the little body into her arms.

Torchlight flickered across her cheek. A Rose Knight rode toward her, a burning branch in his hand. She stumbled back a step. Even in his black mask, she recognized Duke Jordis.

"Give me your hand." His voice sounded different, stripped of its sneer by their peril. "I'll get you to the castle."

"She's got the dragon," Nicolas told him. "I'll help her up."

Jordis tossed his crude torch to the ground and reached his hand toward Jax. Why? Was it a trick? He'd made no secret of his disdain for her.

"By all that's holy, come *on*," he snapped, sounding more like himself. "The boys can't hold them off all night."

Jax looked around in surprise to see that the other Rose Knights had managed to mount and were doing their best to distract the giants from Jordis's rescue.

"Princess." Nicolas's steady voice grounded her.

That was the answer, of course. The exasperating, irresponsible, gallant Rose Knights would never leave behind a princess in distress, however poor of a princess she might be.

"But, Nico—"

"I'm quick on my feet, Princess. Don't worry about me." Even in the impossible light, Nicolas's intense blue eyes held hers.

She knew he was right. If she stayed with him, carrying Tenzin, she would only slow him down. Besides, she had to get the dragon to Anara, the only one who might know how to help the little creature.

With a quick prayer to any god that might be listening to keep Nicolas safe and Tenzin breathing, she grabbed Jordis's hand and put a foot in Nicolas's cupped palms. Together, they swung her up on the horse.

She wrapped her free arm around Jordis's waist, tight as she could without crushing Tenzin.

"Run!" she cried to Nicolas. She caught only a glimpse of him as Jordis's horse leaped forward—a glimpse of his gaze still on hers before he disappeared into the dark as swiftly and completely as the giants.

Then she could focus only on keeping her seat. Riding Bruno hadn't prepared her for a wild gallop through the dark on a knight's palfrey. She clung to Jordis and tightened her legs on the horse's ribs, hoping she wouldn't crush the breath out of either one.

Tree branches whipped past, snagging her hair and cloak. The other knights' horses pounded behind them. When they reached the road, bright in the moonlight, Jordis swung his horse up the hill toward Lukos, away from Newport Castle and the giant encampment. It had seemed a goodly distance on foot, in the dark, but Jordis's palfrey covered it in hardly any time at all.

As they neared the fortress gates, Jax saw the great wooden doors had already been opened for Theo and Hajni's wild arrival. Dirk and Marshal Oswald stood at the entrance, swords in hand. There would be archers on the walls with arrows nocked.

But the marshal recognized Jordis's galloping mount and waved them in. Jordis pulled the horse to a skidding stop in the center of the courtyard. With practiced grace, he swung a leg over the animal's neck and leaped to the ground, then turned to help Jax slide down beside him. She might have collapsed if he hadn't kept a firm grip on her free arm.

"Don't vomit on my boots," he said curtly.

That stiffened her legs. She pulled from his grasp as the other Rose Knights pounded into the courtyard. The horses swam in her vision, their rolling eyes and foam-flecked sides, but she counted four—Ralf and the three Sirs. They'd all made it back. Sir Edgar roared at Marshal Oswald to close the gates.

"Princess Jaclyn!" Sister Ursel bustled to her side, Princess Hajni stumbling in her wake. "Are you all right? Are you hurt? You're bleeding!"

"Tenzin's blood." The dragon still hung limp in her arms. Jax wasn't hurt in any way anyone could fix.

"Prince Theodor." Hajni's face was pale as moonlight, her eyes wide and dark as she stared at Jax. "Is he all right? Did Havoc hurt him?"

"What? I don't know. I just got here." Jax looked around at the dismounted knights milling in confusion, heard the marshal's rumbling voice rising in alarm. "Where is he?"

"Havoc was terrified of the giants. Of *us*," Hajni said, her voice breaking. "All the fire and shouting made it worse. He reared up, and I think he kicked the prince. I heard Theo cry out, and he fell—"

Jax realized she actually was in danger of vomiting on someone's boots.

"—Havoc jumped, and I almost tumbled off. All I could do was grab his neck and hold on. By the time he slowed down, we were at the gates, and that man Dirk grabbed the reins—"

"Theo's not with you?" Jax heard the Rose Knights shouting. Her chest heaved as she pulled in more air. "*Prince Theodor didn't return to Lukos with you?*"

"That demon horse ran away with the poor child," Sister Ursel said. "We had to pry her fingers out of his mane—"

"No." Jax's voice broke a little louder. "You don't understand. *We thought Prince Theo was riding Havoc.*"

Sister Ursel's face blanched pale as Hajni's.

A hand gripped her shoulder and spun her around. Jordis stared down at her, his eyes nearly as white and panicked as Havoc's had been.

"By all the gods, girl. *Where the hells is Prince Theodor?*"

CHAPTER THIRTY-FIVE

I don't know why my father says I'm stubborn. He's so much worse.

— Princess Hajni of Fairföld

It took an eternity of horrified shouting for everyone in the courtyard to reach the obvious conclusion: The prince had been left behind in the woods with a band of raging giants. Possibly injured. Possibly worse.

Jax acquired a newfound respect for Marshal Oswald's battered crew of castoffs as they assembled in the yard to begin the search. It took true courage to hunt the night for legendary foes half again the size of even their huge, one-eyed leader.

The Rose Knights remounted with a grim bravery of their own, though their bold war faces couldn't hide their terror for their friend or their bewilderment at how things could have gone so wrong.

"This is your fault," Jordis snarled at Jax as he whirled his horse toward the gate. "You're the one who told him he had to return that brainless giantess to her father. If anything happens to him, I'll carve you up and feed you to the giants myself."

"Come, girls," Sister Ursel said quietly. "We can't do anyone any good out here."

Still clutching Tenzin, Jax stumbled after her and Hajni, her mind a maze of dangerous, disconnected thoughts. As they entered the roiling, anxious buzz of the keep, she couldn't pull her senses together. She floated in a blur of hazy misery punctuated by sharp jabs of others' pain.

The sound Anara made when she took Tenzin into her arms, before Sister Verena rushed them to the infirmary where Jax was not allowed to follow.

Abbess Sofia's anguish when she heard her only remaining son was missing, a grief that rang in Jax's ears even after Sister Ursel ordered all the girls to their rooms.

The look in Hajni's eyes as she paused at the door to Isolde and Pia's room—not even Isolde had dared to object to housing her, in the face of Abbess Sofia's fathomless distress—and asked Jax, "Is he dead?"

"Prince Theodor?" Jax stood stiffly, trying not to touch Tenzin's blood on her clothes. "Try not to worry. Marshal Oswald will find him."

"*Gergely.*"

"Ger-gay?"

"The captain of my personal guard." Hajni's eyes were more black than violet in her grief. "You hit him with your hammer. He would have taken me home if you hadn't … Did you kill him?"

The icy blade of fear and guilt dug deeper into Jax's heart. "I don't know."

She could have added, *I hope not.* She could have asked, *What did you think would happen when you ran away from your father?* She could have said, *My friend Nicolas might be dead, and no one cares,* or, *if Tenzin dies, Anara will never be able to return home.*

Instead, she choked back the unsaid words and crossed to her own door. Eira and Beatrix caught her as she staggered in. They stripped her of her torn and bloody clothes, dressed her in her night shift and wrapped her in warm blankets because she couldn't stop shivering, despite the oppressive heat.

Eira put an arm around her shoulders, Beatrix pressed a cup of mulled wine into her hand, and they sat and listened as she told them everything that had happened. Everything she could remember.

They didn't try to reassure her that Tenzin would be fine, that the giants had no reason to harm Prince Theo, that Nicolas was smart and quick enough to escape pursuit. They only hoped those things with her.

"I'll light candles to the One Goddess," Eira said when Jax finally ran out of words. She moved to the table beside her bed, where she'd set up a small altar. "One for Tenzin, one for Nicolas, and one for Prince Theodor."

"And one for Gergely," Jax said, her voice like jagged glass in her throat.

"And one for Gergely," Eira agreed.

Beatrix took Jax's cup. "Sleep now. There's nothing more to be done tonight."

Jax couldn't imagine sleeping. Even if she could stop reliving Gergely's fall, her last glimpse of Nicolas's face, the sight of Tenzin's blood, surely every muscle in her body—not just her heart—ached too much for sleep. But maybe Beatrix had slipped one of Dora's tinctures into the wine. Or maybe her exhaustion, and some animal instinct to escape her devastating misery, simply overwhelmed her.

She was deep in black, dreamless sleep when the door to their room crashed open, slamming violently against the wall. Jax woke to startled shouts and lantern light. For an instant, she was back in the clearing in the woods, her tangled blankets some deadly trap of the giants' devising.

"What is the meaning of this?" Beatrix's imperious voice brought her back to her room.

Two soldiers dressed in King Wulfric's livery pushed through the door. A black-clad shadow followed a step behind. In the flickering light of the lantern he carried, he might have been a Santian demon god, risen from the caves beneath Lukos on the breath of a curse. Then the light stilled, settling on Castellan Kenrick's shrewd, narrow features.

"Not one more step if you value your life." Eira's voice rang cold and steady as the ice in her eyes. She stood beside the hearth, a borrowed bow from the training yard in her hands, an arrow nocked and ready. Even with mussed hair and bare feet, her deadly intent was clear.

No question that in such close quarters, three sturdy men had the advantage over one slender archer. There was also no question that one of them would get an arrow through his eye for his trouble. Neither of the guards looked eager to get skewered by a girl in a nightshift.

"Princess Eira! Put that down." Sister Ursel pushed past the castellan, carrying a lantern of her own. Exhaustion pulled her face into dark, shadowed lines, but she glowered fiercely at Kenrick. "When I warned you not to barge in here, it wasn't just to protect their Royal Highnesses' modesty. We don't need any more violence tonight."

Eira held her aim steady on Castellan Kenrick's heart. "He's not taking Jax."

In that moment, Jax understood Eira wasn't simply reacting to unexpected danger. She'd had the bow ready by her bed. She'd guessed guards might come tonight. She'd foreseen why. And she'd decided that, this time, staying silent wouldn't save Jax's life.

Of course, neither would killing Castellan Kenrick.

Surely Beatrix would tell her ... Jax's quick glance caught the glint of the knife blade her other friend held hidden beneath her coverlet.

"No!" Jax finally freed herself from her blankets and tumbled to her feet. "It's all right, Eira. I'll go with them."

"I'm not letting them take you away!"

"Hush, girl." Sister Ursel put her sturdy form between Eira and Kenrick. "Abbess Sofia won't allow him to take

Princess Jaclyn from the keep. They're only moving her to a more secure room, higher in the tower."

Eira hissed like a cat, but she slowly lowered her bow.

"Excellent choice," Kenrick said dryly. "Come with us, Princess Jaclyn."

At least he was still calling her "princess."

"She's not going in her night shift," Sister Ursel said indignantly. "You can wait in the hall."

The castellan's calculating gaze assessed the princesses. Judged the deadly drop from the windows. He finally nodded. "Very well. You have five minutes."

The moment the heavy door closed behind the guards, all three girls whirled on Sister Ursel.

"Prince Theodor?" Eira demanded.

"I'm not allowed to tell you anything. Get that shift off, Princess Jaclyn. Help her, girls." Sister Ursel directed Beatrix to Jax's trunk. "That man won't give her a minute more than he said."

"Please." Jax's voice cracked. "If the searchers had brought Prince Theo home safely, the castellan wouldn't be waiting for me in the hall."

Sister Ursel's expression softened. "He's alive, as far as we know. Lift your arms. We'll get that shift off."

"The giants?" Beatrix asked grimly.

"They've taken him to their camp. King Frigyes has threatened to throw his head over Newport Castle's walls with his bare hands if a single hair on Princess Hajni's head is harmed."

Jax sucked in a shaky breath and let Sister Ursel help her into the soft blue gown Beatrix pulled from her trunk. "Tenzin?"

"The little beast is also alive, last I heard. I've been a bit busy with other things. Quit twisting and let me tie this up." Relenting at their anxious faces, Sister Ursel added, "Princess Anara has extensive training in dragon care, and Sister Verena is a skilled herbalist. We must leave it in their hands and, of course, the hand of the Mother Goddess."

She pressed three fingers to her lips and touched them piously to her heart.

"Did the marshal find *anything* in the woods?" Beatrix pressed, so Jax wouldn't have to ask about Nicolas—or Gergely.

"Not that he shared with me." Sister Ursel handed Jax her cloak. "Take this. It might cool off yet."

"But why is Castellan Kenrick moving Jax?" Eira demanded. "It's not her fault Prince Theodor was captured. She was only doing what Abbess Sofia asked."

"Enough," Sister Ursel said. "You know as much as I do, which is little indeed. I have no intention of speculating."

The door swung open. The castellan, dark as Jax's fears, filled the opening, though he wasn't a particularly large man. "Do I need to search her, Sister, or will you pledge that she is unarmed?"

"Of course she is unarmed, you—" Sister Ursel bit down on the rest of her opinion.

Jax reached reflexively for her hammer, her hand closing on its empty loop. Her stomach pitched with grief and loss. She'd been so horrified at Gergely's fall that she hadn't thought to retrieve it. Her one solid connection to home, to her father, and she'd literally thrown it away.

Eira squeezed her hand. Beatrix straightened her gown. And then Jax stepped to the doorway, eye to eye with the castellan.

"Jax saved Prince Theo's life," Eira said.

"I will take that under consideration." Kenrick's expression changed not at all as he stepped aside. "After you, Your Highness."

Hajni waited in the hallway with the guards. She wouldn't have needed time to change. Not even Jax had night clothes that would fit her. She must have slept in her traveling gown.

If she'd slept. Her eyes were dark as bruises.

"That's right." Isolde stood in the doorway to her room, eyes flashing. "Lock the ugly giant up with the girl who kills giants. That's some kind of justice."

"Jax was protecting Prince Theodor," Eira spat over Sister Ursel's shoulder. "Which is exactly what King Wulfric brought us here to do."

"She didn't do a very good job of it, did she?" Isolde snapped back. "And what about me? I had to spend all night with a monster in my room because of her." She looked Jax up and down, her lip curled with a disdain not even golden hair and a perfect complexion could make attractive. "I hope you get what you deserve, Jax the Giant Killer."

CHAPTER THIRTY-SIX

Poor Prince Theodor! I hope he's not hurt. I wish I could be there to tend to him. Except for the giants. I would just die of terror if I were captured by giants, wouldn't you?

— Princess Pia of Capra

We were brought here to marry a prince. What are we supposed to do if there *is* no prince? Compete for the king's eight-year-old bastard? I'm a princess, not a nursemaid.

— Princess Raisa of Ravnina

Jax and Hajni followed Sister Ursel up the winding stairs, Castellan Kenrick and the two guards close behind. They passed the abbess's chambers and the sisters' rooms, arriving at the tower's top floor where the still air smelled faintly of candle wax and incense.

"There's a set of unused rooms behind the chapel," Sister Ursel explained. "We'll settle you in one of those."

She led them by a small, bare room where a single candle burned on a low stone altar. Apparently, Lukos's chapel was not high on King Wulfric's redecorating schedule. At the next door, the sister stopped and pulled a ring of keys from her belt. Jax's stomach twisted. Not even the princesses' rooms had locks.

"The workers used this as a storeroom," Sister Ursel explained. In the lantern light, the small room was even starker than the chapel. "It is not appropriate accommodation for royal ladies."

"Abbess Sofia seemed to believe it was preferable to accommodations in Newport Castle," Castellan Kenrick reminded her.

"She was not going to let you put these girls in the dungeons!"

"The king is not in the habit of imprisoning young ladies in dungeons," the castellan said.

Sister Ursel's eyes narrowed. "It would be better if he were not in the habit of imprisoning young ladies at all."

Hajni swallowed hard and tilted sideways. Jax caught the girl's arm and wrapped it over her shoulder. Together they staggered through the door. Hajni was so young, Jax kept forgetting how tall she really was.

"It's all right," Jax said, helping her sit on the floor. "We'll be fine here. Won't we, Hajni?"

The giant princess managed a nod, though her eyes refused to focus on Jax's face.

"The poor child!" Sister Ursel turned on the castellan. "See what you've done?"

"Some watered wine," Kenrick prescribed calmly. "Perhaps a little food. And you'll want to fetch some bedding to make them comfortable."

The indomitable sister gave him a look that would have cracked a less hardened soul. She squeezed Hajni's shoulder. "We'll have you comfortable in no time. Never fear."

It was too late for that, but Jax nodded anyway. It was the best she could do.

Kenrick stopped Sister Ursel at the door. "The key."

The sister's mouth thinned, but she pulled the key from her ring. "We sisters will need to attend to the princesses."

"Of course," Kenrick agreed, handing the key to one of the guards. "The princesses may not leave this room, but you and your sisters may come and go freely."

"I will return soon," Sister Ursel said. Whether she meant to comfort Jax and Hajni or to warn Kenrick, Jax couldn't be sure. She bustled away, taking only one of the lanterns but everything that kept the dark at bay.

"You may ask the sisters for whatever you require," Kenrick told Jax and Hajni, "as long as it is reasonable."

Jax swallowed around the fear lodged in her throat. "What will happen to us?"

"I cannot say."

"We haven't done anything wrong." Anger filled her mouth like ash, bitter and suffocating. "Abbess Sofia must have told you what happened. King Wulfric can't believe it's our fault."

"I am not privy to what the king believes." Kenrick's eyes glittered almost black in the dim light. "I imagine he thinks it unlikely an ignorant peasant girl could invent such an audacious plan. Still, he needs someone to blame, and you are convenient."

His eyes narrowed as he appraised her. "*I* have no doubt you are capable of unprecedented audacity. Indeed, your boldness with those above your station, your ability to assess rapidly changing situations, your cleverness ... You remind me of myself. When I was much younger and more foolish."

With a short bow, he left the room, closing the door firmly behind him. The scrape of the key in the lock, loud in the sudden darkness, sent a chill down Jax's spine. She sank gracelessly to the floor beside Hajni.

The younger princess sucked in a deep breath, something between a shudder and a sob. Then let it out with a long, prickly word in her native language that sounded exceedingly impolite.

The room wasn't completely dark, after all. Pre-dawn light

seeped heavy and gray through the narrow windows, illuminating the pale oval of Hajni's face as she spoke.

"Thank you for not letting me faint in front of that horrible man. I don't know how you stood up to him. He's terrifying."

"He is," Jax admitted. She leaned back against the cold stone wall. "But King Wulfric is the real monster."

Hajni swiped a sleeve across her eyes. "He won't harm us while my father has Prince Theodor. They'll work out a trade."

"Of course they will," Jax said.

Hajni sighed and rested her head on Jax's shoulder. There seemed no reason to remind her that neither King Wulfric nor King Frigyes had any incentive to trade for Jax's safety.

~

Sister Ursel proved good as her word. By the time a rosy dawn warmed the windows, she and the other sisters had filled the bleak room with fresh straw mattresses and soft sheets, a chamber pot, chairs, a table and food to serve on it. They even brought a clean shift for Hajni to wear while they cleaned the dust and burrs from her traveling gown.

"It's Sister Verena's," Sister Ursel explained as Hajni slipped it on. "She's the only one of us with shoulders wide as yours."

The shoulders fit perfectly. The shift's hem barely reached Hajni's knees.

"Sister Verena is not much taller than she is broad," Sister Ursel admitted. "But it will do to sleep in. Into bed now. You didn't get much rest last night."

Jax couldn't argue. Exhaustion pressed her to her mattress, heavy enough it might crush her bones. Yet her mind fluttered like a moth against a windowpane, unable to escape, unable to settle in confinement.

She could imagine Constable Anatole's scolding. "I said,

'whatever you do, don't draw attention to yourself.' For gods' sake, girl, how do you lose a bedamned prince?"

She almost smiled, a crack that let the tears leak through. She curled on her side and stuffed her fist into her mouth to stifle her sobs. She wept for Theo and Hajni, each captive to hostile, inflexible men. For Nicolas, who might be captured, too, or even dead. For her homeland, failed by its sham princess whose only job had been to keep King Wulfric's wrath at bay. And for herself, imprisoned and forsaken.

Once again, emptiness finally dragged her into sleep. Once again, Castellan Kenrick's arrival dragged her back.

This time he brought a cold tisane of barley and herbs and a plate of small cakes. He arranged them on the table by the empty hearth while Jax untangled her skirts and swiped damp hair from her face. The afternoon heat pressed down on Lukos like a wet, smothering cloth.

Hajni lay loose-limbed as a toddler on her mattress nearby, her face smooth and peaceful in sleep.

"No need to wake her," Kenrick said. In the dusty sunlight, his dark eyes looked sunken and tired.

Well, hers probably did, too.

"Why are you here?" she asked flatly. "If the kings had reached an agreement for exchanging their beloved children, you'd be taking Hajni back to her father."

"King Wulfric has sent me to interrogate you, to make you divulge how you conspired with the giants."

Interrogate. Such a bland word, in such a bland voice. Of all the terrors that had dogged her overnight, this one had not occurred to her. How was this man accustomed to making prisoners talk? Threats? Beatings? The rack?

"I can't divulge something I didn't do." Her voice was thin but steady. "You mean you're going to torture a confession from me."

He sighed. "I suppose I do cultivate that impression. Fortunately for you, the law is clear on the immunity of visiting royalty from physical coercion. A few words in the right ears have provoked King Wulfric's councilors into reminding him of that fact."

"I'm supposed to thank you for those 'few words'?" Jax asked. He couldn't think her fool enough to lower her guard because he refrained from striking her. She gestured at the table. "And then you buy my trust by offering not to starve me?"

"I encountered Sister Ursel in the hall," he responded dryly. He poured them each a glass of barley water. "Please sit. I must stay long enough to convince the king I did my best to drag the information from you."

She sat. Better than her shaky legs collapsing beneath her.

"You believe me." If there was anything she trusted about him, it was that he was no fool, either. "That I'm innocent."

"Your innocence is immaterial," he told her, his words blunt as his manner. "All that matters is getting Prince Theodor back, and your confession would only complicate the negotiations. The king is resistant enough to bargaining with Frigyes already."

"He must be desperate to get Prince Theo back," Jax objected.

"If it were Prince Guntram, there would be no question," Kenrick agreed. "But Theodor … He will never be the cold, brutal despot Guntram would have become."

"He's Wulfric's only heir," Jax said, not bothering to hide her disbelief. "Prince George is illegitimate. He could never rule Aldforth."

"Not while the king is still legally married to the former queen," Kenrick said. "If she were to agree to an annulment, he could marry Duchess Bianka and legitimize George."

"But that would make Theodor a bastard. Abbess Sofia would never agree to that." And then Jax understood. "Unless Theo were dead …"

Kenrick raised his glass of barley water to her. "I'm sure it wouldn't be the king's first choice. An eight-year-old is a risky prospect to wager a kingdom on. But George is malleable.

Wulfric might have a chance to mold him into another Guntram."

Jax clasped her chilled fingers beneath the table to hide their trembling. Constable Anatole had warned her Aldforth was a wolf's den, but the humans here were worse than wolves. "Why are you telling me this?"

"I told you, I must pass the time." Yet his dry manner did not hide the layers of frustration, exhaustion and calculation lining his face. "Impetuous as he may be, I believe Prince Theodor is Aldforth's best hope for a thoughtful, stable leader to follow Wulfric. Perhaps our *only* hope for a safe, prosperous future. My first priority is his safe return."

Despite herself, she believed him. She had seen him first-hand try to curb Wulfric's worst impulses in order to protect the kingdom.

"At the same time," he continued, "I would prefer Theodor to inherit a kingdom not at war with yours. You have displayed a rare talent for getting under King Wulfric's skin, but you're a smart girl, and I believe you can turn that to your kingdom's advantage. At some point, the king will call you to account for yourself. He must be convinced to pardon you—"

"I don't think King Wulfric can be convinced he *must* do anything," Jax said bitterly.

"That's why we must convince him the pardon is his idea." Kenrick rose from his chair. "He would rather lose his son than be seen as weak, as bowing to pressure, but he loves to be seen as pragmatic, crafty, smarter and stronger than anyone else around him. Show him that vision of himself, and you may yet return home a free woman."

"That's all?" Jax stood to face him, forcing her legs to remain steady. "That's all I have to do to … what? Keep him from executing me?"

"To *pardon* you, not lift the punishment," the castellan corrected. "The king has already decided that Prince Theodor's capture requires a very public, very bloody response. However, due to that inconvenient matter of royal immunity, he has allowed himself to be persuaded that it is not necessary that the response fall on *you* specifically. The actual punishment may be meted out on a sort of whipping boy, as it were."

"What do you …" Jax suddenly remembered Presentation Day, the king's anger at Theo's late arrival, his brutal response. Horror rose like bile in her throat. "He would execute someone in my place?" She could still hear the sound of Wulfric's fist striking Theo's esquire. "Not *Ralf*."

"What?" Kenrick frowned at her. "Of course not. A Venian committed the crime—"

"There *was* no crime!"

"A Venian must suffer the punishment," he finished, something almost like pity in his hard gaze. "We have a suitable replacement in custody. Marshal Oswald's men may not have retrieved the prince last night, but they did not return to Lukos empty-handed."

Time stopped. "What do you mean?"

"Last night, you were accompanied by a young man whom you claimed Dirk sent with you from the castle. A young man with a poorly disguised accent. You didn't really think we wouldn't find him, did you? Everyone in Newport knew where the overly educated Venian dockworker was staying."

"*Nicolas*." The name tore from her throat, and she clutched the back of her chair to keep from falling. "What have you done with him?"

"He is safely locked away in Newport Castle—in accommodations not so much worse than yours. The king wants him healthy enough to walk to his beheading."

CHAPTER THIRTY-SEVEN

It serves her right! It's her fault I don't have a prince to marry. I always said that Venian peasant doesn't belong here, and I've been proven right. Oh! I could just scream.

— Princess Isolde of Montaine

They say this castle is cursed. I say this whole kingdom is cursed.

— Princess Marjani of Almasa

Castellan Kenrick's genteelly tailored clothes hid the solid muscles of a street brawler, but Jax's attack caught him by surprise. She dug her fists into the crushed velvet of his tunic and shoved him against the solid oak door.

"How dare you?" They were the same height. She was shouting directly into his face. "You can't imprison an innocent man for a crime *no one has committed*."

His shifting shoulders were her only warning before he shoved her away, breaking her hold. Training with the other girls had improved her footwork, and she kept her balance as she stumbled back, though her hip struck the table. Her hand landed on the pitcher of barley water—not an ideal weapon, but it was heavy ceramic. And she'd already felled a giant with a hammer.

Gergely's memory stayed her hand. The castellan wasn't coming after her. And judging from his confident defensive stance, it wouldn't be the first time he'd had to dodge a pitcher thrown at his head.

"You should be grateful, girl," he snapped, jerking his tunic back into place. "If we hadn't found your man, your own life would be forfeit, princess or not."

"You can't hurt him." Her voice cracked with helpless fury. "He's done nothing wrong. *Nothing.*" She lifted her chin, refusing to break. "As princess of Venia, he is *my* subject, not King Wulfric's. I order you to release him."

His teeth showed in frustration—or amusement. "*Now* you decide to act like a gods damned princess. Well, it doesn't work that way, Your Highness. Wulfric is the ruler here. He is the one with the power. *That's* the way the world works."

"You're a coward," she spat. "You said I reminded you of yourself? I am nothing like you. I would never allow an innocent man to die to appease a monster."

"The only way your man leaves Aldforth with his head on his shoulders is if you confess to conspiring with the giants and take his place. That doesn't just end you, it endangers your kingdom." Kenrick reached behind him for the door, too wary to turn his back on her. "I've told you what you must do to preserve the peace. I've learned how to survive the hard way. If you can't emulate that, you're a stiff-necked, naive fool, and you won't live to be my age."

"I'd rather be dead!" Her pitcher hit the closing door and exploded into a dozen pieces, splattering water across the room.

"Princess Jax?"

She had utterly forgotten Hajni was in the room. The giant princess sat on her straw mattress, pressed against the wall. Her eyes looked bruised with fear.

Jax's nails dug into her palms. Her jaw clenched so hard

she feared it might break. She must look capable of murder. She felt capable of it.

"I'm sorry." Tears slurred Hajni's words. "It's all my fault. I shouldn't have begged my father to bring me here. I shouldn't have listened to Prince Theodor. I shouldn't have—"

"You're a fourteen-year-old girl locked in a tower by a brutal tyrant," Jax said, her voice so savage she scarcely recognized it. "You didn't assassinate Prince Guntram. You didn't plan this travesty of a ball. In what kind of a world does a man's life depend on your having better judgment than a pair of pigheaded kings?"

If only she still held the pitcher. She wanted to throw it again. And again.

"If you confess …" Hajni's knuckles were white where she clutched her blanket. "If you tell them you helped get Prince Theodor kidnapped, King Wulfric would think I helped you. He might execute me, too."

"Yes." Jax lurched to the nearest window and leaned on the narrow sill. The air was thick, but at least it smelled of the woods far below, smelled of freedom. The closest to freedom she might ever get again. "Yes, he could use my confession as an excuse to execute you. Or to declare war on my mother and invade Venia."

"But he might execute me and attack Venia, even if you stay silent," Hajni said, her voice small. The naive young princess learned fast. "Do you think he'd really let Nicolas go free if you said you were guilty?"

"I don't know," Jax admitted. Castellan Kenrick might push for his release, for form's sake, if nothing else, but King Wulfric … Everything hurt. Her body, her mind, her heart.

Would confessing condemn Hajni, as well as herself? And then what would happen to Theo? Could she trade their lives for Nicolas? Nicolas, her … what? Guardsman? Swordmaster? Friend? None of those touched how she'd felt hearing Nicolas's voice the night before. *Her heart's refuge.* Sentenced to death because an angry despot was too proud to make a simple hostage exchange.

There had to be a way for her to save Nicolas without endangering Hajni or Venia.

She placed her hands on the window sill. It was narrower than the one in her room downstairs. Ziva could probably squeeze through, but not a big, healthy peasant girl. She pictured herself dangling down the keep wall, her hips wedged in the window. Not exactly a dignified exit.

With a snort, she turned away and sank heavily to the floor. She couldn't help Nicolas locked up in this tower, but jumping to her death wouldn't free him, either.

She dropped her head to her knees. He'd come looking to rescue her last night. Why hadn't she abandoned Hajni and let him? Why had she pulled away when he embraced her?

Why hadn't she been brave enough to let him know how she felt?

Hajni sat beside her. "Don't give up hope."

Jax shook her head. She hadn't given up hope. Hope had been brutally ripped from her.

Still, she wiped her sleeve across her face and squeezed Hajni's hand. It was as large as her own but slender and soft. The hand of a child who needed her to keep the darkness at bay.

She pushed herself to her feet, hauling Hajni up with her. "Let's get you dressed, and then we should eat those cakes the castellan brought."

"We need to keep up our strength," Hajni agreed. "Next time you throw a pitcher, you want to make sure it hits Kenrick, not the wall."

She flashed an irrepressible grin that made Jax feel heart-breakingly old.

The day stretched on, growing hotter and damper and more stagnant. Late in the afternoon, a guard cracked open the door and shoved through a tray of food.

"These ignorant buffoons won't let me in!" Sister Ursel

complained from the hall. "Some poppycock that you girls might be dangerous. Of all the ridiculous … Just wait until Abbess Sofia hears about this. We'll see what—"

The door slammed shut, cutting her off.

Jax forced herself to eat to set a good example for Hajni. She knew she should distract the girl by asking about Fairföld, about Hajni's family, about life deep in the heart of the Serpents Teeth, behind the High Gates of Elhalad. Or she should tell Hajni about Dormance, about her father and Agnes and the children.

But she couldn't bring herself to speak. Couldn't bring Siddy and Lili and Denis out of the safety of her thoughts into this horrible place where her heart felt blackened by despair.

So they sat in silence, side by side, as the light from the windows grew heavy and gray.

The king could call for Nicolas's execution at any moment, before she ever got a chance to choose to confess and take his place. Would she hear the shouts of the crowd from Newport Castle? Would she learn he was dead hours too late?

Hajni collapsed once more into boneless sleep, but Jax continued her watch. She found herself whispering prayers from the sisters' service to the Mother Goddess.

"Hold us in your arms, that we may weep for the sorrows of this life … When darkness closes around us, rest your hand on our hair while we sleep …"

She didn't have the words exactly right, but she sent them out for Nicolas anyway.

Night fell, thick and black, with no news, no change in the damp heat or the pain in Jax's heart. In the darkness, she felt half outside time, as if she might be able to float unmoving on the path between dusk and dawn, so the morning might never come, and she could keep Nicolas alive forever.

CHAPTER THIRTY-EIGHT

I was in the infirmary all night. You can ask Sister Verena.
— Princess Anara of Kherem

When the door opened, piercing the dark with lantern light, Jax jolted with fear that she'd failed in her vigil and fallen into a dream. She pinched her arm to wake herself up. "Ouch!"

The lantern jerked, and a stifled gasp came from the half-open door.

"Leave her alone, you beasts!" Eira swept through the door, pulling a sword from beneath her white priestess's robes. The lantern Beatrix carried silhouetted the priestess-princess, making her look like the Warrior aspect of the Mother Goddess herself.

Jax raised a hand against the light—and the fear Eira might be a little too quick with the sword. "Hajni and I are alone. You startled me. What is it? Why are you here?" Her breath caught in her throat like a knife. "Nicolas?"

"Still locked in Wulfric's dungeon," Beatrix said. "No way to reach him there. Getting to you two, on the other hand, wasn't even much of a challenge."

"Who's that?" Hajni rolled over, her voice thick with sleep. "What's going on? Where are the guards?"

"They're right outside."

"But … You didn't …" Jax glanced nervously from Eira's sword to the cracked-open door. "They let you in?"

"They didn't try to stop us," Beatrix said. "That's as good as permission."

"They're asleep." Eira slipped the sword back under her robes. "Poor things. Guarding you two trouble-makers would exhaust anyone."

Jax scrambled to her feet. "You can't stay," she hissed. "This isn't a game. If they catch you, you could end up locked in here with us. *Or worse!*"

"Oh, I don't think that will happen." Beatrix's mouth twisted smugly. "They're *very* sound asleep."

"We brought you a jug of mulled wine earlier," Eira explained. "Anara borrowed a few things from the infirmary so Dora could brew a sleeping draught her old nurse taught her—"

"Dora?" Jax asked.

"And if that Rigan potion-brewer thinks I'm going to believe it was 'mostly just chamomile' …" Beatrix muttered, as a sonorous snore echoed from the hallway.

"Who would have guessed those two honest, law-abiding guards would keep the wine and drink it themselves?" Eira asked, eyes wide with innocence.

"You've come to help us escape!" Excitement bloomed in Hajni's pale cheeks.

"What?" Jax felt slow and stupid compared to the thrumming energy of her friends. "You can't mean it."

"What else would we mean?" Beatrix demanded. "Unless you're planning to wait until one of you grows enough hair to climb down from this tower? We've put a lot of effort into this rescue. We're not drugging guards and sneaking around in the middle of the night for a lark."

"It's too dangerous. I won't be responsible for your deaths."

"Then you'd better stop arguing. Those guards won't sleep forever." Eira wrinkled her nose at another snore. "At least, I hope not. You don't suppose Dora could have misjudged the dosage? I told her they were big men."

"I'm ready," Hajni said. She shoved Jax's cloak into her arms. "Let's go."

Eira poked her head around the doorframe. "All clear."

"But the sisters," Jax objected, "you didn't drug *them?*"

"Ellycia suggested an all-night prayer vigil for Prince Theodor in the Abbess's rooms," Beatrix told her, pushing her out the door. "Ziva and Pia helped organize it. Sister Ursel made sure all the sisters are attending."

The two guards lay sprawled on either side of the door, resting in easy slumber. An empty jug lay on its side nearby, the dregs of the mulled wine staining the floor beneath it.

Hajni snatched up the guards' lantern. Eira locked the door and hooked the key to a ring on one guard's belt before following the giant princess down the hall.

"Stop," Jax hissed. "Castellan Kenrick must have guards posted downstairs, too—"

"Sleeping like babies," Eira said brightly. "Isolde was wearing that blue dress of hers. Those guards would have drunk anything she offered."

"Isolde?"

"Shh! We need to hurry." Beatrix took the lead down the stairs. They padded silently past the sisters' rooms down to the landing on the princesses' floor.

"There it is," Eira whispered triumphantly, grabbing a knapsack tucked in the shadows of the stairwell. She peered inside. "Food and water, a knife, flint and steel, the coins Lidia collected. Even a couple of moon time rags." She grinned at Beatrix. "I told you Raisa would come through."

"*Raisa?*" All those girls Jax had been so certain would disdain and shun her—some of whom *had* disdained and shunned her—coming together to try to save her life. She couldn't quite take it in.

"What can I say?" Beatrix asked. "She's eager to be rid of the competition."

"Competition? I'm under sentence of execution!"

"And look how much attention you've grabbed with that." Eira handed Jax the knapsack. "I bet Raisa wishes she'd thought of it herself."

"It's not funny," Jax snapped.

"Keep your voice down," Beatrix said. "And you and Hajni put on your cloaks. If any of the kitchen staff come into the hall, we don't want them to recognize you."

Jax shared a glance with Hajni. They weren't just the two tallest women in Lukos Castle. They were *by far* the two tallest women in Lukos Castle. A pair of cloaks wasn't going to change that. But they did as they were told.

The night was warm and thick, yet the enveloping folds offered Jax an unexpected comfort, as if all the individual acts of aid the other princesses had given were woven into the fabric. Everything they had done to give her this chance. She had to seize it and make it worth their gamble. She was the only one who could make things right. For Nicolas, for Theo, for all of them.

A shadow moved in the hall at the bottom of the stairs. Eira reached for her sword, but the black-clad figure stepped into the lantern light, revealing a familiar frown.

"*Anara.*" Jax brushed past Eira to grab the Kheremese princess's hand. *Please.* "Tenzin?"

"She lives." Exhaustion bruised Anara's eyes, and her skin looked stretched and pale, but a fierce will steeled her voice. "She woke this afternoon and has kept down some medicine and a little broth."

Tears stung Jax's eyes, and she squeezed Anara's hand. Maybe a little hard. Anara winced and pulled it free.

"She is strong. If the gods are good, she will survive. Her wing—" Anara's breath hitched. "Sister Verena thinks she may have torn a tendon. We will have to wait to see if she will fly again."

"Oh, Anara." Jax swallowed a sob. "I'm so sorry. I hope someday you can both forgive me."

"Why should you need to be forgiven?" Anara demanded. "You did not ask her to go with you. You did not make her foolishly bold against the giants."

"I shouldn't have let her fight the giants. I should have protected her."

Anara's eyes narrowed. "Tenzin is a dragon. She protects! She does not ask for protection. You forget yourself."

"*You* protect her."

"That is not the point." Anara waved the subject away with an imperious hand. "You saved Tenzin's life. She said I must give you a gift before you leave."

"A gift?" Jax shook her head. "But I can't—"

"Just take it," Beatrix hissed, "or we'll never get out of here."

Anara placed a small bag in Jax's hand. "Open it."

Jax pulled apart the drawstrings. Three perfectly formed red candy blossoms lay nestled in the black silk.

"Fire sweets!" Eira breathed, her voice a mixture of delight and envy.

"Oh, Anara," Jax said again and then could say nothing else through the lump in her throat.

"Tenzin says they might be to hand."

"Handy," Hajni put in helpfully.

"Whatever," Anara said with an airy sniff. She slipped away toward the infirmary without a backward glance.

"Lovely," Beatrix muttered. "Lovely dragon. Lovely moment. Now let's *go*."

She strode off, Eira and Hajni close behind. Jax tucked the little bag of fire sweets into her knapsack and followed. They met no one else in the hall, and Jax didn't ask where the girls had put the drugged guards. When they reached the keep doors, Beatrix paused to blow out her lantern.

"Yours, too," she directed Hajni. "If we're seen in the courtyard, we're done."

Once the hall was safely dark, Beatrix cracked open the doors, and they stared into the murky gloom outside. Clouds hung low in the unsettled sky, and only the faintest scattering of broken moonlight hinted at the contours of the courtyard.

"You have them?" a low voice demanded from the murk.

Hajni gasped, and Eira slapped a hand over her mouth. "It's just Marjani," she whispered. "I said we didn't need *her* help, but no one listened to me."

"I have scouted the courtyard," Marjani murmured, a swirl of dark robes in the doorway. "The sentries care only for threats from outside the walls. They will not notice us if we are quiet."

Eira stepped forward, but Marjani pushed her back. "Not you, white witch. The guards would see you coming from a league away."

Eira reached for her sword belt.

"What are you doing?" Jax yanked her back. "Marjani's right."

"This once," Eira agreed grudgingly. "Don't worry. Princess Gloom-and-Doom has nothing to fear from me. I've been sent by the Temple of Peace, after all."

She unbuckled her sword belt and wrapped it around Jax's waist. The scabbard slapped against Jax's thigh, and she dropped a hand to the sword's hilt, unnerved at how familiar it felt.

"I can't take your sword."

"It's not mine," Eira said. "After I threatened him with that bow, the castellan made me turn all my weapons over to Sister Ursel for 'safekeeping.' I took this one from your trunk."

Jax stifled a laugh. Her mother's sword. *Protector*. She and Hajni could certainly use protection.

Eira gave her a fierce hug. "We will see each other again."

"Are you an oracle now?" Beatrix asked. "I thought the Temple of Peace disapproved of prophecy."

"It's not a prophecy." Eira's voice was threaded with steel. "It's a promise."

"I'll hold you to it," Jax lied. If—most likely, *when*—the sentries recaptured her and Hajni, she doubted Castellan Kenrick would make the mistake of allowing the other princesses near them again.

"The gate to the cliff stairs has only one guard," Marjani whispered. "He will not hear me coming. I will immobilize him while you escape."

"Not the cliff gate," Jax said. This was the chance she had to seize. "The hidden courtyard."

CHAPTER THIRTY-NINE

Works woven in wicked darkness—
Can bright purpose yet prove bright?

— From "Death's Rule," an epic from the time of the Devastation, Author Unknown

Jax slipped past Marjani and hoped the others would follow. She could almost hear their mute confusion, but they didn't dare risk an argument, with only the shadows of the clouds and the bulk of the keep to hide them. Hajni faded from her sight like a mirage. Marjani's dark skin and robes blended into the wavering shadows. Trained to gather secrets, Beatrix scarcely made a sound.

Jax's own footsteps, on the other hand, rang in her ears like a plow horse's hooves on the hard-packed courtyard. She wished she had worked midnight stealth into the princesses' training schedule.

Still, they reached the passageway between the keep and the curtain wall without raising an alarm and scrambled awkwardly over the rubble to the abandoned garden. The scent of wild roses hung faintly in the air.

"We're lucky we didn't break our necks," Beatrix hissed. "We can't go any farther without light."

Even as she spoke, the clouds shifted, and ashen moonlight spilled across the garden. If the ancient, twisted trees and headless statuary had raised fears of monsters by day, the sickly moonlight brought them alive with horrifying menace.

Hajni stifled a moan of dismay.

"There's our light." Jax set off into the sinister tangle—no point giving anyone time to raise objections. If she tried to explain her plan, the others would think she had lost her mind. Jax half thought so herself. Just a harebrained idea inspired by an offhand comment from Hajni the last time they'd escaped the fortress under cover of darkness.

Disquieting shadows altered the writhing briars and amputated stone limbs almost beyond recognition. Yet, as with the sudden appearance of the moon, the path into the hawthorn thicket opened before her feet just where she needed it to be.

"We should be hidden from the sentries now," she whispered as they crept into the dark covert.

Beatrix lit her lantern and then Hajni's.

Marjani eyed the thorny branches lining the path. "If you crawled in there to hide, not even dogs would follow."

"I don't want to hide," Hajni objected. "I want to go home."

"I'll do my best to get you there." Jax led the way through the thicket, around the sudden, looming rock formations.

There was only one path, but it seemed longer than it had by daylight. Just as Jax began to imagine the hawthorns were under some enchantment that allowed them to shift at will, sending victims ever deeper into a deadly, inescapable maze, the path spilled into the small clearing she remembered.

She hurried to the rugged spire of rock. Even knowing the opening was there, it took her a long, tense moment to find the entrance to the cave. The lanterns filled the small space with light, revealing the others' consternation.

"You can't hide in here," Beatrix said, staying as close to the opening as possible. "Prince Theodor and his lackeys met us on this path. They must know about the cave."

"I'm counting on it," Jax said, with more confidence than she felt. If she were wrong about her tenuous theory, they would all be caught and imprisoned. Of course, the chances of descending the exposed staircase at the cliff gate right under the sentries' noses had been almost nil.

Even this wild wager of hers offered better odds than that.

"You must have a reason to bring us to this death trap," Beatrix said, more of a command than a statement. "You're not a fool."

That remained to be seen. Now that it came to it, Jax's hands were cold with doubts.

"Why did Prince Theo and his friends come searching for us that day we went exploring?" she asked. "Telling us about curses and weird noises. Why didn't they want us here?"

"Curses?" Hajni squeaked.

"The manticore that killed the devil prince came from somewhere," Marjani said darkly.

Beatrix rolled her eyes. "They just wanted to scare us."

"A prank," Jax agreed. "They reminded me of my little brother trying to convince me he's not holding a big, slimy slug behind his back."

A smile flickered across Marjani's face as if maybe she had a brother, too.

"What does it matter if it was just a game?" Beatrix asked. "Marjani has a point. A vicious, man-eating manticore could climb out of that hole over there any minute."

Hajni lifted her lantern, illuminating the shadowed pit at the far end of the chamber. She and Marjani took an instinctive step back toward Beatrix.

"What if frightening people—us, the workers, the sisters— was a means to bigger, better pranks?" Jax's mouth felt dry. "Hajni, you said that when you were blindfolded, the forest was so close around you it was like walking through a tunnel. What if it really *was* a tunnel?"

The giant princess wrinkled her nose in thought. "It did smell kind of … musty."

"And last night, you said you had to climb over rubble blindfolded. Like the rubble we climbed over to get to the hidden garden?"

"I don't … Maybe. They didn't remove the blindfold until we were inside the courtyard."

"How many times have the Rose Knights appeared out of nowhere while we were training?" Jax pressed, her pulse quickening. "Think about it. They have a secret way into Lukos."

They all looked toward the hole in the chamber floor.

"There was a new chain and padlock on the gate in that tunnel," Jax said. "*Someone* has been down there."

"If you're wrong," Beatrix warned, "if the tunnel dead ends, you lose your chance to try the cliff gate."

"Bee, *this* is our chance. We have to take it."

"All right." Beatrix took a deep breath. "Let's go."

"No." Whatever caused the fear in her friend's taut face, Jax couldn't ask her to enter that cold, dark tunnel. "You and Marjani return to the keep. If Hajni and I end up trapped down there, best we're found alone."

Beatrix's gaze snapped to hers, the familiar spark flaring. "That's noble of you, but not terribly bright. How are you going to open that padlock without me?"

"You've taught us some lock picking," Jax said. "Give me a key—"

"Which one?" Beatrix demanded. "What size is the hole? What is the lock's design? I'm sure as hells not letting you take my entire ring just so you can fumble around with them like a cat with a knitting needle."

"I will come, too," Marjani said. "You will need me if we find a manticore instead of an exit."

Jax didn't know how Marjani would fight off a manticore with her bare hands, but there wasn't time to argue.

"Take out that sword," Beatrix said grimly.

Jax slid Protector from its scabbard and made her way down the narrow steps, Beatrix close behind to light her way. Hajni followed with the other lantern, and Marjani took the rear. Despite the steady light, the tunnel felt colder and grimmer than the first time she'd come this way, haunted by the lives hanging in the balance of her gamble.

They soon reached the cavern, with its rough floor and bat-hung ceiling. Jax wished she hadn't remembered the bats. She hoped they'd already left for the night. The darkness waiting beyond the iron gate made the hair on her arms prickle.

"Here." Beatrix thrust her lantern into Jax's free hand, then lifted the padlock to examine its mechanism. She sniffed in contempt. "You would think a prince could afford better than this."

Jax pretended not to notice the way her hands shook as she pulled out her ring of picks and started work on the lock.

"Evil has been worked in this place," Marjani said, her voice low. "Malevolence lingers here …"

The chain rattled sharply in the still air as the lock slipped from Beatrix's fingers. "Thank you, Marjani. I really needed someone to voice that thought out loud."

As Beatrix started over on the lock, Marjani stared pensively around the cave as if looking for unnatural shadows thrown by some invisible darkness.

"Wickedness is a creation of the human heart," she stated. It sounded like something Eira would say. Strange how the two of them could believe something so similar and loathe each other so intensely. "It fades with the deaths of those who hold its memory. The darkness here barely remains, the faintest whisper. And yet, it feels terribly ancient … it must have been a monstrous evil."

The chain rattled again, but this time Beatrix lifted it free with a grunt of triumph, the lock dangling open from one end. She tossed it to the ground and jerked on the rusted gate. It opened so easily, she almost tumbled into Jax.

"*Caco*," Beatrix spat, catching herself on the bars. "Someone has oiled these hinges in the last thousand years."

They peered into the tunnel beyond.

Hajni swallowed hard. "Marjani, do you think that whatever it is you felt … do you think it's waiting in there for us?"

"Whatever I sense, it has no power to cause direct harm," Marjani said. "Still, it would not be wise to prolong our exposure."

Well, *that* was reassuring.

"You heard the spooky hex detector," Beatrix said. "Let's go."

Jax handed her the lantern. "Hajni and I go alone from here. You and Marjani need to return to the keep before anyone discovers we're gone."

"What if you're wrong? What if there's no way out?"

"Then it is even more important for us to be far from this tunnel when the search begins," Marjani said. "For their protection, as well as ours."

"*Caco*." Beatrix's steely control slipped. "Truthfully, I'm not sure I could force myself down there. Still, I almost wish I were going with you. Getting out of this place …"

"You could come with me to Fairföld!" Hajni exclaimed. "That would be a wonderful adventure—for you, at least."

Beatrix laughed, shaky but genuine. "I appreciate the invitation, but my duty here is too heavy to allow me to fly."

"What duty?" Hajni demanded. "I don't understand why you can't just—"

"Go now." Marjani pushed her through the gate.

Jax followed. "Lock it behind us. The longer they believe we're still on the castle grounds, the farther we can run."

"If you can get out at all." Beatrix met Jax's eyes as if gauging her resolve, before snapping the padlock closed. "You've got food and water. We'll come back as soon as the search dies down to make sure you're not trapped. A day. Two at the most."

Suddenly, being locked in the bare, stuffy priest's room didn't seem so bad. Jax fought down the urge to throw herself howling at the gate.

"Go," Beatrix commanded, her voice threaded with fire. "Find Margrit in Newport. She'll book you passage across the Saber to Venia. Get out. Fly for all of us."

Jax turned and walked into the darkness without looking back. She squeezed the hilt of her sword. She wasn't flying anywhere. She was marching.

CHAPTER FORTY

I don't see why you think I might know where they've gone.
I was at the prayer service for Prince Theodor. Of course, I
also prayed for Princess Jaclyn and Princess Hajni.

Wait, you don't think *that's* how they escaped, do you? I
always knew prayer was powerful …

— Eira, acolyte of the Temple of Peace and (former)
princess of Nordmark

In the end, Jax and Hajni's journey through the tunnel
proved anticlimactically uneventful. The main
passageway remained easy to follow. No rockfalls or
gates impeded their progress. Nothing menaced them from
the shadows—living or dead.

Even the chill, creeping breath of malevolence eventually
fell behind them, and a curl of warm air moved the stillness.
At the scent of wet leaves and living earth, they picked up
their pace, coming around a bend into a shallow chamber
strewn with forest duff. Roots gnarled the ground. The walls
became trunks and tangled branches. They found themselves
suddenly on a narrow path through thick forest, nothing above
them but branches and dark, cloud-covered sky.

Jax sucked in the sweet air, nearly gasping with relief.

294

"You can't even see the cave entrance from here, and we just stepped out of it," Hajni said. "Prince Theodor must have discovered the tunnel from the castle side like you did. Just think. He helped us escape."

"He also got us locked in a tower condemned to die," Jax pointed out.

"Do you always focus on the negative?" Hajni demanded. "We've escaped! The path splits here. Left or right?"

When had people started expecting Jax to know what to do? And when had she started expecting it of herself?

"We must be on the north side of Lukos," she reasoned. "Kenrick said your father moved his camp to the upper meadow, northeast of the castle. That's to our right."

She shot Hajni a wry smile. "With our luck, it will lead straight to the manticore's den."

Hajni rolled her eyes. "Or to the cottage of a fairy godmother who's looking for someone to grant wishes to."

"Or over a cliff."

Hajni laughed and blew out the lantern. "There. At least you won't see it coming. "

Jax's hand clenched on her sword, remembering the terror of the giants attacking them in the clearing. Remembering the sound of Tenzin hitting the tree.

And then she remembered Gergely, Hajni's guard, falling to the ground.

She slipped Protector back into its scabbard.

"Hold onto my cloak," Hajni ordered, pressing the fabric into her palm. "I want my hands free."

Despite the disorienting darkness, Jax felt the trees pressing close and thick on either side. It was no wonder Hajni hadn't recognized the transition from forest to tunnel with a blindfold on.

"*Yuck*," Hajni whispered, a moment before Jax's shoe slipped in something slick. The unmistakable scent of horse manure suffused the heavy, wet air.

"At least we know we're going the right direction," Jax

whispered back. "This must be where the Rose Knights teth-ered their horses."

Not much farther on, the forest opened, spilling them into a familiar clearing. In the absence of moonlight, Jax couldn't see much, but she could *smell* reminders of the battle with the giants—crushed grass, churned earth. She shuddered.

In her memory, the giants were the monsters of fairy tales. She could picture them crunching human bones between their teeth. Yet, she'd come to admire the brave, sweet, giant princess before her.

What kind of welcome would she receive at the giants' camp?

You're clever enough to deal with Wulfric. You have a talent for defusing fraught situations, and you'll keep your head if things get dangerous.

She hadn't outwitted King Wulfric. Had only made Theo's abduction of Hajni worse. And the man who told her she knew how to keep her head was about to lose his because of her.

As they trudged on, Jax strained her ears for the sounds of pursuit but heard nothing except their own ragged breathing and the tree branches creaking in a restless breeze far above their heads.

"Shh." Hajni breathed. "I think … Here."

She pulled Jax off the path, through a stand of whispering trees. A moment later, they stood at the edge of a sweeping meadow. Below them spread the giants' encampment, marked by watch fires and the glimmer of lanterns. A horse whickered somewhere in the darkness, but the rest of the camp lay silent and motionless.

Someone with no knowledge of giants might assume the sentries had fallen asleep. Having just walked miles through the dark behind a towering girl she could barely see or hear, Jax wasn't fooled. She wouldn't notice any sentries until they were close enough to club her.

"You don't need to come any farther," Hajni told her.

"You've brought me safely to my father. I know you were just protecting Prince Theo when you struck Gergely, but the others might not understand. Good fortune and good faith, Princess Jax. Find Bee's friend in Newport. Go home."

Home. Walking across the village square toward her father's house. Lili slamming open the door, running to throw herself into Jax's arms, Siddy and Denis close behind. Agnes with a tart word and a quick hug. Her father wrapping all of them into his arms …

She pressed the heels of her hands against her eyes and swallowed her tears. She would give anything to see them all again. Even for an hour. A minute.

Almost anything.

Not Nicolas's life.

"I appreciate your kindness," she said when she could trust her voice. "But I must ask more of you than that. I need your help trading your freedom for Theo's. I must return the prince safely to King Wulfric."

"But that's not necessary!" Hajni rushed to assure her. "Father will let Prince Theodor go as soon as I arrive."

"Are you certain? Certain enough to risk his life?" Jax didn't have time to tread gently on the girl's feelings. "Your father believes Prince Theodor kidnapped you from your bed and attacked your men when they tried to rescue you. King Wulfric imprisoned you and threatens war against Fairföld. Do you really think your father will just let Theo go?"

"I'll tell him what really happened," Hajni said testily. "My father would never kill an innocent prisoner."

"Maybe not." Jax hoped she was right. "That doesn't mean he will return the prince. If I were your father, I'd take Theo back to Fairföld with me, as a hostage to guarantee my safe passage home. And I would enjoy thumbing my nose at King Wulfric while I did it."

Truly, she would. Had she changed so much in such a short time at Wulfric's court?

Hajni scuffed her toe in the dirt. "So what if he did? King

Wulfric is a beast. It probably *would* be wise for Father to take Prince Theo with us as a safeguard against attack."

"Yes. Unless Wulfric decides Theo's death is an acceptable risk and attacks you anyway." Jax let that hang in the air. "Either way, King Wulfric will execute Nicolas. Probably today."

She didn't remind Hajni that Nicolas had risked his own life to help her. She didn't remind her that if not for Hajni and Prince Theo, Nicolas would be safe in Newport, and Jax would be sleeping peacefully in her bed. She did not remind her of the possibility Tenzin might never fly again.

The young princess was smart—and honest—enough to think of all that for herself.

Hajni took a deep breath. Held it. Nodded. "I owe you and Nicolas a great debt. I will do my best to repay it. What do you want me to do?"

Jax took a breath to steady her racing heart. One hare-brained plan had succeeded already tonight. Time to try another.

Thunder rumbled overhead, and every nerve in Jax's skin prickled as she and Hajni started down the rise into the meadow. Nothing moved in the giant camp, but she felt the sentries watching. With one hand on Hajni's arm, one waving her fine white handkerchief, she hoped she looked like a confident emissary. No one need know Hajni was guiding her so she didn't trip on a hummock of grass and fall flat on her face.

As they drew closer, Jax saw the giants had erected a crude fence around their camp. They had felled and stripped entire trees and driven them into the ground at two-foot intervals. A stealthy scout might slip between them undetected, but they would slow a direct assault, and no knight on horseback would be able to ride through.

"There's an entrance between those torches," Hajni murmured, guiding her toward the opening.

With barely a flicker of movement as warning, a mountain-shouldered, ten-foot giant appeared between the entrance posts. His eyes widened when he recognized Hajni, then narrowed on Jax and the kerchief in her hand. He thunked the butt of his spear against the ground.

"Who are you, girl, and what is your business with Fairföld?"

"My name is Jaclyn, Princess of Venia." She stuffed her handkerchief into her pocket, so he wouldn't see her hand shaking. "You may address me as Your Royal Highness. I have come to parlay with King Frigyes for the exchange of his daughter for his prisoner, Prince Theodor, Crown Prince of Aldforth."

The guard's gaze shifted to Jax's companion. "Princess Hajni. You are well?"

"I am well, Akos," Hajni said, playing her part gravely. The whole plan hinged on the giant king believing Jax had the authority to trade her for Theo. "No harm has come to me in King Wulfric's custody."

The guard's stoic face melted in relief. "What is your command?"

"Take us to my father. He will wish to hear what Princess Jaclyn has to say."

"Very well. Follow me."

As Akos guided them through the encampment, Jax felt eyes watching from the darkness. When they reached the huge tent at the center, she was not surprised to find fresh torches blazing. They lit a looming sweep of oiled canvas held aloft by massive poles carved with images of bears and fish and catamounts. Two guards stood at attention, awaiting their arrival.

"I must take your sword," Akos told her. "No weapons are allowed in the king's presence. Your Royal Highness."

Jax unbuckled her sword belt and handed it to him with a mixture of reluctance and relief. Akos might be a terrifying size—Protector looked like a child's toy in his massive hands—but he showed no inclination to eat her. Given what had happened with Gergely, it was better she not carry a weapon around giants.

I raised you to slay your own dragons, her father had told her. But he'd given her mother the sword. He'd given Jax a hammer, to create her place in the world. *Your greatest strength comes from your mind and your heart, not your muscle.*

Akos stepped aside. "You may enter."

The two fractionally less … *gigantic* … entrance guards pulled aside the tent flaps, allowing the light inside to spill out. Jax took a deep breath and shot a glance at Hajni. The giant princess grinned, violet eyes glimmering with adventure. Before the guards could wonder at her hostage's high spirits, Jax marched into the tent to challenge the giant king.

CHAPTER FORTY-ONE

Most people assume being a diplomat requires less courage than being a warrior.

They don't understand that entering a hostile negotiation is like stepping into a peat bog. It takes knowledge and instinct to keep you on the safe path when all choices look equally dangerous. One wrong step will plunge you into the murk to be sucked down and never seen again.

— Princess Beatrix of Bellis

From the outside, the tent appeared enormous, an ostentatious display of royal excess. Inside, it showed itself to be a practical height and breadth for a modest gathering of exceptionally large people.

At the moment, quite a number of exceptionally large men and women lined the sides of the tent, most of them glaring at Jax, many holding various kinds of massive weapons. They appeared more than capable of crunching her bones, and she could hardly blame them. But as their gazes settled on her companion, relief and joy warmed their hard eyes. Hajni's eyes glowed, too, though she struggled to look solemn.

In the center of the tent sat a great oak chair. Wooden fish seemed to leap from the tall back, and carved bears snarled from the armrests. But it was the man sitting in the chair who drew Jax's attention. Many of the giants appeared to have risen hastily from their beds, disheveled and sweating in the oppressive heat; King Frigyes looked as at ease as if holding court in his throne room in Fairföld.

He was shorter than many of the giants, though his shoulders were broad. The rough waterfall of his grizzled hair obscured the simple circlet on his head. His wide nose hitched to one side as though it had been broken—maybe more than once—and his face could not be called handsome. Yet, he wore self-assurance like a cloak of royal ermine.

Jax saw nothing of Hajni's sweetness in his square, rugged features. Only the intensity of his eyes, an even darker violet than his daughter's, showed their kinship.

"Daughter!" His voice boomed so loud, Jax felt it in her bones. "Are you truly well? You have not been harmed?"

"Yes, Papa," Hajni said earnestly. "I am well. I have not been mistreated."

The rocky crags of the king's face softened, hinting at the desperate fear he must have suffered since discovering his daughter's disappearance.

"Well, then, what is the meaning of this?" he demanded. "The Aldforthian tyrant has tired of his game and sent you home? Does he think he can abduct and insult you and then throw you away in the dark like night soil?"

The king waved his hand, and a guard stepped from behind the throne, dragging a bedraggled young man into the light. "Does he think I will just release his gormless little bastard?"

"Prince Theodor!" Hajni cried.

Despite the rumpled state of his clothes and a bruise across one cheek, Prince Theo's head was high and his eyes bright. He looked as though he'd been bathed and fed. He'd obviously been treated at least as well during his captivity as Jax and Hajni.

His gaze fell on Jax, and his eyes widened in comic disbelief. He shook his head and mouthed, *You again.*

As quickly as it had come, Jax's relief gave way to exasperation.

Hajni dropped to her knees before her father. "This wasn't Prince Theodor's fault, Papa. I ran away. I wanted to join the ball."

"No, Your Majesty," Prince Theo said. "It *was* my fault. Princess Hajni is only a child. I take full respons——"

"*Silence!*" The king's voice fulfilled its own command, hushing everyone in the tent. "Do not speak again, boy. I have listened to more than enough of your prattling since my men caught you carrying off my daughter."

"He was bringing me *back*, Papa." Hajni rose to her feet. "He was planning to return me to the camp."

The king's face darkened. "Is that why his band of cowards attacked my men and bore you off to that snake, Wulfric?"

"That was a misunderstanding." Hajni's composure finally shattered. Her eyes shimmered with misery. "If everyone had only *listened* to me, I could have explained … Oh, poor Gergely. If I hadn't run away, he would still … still be …" Her voice broke.

"For gods' sake. Don't cry." King Frigyes's frown turned uncomfortable. "There, there, child. Stop. Put your mind at rest. *Gergely!*"

His roar blew a pathway through the giants nearest his chair. From among them stepped a massive bald man. Jax would not have recognized him without his mane of wild red hair, but the thick bandage around his head gave her a pretty good idea of who he must be. Her skin flashed cold with both relief and terror.

"Princess." He dropped to a knee and still towered over

Hajni and Jax. "Forgive me for not fulfilling my duty to protect you."

"Gergely!" Hajni threw herself at the huge man and wrapped her arms around his neck. "You were willing to give your life for me. No one can ask more of you than that. You must forgive me for running away like a sulky child and putting you in danger."

"Yes, yes, that's all very good," King Frigyes interrupted, looking put out that he had not yet had the chance to embrace his wayward daughter himself. "We are all grateful Gergely is not dead. That does not answer my question. Why has Wulfric sent you back to me in the dead of night without a proper escort?"

"Why, isn't it obvious?" Prince Theo burst out with a laugh. "They've escaped!"

Jax would happily have risked another death sentence if she could have gotten close enough to strike his royal person.

"Escaped?" King Frigyes leaned forward, cunning delight creeping across his face. "Is that right?"

"We have not come here as fugitives, Your Majesty." Jax felt the eyes of every giant in the tent turn toward her as though she were a fly that had landed on their supper. She gave the king the regal nod Constable Anatole had taught her. "I am Princess Jaclyn of Venia. I have come to restore your beloved daughter to you and to parley for the release of Prince Theodor."

All of which was strictly true. She didn't intend to tell any unnecessary falsehoods. Especially since the necessary ones were liable to be rather large.

King Frigyes scowled. "This is who Wulfric sends to talk terms with a king? He tosses my daughter into the night without a proper guard and expects me to treat his son with respect?"

"Princess Jaclyn is a proper guard!" Hajni objected. "King Wulfric could hardly have sent anyone more likely to get your attention, Papa. At the castle, they call her 'Jax the Giant Killer.' "

Jax heard Theo's stifled snort, but she refused to look at him.

"Giant killer?" the king scoffed.

"She is the one who struck Gergely down," Hajni told him.

Unable to stop herself, Jax glanced toward the hulking captain of Hajni's personal guard. He peered back at her with an uncertain frown.

"This little girl felled Gergely?" King Frigyes asked in disbelief.

"It *was* a little hammer," another giant called out. A rumble of snickers rippled around the tent.

"It wasn't the hammer that disabled me," Gergely grumbled. He rubbed the back of his head. "It was the rock I landed on. A lucky blow."

"*Lucky?*" Theo protested. "This young woman knocked down seven knights with one blow of that hammer."

Gergely turned slowly toward him. "Are you mocking me, boy?"

"It's true," Jax broke in, sure her face would burst into flame. *Couldn't the prince just keep his mouth shut for five minutes?* "Princess Eira marked the seven notches on my hammer, one for each knight."

"Where is the hammer?" King Frigyes demanded. "I want the truth of this."

"I kept it." Gergely frowned at Jax. "I meant to use it to kill the one who prevented me from rescuing Princess Hajni."

He thrust his hand into a leather pouch at his waist. "I know I had it in here somewhere ..." He pulled out a kerchief the size of an apron, a coil of rope, a ring of keys that could have doubled for serving utensils, a handful of coins ... "Here!"

He lifted his fist into the air. At first, Jax thought he had grabbed the wrong hammer. It looked like a delicate goldsmith's tool in his massive hand. Then he took the head between his thick fingers, exposing the dark notches on the handle.

"She tells the truth," Gergely acknowledged. "At least about the hammer." He thrust it toward Jax, haft first, and she just managed not to shrink back. "Prove the rest."

She had to swallow before she could speak. "What?"

He pushed it toward her again. "Show us how hard you can hit something, little girl."

A giant laughed. Another whistled. "Get her something to clobber!"

After a moment of scuffling and shouting, a giant woman stepped forward. A mace hung from her belt, and bones adorned the ends of her numerous glossy black braids. She tossed an enormous chunk of rock to the ground at Jax's feet as though it were an apple core.

The giantess grinned. "Go on. It can't be as hard as Gergely's head."

As laughter rumbled around her, Jax took her hammer from Gergely. It felt right in her hand, much more comfortable than her sword.

She hefted it, grateful to have it back, but also ashamed. She'd used the hammer her father had given her, a tool meant for creating, to nearly end another person's life. And now it was being used against her, to thwart her attempt to avert a war and save innocent lives.

None of this audience with the king had gone the way she had planned. What had made her believe she could convince him to release a prince?

And yet, the consequences if she failed …

The giants were smiling now, with joy at the return of their princess and good-natured amusement at Gergely's expense. Eager to be entertained by a stranger's exhibition of skill.

But they didn't care that she could turn a piece of raw metal into a plow or an axe or a horseshoe. They wanted her to break open a worthless chunk of stone, and when she couldn't do it, they would decide she was nothing more than an unimportant little girl. She would be dismissed by the king. He might turn her loose, but Prince Theodor would still be a prisoner. Nicolas would not be freed.

"Is it too big for you?" Gergely asked. "Gizi, may I?" He took the iron-headed mace from the female guard and swung it over his head.

Jax flinched as the weapon whipped past her. It struck the rock with a crack that made her ears ring. Gergely poked the stone with the toe of his boot. It fell into two halves, split cleanly down the center.

The giants roared approval. One began a chant in the giant language, and others stomped their feet, making the ground shake.

Hajni laughed and clapped with the rest until she caught Jax's gaze. She bit her lip and made a sympathetic face. *Sorry,* she mouthed.

Theo gave her a brave shrug as if to let her know he didn't blame her for her inevitable failure.

"There. I made it easier for you." Gergely grinned down at her and wriggled his shaggy eyebrows, making them dance. Jax was sourly pleased to see they were still singed from Tenzin's attack.

Tenzin.

Jax's hand clenched on her hammer. The giants wanted a show? Well, she could give them a show, all right.

"Is that the best you can do?" She pitched her voice high to cut across the low thunder of laughter. As the noise subsided, she tossed her hammer, sending it spinning almost to the high tent ceiling before it fell back easily into her left hand.

With the full attention of her audience, she reached into her knapsack and fumbled open the small velvet bag inside. Thrusting out her fist, she slowly uncurled her fingers to reveal the gleaming ruby-colored flower on her palm.

"A soldier can split a common stone if he likes," she said,

mimicking Raisa's hauteur. She placed the fire sweet on the flat surface of one half of the broken rock. "But I am a princess."

"You plan to break a little gem?" King Frigyes asked.

Gergely gave a contemptuous grunt. "Such a bauble may be hard to scratch, but it doesn't take great power to cleave it."

"I don't intend to cleave it." Jax gave her best Isolde head toss and switched her hammer to her right hand.

She had been asked to demonstrate many skills in Aldforth, knowing her best effort would lead only to humiliation.

For the first time since leaving Dormance, she felt no self-doubt, no embarrassment. She knew her hammer as well as she knew her own arm. She did not know what the result of her strike would be, but she knew it would be the precise strike she wanted to make.

"Show us, little girl!" Gergely called.

The giants began to laugh again, and she let the noise build for a moment. Then, with the relaxed, confident stance she would use at her father's anvil, she swung her arm and brought her hammer down.

CHAPTER FORTY-TWO

The whole thing is a scandal. Colluding with giants! And you heard about that Venian boy, didn't you? They call him a lord, but I've heard he's a jumped-up peasant, just like she is. What can you expect from the lower classes? It's no wonder the king plans to execute him.

— Princess Isolde of Montaine

Oh, it's terribly sad. Everyone says the giants will kill her. And I saw that poor, doomed boy on Presentation Day. You couldn't miss those eyes. So dreamy.

— Princess Pia of Capra

Her blow struck true. Jax felt an instant of pride before the explosion of noise and flame nearly blew the hammer from her hand. She stumbled back, ears ringing.

Around her, giants yelped and shouted. Huge feet stamped out sparks that flared in the trampled grass. All that remained of the fire sweet was a black smear across the face of the rock.

"It's a trick!" Gergely shouted, his face redder than his missing hair.

The canvas overhead flashed with light, and thunder

rocked the tent. A moment of sudden, silent anticipation. Then a faint spatter, a hiss, a drumming of water drops falling on the peaked roof. The storm had finally broken.

Wind tugged at the tent flaps, and cool, rain-scented air swirled in.

"Ha!" King Frigyes threw back his head and laughed. "Ha! Of course it was a trick! But what a *marvelous* trick! The look on your face, Gergely!"

Gergely scowled so blackly, Jax thought his eyebrows might start smoking again.

The female guard, Gizi, smacked his arm. "The two of you know how to put on a show."

Gergely growled at her. Then snorted. Then raised his borrowed mace and slammed the butt into the floor.

"I yield!" he cried, a grin splitting his face. "I yield to Jax the Giant Killer!"

The other giants roared with laughter. One began a raucous song in rumbling Fairföldian. Based on the hilarity with which the others joined in and Gergely's good-natured growling, Jax guessed it wasn't entirely polite.

The king rose to his feet, and his people slowly settled, though murmurs of laughter spilled around the tent.

"Very well," Frigyes declared. "King Wulfric is an under-handed bastard, but sending this girl as messenger was a stroke of brilliant diplomacy. I hereby acknowledge you, Princess Jaclyn of Venia, as a worthy escort for my daughter and advocate for Prince Theodor. You may take the impudent pup away, and good riddance!"

More cheers and laughter. With a loud whoop, Prince Theodor joined in. Hajni threw her arms around Jax's shoulders for a quick hug, then ran to her father.

He lifted her effortlessly off the ground in a crushing embrace. The laughing, crying princess suddenly looked every bit the young teenager she was.

"If you ever pull anything like that again ..." The rest of the king's words were muffled as he pressed his face into his daughter's hair. He glanced over at Jax with a curt nod of thanks, and she saw tears in his eyes.

"You have my gratitude," a low voice rumbled beside her.

She looked up—and up—to find Gergely staring down at her. Despite the injury she'd inflicted on him, she saw no malice in his eyes.

"For bringing our girl home," he added. He nodded toward Prince Theo, who was hefting a massive tankard of some foamy beverage. "And for taking that one back. He's callow and impulsive, but the whole time we've held him, he's been more worried about Princess Hajni's danger than his own. He could be a better king than his father—if he lives long enough."

He clapped her on the back, just hard enough to knock the air from her lungs. His grin was a little wicked. "Not bad for a night's work."

Jax wanted to return Theo to his father immediately. Knowing the sentence Nicolas faced, she dreaded any delay. King Frigyes, however, insisted on waiting for daylight, when she could "parade the boy back to his father before an abundance of witnesses."

He was right, of course. They needed everyone to see the truth of Theo's free return. They could leave King Wulfric no pretext for executing Nicolas to conceal his own embarrassment.

For his part, Prince Theo seemed delighted to delay his homecoming and join the giants' celebration. Weighed by her dread for Nicolas, Jax excused herself to the pallet King Frigyes assigned her in Hajni's own tent.

The structure was covered in the same drab canvas as all the giants' tents and furnished simply with low cots and simple chairs. Yet radiant fabrics of reds and oranges, yellows and deep blues shimmered on the walls and draped the beds. Big enough for Hajni and her giant attendants, it still felt welcoming and cozy, a glowing contrast to the stark, bare tower cell where Jax had begun the night. Despite her worries, she fell into a bottomless, dreamless sleep for the brief hours until dawn.

After a hearty breakfast—giant oatcakes were, indeed, gigantic—King Frigyes assigned a full escort of his tallest guards, including Gizi and Akos, to conduct Jax and Theo to Newport Castle. Gergely led them, towering over even his massive companions, his bronze helmet glinting in the fresh morning sunshine—and hiding his bandages. Apparently, the king intended to make good on his pledge of a spectacle.

As they prepared to leave, Hajni grabbed Jax and Theo each by the hand. "Thank you," she said. "Thank you both from the bottom of my heart."

"For what?" Theo asked ruefully. "Abducting you? Throwing you on a runaway horse? Almost getting you killed?"

"It was the greatest adventure of my entire *life*." Hajni shot a guilty look at her father and lowered her voice. "Maybe enough adventure *for* my entire life."

But her violet eyes gleamed, and Jax doubted her life would ever be as boring as she feared.

Hajni squeezed their hands. "You have risked so much to help me. Whatever happens between our kingdoms, you will always have friends in Fairföld. I hope you will visit one day."

Despite the dire consequences of Hajni and Theo's "adventure," the girl's earnest warmth touched Jax's heart.

"I'd like that," she said, finding she meant it.

"It's good to know I'll be welcome *somewhere* if my father exiles me for stupidity," Theo said wryly. He lifted Hajni's hand to his lips. "You are a remarkable young woman, Your Highness. My father is a fool not to welcome you to his ball. Should the time come when you and I rule our respective kingdoms, I assure you of Aldforth's enduring friendship."

Hajni blushed brightly but held her head regally as any

queen. "May it be as you say, Prince Theodor. And, Princess Jax—" She bit her lip and ducked her head. "I will pray to the Mountain Gods for your Nicolas."

"Nicolas? Who's Nicolas?" Theo asked, but Hajni cut him off with a hug that squeezed the breath from him.

Jax laughed at his wide eyes until the giant princess hugged her in turn. "Good fortune and good faith, my friends," Hajni said, tears in her eyes.

Heartened by the rowdy farewells of the giants, Jax and Theo departed for Newport Castle, their towering escort falling in behind them.

As they made their way down the sloping meadow, Lukos rose on their right. The night's storm had washed away the dust and heat, and the spire of pale stone glowed in the morning sun. Ahead, Newport Castle sprawled at the end of the broad lower meadow that stretched between the fortress and the town.

A fairy tale castle. Well, fairy tale castles often housed cruel monsters.

Theo edged closer, his voice pitched low so the giants couldn't hear. "Just for the record, I *know* you and Hajni escaped. You found the tunnel."

She shot him a sideways glance. "You thought I'd be frightened away by scary stories?"

"I didn't know you very well back then." He eyed her thoughtfully. "Speaking of which, don't think I haven't realized that you didn't have to come back with me. You could be on your way home right now. Which means exchanging me for Hajni isn't the endgame of whatever scheme you're running ..."

"I don't know what you're talking about."

He grinned. "My admittedly healthy vanity would love to believe you're returning out of a desire to win my hand, but I very much fear it has more to do with this fellow Nicolas that Hajni was on about. Why does that name sound familiar? Nicolas ... Nicolas ... Wait!"

He bumped her shoulder with his. "I've got it. Nicolas is the fellow Dirk sent with you and Hajni that night … No. That accent. Dirk *didn't* send him, did he? He's your mother's man. He came with you from Venia. My father's caught him, and—"

His eyes drained of humor. "And you can't just run off home, can you?"

"No, I can't."

"Blast it." He clenched his fists and looked down at his boots, all mischief gone. "This should be my mess to clean up, not yours."

His remorse seemed more genuine than any of his glib irreverence. Yet, could she trust the irresponsible, impulsive Theo to follow through on her plan?

She touched her hammer. *Your heart won't steer you wrong.* "If you really mean that, I could use your assistance."

The prince placed a fist over his heart. "I owe you my freedom, Princess Jax. Quite possibly my life. How can I serve you?"

As they neared the castle, Akos lifted a horn and blew a long, wild note that echoed back from the high stone walls. Sentries must have been watching them since they'd left the giants' camp, but only now did the drawbridge begin to lower.

Thank the gods. Jax had harbored a possibly-not-so-irrational fear the king might refuse to allow her through the gates, even with the crown prince of Aldforth in tow.

The drawbridge thumped into place.

"Thank you for seeing me safely home," Theo told their escorts. "Please relay once again my profound apologies to King Frigyes for my father's imprisonment of his daughter. And for my part in it."

Gergely frowned. "We are returning a hostage. The

exchange is not complete until we present you to King Wulfric."

"I don't think that's a good idea." Theo flicked a glance toward the gates, where the portcullis was slowly rising. "I would hate for my father to do anything … ill-advised that might jeopardize the peace King Frigyes has made possible with his generous return of my person."

Gergely's singed eyebrows rose. "Do you people make up for your lack of stature with an excess of words? *I* am here to speak for my king. Not you."

"Prince Theodor is right." Jax had almost killed Gergely once. She wasn't about to risk his life again. "King Wulfric might use your presence as a pretext for more violence."

It might also make it more difficult to convince the king that lifting Jax's death sentence from Nicolas's head would bring him more respect than looking ruthless in front of the giants.

"Princess Jax will speak for King Frigyes," Theo pledged. "I will ensure her voice is heard."

A bold promise. But a thousand times less preposterous than her own pledge to free Nicolas. Nicolas had told her she was clever enough to deal with Wulfric; his imprisonment was proof he'd been wrong. Yet her wits were all the hope he had.

She rested a hand on her hammer to steady herself. "All of Aldforth will know of King Frigyes's benevolence in agreeing to exchange Prince Theodor for his daughter."

Gergely considered her for a moment, then nodded. "I trust it will be so. You know how to get a king's attention, that is certain, little girl."

Theo laughed. "Don't make her regret she didn't kill you, giant."

"Don't make me regret I rescued you," Jax warned the prince.

"From here on, he's your responsibility," Gergely rumbled cheerfully. He clapped her on the back, gently this time, barely lifting her off her feet. "Good fortune and good faith, my friends."

The other giants stomped in unison. "Good fortune and good faith," they echoed.

Theo put his fist to his heart. "Good fortune and good faith, to all our giant brothers."

"And sisters," Jax added.

Theo dropped a military bow to Gizi. "Especially sisters."

The giants stomped again, and Akos blew another blast on his horn.

Theo turned to Jax, his expression utterly sober for once. "Time to face the wolf. Do you want me to go first?"

"No." She knew enough about wolves to know she couldn't show her fear. "I'm the one responsible for the exchange. I have to take the lead."

She drew one last deep breath and strode toward the drawbridge.

CHAPTER FORTY-THREE

With hammer held high in her hand,
to foreign shore she came striding.
To win a prince was her intent,
but different tests were biding.

All hail the smith princess,
Her head held high, in peasant dress.
Iron, anvil and fire her tools,
The maid, princess of Venia.

—From "The Song of Jax the Giant Killer," by Foolscap
the Bard

As Jax and Theo crossed the drawbridge, two guards
stepped from the gateway, blocking their path.

"The king commands your presence in the great
hall, Your Highness," the older man said with a stiff bow to
the prince. "The girl is to be returned to Lukos."

"This 'girl' is the daughter of the queen of Venia," Jax
reminded him. She'd just saved this pompous blowhard's
kingdom from war. She refused to let him silence her. "I have

been charged by King Frigyes of Fairföld to return Prince Theodor to his father."

"You are King Wulfric's prisoner, *Your Highness*," the guard said, not hiding his disdain.

"Obviously, I am not." Jax gestured at the drawbridge she'd crossed so freely. "I spent this past night negotiating the exchange of the king's son for the giant princess. He should be expecting me."

"He certainly should, by this point," Theo murmured.

"If he wants you, he will send for you," the guard dismissed her. "I will take you to your father, Prince Theodor."

"I'm afraid that's not possible," Theo said gravely. "I gave my word that my father would hear of King Frigyes's noble generosity directly from Princess Jaclyn. If she is not allowed to deliver that message, I am unable to give up my status as a hostage. Sadly, I will have to return to the giant camp."

The scamp didn't manage to look particularly sad. "You may tell the king his heir has returned to King Frigyes's custody, and the giants have gained the advantage in the hostage negotiations."

The guard stiffened, undoubtedly envisioning King Wulfric's wrath. In the end, he gave Theo another bow. "As you command, Your Royal Highness. Follow me."

Jax ignored Theo's wink, fighting a surge of nauseated terror as they passed through the gateway into the courtyard. But there was no sign of an execution stand. No gallows or chopping block.

Maybe, just maybe, they were not too late.

Memories of Presentation Day flooded over her. Isolde and Pia with their fancy carriage. Beatrix, striding first to the dais, Theo's young half-brother demanding to know what was wrong with her face. Anara and her dragon.

King Wulfric brutally clouting Ralf to the ground for Theo's tardiness.

Jax and Theo followed the guard up the keep steps to the

entrance hallway. Once again, Jax was forced to hand over her mother's sword before an audience with a king. If only she were facing King Frigyes again, a man whose love for his daughter was stronger than his pride, whose people admired rather than feared him.

The guard led Jax and Theo into the cavernous great hall. Hushed and empty on Presentation Day, now it swirled and rustled with lords and ladies, knights and pages, a riot of clashing colors and incompatible perfumes, none of it quite enough to cover the cold, gray stone underneath.

All eyes turned toward them in eager anticipation. Jax saw the Rose Knights, exiled to a place of shame at the side of the hall, craning their necks to see for themselves that their prince, their friend, had truly returned alive and unharmed.

King Wulfric waited in a great, carved chair on the dais at the head of the hall. Duchess Bianka sat beside him, resplendent in a lace-trimmed, white velvet gown. And arrayed behind them, eleven princesses stood in a semicircle of shimmering finery. The king must have summoned them when he received word the giants were releasing the prince.

"True to form," Theo muttered as the guard waited for the crowd to part down the center of the hall. "Only my father would gather the entire summer court to witness my humiliation."

Jax couldn't argue. Prince Theodor was being returned only because King Frigyes no longer needed him. How else would a man like Wulfric manage such an embarrassment, other than heaping it on his unsatisfactory son in the most public way possible?

Still, there was a crack in the king's command of the stage setting. The princesses stood in the same order as they had on Presentation Day, with Beatrix and Raisa in the center, sweeping out to Anara and Ellycia on the left and the right. Yet, the girls were not evenly spaced. They had left a gap between Ellycia and Eira. Jax's place.

The gesture restored a flicker of her courage, even as she had to blink back tears.

Of course, all eleven princesses were glaring daggers at her, some in outrage, some in concern, one or two in exasperated unsurprise. Beatrix actually rolled her eyes … then shot her gaze sideways, guiding Jax's attention to Castellan Kenrick lurking at the side of the dais. Two guards stood behind him with a tall, still figure who stared at her with an expression of such despair it almost buckled her knees.

Nicolas.

She must have breathed his name aloud, because Theo turned to look.

"He's alive," the prince murmured in relief. "Looks in rather better shape than I do, all things considered."

Indeed, his clothes looked clean, his hair trimmed. No obvious bruises. Jax's heart squeezed with relief. Of course, he was to be executed in place of a princess. King Wulfric would want him to look the part.

Jax held his midnight blue gaze like a lifeline, memorizing his features, the way he stood, the look in his eyes that said that even under threat of death, his first concern was for her safety.

The guard motioned for her and Theo to follow him down the center of the hall. He stopped a yard before the dais, bowing deeply.

"Your Majesty, I bring you His Royal Highness, Crown Prince Theodor."

The king waved him away, his ire focused on Jax and Theo. His eyes shone with the anticipation of a cat spying a wounded mouse. He obviously meant to enjoy every moment of eating Theo alive, with Jax a tasty appetizer.

"The giants threw you back on my mercy, did they, girl?" he snarled.

Jax's breath caught in surprise. *He'd asked her a question.* So eager to enjoy her powerlessness that he'd unwittingly given her the slimmest of openings.

"Indeed, Your Majesty." She leaped on it before he could continue, ignoring his indignation that she'd dared to answer, fighting down the fear threatening to steal her voice. "King Frigyes has tasked me with expressing his profound gratitude for the return of his beloved daughter, Princess Hajni. He agrees that while Princess Hajni and Crown Prince Theodor's actions may have been foolhardy—"

Theo shifted beside her, but for once held his tongue.

"—youthful indiscretion should not be taken by older, wiser men as a cause for hostility between their kingdoms."

"He *tasked* you with reciting this drivel?" The king leaned forward, his hands gripping the arms of his throne hard enough to make the wood groan. "*Youthful indiscretion?* Shall I demonstrate the punishment such 'indiscretion' deserves? You would not survive it, I assure you."

Jax no longer believed in man-eating giants, but she could almost feel Wulfric's teeth at her jugular.

You're a stiff-necked, naive fool, and you won't live to be my age.

Castellan Kenrick might have had a point.

"I'm sure I would not, Your Majesty." She forced herself to bow her head, though it meant she would have no warning if he decided to strike. "It is only by your great mercy I am not already dead."

She had to swallow hard before she could continue. How had she ever thought this ridiculous plan could work? But she had to try.

"King Frigyes was not initially inclined to listen to my appeal for Prince Theodor's release. Yet, with the ... *explosive* materials I was provided to complete my mission, I was able to convince him of the authority of my petition." A muffled cough broke the silence on the dais, but Jax didn't dare glance at Anara. "He acknowledged before all his people the brilliance of the one who chose to send me."

From the murmurs of the courtiers, she could tell her ambiguous statements had convinced many of them that Wulfric himself had done the sending. But the flare of hostility in the king's eyes showed he'd recognized her snare, and her carefully crafted sop to his vanity would not sway him. She had tried to follow Kenrick's advice and made the desperate wager that the opportunity to save face, to avoid admitting that two mere girls had escaped his clutches and pulled off a diplomatic success, might tempt the king to join her game.

But Wulfric was not King Frigyes, moved to generosity by his joy at his child's safe return. No simple trick would delight this man into letting go of his resentments and cruelty.

Well. That was what she had expected, after all. She hadn't come back to Newport Castle to defeat Wulfric. She'd come for Nicolas.

She held her head high and her gaze steady. If the king exposed that she hadn't acted on his orders, the conclusion was obvious. She had stolen Princess Hajni from his custody, and this time she really *had* colluded with the giants. She had admitted it.

The only way your man leaves Aldforth with his head on his shoulders is if you confess to conspiring with the giants and take his place.

If the king wanted to punish her for returning his son, he would have to execute a princess.

CHAPTER FORTY-FOUR

Of course I do not agree with Princess Isolde that Princess Jaclyn is made of bronze! Is that not what "brazen" means?

I see. Well, then yes, it is an appropriate description. It's one of the things Tenzin and I like about her.

— Princess Anara of Kherem

"Ralf!" The king barked. "Come here, boy!"

Hot horror washed down Jax's throat. He already had her to punish. He couldn't hurt anyone else. A hand at her wrist held her still. Prince Theo's expression begged her to silence. *Anything you say will make it worse.*

The prince's esquire came forward through the crowd. The remnants of Presentation Day's bruises showed stark on his cheek, yet he stood unflinchingly before the king.

"Tell me, young Ralf," Wulfric said. "Here we have the bastard princess of Venia, standing in my court, calling herself a brilliant negotiator. Do you believe I would send a jumped-up peasant to bargain with a king? Even the king of a backwater like Fairföld?"

Ralf flicked his gaze to Theo as if seeking the prince's answer. But there was no good answer. The king wanted blood, and whatever answer Ralf gave, the king would take blood.

"No one would believe it, Your Majesty," Jax said, stepping up beside Ralf on shaky legs. She could not—*would* not—let him take blows meant for her. "I confess—"

"Of course no one believes it!" Castellan Kenrick crossed the dais to the king's throne. "Even if such a throw of the dice resulted in Prince Theodor's return and put that oaf Frigyes in Your Majesty's debt, that was a one in a thousand chance."

He threw Jax a look so hooded and dark, she might have stepped into shadow. He'd been the one to tell her how she could save Nicolas. Could he really be so shocked that she would try it? Whatever else she'd done, she'd returned Theo for him. And however little she trusted him, she believed he would use that to prevent Wulfric from declaring war on Venia, whatever happened to her.

"You are much too cautious to take such a foolish risk for so little promise of gain, Your Majesty," he assured the king.

"Too cautious?" Wulfric's voice hung in a sudden hush, his expression still, his eyes narrowed.

Jax's heart fluttered with fear. Hope? How close were the two? *He loves to be seen as pragmatic, crafty, smarter and stronger than anyone else around him. Show him that vision of himself* ... Did she dare? Kenrick's dark eyes gave nothing away.

If she didn't take this chance, no one would.

"Your councilors are prudent, sensible men, Your Majesty," she said. "They would never recommend something so risky. They could never even *imagine* such a course of action."

The acid seething behind the king's stare threatened to burn her, but she held her head high. *She* was bold. *She* took risks. Not like those meek councilors ...

"There!" Wulfric boomed finally, throwing himself back in his chair. "That's it exactly. That is the precise difference between a castellan and a king." He smirked, his predatory gaze settling on Kenrick. "You skulk, and you plan, and you *calculate.* Every last step. You never risk. You never dare. You never make the bold move."

The cunning gleam in the king's eyes was as unsettling as his rage. "I brought these girls from all corners of the known world to prove their skills. Why should I not make use of them? Success transmutes risk into triumph."

Particularly if it made the king look shrewd and fearless. Jax risked a glance at Kenrick. His eye twitched. Was he *winking* at her?

Balanced on a knife-edge, she once more bent her head to the king. "Your Majesty, I did only what I thought would accord with your command to protect Prince Theodor."

"Indeed," Wulfric murmured acerbically. "It's little wonder King Frigyes said my negotiating tactics were brilliant.

"You, boy!" He gestured at Theo. "I don't suppose he was quite so impressed with *your* cleverness. Interfering in the affairs of kings without a serious thought in your head."

The prince managed a self-deprecating shrug. "He did seem relieved to be rid of me. He thinks he got the better end of the bargain."

"He's not far wrong!" Wulfric roared, and the courtiers broke into relieved laughter. "So, Ralf. There's your answer. A true leader isn't afraid to do things that sound unbelievable to win the day. Go. Take that wisdom back to your fellow hare-brained pups."

"Arf, arf, Your Majesty." As Ralf made a show of bowing himself through the chuckling crowd to the Rose Knights, Jax took the moment of distraction to step back beside Theo.

"That seals it," he murmured in her ear. "I've pulled you off the hook. You owe me."

"I owe *you?*"

He flashed his rakish grin. "All right. You did ransom me from King Frigyes. We're even."

"I *saved your life*," she hissed. "*Twice.* Have you forgotten Gergely?"

Theo shuddered. "And his tree trunk of a club? Not likely. I intend to even that score, as well. A life for a life."

He approached the dais and dropped to one knee before his father. The laughter died down as courtiers craned their necks to see him. They looked delighted the spectacle wasn't over, but apprehension clawed Jax's throat. She needed this moment to plead for Nicolas's release.

"Sire," Theo said. "I apologize for my foolish behavior stealing Princess Hajni for your ball. I am in your debt for ransoming my reckless behavior."

Wulfric sneered. "You can repay it by pretending to be a crown prince, like your brother was, instead of a spoiled child."

"As you say, Sire." Theo's voice sounded blunted, as if he had filed the edges off before using it. "Yet, I owe other debts, as well. On the night I was captured, my men fought bravely—"

"They left you behind!" the king barked.

"Thinking I had safely escaped danger."

The Rose Knights stood with heads bowed, abashed. Jordis appeared ready to fall on his knees and beg forgiveness for not giving his life for his prince. Gergely had said Theo could be a better king than his father. The honest devotion of his friends strengthened that case.

"And Princess Jax—"

"Jax the Giant Killer," Wulfric scoffed, but he sounded amused. "She's got her reward. The peasant bastard gaining a chance to be a prince's bride."

"But there was another who fought to protect me that night." Theo rose to his feet. "One who had no personal obligation to Aldforth and who has received no reward for that courage, only pain."

On the dais, Anara brightened, but Jax didn't think he meant Tenzin.

"I speak of Lord Nicolas of Venia," Theo intoned, "who chose to fulfill his duty to Princess Jaclyn rather than return safely home. He had no quarrel with the giants, and yet he risked his life for mine. Now that Princess Jaclyn has proven her loyalty, Lord Nicolas must be released."

Jax stifled a moan as sullen resentment seeped across Wulfric's features. *No, never* tell him *"must."* Theo's willingness to sacrifice his dignity to make things right touched her heart, but he had such a talent for saying exactly the wrong thing.

Before Wulfric could vent his anger, Castellan Kenrick edged closer to the throne to whisper in his monarch's ear. Slowly, the king's glower began to soften. His mouth curled in a smile that could slice flesh.

Jax fingered her hammer. Nicolas's guards carried only heavy sticks in their belts—meant to subdue a troublesome prisoner, not ward off an attack. If she could reach Nicolas and remember the route through the gardens to the postern gate …

"As you wish, boy," Wulfric boomed, interrupting her desperate plans. "Lord Nicolas has indeed proven his devotion to his royal patron. His origins may be as humble as those of his princess, yet he has not fallen prey to the errors in judgment made by more high-born young men, such as yourself. Surely a benevolent king and *brilliant* strategist can do better than simply accord such a man his freedom. I hereby grant Lord Nicolas permission to remain in Aldforth until the Solstice Ball."

For a moment, Jax couldn't understand the words. Did he really mean …? She looked to Kenrick.

The castellan's lips curved in an almost imperceptible smile. *See how it's done?*

Nico. Staring at her from between his guards, Nicolas appeared as dazed by the possibility of hope as she. Jax swallowed her tears. She was willing to bet any show of joy would only annoy the king.

Indeed, if Wulfric had sprouted fangs and a tail, he could hardly have looked more wolfish as he spoke to his son. "Moreover, I appoint Lord Nicolas to your service, Theodor. He shall be your noble companion and esteemed advisor, tasked with preventing such egregious displays of idiocy as we have been privy to these past several days."

Sniggers rose from the surrounding courtiers as they watched to see how the prince would react. After a frozen moment, Theo offered his father a crisp bow, though it couldn't hide the mortification flaring in his cheeks.

The king stood and clapped his hands. "Enough. My wayward son has returned! Custom calls for a celebration, and I would hate to deprive you all of an excuse to eat and drink at my expense. Kenrick! I trust your staff can provide us with something adequate on short notice."

"Of course, Your Majesty." The castellan made a quick gesture, and servants appeared, carrying trays of drinks and platters of sweetmeats. From one of the overhead galleries, a group of musicians began to play a rousing tune. "More substantial fare will be served shortly."

Jax wondered grimly if he had a man with a black hood and an ax stashed in some nearby niche in case the king's temper had gone the other way.

Duchess Bianka glanced around at the smiling, relieved crowd. "Isn't it early for a feast?" she asked in a vague, breathy voice.

"It's past time for a drink." The king grabbed a flagon from a tray, and the onlookers broke apart into laughing, chattering groups.

"There." Theo moved to Jax's side. "*Now* we're even."

It wouldn't do any good to argue that technically it was Kenrick who got Nicolas freed. *Nicolas was free.*

"Thank you, Your Highness," she said, searching the crowd for Nicolas's face. "I don't know how to express my gratitude."

He gave that irrepressible grin. "You could kiss me. That might do it."

She snorted with laughter. Based on his expression, that was not the response he was used to receiving for such an offer. "I wouldn't dare. I'd wind up with one of Isolde's arrows through my eye."

He followed her gaze to the Montainan princess sweeping toward them. Isolde's merciless beauty parted the crowd like an avenging sword.

Theo blanched. "I see what you mean."

Jax grabbed his arm before he could escape. "She'll want to see for herself that you're all in one piece."

"I might not be, when she's through," he gulped.

"Raisa's right behind her. You can reassure them both at once. And *then* we'll be even." Jax flashed him an impish grin of her own before an arm hooked hers and pulled her behind a group of glittering courtiers.

"Well done," Eira said, guiding Jax to the walkway beneath the side gallery. "Return the princess, rescue the prince, impress the king. If we can keep Isolde and Raisa from murdering you in your sleep, you could end up a queen."

Jax shuddered. "Not a chance. From this moment on, I am going to keep my head down and stay out of Wulfric's sight."

Eira's pale brows rose in disbelief. "All the better for my chances, I suppose. Then again, if I had those gorgeous eyes looking at me like that, I might forgo a prince, too."

Jax followed her gaze.

Nicolas.

CHAPTER FORTY-FIVE

Sooo romantic.

— Princess Pia of Capra

Nicolas walked toward her along the gallery. Anara gripped his elbow, clearly intending to release him only to Jax's custody.

Eira was right about his eyes.

A princess would never run through a great hall, but Jax had long strides.

A princess would never throw her arms around a young man, but she took his hands, holding on as if they were the only real thing in the world. He gripped hers just as hard. A bruise purpled his jaw, and shadows haunted his eyes from the ordeal of the past two days.

Yet the warmth in his gaze reached all the way to her heart.

"*Nicolas,*" Eira sighed. Jax managed to elbow her in the ribs without letting go of Nicolas's hands.

"Princess Eira." Nicolas bowed his head. "I am so glad to finally meet you and Princess Anara. She tells me our brave draconian friend is recovering from her battle with the giants."

Anara's expression softened. "I thank you for your kindness toward her. She will be insufferable when she discovers *her* Nicolas will be staying at the castle in service to the prince."

Jax grinned. "Just wait until I tell her about the giants and the fire sweets."

"There you are! Exactly what part of 'escape' did you not understand?" Beatrix scowled at Jax and Nicolas's clasped hands. "The stairs at the end of the hall lead to the castle battlements. You should look across the river at Venia and the freedom you threw away before we all get locked back up in Lukos again."

"How do you know your way around this castle?" Eira demanded. "Have you got the entire floor plan memorized? Why haven't you shared it?"

Jax heard Beatrix respond and Anara join in the building argument, but she and Nicolas were already walking away. Servants gave them curious looks as they hurried down the gallery, but no one stopped them. Even climbing the narrow spiral stairway, Nicolas did not release her hand, as though afraid she might disappear.

Or run off to fight giants.

They found the landing that led to the castle's outer wall, just as Beatrix had promised. Perched above the Aldforthian cliffs, a small alcove on the battlements looked out across the Saber, the river running wide and darkly glimmering in the summer light. Hautberge was visible on the far bank, and the rest of Venia spread beyond, rolling green hills patched with fields of wheat, rye and barley, and pastures dotted with sheep and cattle.

"Home," she murmured, though in truth Dormance lay farther still, past the fields and forests and more fields and more forests … Yet she felt closer to home than she had since she arrived in Aldforth. Almost close enough to see her father and Agnes, Siddy and Lili and Denis.

"We could still go," Nicolas said.

"Out the postern gate?" The celebration of Prince Theodor's return could run all afternoon and into the night.

With luck, no one would even notice they were missing until morning.

So tempting …

Jax shook her head. "All King Frigyes did was bring his daughter to a ball, and you saw Wulfric's reaction. I came to Aldforth to protect my family. I have to stay."

"Do you want to go home?"

What kind of question was that? "Of course I do! That's all I've wanted since I got here, to go home where I belong—"

Where she *wanted* to belong. Could she belong in Dormance? Enduring the villagers' mistrust and Hubert's taunts. Facing a future that had troubled her long before Nicolas and Constable Anatole arrived.

She touched her hammer and remembered her father's words when he'd given it to her. *I knew when I brought you here, Dormance couldn't hold you. It was only a place I could keep you for a while.*

He'd told her to create her own place in the world.

"Maybe I don't," she admitted softly. "Maybe that's not where I'm meant to be."

Nicolas let go her hand and leaned on the battlements, gazing fixedly at the horizon. "I was wrong when I told your sister you couldn't win King Wulfric's challenge. He wasn't just goading Prince Theodor today when he said you could be the prince's bride. He was sizing you up. You could be the crown princess of Aldforth."

"That's not funny."

"It's not meant to be." He glanced at her from the corner of his eye. "The prince seems like a decent fellow. He obviously likes you. You might enjoy his company."

Her indignant denial died in her throat as she studied Nicolas's stiff profile. Was his voice a little *too* neutral?

She turned to stare at the view before them, hoping he couldn't see the heat rising in her face. "When I first got here, Eira said she wanted to marry Theo because it would give her the power to make a real difference in the Blessed Kingdoms.

I've been thinking about that ever since. One of these princesses will have that opportunity, but it will be hard for any one of them to improve things on her own.

"When he becomes king, Prince Theo will be surrounded by powerful men who like things as they are. Giving peasants a voice means they might say things you don't want to hear. If you let women choose their own paths, they might not follow the one you'd prefer. War is profitable—for the victor.

"What if—" She *had* been thinking about it, but she hadn't tried to put it into words before. "What if the princess who married Prince Theo didn't have just one voice to raise, but a whole chorus of voices? What if she had her own advisors by her side, her own high-ranking diplomatic allies all over the Blessed Kingdoms and beyond?"

Jax watched him, suddenly anxious about his response. She could imagine King Wulfric's outrage, Hubert's laughter, Duke Jordis's scorn.

Nicolas's brow furrowed in thought. "What if an entire generation of princesses could work together to resolve conflicts and improve conditions in their respective kingdoms ..." One side of his mouth turned up. "And who better to encourage them to come together and see each other's value than someone with no political ambitions of her own?"

"I'm sure there's someone better, but I'm the one who's here." She bit her lip. "Is it too implausible?"

"Implausible isn't the word I'd use." His smile hitched higher. "Impossible? Preposterous? So inconceivable that it would never occur to King Wulfric in a thousand years. Not even that old fox Kenrick would suspect the scope of what you're up to. You're the only one I know foolhardy enough to try it. And tenacious enough to have a chance at pulling it off."

It was Jax's turn to glance at him sideways. "Now that you've been assigned to the prince, you could try to warm him to the idea ..."

Nicolas snorted. "The king all but called me his babysitter. I don't think the prince is thrilled to be burdened with me."

"He'll grow to like you." Not that Jordis would make it easy. But she didn't believe Theo would hold a grudge against Nicolas for his father's cruelty. "And you'll like him. There's a genuine person under all that charm. He's not his father."

"Is that why you rescued him from the giants instead of escaping when you had the chance? Did you think his life was worth yours?" The intensity of his gaze captured hers, his dark blue eyes almost black with emotion. "I've never been so terrified in my life as when you walked into the great hall this morning. I thought the king was going to grab a sword and run you through himself."

This time there was no hiding the red that flooded her cheeks. "I didn't come back for Prince Theodor, you idiot."

Nicolas stared at her as if he couldn't quite understand her words. Then his eyes warmed as if the sun itself were rising behind them. "That was a *stupid* thing to do."

"You dare speak to a royal princess that way?"

He grabbed her arms and shook his head, losing the struggle to subdue his grin. "I think I would dare anything for you, Princess."

She dared a step closer. "I won't marry Prince Theo."

"You can't say that," he cautioned, even as his hands moved to her shoulders. "If King Wulfric heard you—"

"I don't need to say it. You're the only one who needs to know."

He was so close now, she felt the breath from his whisper. "*I* shouldn't know. I shouldn't be here with you now. We can't even look at each other like this."

"No," Jax agreed.

He touched her cheek. "If I kissed you …"

She hardly had to tilt her face at all. "We would have to wait until after the solstice ball to kiss again. We should make sure it's memorable."

He pulled her to him, and his lips touched hers. It wasn't a fairytale kiss. The kiss burned through her, tender and hungry, joyous and sad. Even with the euphoria of Nicolas alive and in her arms, even as their kiss pushed back the world around them with the light of hope and belonging, she knew it wouldn't end with happily ever after.

Grave peril and daunting challenges waited for them just inside the keep. Loving Nicolas, even Nicolas loving her, didn't diminish the danger. It only increased it.

He pulled back, just far enough to hold her with his gaze. "You can do this."

A smile tugged the corner of her mouth. "I know."

Because she'd come home to who she was. Not Princess Jaclyn, though that name had its uses. Not Jax the Giant Killer —thank the gods, she hadn't killed anyone.

She was Jax Smith. And she was ready to forge her place in the world.

EPILOGUE

Their names are legend now, but then
Each one had yet to prove,
Her sword, her bow, her heart, her hand
Were worth a prince's love.

—From "The Ballad of King Wulfric's Ball," by Foolscap
the Bard

The celebration of Prince Theodor's safe return lasted all day and into the evening. The resentment, distrust and fear bottled in Newport Castle might easily have overflowed with the wine and the ale, yet, by some blessing, the mood remained merry.

The king's sentries brought news the giants had decamped and were returning to Fairföld. Castellan Kenrick's kitchens provided a feast fit for … well, a king. The king's courtiers, beginning to chafe at their summer exile from the capital in Cadesleigh, welcomed the diversion.

The princesses rose magnificently to the occasion, so delighted to have company other than themselves that even Princess Isolde forgot to snipe and backstab. Castellan Kenrick called for dancing, so they might display the skills they claimed to be practicing so diligently—and none could fault their grace.

A fairy tale would end there, with Prince Theo partnering each princess in turn, charming even apprehensive Princess Ziva into shy smiles. With Princess Jaclyn and Lord Nicolas stealing glances that made Princess Eira laugh and Princess Beatrix warn them to behave themselves. With the king patting Duchess Bianka's hand with an expression of such unaccustomed fondness that it made the courtiers smile indulgently.

But this is not a fairy tale, and, as Princess Jaclyn so astutely realized, one good day is not happily ever after.

As the sun descended behind the eastern hills, a small company of men, dust-covered and weary from their journey, approached the castle gates. Their leader showed the guard the earl's seal he carried. Grooms hurried to take the men's spent horses, and the guard brought their leaders to the great hall where the revelers had just taken their seats for another round of feasting. He led the two men to the high table, which was laden with rich food and overflowing with royalty.

"Your Majesty." He bowed. "I present Steward Tarben of County Saebern and Reeve Hartwin of Saebern Town. They have come to beg your assistance in their people's distress."

"Saebern, you say? Earl Hallborn's lands? Bit of a prig that one." Prodigious consumption of food and drink had mellowed the king nearly to somnolence, but some dim memory made him sit up and squint at the visitors. "No, Hallborn's dead. And his boy, what's his name—"

"Berengar," his castellan supplied. "Earl Berengar. He vanished without a trace while out hunting, nearly a year ago now."

"That's right." The king frowned. "Who's the earl now, then? Who's this fellow the steward *for*?"

"Your Majesty." The older, narrow-faced stranger bowed stiffly. "Berengar remains the earl of Saebern County. His heir, his niece—my stepdaughter—is yet a young child. You saw fit to delay the transfer of his title to her for a year, to leave time for Berengar to return or his body to be found."

"You think to request a shorter term?" King Wulfric's tone made his counselors flinch, but our unwary steward had never been to court before.

"No, Your Majesty. We are here about the bear." Steward Tarben stared at the puzzled courtiers. "Have none of you heard of the bear terrorizing Saebern these past months? It has killed our sheep, torn down our fences, walked the town streets in broad daylight. It climbed over the manor walls one night, came all the way to my door and tried to break in!"

"A *bear*." The king guffawed. "Have you no hunting dogs in Saebern? No spears? No brave young men?"

He shot a scornful look at Tarben's broad-shouldered companion, and a number of courtiers laughed outright, delighted at the unexpected entertainment.

The steward reddened. "This is no ordinary bear, Your Majesty. The beast is the size of a bull, and its claws are like knives. Our hunters cannot harm it. Some sorcery has rendered it impervious to our weapons. Please, Your Majesty. Supply us a company of heroes to rid ourselves of this animal."

"Like a child's tale of noble quests?" the king scoffed. "My heir is dead, my neighbors treacherous. I cannot spare men for such a trifling affair."

"You should send Princess Jaclyn, Your Majesty." Princess Raisa had secured the prized seat beside Prince Theodor at the head table. She smiled coyly. "She rid us of the giants. Surely she would make short work of a bear."

"No, Princess Jaclyn has proved her worth." The king's eyes lit with sudden anticipation. "It is only fair we give her rivals the same opportunity."

He leaned forward, scanning the nearest tables for his twelve royal guests. "These men require a champion. I will grant leave for one of you to accompany them and rid their people of this scourge. Which of you is brave enough to take this quest?"

It took only an instant for each princess to calculate the risks. A fortnight of training with wooden swords was no preparation for killing a bear, even if the talk of sorcery was surely nonsense. Besides, supposing the girl who took this quest actually killed the beast, who knew how long she would be gone? Better to remain in Aldforth and keep oneself in the prince's eye—and the king's. No, there was no profit in taking on such a dangerous—

"I'll go." Princess Eira rose from her seat, ignoring the hissing and head-shaking from her friends. "I can kill a bear for you, Your Majesty."

"A *girl?*" Steward Tarben sputtered. "You can't mean to send us away with a single *girl.*" He suddenly remembered himself and bowed his head. "Your Majesty. *Please.*"

"She is a Nordish princess," the king pointed out, well amused at the man's shock—fortunately for Tarben's petition. And his neck. "Nordish warriors hunt ice bears for sport. Your measly forest bear shouldn't be a challenge. Still, if it will make you feel better, I can send two girls.

"You." He pointed a heavily ringed finger toward a princess at the table opposite Eira's. A problem he would need to deal with at some point. Might as well give the bear a chance to take care of it for him. "Wasn't your brother a sorcerer, girl? Didn't do him much good against an Aldforthian wolf, but perhaps you can handle an addled bear."

Princess Marjani of Almasa stood, her robes red as blood against her dark skin. Her unmatched eyes glittered in the torchlight. "It would be my pleasure to kill *any* savage Aldforthian animal, Your Majesty. The Nordish barbarian may stay behind. The limited assistance she might provide is unnecessary."

"I don't need any help from a sullen doomsayer—" Princess Eira drew herself up short, her pale cheeks tinged with red. "But the Temple of Peace teaches that we are more powerful when we work together. Of course, I would be glad of whatever slight aid Princess Marjani can offer. Protecting her will be proof I can protect Prince Theodor."

Princess Marjani lifted her chin. "You can be sure I will see the bear does the white witch no harm."

"Excellent," the king drawled. "There, Steward. The solution to your dilemma, offered by your generous king. Their charming company is only an added gift."

As the two princesses glared at each other across the great hall, Steward Tarben might have been forgiven for thinking these two young women were more likely to be a curse upon him than the answer to his prayers.

It would take a more discerning eye than his to see how very dangerous the two of them could be—to the unsuspecting bear, to the earldom of Saebern, and to each other.

The king smiled. "Let the hunt begin."

THE TWELVE DANCING PRINCESSES

THE BLESSED KINGDOMS

Bellis
Princess Beatrix
Rigas
Princess Dora
Ravnina
Princess Raisa
Aldforth
Princess Ellycia
Venia
Princess Jaclyn
Ilhavair
Princess Lidia
The Fair Isles
Princess Ziva
Montaine
Princess Isolde
Princess Pia
Nordmark
Princess Eira

Almasa
Princess Marjani
Kherem
Princess Anara

ACKNOWLEDGMENTS

This is my chance to thank all the people who helped me take the book I wrote and move it closer to the book I saw in my mind's eye when I imagined Jax and her story.

Thank you to my wonderful critique group—Jennifer Sowle, Sharon Brown, and Georgia Salmon—for all the support and suggestions over many books over many years (and many cups of coffee).

Thanks to Beth Hull for seeing where I wanted to go with this story and nudging me toward it.

Thanks to Ari, my dear child, for reading that endless first draft and making me cut the boring bits. You can quit complaining about them any time now …

Thanks to my mom, Judy Longshore, for loving books and stories enough to let me bury myself in them for days at a time as a child and not telling me I was crazy when I decided to try writing my own.

And finally, a huge, heartfelt thank you to Katherine Longshore for reading multiple drafts, for ruthlessly pointing out holes and inconsistencies, for making every word work harder. Every author should be so lucky as to have such an incredible writer and book coach for a sister. But mostly, thank you for supporting me through all the ups and downs of my life.

ABOUT THE AUTHOR

Rowan Mallory grew up on the northern California coast, in a world of giant, ancient trees and swirling mists, which may have subtly altered her brain to gravitate toward tales of mystery and adventure. She's in her happy place in the forests and the fog, writing stories about strong, smart, flawed heroines who believe the world can be a better place if they just make it so.

She and her daughter share their home with a dog and cat with massive amounts of personality who may or may not have provided inspiration for a certain cheeky little dragon.

Rowan is the author of *The Twelve Dancing Princesses* series, including *The Blacksmith Princess*.

www.ingramcontent.com/pod-product-compliance
Lightning Source LLC
Chambersburg PA
CBHW020906060726
47591CB00004B/1106